Regina Maria Roche

Rev. John Alexander Roche

Autobiography and sermons together with the expressions elicited by his death

Regina Maria Roche

Rev. John Alexander Roche
Autobiography and sermons together with the expressions elicited by his death

ISBN/EAN: 9783337114442

Printed in Europe, USA, Canada, Australia, Japan

Cover: Foto ©Raphael Reischuk / pixelio.de

More available books at **www.hansebooks.com**

John A. Poche.

REV. JOHN ALEXANDER ROCHE

M.D., D.D.

AUTOBIOGRAPHY AND SERMONS

TOGETHER WITH

THE EXPRESSIONS ELICITED BY HIS DEATH

COMPILED BY HIS CHILDREN

PRINTED BY

EATON & MAINS

To the memory of

Mary Caroline Roche, our mother,
and of
Mary Caroline Roche, our sister;

Whose lives were inwoven with the one here described
like beauteous threads in cloth of gold;
Whose presence diffused joy, whose sympathy gave strength,
whose lives ministered inspiration;
Two Marys who reached the sepulcher before the disciple,
These pages are inscribed.

CONTENTS.

Contents.

A FILIAL OFFERING.

GOODNESS and greatness cannot be denied posthumous fame. The reverence that the living have ever paid to certain elect spirits among the departed proves that homage to virtue is an instinct, and that immortality is the inheritance of the worthy. The intuition of the race is reflected in a law of the Church. Where the dust of the child is restored to the earth we cut in stone at least the three lines that preserve the name and those dates whereof one tells when the soul entered this order of existence that we call life, and the other when it went hence. With all the more justice may we seek to preserve the words and to perpetuate the virtues of those that with lifelong efficiency, ability, and consecration served God at his altars and gathered souls into his kingdom.

For many a reason the life and teachings of John A. Roche are entitled to record. He possessed a marked and fascinating personality. His intellectual robustness struck everyone. The freshness and force of his mind were always noble and stimulating.

While open, candid, trustful, and charitable in his judgments, he had strong confidence in his opinions when once formed. He came near to being immovable in his conclusions, especially as to character. Prejudice never wrote a man down with him, but when a man had written himself down it was next to impossible for him ever to confide in him, or even to speak of him with patience. Though one of the most urbane and diplomatic of men, he was at times severe. His anger was of the kind that shot forth at the spectacle of injustice, and it was united with a courage like that of Achilles, sufficient to challenge all the armies of Troy, and, in addition, all the men of Greece, his own companions. To speak when every man of the Preachers' Meeting thought him wrong, to plead when an entire Annual Conference differed, had for him the inspiration of exertion, and not seldom the joy of victory.

He was the sincerest of men, and sublimely free from affectation. Uninfluenced by bias, independent of mean and petty considerations, possessed of rock-ribbed courage, such qualities as sourness, cowardice, treachery, mercilessness could no more be asserted of him than poison could be predicated of sunshine, or ugliness of the flowers.

He had Chesterfieldian courtesy. He was one of those men in whom, to use the expression of Addison, wisdom and virtue were seen to be far from inconsistent with politeness and good humor. Here spoke not simply his Irish blood, but as well his Virginian culture, his tender heart, and his Christian calling. Yet no one could say that the gracious side of his character had been cultivated at the expense of consistency. In him were found both dignity and condescension, both ceremony and simplicity, as though he had set himself to learn well Bacon's maxim, "Amongst a man's peers a man shall be sure of familiarity; and therefore it is good a little to keep state: amongst a man's inferiors one shall be sure of reverence; and therefore it is good a little to be familiar." While he was unsparing in his condemnation of evil, and while instances are not lacking when to his opponents he exhibited great severity, his attitude toward everyone he did not know and toward ninety-nine hundredths of those he did know was one of childlike, bland, unsuspecting kindliness. His life illustrated Burke's apothegm, "All the possible charities of life ought to be cultivated, and where we can neither be brethren nor friends, let us be kind neighbors and pleasant acquaintances."

The spring of his politeness was in the gushing fountain of his genuine respect for humanity. The social station of people made no difference in his manners. No one could have had less agreement with Byron, who was deferential in degree matching the rank of the person he addressed. Dr. Roche's services were placed as generously, as effusively, at the command of the apple woman in distress as they could have been at the request of the heiress. The cobbler who had lost a child was the recipient of as sincere attention as the merchant prince.

He was like a child to him who by genius, by sanctity, or by achievements commanded his respect. With the strongest admiration for the character of the late Dr. John Hall, of New York, it is scarcely possible that the humblest member in that parish listened with more reverence than he to Dr. Hall's discourses. When, in 1869, this noble Irishman came to the Fifth Avenue Church, Dr. Roche instantly recognized his princely powers, and for several years was accustomed to attend his Sunday afternoon services.

He was an ardent friend. It is doubtful if his mind ever threw off a kindly estimate that he had formed concerning anyone who had displayed marked ability in speech or writing, anyone who had served the Church of Christ effectively, anyone who had performed a generous act for himself or for anyone dear to him. What may be called his happy prejudices were ineradicable.

No man held his friends by a stronger or more deathless tie. When eighty-four years of age he received the most eloquent testimonials of regard from the children and the grandchildren of those who had known him in Smyrna, Del., in the days of his apprenticeship. Leaving the Philadelphia Conference in 1857 and returning to the city for the Centennial Exposition nineteen years later, it was impossible for him to give his attention to the exhibits by reason of the large number of his old friends who crowded around and would not be denied conversation. On this visit he was gratefully addressed by conductors on street cars, who recalled the texts of some of his sermons. He himself traced many of these instances of interest to scenes in sick rooms, illustrating the fine remark that "the firmest friendships have been formed in mutual adversity, as iron is most strongly united by the fiercest flame."

That amiability, confidence, and hopefulness with which he looked upon almost every person that lived inspired him in an extraordinary degree with each of his children. As the eagle teaches her young to fly, he lifted up each of his offspring by faith and hope and love into something infinitely better than the child could have been without that self-sacrificing devotion on his part.

What a home was that over which he ruled! The entire atmosphere was one of mingled helpfulness and stimulus, and the youngest child, from the dawn of reason, had his

responsibilities and privileges. Each was taught that with
the application of his energy and the blessing of God he
was sufficient for all his tasks. Not only filial respect was
insisted on, but fraternal respect. When the youngest
spoke the eldest might not interrupt. On matters of grave
domestic concern it was the custom to assemble all around
the board and listen at length to the opinion of each, beginning with the eldest and allowing the youngest to speak
fully. Soundness of judgment, directness of method, precision in speech were at all times enforced. No error as to
fact, no slip in grammar, no rhetorical blunder went for
an instant without correction. From an early age the
children were permitted to visit friends for a few days at
a time, the rule being that the absent one should write
home once a day. These letters were carefully answered
by the busy father. Birthdays were studiously observed,
and without a word of what would be called counsel or
preaching the child was made to feel that the new year
called to greater sobriety and fidelity.

Not the least of his injunctions had reference to fru-
gality. Just as he and the sainted mother inculcated
earnestness, with the indulgence at proper seasons of mirth;
and industry, with the permission of wise recreation; so
there was due provision for every just need, but not so
much as a penny a year for waste. Having in one of the
early years of their married life saved fifty dollars out of
an annual salary of two hundred and eighty, it became a
principle with them that everyone could live within his
income if he would. From whatever money was earned
he demanded that the first part should be taken for the
service of God, and the second part be laid by in savings.

He had few more contemptuous terms of reproach than that one lived up to every cent that he received.

In nothing else appeared more clearly his magnanimity and consecration. While he spent money recklessly, as some might say, for books, education, missions, he maintained very strong ideas about what he called stewardship. Though not unwilling that his household should have such things as comfort and even fashion demanded, so far as his immediate and personal wants were concerned he had a Spartan's disregard of luxury in dress, furniture, and living. Methodist tradition more than early straitness in means kept him from ever having a gold button or a stud: and to the last hour of life his rule for himself was as absolute and austere as the regulation for the inmate of a monastery. If he ever spent a quarter of a dollar for his own individual gratification the item is unknown to anyone of his family. Consistently he illustrated his belief that a good name is better than gold, and that all money that does not contribute to lofty aim is naught but ashes and wormwood.

Those who knew him intimately could scarcely think of him apart from his library. With only that education that could be obtained in the village school on the Eastern Shore of Maryland, in the second decade of the last century, yet possessed by an insatiable yearning for culture, Providence, denying him the college, bestowed on him a hearty and lifelong love of books. His library was far more to him than a university is to most of its alumni. To him his library was rest after labor, joy in the midst of difficulties, inspiration to toil. When wearied out by study, visiting, or preaching he found recreation in going through the old book repositories or in rearranging his shelves. No poacher ever changed his plow for his gun with more avidity than he would break away at seasonable times from Church work to pore over catalogues of the London dealers in old books, or to examine the offerings at auction sales. He had an unerring scent as he swept through piles of literature for whatever had to do with Bible interpretation, Christian experience, the composition and delivery of sermons, or what he would have called orthodox theology.

His frequent movings, especially under Methodist law sixty years ago, and the meager salaries of young itinerants, had little influence in limiting the number of volumes. Early in his ministry he made the important discovery that new clean books from the publishers' tables cost dollars, while the same works could be had a little later at auction or in old bookstores for a few cents, with the added advantage that by that time one knew whether he cared to read the volume or not. These regular purchases excited the grave anxiety of his wife. She herself was a great reader of history, poetry, and romance, but found little to interest her in the strictly theological avalanches, payment for which interfered with other desirable outlays. Her vigilance demanded no slight degree of judicious management on his part. He would bring home the books from auction, a few at a time, in the pockets of his coat-tails, surreptitiously crowding them out of sight on back shelves and waiting months or years to place them in front, if they happened to have striking bindings. The peace of the household was never disturbed. though the constant increase of the library and the frequent tearing of the pocket linings each demanded periodical explanations.

As no parsonage ever had shelf room enough, he was
ever racking his brain to crowd into a space as long as his
hand a row as long as his arm. One of the churches he
served set out to give him as much book space as he desired. A tasteful design was made, some walnut moldings
being prepared for the face of the plain pine shelves. This
faint show of elegance was suppressed at his desire, that
the money saved might be expended on more shelves. The
church authorities succeeded in giving him for the first
time in his life more shelves than his books would fill. But
at the time some gold mine stock he held was paying good
dividends, and it took him not long to catch up with the
shelf room. He was soon, of course, as crowded as ever.
Succeeding pastors gazed in wonder at the vacant book-
cases, curtained them, and used them as cupboards for
china or storage for jellies.

His books filled about all the house, overflowing his
shelves, covering the floors, tumbling over mantels, tables,
and chairs. Books were set back of others, a volume or
two of an author indicating more behind, and a famous
Unitarian or Baptist preacher showing where more of his
brethren were. He had a vast collection of sermons, no
Church or school of thought among English, Scotch, Irish,
Welsh, or American divines being without full representation. His hunger for sermons — Protestant or Roman,
evangelical or radical, mediæval or modern, didactic or
emotional — was like the fondness of Polyphemus for
travelers.

Of Julius Hare, the friend of Bunsen, it was said that
though his books were scattered everywhere through the
rectory at Hurstmonceaux, whichever was wanted he could

find instantly without trouble. So with Dr. Roche; it was rare indeed for his law of association to be defied by any book among his thousands getting lost. Still it must be owned that his back shelves were to him much that Israel's stiff-neckedness was to Moses, or the thorn in the flesh to St. Paul.

No scholar ever set a higher value on the contents, the soul of a volume; none ever cared less for its body, its dress. He was at once bibliophile and student. Not seldom great collectors are book neglecters, but he brought home no book he did not master. He was that often described but in reality rare person, an omnivorous reader. From fourteen years of age till eighty-four it may be said that he read more pages than any three of the most indefatigable literary drudges in the library of the British Museum. Tables of contents and indices were rapidly yet thoroughly mastered, and in a single evening he could satisfy himself as to the contents of from a dozen to a score of goodly-sized volumes.

As his life advanced he felt greater pleasure in his books, knowing his sons were in the ministry, and that the breaking up of his library would not be necessary. Certain of the volumes were given to his daughter, but the great bulk was divided between the two sons, his own choice arranging, down to the smallest pamphlet, what each should have.

He was a good talker. On every subject he had an opinion, and a strong one, and in an impromptu utterance he would express it with singular felicity and power. He had a radical directness that pressed its way into his chance conversation. Hearing a nervous person say,

"Every time I look at that crack it grows wider," he retorted dryly, "Then don't look at it." He would have said, with Jeremy Collier, that "the advantage of conversation was such that for want of company a man would better talk to a post than let his thoughts lie smoking and smothering." When his mind was full of a subject he embraced every opportunity to speak on the matter. Whatever his mind gained from a talk with a friend he would at once put upon paper, enriching it with his own lines of thought. On a variety of subjects connected with his profession, and especially upon sermons, homiletics, and oratory, he was full, one might say, inexhaustible.

On his favorite authors Dr. Roche would talk with the greatest enthusiasm hour after hour. He knew the English divines of the seventeenth and eighteenth centuries as merchants know their clerks. The contemporaneous schools of theology, the historic periods of American preaching, he knew in their doctrines, their influence, and their leading specimens of pulpit literature.

Bunsen, when he represented Prussia at Rome and lived in a house at the top of the Tarpeian Rock, had not Roman history and antiquity more at his tongue's end than had Dr. Roche in his library the various periods of English and American makers of sermons.

He was an elegant letter-writer. His earnestness in correspondence was founded on philosophic principles, and was advantaged by careful study of the best models. In his mind judicious correspondence was one of the most efficient methods for influencing men to wisdom and righteousness. If one of his own people was in distress or had met great prosperity; if a friend was in doubt or desired information on some passage of Scripture or on some theme of current interest; if one in authority was to be addressed with reference to some place sought for an applicant; if a young clergyman wanted counsel; if a member of the Cabinet or the President of the United States could, in his opinion, be addressed with effect, he would throw off communications — weighty in reasoning, exquisite in deference, and graceful in manner—that cost him more labor than the Sunday morning sermon costs many a clergyman.

His correspondence was large, and he left among his papers an interesting collection of letters from some of the most prominent Americans of his day, and particularly from the most eminent divines of New York and Brooklyn during the last forty years.

As a debater he attained high excellence; his readiness, fullness of knowledge, strength in retort, and fluency of utterance calling often for admiration. His powerful logic and his analytical acuteness appeared in discussion to great advantage. No one was clearer in detecting the lurking sophistry in a spurious argument; no one more infallible in discerning the practical result of a novel proposition. In an erroneous statement he could take out the ideas or words that left the proposition agreeable to him. From any complicated, overlaid matter he could at once single out the element of right. As by instinct, he discriminated the main point from immaterial adjuncts, and, while he cared nothing for details, no wording or rewording of a proposition could cause him to lose sight of the principle for which he contended.

In a discussion he preferred to be either the first speaker
2

or the last. As a debater he was liable to criticism at the points of prolixity and personality—faults only too common in the discussions both of courts and legislatures in the earlier part of the last century.

His principal opportunities for the exercise of his skill were presented by the Annual Conference and by the Monday morning sessions of the Preachers' Meeting, which for a long time has gathered, at the great publishing house of the Methodist Church in New York city, the preachers from Trenton to Montauk Point, and from Albany to Atlantic City. Here, he would say, a keener discussion could be had than the floor of the General Conference would allow.

Whatever greatness he possessed came out with radiant clearness in his lifework. As a pastor he reached a high standard of excellence. His fidelity had two powerful helps. One was his great physical strength, or better perhaps, a toughness of frame that threw off fatigue as the duck sheds water. He could make calls almost without limit. During an early ministry in Philadelphia, in a society where a large number of families were massed near the parsonage, he started along the squares, calling up one side the alleys and down the other side till by nightfall he had made visits on seventy-five families, praying, according to the custom of Methodist preachers of that day, in almost every home. On coming to New York, in 1857, and learning that on New Year's Day many of his people expected their friends, he went with Samuel Halsted in his carriage and by night had completed a list of seventy calls. It must be admitted that one such day convinced him that the custom for pastors at least might be more honored in the breach than in the observance. When his members were in a critical condition he would make daily calls even at the extreme limits of the city.

Here too appeared the man's symmetry of service. Many a minister with his lusty strength and social nature would have been content to live, move, and have his being in a constant round of visits. None could have seen more clearly the inexorable limitations of a house-to-house activity. None could have recalled more cogently that in St. Paul's address to the elders at Miletus teaching publicly was mentioned before the teaching from house to house. "Good pastors," he would say, "are often invited by their people to resign; good preachers, never."

With such tireless service he appeared to be not the least disqualified for study or for public ministrations. After spending the daylight in visiting the sick or religiously awakened he would sleep for half an hour, eat a hearty meal, and work, for week after week, at "extra meetings," or read and write till eleven o'clock, which was, as a rule, his latest night study.

Again, in his private ministrations to his people he was helped by a sincere and sympathetic heart. Nothing roused his sensibilities so quickly as the pain, loss, or bereavement of his people. There were failures in Wall Street which, though costing him not a shilling, sent him to bed sick on account of the humiliation to some layman and the unavoidable loss to the Church. In the hearts of his people his tireless devotion in their hours of distress created the strongest gratitude. He declared that many a man had been recovered from backsliding, many an instance of coldness overcome, and many a missionary collection increased by timely pastoral calls. When there came sickness or death into the household of the fretful official or of the successful and worldly merchant he would say, "There is my opportunity."

The recovery from dangerous sickness of man, woman, or child was in some instances more strongly retained in his memory than in that of the person. When over eighty he recalled with vivid affection the leading back from death, as he believed in answer to prayer, of some whom he had known in his early ministry.

His regard for his people as a whole was in proportion to his devotion to individuals. In his early ministry pastorates were at the most but two years; yet so endeared to him did a charge become in that time that he could never break off from the Church he was serving without a period of depression lasting for several days.

His great success in the pulpit is to be ascribed to his evangelical doctrines, his logical acuteness, his mental ardor, and his affluence of diction. Under all his utterances lay a creed solid as granite. He would say with St. Paul, "We having the same spirit of faith, according as it is written, I believed, and therefore have I spoken; we also believe, and therefore speak." In all his preaching no place can be found where he dislocated one stone from the wall of the ancient faith. His deep and ardent trust, his force of mind, his sturdy theological attainments left him no sympathy whatever with the complacent radicalism and ambitious destructiveness of certain modern teachers. The refurbished systems, the airy apologies offered by some for God's word, were to him naught but vanity. The rationalist, pantheist, transcendentalist, and agnostic had no attraction for him. He had no prayer gauge, but a thousand proofs of prayer's efficacy.

He rested with sublime faith in the word of God, and this voice once fairly interpreted was for him final, unalterable. He spent his life in trying to impress on men what Revelation had said to him of God's omnipresence, omnipotence, holiness, justice, and love; of man's guilt and helplessness; of the overreaching sublimity of the moral law; of the Father's sending Christ, and Christ's coming in obedience to his Father's will; of the fullness of Christ's redemption and its perfect adaptation to every element of the sinner's nature; of the regenerating power of the Holy Ghost; of the tremendous reality of judgment, the irrevocable nature of its decisions, the eternity of the sinners' suffering and the saints' bliss. These were the themes on which he oftenest dwelt. In their justice, reasonableness, and absolute bearing on every soul he had the same kind of faith that he had in the cleansing nature of water or the life-giving power of sunshine.

His spirit was steeped in knowledge of the Holy Scriptures. Reading with difficulty in the Greek, and having scarcely any acquaintance with the Hebrew, he felt under the greater necessity of being well acquainted with the English Bible. If St. Luke could say of Cornelius that he prayed to God always, it might be said of John A. Roche that he was always occupied with the word of God. Few men had so thorough an acquaintance with the book from the point of the margin and the concordance. Nor were the divine oracles simply in the mind of the scholar; they were on the tongue of the speaker. In ordinary conversation he could hardly utter a hundred words without some quotation from Scripture or some form of allusion or suggestion derived from its study. Current themes were conceived by him in terms of scriptural expression. He often said that if he wanted to ransack his brains on any subject it was his custom to select a pertinent text and make a sermon. Many an airy and pretentious address, launched and sailing aggressively aloft like a balloon, did he penetrate and collapse with successive quotations from the New Testament. He well illustrated the exhortation, "To the law and to the testimony: if they speak not according to this word, it is because there is no light in them." Preaching—indeed, every form of speech—was a joy and inspiration to him. He would have felt ashamed if he could have been surprised when he had not a text and a subject ripe if speech were in order, or when he was not ready to pray if supplication were timely.

Always there was the subordination of self to truth. Archbishop Whately, commenting on Bacon's essay "Of Discourse," reminds us that there are two kinds of orators— those whose utterances may be compared to moonlight, a thing admired for its own beauty and not for the objects it illumines, whereas the very greatest orators resemble sunlight, which causes us to see all objects with clearness, never calling our attention to itself. Of Dr. Roche it might be said that as a preacher he sought to sink himself and show only his Lord and Master. Ever before him was the overwhelming conception of the glory of Christ, and before that radiance humility taught him to sink deeper and deeper into the dust.

Divine grace, natural gifts, and extraordinary industry were united in him. Endowed originally with clear tokens of power in oratory, he yet set himself to gather from books and experience the soundest principles and broadest intelligence. The light of genius never saved him from weary trudging. Like the creatures the prophet saw in vision, his nature had both wings and feet, and there were times when he was content to fold the wings and go afoot. From the very first day in the ministry he gave himself to thorough, unwearied, holy exertion. Archbishop Trench recalls Fuller's exclamation on the death of a famous divine, "O, the painfulness of his preaching!" By which was meant not the pain his sermon caused his hearers, but the labors they had caused himself. No better illustration of Dr. Roche's toilfulness can be found than his exertions to acquire and improve literary style. It might be said of him, as of Palmerston, that "he read everything and wrote an immense quantity." For every call he prepared himself with tireless industry. A speech in debate, an estimate of the character of some divine or of some lay worker, a funeral address, a prayer meeting talk, a sermon, and particularly discourses on missions or on anniversaries of the churches that invited him to their celebrations, would be written over *de novo* ten, twenty, even fifty times. His corrections of his own composition were innumerable. His principal sermons he rewrote at least once a year; and he has been known to recast entirely the same sermon six days in succession. Delivery of the discourse, instead of stopping, stimulated the process. His mind wrought with his ideas as the winds struggle with the clouds, producing in endless succession original forms. Every time he saw his own work he changed, omitted, underlined. Of him, as of John Ruskin, it is true that later touches sometimes wrought no improvement. His style was affluent, deeply analytical, rich in shades of thought, and steeped in scriptural phrasing. He was direct, hortatory, strenuous. Primarily a revivalist, he was next a rhetorician and theologian. His mind craved earnestness in its every form of expression, and he abhorred the commonplace and trivial.

In the preparation and delivery of each discourse there was seen a sublime intellectual energy. Plutarch compared the poetess Sappho to Casus, the son of Vulcan, who breathed out nothing but flame. In Dr. Roche's sermons we find only the ardor of a soul on fire to save other souls. He was intense in appeal and intolerant of apathy. He threw himself with all the energy of soul, with all the faculties of mind, and it might be said with every nerve and muscle of his body, into the labor of making God's truth plain and persuasive. There was in him that fullness and vehemence of action, that *laterum contentio* which was so marked a trait in Cicero. The words applied by Burke to one of the greatest of orators were true of him: "His enthusiasm kindles as he advances; and when he arrives at his peroration it is in full blaze."

His sermons produced instant and profound effect. When he probed conscience, convicted men were haunted day after day with the terrors of the Lord, and found no peace till they surrendered to the God of all grace. When he consoled, unlettered men and women carried his sentences and his beautifully enunciated texts of Scripture to the workbench and the home. When he preached to the great congregations at the Eastern Shore camp meetings, it was as when Brougham spoke for Queen Caroline to the House of Lords, his argument and oratory beating down all opposition. After one of his fervid appeals twenty and thirty persons would present themselves for prayers, many of them strong men.

His public labors had a most remarkable close in his octogenarian activity and popularity. Of many preachers it is said that the public tire by the time they are fifty, while Sydney Smith said that intellectually men never improved after they were forty. The eagerness of Dr. Roche's former congregations to hear him, their invitations to preach on their festival occasions, and his own enjoyment and effectiveness had extraordinary and increasing illustration for nearly ten years after he had entered his seventy-fifth year. It was as though the interest and enthusiasm of the people whom he had served fifty years before knew no abatement. How long this feeling would have continued it is impossible to say, had not one of the visits resulted in a weakness that rapidly reached a point from which there was no return to health.

His whole nature went out in the enterprise of rescuing men from the temporal and eternal results of sin. No preacher could have a stronger passion for sinners. His absorption in the work of the ministry was unworldly, saintlike. In a sublime sense he could have said with St. Paul, "One thing I do." To those who were closest about him it seemed as though he literally did nothing but eat, sleep, visit, write, read, and talk. As he dressed he prayed, as he walked he committed and often soliloquized, as he rode he composed sermons or noted on the back of an envelope the rising thought. He worked at the saving of souls with a zeal that proved him in the apostolic succession of grace and achievement. Something of what St. Bernard showed

when he traversed Europe and appealed to apathetic believers; something of what Wesley and Whitefield and Ed-
wards showed when, trampling on worldly advantages, they
gave themselves up to proclaim the Gospel, John A. Roche
manifested, in his lofty and whole-souled consecration, in
his absolute forgetfulness of self, in the constant bent of
his gaze on the glory of God, in his boundless enthusiasm
in the service of Jesus Christ.

Measured by any standard he was both a good and a
great man. With no assistance from fortune or circumstance, he educated himself and devoted a long life to what
he felt to be the highest interests of his fellow-men. He
was a preacher of righteousness, but none the less a gentleman, a philosopher, a hero, and a saint. His old-time
courtesy, his diligence, his simplicity and *naïveté*, his
fluent, sparkling, trenchant, epigrammatic conversation,
his candor and magnanimity, his white heat of earnestness,
his loyalty to his friends, the gracious character of his domestic life, his freedom from "envy, hatred, malice, and
all uncharitableness," his exalted aim as a minister, his
success as sermonizer, debater, and author, and, above all,
his tireless and joyous direction of all his powers to the
rescue of sinning men and to the magnifying of the glory
of God invested him while living with an honorable distinction, and demand for him dead the memorial of these
pages.

While he served God, his activity took on as many aspects as he himself had endowments. One of the very last
utterances from his lips was, "Do all you can for the glory
of God and for the good of men." It was the first time
that the sentiment was ever heard by those then around

him. In its circumstance it was scarcely other than the involuntary, unpremeditated utterance of a fevered mind, but with the utmost appropriateness it summed up all the endeavors of his life and the culminating earnestness of his soul.

Such as it was, his work is done. He spoke to souls that received from God through him a new impulse and that will live forever. The influence which he exerted must be carried through generations yet to come. His grand work was wrought not by chisel, but by pen and tongue, on the hearts of thousands of men and women. They themselves have been living epistles, known and read of all men, and in their regeneration, and in the countless influences for holiness and for eternity that have proceeded from them, John Alexander Roche had and has his crown of rejoicing.

AUTOBIOGRAPHY.

TILL the closing years of his life Dr. Roche committed nothing to writing concerning his family, childhood, or labors. After repeated and urgent requests from his children and from the churches and the Conferences he had served he gave some reminiscences. Those intended for the children were given in the form of a connected narrative, which bears the date January 1st, 1894. The others became contributions to some of the Methodist journals. Selections from both sources are here presented:

"I was born in Still Pond, Kent County, Md., on August 30th, 1813. My father, John Roche, was a native of Ireland. His ancestors came from France. He came to this country in his youth, and died in New Market, now Chesterville, Kent County, Md., in December, 1824. My mother was born near the 'Head of Chester,' now Millington, Kent County, Md.; her maiden name was Sarah Fisher. They had seven children: Alethia, Sarah Ann, David, Ellen Maria, John Alexander, Mary Jane, and Elenora, the last two being twins. These and David died in infancy. I was the youngest of those who attained maturity. At or about the time of my birth my father kept store at Still Pond Cross Roads, and also carried on a farm known as 'Camels Worth More;' on this farm I was born. It is near the 'I. U.' Church, St. Paul's parish, Chestertown, where probably I was baptized in my infancy. In the absence of my mother and not certain as to the fact, I was baptized after my conversion by the Rev. Solomon Sharp, in Smyrna, Del.

"When in my second year my parents removed to Baltimore, where we remained about six years. In Baltimore I first attended school. When I was eight years old my parents returned to the Eastern Shore, and my father taught school in New Market, where, when fifty-four years of age, he died from bilious fever. Young as my father was when he came to this country, he had what in those days would be considered a superior education. His family in Ireland, with which he corresponded till he died, were wanting neither in reputation nor means.

"Young as I was when he died, I know he was a careful and constant reader of authors of the highest character, and such as wrote on the weightiest subjects.

"As a man he was genial in spirit and generous in his habits. He was warm in his friendships and maintained a high sense of honor.

"While we were living in Baltimore the brother of my father, the Rev. David Roche, a Roman Catholic priest in Ireland after whom my brother David was named, desired my father to give me to him, to be educated by him, I suppose, for a priest. This my father declined, but, placing my open hand on a blank page of a letter he wrote, drew the size and shape of my hand, and sent it to my uncle.

"It was my father's ambition to see me a naval officer. He called me Alexander, after the Macedonian conqueror.

"The death of my father was my first great sorrow. It filled me with sadness; I refused to go to the grave and hear the clods fall on his coffin. I was the only son that lived, and my father, from my eighth year, would hardly go anywhere without me, and some of the sweetest memories of hospitality that my life has known were in my native county at my father's side in his visits to friends and the patrons of his school. He watched the tendencies of my mind, was my guard against the vices that youth often contracts, impressed the integrity and taught the honor that would distinguish coming years. Though not literally a member of the Church, he read the Bible with reverence and taught his children to walk by its rule.

"When with the rod he had occasion to correct my wrongs the severest part of his reformatory process was in the lecture he gave, telling me with ardor and eloquence of the benefit I would reap by following what he was then to impress with the switch.

"My mother was my father's second wife, and was much younger than he. She was about thirty-eight years of age when he died. Some five years after my father's death she married Mr. Daily; through this marriage she became possessed of slaves, who remained with her after Mr. Daily's death. He was a farmer, but lived only a few years. She was again married to Mr. Short, who also was a farmer. At her death, in 1851, she was and had been for years, a widow. She died from pneumonia, near Smyrna, Del., in her sixty-ninth year.

"She was a woman of sound intellect, excellent taste, refined manners, boundless energy, and great tact. Left at my father's death with no means of support except what her energy and skill supplied, she was always equal to the necessity that pressed her, and had the cheer that makes all easy. She was the light that dispelled the gloom that a husband's and a father's death threw over the household. My eldest sister, Alethia, had married Thomas Woodall, who, with his brother, owned a large part of the small village of New Market. With her we lived for several years. My younger sister, Sarah Ann, was married to John Woodall, the brother of Thomas. My youngest sister, Ellen Maria, when about eighteen years of age, was married in Smyrna, Del., to Reese J. Bell.

"My eldest sister, Alethia, died when about thirty years of age. Just before her sickness she sought God, and her death was in the triumphs of faith. With her husband she left two children, Sallie Ann and Mary Augusta. Sallie Ann married Mr. Gamble and died early. Mary Augusta married a Mr. Darling, and is still living in Baltimore.

"My sister Sarah Ann had a numerous family by her first husband, John Woodall, and was left a widow when about thirty-four years of age. After some years she married a Mr. Raughley, a farmer, near Smyrna. He lived only a few years. She died when seventy-seven years old. The children who survive her are Mrs. Hannah Spruance and Mrs. Mary Hoffecker, both of Smyrna. Del., and Mrs. Frances Bradley, of Elkton, Md.

"My sister Ellen Maria Bell died in Millington, Kent County, Md., and left two children, Sallie Eliza, who married Mr. Megear, of Smyrna, and Ellen, who married Mr. Allen, of Wilmington. Del. My sister Ellen Maria died when thirty-six years old. I alone of my father's family survive!

"Both father and mother had excellent constitutions, and died from acute diseases.

"My sense of obligation to my mother has increased with my years. The thought she gave to her children, the lessons of wisdom she impressed on our youthful minds, the guards she threw around our steps, the example she furnished in illustration of the principles and practices she taught, and her constant care for me, her only son, disclosed a wonderful devotion. All the thought that so active a mind could take, all the care a mother's heart could show, all the effort that one of her sense of right could prompt, were manifest in all the days of my childhood and youth. The teachings of the household were virtue, honor, and usefulness, and by the means at command she impressed the truths that were the best calculated to crown all our future lives with favor before God and the world.

"Being the youngest of the family that lived, the love and care of my three sisters for me, and their own womanly circumspection, compelled in me a devotion to them that was one of the greatest joys of my youth and early manhood—a joy that remained with me till my last sister, Mrs Raughley, died.

"We, as a family, had few near relations in this country, and those of my father's family, though numerous, were unknown to us. My mother had one half-sister and also one half-brother. The sister married a Mr. Mott, and she had two sons, William and Thomas Mott, and a daughter, Nancy. The daughter grew up in my father's family and was there married to a Mr. Grace, in Baltimore. My mother's half-brother was John Medders, of Georgetown Cross Roads, as the village was then called, now Galena. He had many children by his first and second wives. His eldest daughter, Hannah, married Joseph Ireland, Esq., member of the Legislature of Maryland; a younger daughter, by his second wife, married Wright Spry, of Chesterville. The eldest son of my uncle, George W. Medders, became sheriff of the county. As cousins, these were very dear to me: and the sight of my uncle's carriage at the door, when I returned from school, gave me a gay spirit, as it told me Cousin Hannah was there. My uncle's house was one of real and broad hospitality.

"While living in Baltimore a cousin from Ireland, Dr. William Roche, came over to this country, married in Baltimore, and went South. I thought he was one of the finest-looking men that I had ever seen. I think so now from my memory of his form and features.

"There was an Irish lady in Baltimore known in those days as a 'lady of quality,' with whom my father and family had close connection; but I think relationship was not of blood. In their youth my father and she were close in their friendships, and possibly in education.

"My education began when I was very young. I do not remember when I learned the alphabet, the Lord's Prayer, or the Apostles' Creed. The Bible in the family was the word of God, and had its place on the stand and was held in highest reverence. My eldest sister, Alethia, in taking it up to read was careful not to lift it 'upside down.' Among the last words my father uttered was a passage from the book of Job. When I crossed the steps of the place of worship I was taught to lift my hat. This lesson has gone through my life as a propriety for observance.

"Up to the time of my father's death he was the teacher of the village school, and my education was with him. In winter the school was large. Then the sons of the farmers

3

could attend. The ordinary branches of English education were taught—reading, writing, arithmetic, grammar, and geography.

"In the school there were bright and beautiful girls, who would make boys study 'to keep up with them,' and there were boys of excellent capacity and some of close application. I am sure my sisters, Sarah Ann and Ellen Maria, who were older than I, were better students and more advanced. I did not like hard study, and I am not aware that I showed any special aptitudes. I was among the youngest in the school, but was not willing to show inferiority in learning to those around me. There was one youth, a farmer's son, who came to school only in winter, and so capable was he that I would find he was getting in advance of me. He made me work. In the exhibitions of the school, after my father's death, when I was twelve or fourteen years of age, whether from aptitude for declamation or not, a good deal more was imposed on me than upon any other scholar. On one of these occasions I was in single speeches and dialogues five times, and it devolved upon me to give the opening piece. At the close I heard for the first time in my life a clapping that I was at a loss to interpret, but was told it meant applause. This reconciled me to it, and I welcomed it when at other times it came.

"I have often thought of the hard time I had in wrestling with the multiplication table. To conquer it by memory seemed about impossible. In the wrestle it would throw me, and for a time I would be prostrate in my hopes. But I would rise and take hold of it, and if it flung me I would try again. At such times that which my father adopted as a motto would come to me—'Don't give up the ship.' The brave Captain Lawrence, who fell on the *Chesapeake* in the War of 1812, about the time of my birth, having received a mortal wound, when he could do no more, addressing his men, used that never-to-be-forgotten language, 'Don't give up the ship.' This my father fairly ingrained into my soul. It is, therefore, with me now when duty faces me and difficulties rise. I conquered the multiplication table. At last it seemed as if I so well knew it that I knew nothing else by comparison. It has remained conquered for about seventy years—a reward sufficient to justify application and persistence. In this country school I obtained, excepting what at an earlier age I had learned in Baltimore, most of my early education.

"As a youth at home and in school, except when about twelve years of age, I was more pleased with play than study. In study I had superiors; in the sports, innocent, I had a supreme claim. I was social and gay, and loved any fun. But I had great respect for religion. Several schoolmasters filled the place my father had occupied, and among them one Erastus Curtis from New England. He and his brother, Leonidas, came from Yale College as students seeking places as teachers. Leonidas obtained a situation at Black's Cross Roads. He was a brilliant young man, but with intemperate tendencies. Erastus, our teacher, was deeply pious and a Congregationalist. He opened school with prayer. He was criticised by a few Methodists for standing; they thought that kneeling was the right approach to God. But his posture was no bar to the entrance of my heart. From some cause he took to me. Then I was beginning to appreciate study, and applied myself. He used to take me round with him when he visited his patrons and collected his bills.

"There was not, in my youth, any church in the village. For a time the Methodists 'held meeting' in Oliver Smith's barn, then in the schoolhouse where my father taught on week days—every two weeks by the preachers on Kent Circuit—occasionally in a private house. My parents were not members. In Baltimore they sometimes went to the Roman Catholic Church, and sometimes to a Protestant Church—sometimes to the Methodist Episcopal. My impression is that I was baptized in my infancy in the Protestant Episcopal Church, by Rev. S. H. Turner, rector of St. Paul's Church, Chestertown—afterward the distinguished professor in the General Theological Seminary, New York, and the founder, in connection with others, of St. Peter's Church, in West Twentieth Street, in that city.

"In my fourteenth year I thought it time to engage in some kind of business for self-support, and went to Smyrna, Del., and entered as a clerk in the store of Messrs. William L. Duhamel and John S. Lambdin. I remained there some ten months, but felt a desire to learn a trade; and not by mother's dictation, but by her consent, I bound myself to Messrs. Benson and Catts, large coach makers, to learn harness making and trimming. It was from no lack of ability that I left the store. Young as I was, I had the opportunity of going into the best store of the town, that of John Cummins. But I wanted a trade.

"This was an epoch in my life. While there, in June, 1829, there broke out in Smyrna one of the greatest revivals of religion that I have ever known, and I was one of the early converts; and both my sisters then in Smyrna, Sarah Ann and Ellen Maria, were numbered with the saved."

The following was contributed by Dr. Roche to the *Penin-

sula Methodist of July 5th, 1884. under the title "Smyrna M. E. Church and Solomon Sharp and Henry G. King in 1829:"

"When our Lord 'called unto him the twelve and began to send them forth,' it was 'two and two.' There was a divine philosophy in it. 'In the mouth of two or three witnesses every word shall be established;' and where there is unity of purpose 'two are better than one;' each can strengthen the other.

"Need enough there was for two preachers on a circuit, when it is considered there might be from fifteen to forty-five appointments to fill in four weeks.

"In 1829 there was no station in the Philadelphia Conference below Elkton. This was then filled by the rising Francis Hodgson. Dover, though the capital of the State, was in a circuit, and its headquarters. Smyrna had the same relation in another charge. In this small village was a Methodist society which all considered, in the judgment of the writer, was, in intelligence, in social position, and in deep piety, equal to any charge of the same size that he has ever known.

"At the time named. Solomon Sharp and Henry G. King were the preachers of this circuit. What laws the wisdom of the episcopacy recognizes in making men colleagues we cannot always judge. It may be a question whether contrasts or resemblances exert the greater power. As a rule, a married and a single man were associated, to prevent too much expense to the charge. As a rule, a young and inexperienced man was placed under one whose age, experience, and wisdom in the administration of our economy made him the proper instructor and guide of the junior in his studies and ministrations. Colleges were unknown as preparations for our work. Theological seminaries did not much more than exist in even the strongest denominations. When spoken of as institutions of the Old World it was with derision, as 'manufactories of preachers.' The Methodist ministers were supposed to be 'God-made.' We were known as graduates of 'Brush College.' The country was sparsely settled. Villages were small. Towns were few and far between. The fields and the forests, the swamp and the wilderness constituted much of the ground we traveled. Thence came many of the people to whom we preached the word.

"But let no one think that the graduates of 'Brush College' were men of unfurnished minds. We had our text-books, the Bible, the Hymn Book, the *Discipline*, Wesley's *Sermons*, his *Notes on the New Testament*, his *Christian Perfection*, Fletcher's *Appeal to Matter of Fact and Common Sense*—a glorious book! Our curriculum was respected. 'There were giants in those days.' George G. Cookman said, 'A Methodist preacher could drive a rousing business on a small capital.' But, with such resources, the world saw mighty men. Under such circumstances an experienced preacher could be of great help to an inexperienced one.

"Solomon Sharp was one of the honored fathers of the former century; Henry G. King had been a preacher for nine years only, but had already made for himself a name. He had filled charges of interest and responsibility in city and country. In his earlier ministry one was brought to Christ upon whom the eyes of the Church were at once fixed, and who in a short time filled some of the first stations in American Methodism, and who, while yet young, was called to the professorship of our first university, and was then elected corresponding secretary of the American Bible Society, and for about a generation served with highest honor in that responsible position. What minister that has labored among us awaits a richer jewel for his crown than Henry G. King, in that precious seal of his ministry, Dr. Joseph Holdich?

"But with all the reputation and experience of King, by the fact that he had lost his wife, he was placed as the junior, because he stood as a single preacher.

"A greater contrast, in some of their characteristics, could hardly be imagined than that which existed between Sharp and King. As a preacher on a circuit, and as a presiding elder in a district, Solomon Sharp had been the means of wonderful revivals. Anyone seeing Solomon Sharp would take him to be a remarkable man. His person was large, his step majestic, his hair was white, ample, and flowing, falling even to his shoulders; his eyes were large and lustrous, his features were intellectual, and his countenance was full of benignity. His dress was neither ancient nor modern. A coat made by a tailor would have been to him like a strait-jacket. His wife was the peerless maker of his garments, and she knew what he needed. Was ever man more indifferent to outward show? But in truth was his coat any more like a bag, except in color, than some of the sacks of ladies, or sack coats of men, at this day? He had broad shoulders for the coat to rest on, and his arms were large enough and strong enough to confine it, if he wished. He carried the best theology in his brain, for the pulpit, and some of the same, bound up in books, he carried in those famous pockets, that thus he might be helpful to the piety of his people. He was anxious that the 'society be duly supplied' with sanctified literature. Who, like his wife, could make coats for that purpose?

"Who discounted Solomon Sharp for his unique dress? Who would have changed it? It was like a part of his individuality. He moved among men as a patriarch— some counted him a prophet. We cannot say that he was not visionary. The people honored his virtues, revered his character, and he would have been a bold man that attempted to criticise his doctrine, deny his logic, or dispute his power. It is rarely the case that any minister attains, by learning or piety or preaching, the power that Solomon Sharp had in the town of Smyrna. He was sovereign in his realm, and no one would shorten or weaken his scepter.

"His preaching was largely expository, as Matt. xi, 7-15: 'What went ye out into the wilderness to see? A reed shaken with the wind?' and for an hour and a half the people would hang on his lips. Isa. vi, 1-12: 'In the year that King Uzziah died I saw also the Lord sitting upon a throne, high and lifted up, and his train filled the temple.' The rapture that this discourse produced lives like yesterday in the memory of the writer. He believed in the millennium, and preached round the circuit on Rev. xx, 1: 'And I saw an angel come down from heaven, having the key of the bottomless pit and a great chain in his hand.' The people heard as if 'the great white throne' was before them. He selected the sublimest themes for his subjects, and an awe rested upon the congregation. This was one reason of his great power.

"James Waddell, whom William Wirt heard in the forests of Virginia, and whose fame he has made immortal in *The British Spy,* could hardly have commanded his audience more by his eloquence than Solomon Sharp did the people of Smyrna by his weighty utterances. They saw, they heard, they felt God in the minister God sent.

"He was not a classic; he was a divine. He was an oracle. His manner in the pulpit was colloquial. Ephraim Jefferson, a local preacher and an excellent judge, said, 'He is the best everyday preacher I ever heard.' Bishop Asbury said he had the best voice of any preacher on the Peninsula. It was as if given for public speaking. It was not a turbulent, a fretted, nor an interrupted, but a steady silvery stream. It flowed out like water from the fountain. There was nothing forced, and it had great compass. As with his voice, so with his matter; as a rule. when he 'opened wide his mouth' God did fill it, and he spoke as easily as the eagle moves when fully on the wing. Flowers do not more readily give their perfume than he preached under the convictions of duty, the impulses of holy passion, and the inspirations of the Spirit of God. Under the divine anointing, truth came from his lips as music flies from the string when touched by the hand of the skillful artist.

"But no one fully knew Solomon Sharp that did not know him in prayer. He walked with God, and his prayers showed they were not strangers. Some would say he was so familiar with the Almighty that he took great liberties with him. It was not irreverence: it was holy boldness. Piner Mansfield was given up to die. Sharp entered his chamber, knelt, and said: 'Lord, thou canst do without him. Thou hast many about thy throne to do thee honor. We have too few such as we need. This is one of those that we want here for thy work.' Then he importuned. He who ever heard Sharp importune knows what it means. He 'took hold of God's strength.' Mansfield lived, and the people said, 'Sharp's prayers would not let him die.' Mrs. William A. Budd, a daughter of Judge Isaac Davis, one of the most intelligent members of his charge, said that if Solomon Sharp prayed for her she was sure of heaven. So spoke the people who knew him best.

"Henry G. King was not less a character. In him there was nothing commonplace. There was little in his labors to remind one of other men. Nature had given him a fine form, a strong constitution, and he was full of nervous energy. He was in his prime, and had the physical ability to do any kind or amount of service that he attempted. He was an earnest Christian: he flamed with light, he burned with zeal, and all his labors showed a quenchless ardor. The caution to 'spare thyself' might have met the same rebuke from him that it received of our Lord. As the patriot spurns the considerations of life's value when he rushes into the thickest of the fight, and asks nothing but victory, so Henry G. King 'counted not his life dear unto him, so that he might finish his course with joy.' To him apathy was damning. Alert, energetic, unqualified, and untiring in his efforts, he could not endure indifference. With a live and consecrated intellect, he was studious of, and fruitful in, the use of means for success. Preaching was with him a means to an end, and if by the subjects Solomon Sharp delighted to treat he revealed some of his characteristics, the same was the case with King. He showed his purpose in his themes. Such were his texts: 'He received him joyfully'—urging conversion; 'Surely I come quickly. Amen. Even so, come, Lord Jesus'—startling men with the terrors of the last day. From 'Gideon's army' he took occasion to tell the supine they were in the way of God's work—that it was not by the thirty-two thousand, but by the three hundred, God would save Israel. He charged nominal Christians to 'get out of the way.' If he was not a 'sensational preacher' he was a preacher to make a sensation, and would so preach as to stir men.

"He held 'watch nights' in summer, or in the autumn, or at any time. He would draw the people to the church. He seemed to say by his labors, 'Give me souls, or I die.' He might declare with Richard Cecil, 'Hell is before me, and thousands of souls shut up in everlasting burnings. Jesus Christ sends me to proclaim his ability and love.'

"These two ministers on Smyrna Circuit were not duplicates. They were each the complement of the other. But there was unity in this diversity. The two showed how diverse are the divine methods in compassing divine ends. If the one was preeminent in tearing down the kingdom of Satan, the other was preeminent in building up the kingdom of Christ. There was contrast. One was serene and uniform: the other was vivid and versatile. One shone like a star: the other shot like a meteor. The one rested in God like a rock in its fastness; the other was 'like goodness in perpetual motion.' If Sharp was an oracle, King was a 'tongue of fire.' If one communicated his wisdom, the other imparted his warmth. Sharp said in my hearing he 'could love God with all his heart as easily as he could drink that glass of water.' Taking the tumbler in his hand, he added he 'could believe God's promise to him as easily as he could turn his hand,' suiting the action to the word. No man that I ever knew seemed to me so fully as King to verify St. Paul's exhortation, 'Rejoice evermore, pray without ceasing, and in everything give thanks.' His prayers were full of praises. As a boy convert my reverence for Solomon Sharp was such that I stood and looked at the ground he walked on, and felt as if it were 'holy earth.' I bought my first volume of Watson's *Institutes,* just out, from him, and obtained other works as he suggested. He did me great good. But there never lived on earth a man to whom, under God, I owe so much for my conversion, and for my spiritual support in my early Christian life, as to Henry Grubb King. O, how I bless his memory!

"On Sabbath, June 13th, 1829, he launched these mighty sentences upon the congregation: 'Sinners, we will have you. We will cast our net upon the right side of the ship, and will inclose a great multitude.' "

For another number of the *Peninsula Methodist* Dr. Roche wrote as follows on "The Revival in the Smyrna Methodist Episcopal Church A. D. 1829:"

"Man has a moral nature that demands his first attention. The faculties with which he is endowed, the passions by which he is moved, and the instincts of which he is conscious do not more clearly show he was not made for idleness, or for the cold and cheerless regions of solitude, but for improvement, society, and companionship, than do his moral intuitions prove that he was not made to 'live without God in the world,' but to recognize the divine glory as 'the chief end of man.' To no part of our physical, intellectual, or social being is there a more positive appeal than to our sense of right. Our spiritual capabilities are the most exalted; they utter the loudest cry, and there are times when they most perfectly absorb thought and direct action. But men may slumber over any of their susceptibilities. There are periods when the sublime passion of patriotism may not assert itself, and yet on a sudden may be waked to the most convincing demonstrations of its presence and power. This was seen in the 'great uprising' of April, 1861. So the mind that has long slept with regard to moral obligations may in one hour wake to the intensest interest, and to the most earnest effort, on the question of eternal salvation. Nothing may transcend this 'great concern.' The philosophy of a religious revival may never be given; speculations as to its cause and progress may prove unsatisfactory, but the reality of the work as truly commands respect as if everything in the labor of man and the plan of God was perfectly comprehended.

"Immediately preceding the revival of which we write there was nothing in the state of the society to indicate its approach. The language of the members was, 'Religion is at a low ebb.' They were without reproach; they had a commanding influence in the community; they were generally plain in dress, in speech, and in manners. There was simplicity in their public service. Modern notions of choirs, organs, and instruments of music they had none. To 'sing with the spirit' was understood to mean to 'sing without note' or the use of any instrument but the human voice. A transient resident had the temerity to attempt singing by note in 'the meetinghouse,' and the look that our old leader of singing gave, and the scowl that his features expressed, are still before me; for a brief space the society was in a flutter. As for manuscript in the pulpit, except as it might be hid away in the head or heart, it was not thought of, and reading sermons was an unknown art. Solomon Sharp, preaching from the text, 'The poor have the Gospel preached unto them,' added, 'The rich have it read.' He placed reading sermons with 'steeple churches.' But on the dawn of June 13th, 1829, there appeared no cloud of the size of a man's hand to foretoken the showers of blessings. The heavens gave no sign. There was no rumbling, no disturbance of an earthquake. The cholera did not appear till 1832. As the sun that rose on Sodom the day the city flamed scattered no vengeful fires to cause the woe, so the sun that rose on Smyrna the day of the revival shed no benigner beams than was his wont, to account for the scene.

"On that Sabbath Henry Grubb King filled the pulpit—every part of it. That day he launched those mighty sentences: 'Sinners, we will have you. We will cast our net upon the right side of the ship, and will inclose a great multitude.' One said for such speech he 'deserved to be taken out of the pulpit.' But these words rang out upon the assembly as from a minister whose trumpet blast was God's signal for immediate and decisive action. Down deep in the caverns of the soul, amid the recesses of disturbed spirits, for hours afterward were heard the reverberations of those words, as if they would not die—as if their authority became more and still more awe-inspiring. That night witnessed scenes of penitence and exhibitions of ecstasy that the memory of fifty-five years reproduces with the vividness of yesterday. The whole church was an altar. Could the terror have been greater the morning after the angel of the Lord smote the camp of the Assyrians than was the triumph of God's people the morning after this revival was ushered in? They recounted the moral victories, and 'then was their mouth filled with laughter and their tongue with singing; then said they, The Lord hath done great things for us.' He had 'turned the captivity of Zion.'

"The news spread; the people came; the church was thronged. Night after night, week after week, for successive months, worship was kept up, and sometimes till the morning hours. The shout of newborn souls again and again broke the stillness of the midnight as they returned to their homes to tell the 'great things God had done for them.' In store and shop and countinghouse, at the corners of the street, in social and business circles, the people of all ages and conditions spoke of the revival. What would be its result? If it could commence under such circumstances, continuance was not incredible. Religion was the ascendant attraction. It was the thought of every mind, the theme of every tongue. Guilt confessed, Contrition wept, Faith struggled, Prayer prevailed. The revival had come to stay till its mission was accomplished. It swept through the town like a tornado. The young readily yielded; the stout-hearted quailed; the obdurate were subdued. Some, sunk in vice, rose to eminence in virtue; the desperate, that defied the sweep, were torn away from the grasp of iniquity; the town was under a moral arrest! O, that day! the tears of joy come while I write.

It was an epoch in the writer's history; it was in the history of many. How sagely did Judge Davis say, 'If these boys will only be faithful, God will make men of them'!

"Though the revival was generally as unlooked for as a bolt from a serene sky, the work was as manifest as when the ancient oak is shivered or the massive tower is riven.

"The exhibitions of power were not confined to the sanctuary; at the family altar hearts received the truth and found peace with God. On one occasion the room filled with apprentices at trades became a scene of agony and rapture. This was at eventide. In another instance, at morning prayer, a lady in the neighborhood, under deepest concern for her soul, rushed into the private dwelling, kneeling there to pray for her pardon; that morning prayer went on till noon, and the house was filled with those who came to witness and profit by the work.

"The field and forest became the resort of penitents. Not while memory has its seat will the writer forget the 19th of June, 1829, when, at a quarter before ten o'clock at night, he found forgiveness of all his sin in the field where he had gone with a burden that had been as a millstone about him for five nights of deepest anguish. He had gone there for seclusion and wrestling with God; but his cries drew many from a distance to the place, and when the light of heaven shone, there were more than a score of persons present to witness his rejoicing. The next day he accompanied a young friend, Joseph Mann, to the woods, where he, too, soon rejoiced in conscious pardon, and in the outburst of his ecstatic spirit gave the early proof of the talents by which nature did so aid him in his subsequent ministry.

"For weeks thereafter it was quite common for boys to go into the fields for prayer. At length one good citizen expressed the thought that while it was right for boys to want to be good it was not right for them to trample down his wheat or corn. It was declared he used some hard language—I will not say 'bad words.' It was to me this lesson, that when we are trying to do our best we may still pray, 'Forgive us our trespasses.' It was not our design, but we did trespass on Mr. Blackstone. As the writer was first in the transgression he was readiest to avoid it in the future.

"Perhaps nothing was more remarkable in that revival than the earnest type of Christians that it made. There was work; there was shouting; there were late meetings; there were many things that might be criticised; but never did the writer see better illustrations of earnest religion than came out of that work. Young converts seemed regenerated to show a new nature—to disclose the highest form of a divine life. They were not those eaglets that required their nest to be stirred before they would try their wings; they more nearly resembled the partridge of that region, that is hardly out of shell before he seems to say, I was disimprisoned to show you that I can run. They were called on to pray, and they did pray: and out of 'the mouth of babes and sucklings God ordained praise.' It was not a question of self-confidence, but of duty. They did not labor because they thought they had skill, but because gratitude to God and love to souls impelled them. Fasting became a habit of every week; self-denial was very broad in its significance; and taking up the cross permitted no parley.

4

"For the increase of their strength a number of the young converts would go on Sabbath morning, before breakfast, and hold a prayer meeting under a tree, at a convenient place for seclusion. After attending church in the morning we would walk from three to six miles in the country to assist in holding meetings in destitute places. Twenty years after this, when the writer was stationed in Asbury, Wilmington, he was addressed in the street by a colored man, who asked him if he did not remember, when a boy, holding meeting in the house of Widow Meredith, in Cypress Swamp. The past flashed in a moment, and he seemed again to hear the cry of the man's distress as he sat on the doorstep, the house being so full as to allow no room. This was one of the early trophies of these useful labors. The late Pennel Coombe took under his special care an old church near his father's farm, and though it had been given up by the circuit preachers, there he saw 'the dry bones live' and an excellent society raised up. Thus the late William Meginnis, James S. Wools, William Nelson, now one of the honored members of Smyrna Church, with Joseph Mann, William Cahoon, and others, delighted to contribute their influence to the cause of Christ. In the church we were allowed a prayer meeting, and as young people we sometimes indulged a taste for hymns not in the book. On one occasion, after singing with much spirit,

> ' Babylon is fallen, is fallen, is fallen,
> Babylon is fallen, to rise no more,'

one who was more mature than we, said he wished it would fall and never rise again—meaning the hymn. We accepted the criticism, and declined singing it afterward. It is God's purpose that 'the strong shall bear the infirmities of the weak.'

"Was ever a revival, though sudden, more opportune? Smyrna had been distinguished for great revivals in other years. But at this time there was much agitation from 'the reform movement' and the organization of the Methodist Protestant Church. One of the preachers who had just left the circuit, John Smith, a man of talent, joined the new society. Besides the excitement that was thus produced, it is a fact that many of the leading members of the church dated their conversion back to the earliest days of our organization. Daniel and James McDowell were soon to pass away. Benjamin Farrow, Thomas Lambdin, Thomas Maberry, and John Gerry were in a little while to be numbered with the departed. There were few young people of either sex in church fellowship. Joseph Farrow, Jr., and Joseph Garey were two earnest young men in the society. The present Mrs. Thomas A. Budd, of Philadelphia, daughter of Judge Davis; the Misses Patterson, daughters of Robert Patterson, one of the strong men of the charge; the Misses Farrow, whose father was among the leaders, and the Misses Mansfield, daughters of Rev. Piner Mansfield, adorned the profession. But the town seemed full of young people, and what were these among so many? The place abounded in 'backsliders.' This was a humility and a hindrance. Solomon Sharp said from the pulpit, 'Nearly all of you have had a pass at religion.' With such a history as Methodism had in that town, could it 'die out'? 'The wood and hay and stubble' of 'decency and order' were swept away by fire from the throne of God. The people were amazed at the grandeur of the result.

"Among the converts were six that gave themselves to the itinerancy of the Methodist Episcopal Church. Joseph Mann entered the Philadelphia Conference, but failing health induced early retirement from the ranks. His smooth and pathetic voice, with his ready utterance, gave promise of popular power. James S. Wools was one of the most pious young men that I ever knew. He went to the Southwest, and was for a time a presiding elder. John Ruth entered the Philadelphia Conference, and after filling highly responsible stations was chosen to the useful post of chaplain to the Eastern Penitentiary, in Philadelphia. William Meginnis married Ann, the oldest daughter of the Rev. Solomon Sharp. and joined the Indiana Conference, where his reputation as a minister, a presiding elder, and a man of God is as 'ointment poured forth.' Pennel Coombe and the writer joined the Philadelphia Conference of April 8th, 1835. Mr. Coombe was too long and too well known in that body and in the Church to need any words from my pen. As a secretary of the Conference, as a stationed preacher, as a presiding elder, as a member of the General Conference, his record places him among the strong men of the Church. Of all these ministers, the writer is the solitary survivor. But for grace that cheers he would indeed be solitary. Alas that so few are in the Church on earth, of the many saved in that revival, who can appreciate the narrative that I give!

"Edmund Wilmer, for many years a distinguished citizen; James McDowell, Jr., who filled some of the most responsible positions in the Church, and was one of its most sensible members, both of whom have passed away—these with the writer were among the youngest professing religion in the revival. What Methodism does may well astonish us.

"How it was with the others who became ministers, I know not; but the writer, before his conversion, had as much expectation of being an angel on the earth as a minister of the Gospel. The young men coming forward to our ministry to-day have, without criticism, as many advantages as those of any other Church. Lack of scholastic training in those earlier times was not confined to our ministry. Some of the most distinguished lawyers, physicians, and statesmen were not linguists. Lindley Murray was known by his grammar, and Hugh Blair by his rhetoric, but many in the professions were ignorant of the rules of the one and the canons of the other. Always remembering that 'our sufficiency is of God,' it may be added we learned to exhort by exhorting, we learned to preach by preaching. Dr. Thomas H. Skinner, professor of homiletics and sacred eloquence in the Union Theological Seminary, New York, told his class the only instruction he ever received for preaching was from the eloquent Dr. Henry Kollock, and that was simply some use to be made of a particular text. Yet Dr. Skinner became one of the ablest of American preachers, and was a distinguished teacher in the 'school of the prophets.' The writer had more help that that. On one occasion that courtly Christian gentleman, Rev. John Durborough, the maternal grandfather of the late Bishop Cummins of the Reformed Episcopal Church, said to James S. Wools and the writer: 'Avoid fear. First, whenever you speak in my presence know that you have one hearer that is praying for you. Second, when you have chosen a text it is fair to assume that you know more about it than those who hear, because for the time you have given it more study.' What could more encourage us?

"It was our custom after going into the country to labor to call on 'Father Sharp.' He would ask us two questions: Were any converted? Was anybody made mad? If to these questions we answered 'No,' he would say, 'Then you did nothing.' This was assuming that if we disturbed the dominion of the adversary, he would stir up wrath; he would be mad if we made such appeals as he could not easily resist. Whether this was a criterion of judging with our fathers, I know not. Certain it is that Christ made them 'fishers of men,' and of all sorts of men. Among these is Leviathan; for him they used the harpoon, and he would make 'the deep boil like a pot.' Thus we were taught to be bold for God, to be fearless in his work, not to 'soften God's truth or smooth our tongue.' The first circuit of the writer showed him the value of this lesson.

"To any eye it was manifest that God made Henry G. King an instrument of amazing power. The general may not only be the head, but the heart, of the army. What were the three hundred without Gideon? Spirits blend, association assimilates, sympathy gives force to action. Is it not still true that virtue goes out of a man? Courage and cowardice are catching. 'Face answers to face in water, so the heart of man.' King transfused himself when he uttered those daring but prophetic words; his 'bow abode in strength;' his soul was in his sentences, and God was in his soul. The arrow flamed as it flew, and kindled what it struck. Solomon Sharp and he were a unit. One could do what the other could not. If one could lay souls prostrate in sackcloth and ashes, the other could edify—build them up as palaces for God. When duty required them both to be out on the circuit never were there better helpers than they had. Piner Mansfield, Ephraim Jefferson, and Dr. John D. Perkins were local preachers in the town. When Mansfield was 'on his high horse' he was a grand warrior. Jefferson knew where the hearts of the people were, and he was a splendid archer. Perkins had a genius for sermonizing, and loved the ministry so well that it seemed a pity that he could not give himself wholly to it. Like Luke, he was 'the beloved physician.'

"These servants of God were at it with all their hearts, night after night, and would refuse furlough. They called to their aid such men as Judge Davis, Denny Stevenson, Israel Peterson, and other mighty men, and 'holy women, not a few,' as Mrs. Rachel Wilmer, mother of Edmund Wilmer and of the first wife of Pennel Coombe. Mrs. Wilmer was one of the most gifted women in prayer that I ever heard; and there was Mrs. Maria Cummins, mother of Bishop Cummins, and scores of others whom I may not give, but 'whose names are in the book of life.' The field is before me as I once saw it, but the reaper has been gathering them in. The few remaining sheaves will soon be garnered; then we will shout the 'harvest home.' "

Regarding his entrance on the ministry, Dr. Roche writes as follows:

"My conversion was indeed a change of heart and life. I, who had had no more thought about being a preacher than of being an angel, was quickly impressed with the thought that I would have to preach. But the possibility seemed an impossibility. How could I be a minister of the Gospel? How could I, who had been so ignorant of God, so great a stranger to the ways of holiness—I, that knew so little about the great truth that the Gospel exhibits? What qualification had I from nature or education? I would turn from the thought, but it would not turn from me. It held me in its grasp, and day and night it pursued me with obligation to try to save sinners. For five long nights of moral gloom I sought forgiveness of God. But then came the light of his countenance, and I had the joy of believing. But for five years continued the mental struggle with regard to entering the ministry. This was not the struggle of unwillingness, but the thought of incompetency. My trade, hope of success in business, my relations, nothing stood in my way but the assumption of inability. I did not then as clearly as now see how God can help one who fully puts himself in his hands. All this time I tried to placate conscience and honor God by labor as I was able. I worked in two churches of destitute neighborhoods, in prayer meetings, in classes, in exhortation. I at once engaged in study, read Christian biography, studied the *Discipline*, the government of the Church, and obtained the first edition of Watson's *Theological Institutes*. In winter I attended night school in the Smyrna Academy, and many a midnight, and two o'clock in the morning, saw me perusing the best works to fit me for the ministry. Meanwhile I neglected no meeting or means of grace.

"Five times during my apprenticeship I read the Bible through. Thus, in reality I was being educated for the work that was to fill my life, and be my glory and crown of rejoicing. And while pursuing my trade the venerable Solomon Sharp came into the shop and put licenses for exhortation into my hand. I pushed them into my pocket, with a feeling, 'It is a humiliation of the church thus to make one of my age and in my position as an apprentice an official member of the church.' But it was the church acting, and I was not responsible. In a little while it was suggested that I should fill the place of a preacher at a 'four days' meeting' in Millington, Kent County, Md., where I was making a visit to my sister, Mrs. Ellen Maria Bell. The late Bishop Scott was the preacher in charge of the Kent Circuit, and it was he who urged and finally constrained me to yield. He had only a little time before been my preacher on the Smyrna Circuit. He took the place (in Smyrna Circuit) of Rev. James Nichols, one of the most talented and eloquent preachers that I ever knew, but who had become insane. This was the period when 'four days' meeting' was the order for revival work. I told Mr. Scott I was only an exhorter. The congregation would be very large—of Sabbath afternoon, when nearly everybody went to our church. I suggested it was unfitting that I should fill the place; when he said, with a figure that told his natural taste and habit with the gun, 'If you were gunning you would prefer to fire into a large flock.' It is just to say Rev. Levi Scott spent little time with the gun, though fond of it, and a good marksman. His ministry absorbed him, as it did all Methodist ministers in that day. Yet when on the Delaware District as presiding elder he went with Frederick Gorman, Esq., of Virginia, a splendid shot; and he acknowledged Scott could beat him, but added, 'He always gets on his knees when he shoots.'

"I yielded to the importunity of this holy man, for in those days it was understood we were to obey orders. At three o'clock I was in the pulpit, and the people filled the house. I took for my text Isa. xl, 6-8: 'The voice said, Cry. And he said, What shall I cry? All flesh is grass, and all the goodliness thereof is as the flower of the field: the grass withereth, the flower fadeth: because the spirit of the Lord bloweth upon it: surely the people is grass. The grass withereth, the flower fadeth: but the word of our God shall stand forever.' This was my text; though I did not tell the people where it was, but said, 'It is not in my province to name the place in Scripture, as I am not a preacher.' The subsequent bishop playfully said to me this was a discrimination between exhorting and preaching that was new to him. Millington was what was then known as 'Head of Chester,' as it was the head of Chester River. My sister lived on the opposite side of the river, in what was known as 'Sandtown.' When I was through my discourse could I have got through the floor of 'the old academy'—for that was then our preaching place—and under the bottom of the river, without having anybody see me in my escape from the pulpit, I should have been more happy than I was. But three things I think I did in the discourse show: 1. Man and the things of earth pass away. 2. God and his word abide. 3. The preacher's duty to proclaim this fact: 'The voice said, Cry.' Notwithstanding my depression I heard much better things of the effort than I had conceived.

"As I recall the facts of my apprenticeship I cannot but feel that it was a great mistake that some friend did not suggest to me to buy my time and go to college, where I could have had the advantages at the start that would have gone with me through life. But the truth is it was unpopular to think that God did not prepare a man who was faithful to his convictions for the work that he wanted him to do. The people of that day and of this might justly think that he who enters the ministry with no other preparation than the college gives, is not God's minister. As it was, I can truly say I did my best under the circumstances to prepare. In those days of my conversion I am not able to name more than five or six men in our ministry that had gone through college. And yet we had mighty men in the pulpit, and they were mighty men of God. In truth, they made the most of God's might, and God in his might certainly made the most of them.

"About five months of the year we worked till eight o'clock at night; beginning October 10th it went on to the 10th of March. My class by Dr. Perkins was on Thursday night; and in the years of my apprenticeship I missed my class meeting but twice, and for reasons that all would accept. My employers thought I could not leave the shop at night without presenting a bad example to others in the establishment; and if done for one purpose it might be claimed for another. To meet this difficulty I asked and obtained 'task work.' But young as I was in the trade, I had given me the 'trim' that a *man* would receive. I was told it would be impossible for me to do the work in the time. I said, 'I will try.' I succeeded, and became a marvel as a fast workman. I spent about three hours a day out of the shop in reading and prayer; I for a time fasted on two days of the week. I was able to do the work of seven days in three and three quarters. But such absence through the day in study and devotion induced criticism by one of the firm, and these were periods of severe trial to me. I went on and worked myself out of my apprenticeship, and left the business before I was of age.

"About the time of attaining my majority I was licensed to preach, after having filled the pulpit with a text in Smyrna, where everybody knew me; and strange enough it was to me. My class leader, Dr. John D. Perkins, moved I be recommended to the presiding elder, Matthew Sorin, as a suitable person to fill any vacancy. To this the junior preacher, Benjamin Benson, objected, saying it was unprecedented, and was calculated to induce pride in one so noticed. The doctor replied that the presiding elders did not always know the men they employed, and gave the case of one who had been sent out, who could not have entered the work from the place where he was better known. The Quarterly Conference recommended me to the presiding elder, after voting my license. In a very few weeks I was sent to Port Deposit Circuit by Rev. M. Sorin."

On the subject of his first circuit Dr. Roche contributed a series of articles to the *Peninsula Methodist* in the spring of 1886, the papers being republished in the *Philadelphia Methodist* during July, 1886. They are here introduced:

"What is the first circuit more than any other? Much every way. Much to the people, who have the first trial of an inexperienced preacher, and who will judge him as fit or unfit for the itinerancy. Nor is it a small matter that they are expected to take his first efforts, with all his immaturity of thought and practice.

"But it is quite possible that this is not the first time that they have had this kind of experience. They have had other beginners. So many, indeed, that they have said, 'We are the circuit for breaking young preachers into the harness.' They see the harness put on, see them in the traces, observe where it rubs, how it fits, whether it can be adjusted. To some extent they train and discipline them. Blessings on the circuits, and people, who for a hundred years have been accepting this responsibility! Honor to them that they have so well performed their work! Let them not be reproached for the inevitable failures of so many of us. But with all this on the part of the people the first circuit of the young preacher is far less to them than to him. Words are too feeble to express his case. It is that of a young man who feels God has accepted him as his child, and who, despite all his early doubts as to the possibility of his ever being a preacher, has reached the conclusion, 'Woe is me if I preach not the Gospel.' By dreams at night, by impressions of the day, by concurring providences, by fruits that have followed his labors, and by the expressions of those with whom he lives, by all the means up to this time at his command, he feels he cannot refuse entering upon the work. It is the one thought of his mind; it is the one great exercise of his heart. That young man would not be diverted from this service if he saw the wealth of a Vanderbilt at his command.

"One thing fills his soul. There is no room for riches. One purpose absorbs him, and he is, at least at present, 'crucified to the world and the world to him.' He now wants to preach Christ, not from sense of mental superiority, but from a conviction of duty that is, to him, more than life.

"The time has come when he is to enter upon his work.

He is young in years and in knowledge, but the presiding elder, that mighty minister, Matthew Sorin, desires him for Port Deposit Circuit. 'Rev. Levi Storks, who has been in charge, is sent to Asbury, Wilmington, on account of the failure of the health of Joseph Rusling; Rev. Edward Kennard is in charge, and you will help him.' The thing is done. Authority has spoken, and subjection knows no delay. It is in the latter part of September, 1834. Here is a new sphere, if not a new service. The aspects of the first circuit are such as no other can ever present.

"Dr. Johnson, in conversation about the merits and demerits of *The Spectator,* said to Boswell, 'One of the finest pieces in the English language is a paper on Novelty.' It was written by Rev. Henry Grove, of Taunton. He begins with a very familiar fact, as an illustration, and says: 'When I have seen young Puss play her wanton gambols, and with a thousand antic shapes express her gayety, at the same time she moved mine, while the old Grannam hath sat by with a most exemplary gravity, unmoved by all that passed, it hath made me reflect what should be the occasion of humors so opposite in the two creatures, between whom there was no visible difference but that of age, and I have been able to resolve it into nothing else but the force of novelty.' To have seen Levi Storks on Port Deposit Circuit, a man for years in the work, and the young preacher who followed him, would have presented as great a contrast in feelings and facts as that which existed in those two irrational creatures that Grove presents.

"There is a sense in which 'familiarity breeds contempt' —if not of real dignity, of real difficulty, and even of danger.

"The first sight of beauty is most impressive, and the grandest things in nature make their strongest appeal when first presented.

"The first day of a physician in his office, the first day of a lawyer at the bar, the first day of a young man just entering into business, or even the first day of a stranger in a great city, is not like other days in the same relations.

"Who supposes that the soldier in his first battle has no experience that later conflicts do not furnish?

"But what are these illustrations of the first day in a profession, in a business, in a city, compared with the 'first circuit'? Though the first day is more memorable, it is not so pregnant with results. Of this we may say:

'The darkest day, live till to-morrow,
   Will have passed away.'

"Impression is one thing, results another. Everything does not hang on these first days in the various departments of life, as it may in the future of the preacher on his first circuit. The physician and the lawyer are in their own command, and the calling of neither is regarded as divine. They can change professions, and, possibly, to profit; but the sacredness of the preacher's vocation takes him out of his own hands, and he feels no liberty to think of anything else.

"The first circuit is supposed to test him, and he who has seen how small a matter will sometimes blast all his hopes will know how critical is the case. If the first circuit speak favorably he has ground for faith. Conference will listen to its voice. If their view is adverse he has little hope. By his first circuit he may stand or fall. It has been the happiness of some by strength of will, by force of character, by repose in God and faithful labor, to survive the adverse report and rise to the highest place.

"But history has shown there is so much in the first circuit as to justify the emphasis we place on it even apart from novelty.

"Yes, there is more in the first circuit to the preacher than to the people. He cannot kill them. There are too many of them, and there is too much in them for him to kill; but he is one, and there is so little of him in the ecclesiastical sense. Though a tornado should leave them unharmed, to him a breath of dispraise might be as deadly as a simoon.

"But what of the preacher's preparations? His external outfit was more than respectable. His mother had presented him with a noble horse of dapple gray, sixteen hands in height, with new saddle, bridle, and martingale. His presiding elder had allowed him the temporary use of his 'saddlebags.' In dress the preacher would have been taken for nothing but what he was, a 'Methodist preacher.' His coat was black and round-breasted, his hat was broad-brimmed, his cravat was immaculate white, and, according to the custom of the time, his only collar was that of his coat. As mounted on his steed, with no critical inspection of features, the young preacher presented an appearance that did not at least shame his sister, from whose residence he departed for his first circuit.

"With such show, he had not gone more than five miles before he was hailed to baptize a dying child. He had to say, 'I have no authority.'

"But in higher qualifications he could not make so good

a show. He had not finished his education by a tour in foreign lands. Colleges were not common, and the graduation of Methodist preachers from such institutions was more uncommon. His journey to his first circuit was the greatest distance he had ever made on land. But his theology was as orthodox as his dress. From his sixteenth year he had been impressed with the duty of preaching. He had been accustomed to help in holding prayer meetings in destitute places. Sabbath after Sabbath he had walked five or six miles into the country for exhortation and any kind of service that was required. Thus he was trying to placate conscience, while it seemed impossible for him to be a preacher. He had also read some of our best authors. Fletcher's *Appeal to Matter of Fact and Common Sense* he had well-nigh devoured; Wesley's *Notes on the New Testament* he had purchased from the widow of one of our Methodist preachers, Mrs. Boyer; two odd volumes of Simeon's *Skeletons* he had obtained from another godly widow in the same house, Mrs. Ann Owens. These were from the library of James Ridgeway, of the Philadelphia Conference. Pollok's *Course of Time* he had bought from R. M. Greenbank, his learned and devout pastor. This he was accustomed to read between sundown and dark, till admonished by the late Benjamin Benson that if he did not take care he would ruin his eyes. The young preacher did not learn this author by heart, but about the whole of that excellent book was at his command. From the venerable Solomon Sharp, the preacher in charge of Smyrna Circuit when he was converted, he had secured Watson's *Institutes,* and many a midnight saw him refusing to retire from their study. Often he read till about two o'clock

5

in the morning. His pursuit of proper knowledge was under real and multiplied difficulties, but it was eager study, and not altogether unsuccessful.

"Two things his class leader, Dr. John D. Perkins, did for his help; nay, a third thing not less important. He put into his hands a mutilated folio copy of Burkitt's *Notes on the New Testament,* saying, 'Take this; you will find it skeletonizes the whole book.' He took it, read it, and derived much help. The doctor was a local preacher of the genius and habit of a sermonizer. When at leisure he would indulge this taste, and looking through his papers he gathered a large number, and said to the young preacher, 'Take these, John; you are welcome to any use you can make of them.' The third kindness was the wise and weighty advice he gave.

"The sketches of the doctor were taken to the first circuit, and, as if the preacher thought physical contact might facilitate mental assimilation, carried in the crown of his hat, near to his brain. The dome of thought after long submission refused the pressure, and the load received a new locality. At what time else did that brain sustain itself under so great a weight of digested theology?

"How much of the plagiarist they could make the preacher, judge from the fact that some of them might not be larger than the palm of a lady's hand. They were hints, not style. If mechanics may have patterns for their work, and artists specimens of the masters to form their tastes, or increase their skill, may not the young preacher have the help of the best minds and models in his work? Thus prepared or unprepared, the preacher journeyed to the land of his future labors and responsibilities. The distance from Millington, Kent County, Md., whence he started, to Port Deposit, Cecil County, of the same State, was forty-five miles, the journey of a day. It was a thoughtful, prayerful, and pensive ride. The mind was full of thought. The heart was full of emotion. The eyes might sometimes well be full of tears. Much of the country was new, but, while sparse in population, it was of interest. The flat lands of his youth disappeared. The undulating landscape of Cecil struck the eye, and filled it with a sense of beauty. The most interesting town in his route was Elkton. It was the county seat, and was a place of lawyers, judges, and distinguished men. It had at one time been connected with appointments now in Port Deposit Circuit. But it assumed a position that to the young preacher gave it ecclesiastical magnitude. At that time there were few stations in the Conference outside of Philadelphia. Below Wilmington there was but one, in the length and breadth of the Peninsula. From the Brandywine to where the Atlantic laves Cape Charles, Elkton stood, the solitary station. It had enjoyed some of the most able discourses of Francis Hodgson, the eloquent ministry of William Barnes, and the elegant sermons of J. B. Hagany.

"While here as pastor Hodgson had met the brilliant Wesley Wallace in a public discussion on the claims of the Methodist Protestant Church as compared with those of the Methodist Episcopal Church. Hence to the fame of a preacher Hodgson added that which his future life sustained, the reputation of a debater.

"In Elkton resided William Duke, who, after William Watters, was the first native Methodist preacher that entered Conference—Watters in 1774 and Duke in 1775. He was majestic in form, venerable in age and virtues, distinguished for theological knowledge and breadth of scholarship, and he excelled as an author. He had left the Methodists before the organization of the Church in 1784, and was now a Protestant Episcopal minister in Elkton. In his love of Hagany he presented him with a choice copy of the Greek Testament, and a copy of Mr. Wesley's Prayer Book. Such a man seemed to impart dignity to the town.

"But with contrast of age, and in my own Church fellowship, in the same town was Benjamin F. Price. The young preacher had been at his father's house only a few days before with the presiding elder, and had learned the anticipations that young Price indulged of entering the Conference. He was young, bright, and devoted; and all the sympathies of the heart went toward him, who was so soon to enter the same work. A good Providence has continued him in the field for fifty years, and now in the Elkton of his youth, where the Wilmington Conference is held, he preaches his semicentennial sermon.

"On the edge of the town stood the magnificent residence of General James Sewall. To the young preacher's eye it would seem as baronial, and give an exalted idea of the people among whom he was to labor. Passing on to his destination, huge rocks arose, and high and steep and rugged hills frowned on him. Night was near. Soon came a descent, and mile after mile the course was downward, till the inexperienced traveler said, 'Where am I going?' It was a day of observation and of emotion, and an hour of weariness had come. By this time the ride on horseback had made as positive, if not as permanent, an impression upon the body as upon the mind. That which at one time weighs as a feather may at another rend like a bolt. Now light things were telling. Nearness to the place was welcome, but there was gloom without and within. If the caravansary at the close of summer, left without guests and music, may have an air of languor, as if the walls were tired of reverberating the sounds of mirth, may we not suppose that a living creature with the susceptibilities of a horse will imbibe some of the spirit of the rider after a journey of nearly forty-five miles?

"Well, sympathizing or unsympathizing, buoyant or depressed, the faithful Fanny fell flat, and flung the preacher over her head—rather, shot him like a projectile. At that moment he felt the expulsive power of a new and greater thought—that of saving his neck; as when a man is about losing his foot he forgets his corns.

"But Port Deposit is reached. As directed, the preacher stops at the residence of Daniel Megrady. It was a mansion, but the hospitality was greater than the house.

"The town was a singular-looking place, and to the preacher one of strange business. Great hills, approaching mountains, towered on one side, and on the other side rolled the Susquehanna. Between them stood the houses. Many of them were against the rocks. The front of the dwelling might be three stories and the back one. This was new. But material objects were less than moral facts. Here was the young preacher, and on him that night devolved the duty of conducting the devotions of that great household. He was to preside at the family altar, reading, singing, praying, where a little while before a Lybrand, a Laurenson, a Lawrence McComb, and a Sorin had officiated. To 'compare ourselves among ourselves is not wise.'

"The young preacher was at the headquarters. The circuit was a remarkable one. The appointments were not numerous, as compared with the circuits generally at that period.

"The following were comprehended: Port Deposit, North East, Hopewell, Ebenezer, Charlestown, Brick Meeting House, Zion, Elk Ridge, House's, Union, Stone Grave Yard, Mount Rockey, Fry's Forge, Trump's, and Rising Sun.

"These were all filled in four weeks, and the classes were led at all the appointments. Every other week was rest from preaching. This was uncommon in those days. At all these places were persons that could take the measure of the preacher. There were fourteen local preachers, and some of them of excellent talent. Thence came and joined the Philadelphia Conference in 1836 the late Dr. Charles Karsner and Dr. T. J. Quigley. Thence in 1839 came the late William McComb.

"Quarrying was at this time largely the business of Port Deposit, as that of coal mining made Pottsville. It brought together, as in the latter place, men of intellect, enterprise, and strong character. Mr. Megrady was one of the most marked of the number. He was direct, outspoken, big-hearted, free from dissimulation, and warm in his attachments. He had the richest quarry in the range, made and gave a great deal of money; he sometimes lost as heavily. But he had a will that knew no surrender. He said he always had at least five dollars to give to one who begged for a new church. He would 'have a brick in every one.' At the camp meeting the young preacher attended Mr. Megrady gave notice through the pulpit to the congregation that any person without provision on the ground could go to his tent for their meals. It was the largest private tent and best adjusted that the young preacher had seen, and the table there spread was such as to induce an appetite in the absence of hunger. This seemed like hospitality on a princely scale, and a prince was the man. At his residence were held official meetings, and there also was conducted a Bible class, composed of such men as Taring, brother of Rev. H. Taring, of the Baltimore Conference; Eli Cameron, an exhorter and admirable talker; Barnes, McClenahan—men of maturity and influence. In the absence of the preacher in charge, the young preacher was once asked to lead it. Of course, he had to obey orders. In the course of the lesson some hard questions arose about Noah and the effect of the wine. After others had spoken the young preacher made some remarks that were noticed with so much favor as to make one think he had some genius if not great scholarship. But he was not anxious to have another opportunity to show his skill.

"No house could have been such a home to ministers if there had not been such a lady as Mrs. Megrady to preside in it. She was refined in her manners and cheerful in her spirit, and, like her husband, enjoyed the prayers and association of the preachers.

"Mr. Megrady, with all his generosity, was sometimes brusque in manners and keen in retort. She was all grace.

"They had an only daughter, Hannah, who married Edwin Wilmer, of Smyrna, Del., who was converted in the same revival with the young preacher. He was State senator for a time.

"The town next in importance was North East. It soon after became a separate charge. At this time it had an excellent membership. As Mr. Megrady was the leading man in Port Deposit, so Thomas S. Thomas was the most conspicuous in North East. He was a contrast in some things to Mr. Megrady. Before his conversion he had held high position as a citizen. He had his education among the Friends, and was of the gentle spirit that so frequently distinguishes their intercourse. For him to speak any other but a soft word would awake wonder. He had a lady's delicacy, and the urbanity of his manners and the hospitality of his home were in perfect accord. He walked in the light of God.

"Mrs. Thomas was his companion in all his pure and noble purposes, and was, like him, ready to every good work. Refined and elevated in tastes, humane in all her instincts and habits, with a heart full of holy aspirations and experiences, eternity only will tell how much the preacher on his first circuit owes to the exalted example of such a lady.

"A more genial hearthstone did not invite the young preacher. The children bore the impress of their parentage, and piety seemed an instinct of the household. God showed his favor to it by calling at least three of their five sons to the itinerant ranks, and at least one daughter as the wife of an itinerant.

"In this town among our leading members were Mrs. Ford, mother of Rev. C. T. Ford, of the New Jersey Conference; Mrs. C. Cazier, mother of Rev. John C. Cazier—a local preacher of great zeal for God—and of a daughter of equal Christian devotion. Here also were Mrs. Wingate and Mrs. Maffit and Mrs. Simpers.

"Toward the center of the circuit were Hopewell and Ebenezer. These, like Port Deposit and North East, were Sabbath appointments. Hopewell had the morning hour. It was full and earnest. Here Rev. J. Goforth attended, Mr. Thompson and family, Mr. White and family, and many others of the best people that the preacher had ever then or has since seen.

"Ebenezer was the church of Edmonson, Reynolds, and Oldham. It was larger than Hopewell, and had a grand congregation and membership. Think of two such appointments, with such attendance and membership and resources, as entering into a circuit of fourteen appointments, and having so little of the care of the preacher. But Methodists did not then give much money to the Gospel. And there was a live church through the labors of those who composed it.

"In these two churches the young preacher made his first efforts. We hear much of the decline of pulpit power. Do we ask if there has been any decline of 'amen' power? The 'Amen' and the 'Glory to God' in Hopewell and Ebenezer made a young man, or any other man, feel, 'We are doing something.' In the days of the 'fathers of the Church,' as well as in early Methodism, responses helped utterance and intensified feeling.

"The power in the pew communicates itself to the pulpit as really as the power of the pulpit falls on the pew.

"Now, in the heart of the circuit there must be noticed as the great home of the preacher the residence of Thomas White. He was as positive a character as there was in the bounds of the charge. His wife was as great a saint.

"It is a curious question what divergencies and dissimilarities in the constitutional make-up of social and domestic character are compatible with the real union of husband and wife. God said, 'They twain shall be one flesh.' They certainly were in the beginning, for the woman was the man's rib. How far this implies they are of the same mind, of the same sympathies, of one style, or of one minute or general conformity, the writer cannot say. But a more perfect contrast in the husband and wife, with the devotion and honor that each rendered the other, is not often seen. Like his wife, he was a member of the church, and attended, and was perhaps one of the best judges of a sermon on the circuit. He was a man among men, and, like his wife, loved to entertain the preachers, and his home was one of their best homes, time immemorial.

"His wife was one of the most gentle, thoughtful, womanly, and heavenly minded in the circuit. He was curt and sharp, and could blurt out almost anything. If the preacher wanted to know anything about a horse he was unequaled. He could tell you if he was as 'sound as a dollar,' and of 'Tom and a mile in 2:40.' She would talk holiness; he talked horse. Approaching the table for a blessing, with a snap of his thumb and finger he said to the young preacher, 'Go it.' But all knew, who understood the man, that it was his way. Among the best friends of the writer was the man whose manner seemed so unlike that of his wife. They had sons bearing the names of Wesley and Fletcher, showing the tastes of the twain; and daughters whose uniform and multiplied kindness blessed the young preacher.

"Experiences of the preacher on his first circuit as relating to his work must be accepted. Some are facetious, others grave. Impressions are sometimes of value, at other times of no account. So much depends upon the mood of him who has them. The one now given may be thus accounted for. The young preacher, with a feeling akin to that of homesickness, was at Mount Rockey, a week-night appointment, and at that time a very different place from what it now is, as it is to be hoped the preacher is now a different man.

"The church was of boards, without ceiling, plaster, or paint; of course, it had no carpets. Fire was rarely used in those days. The seats were without backs, and the preaching stand was not a pulpit, but a platform a few inches high, with a slight board for the Bible. Father Gruber, who was on the circuit two years before, taught ladies not to use veils, and that looking-glasses as well were things of the devil. It may not be a wonder, then, if females came to church without any reproach of the toilet; and 'pow-wow bonnets,' being in use at home, might do for the temple. It looked strange.

"Then for the men! It was a rough region. In autumn, winter, or spring the roads would sometimes be fearful. In all philosophy this would suggest shoes that were adapted. They were heavy. We rarely ask ourselves why we in a city walk as we do, why those in the country walk unlike us. But there is reason. Were they living here they would walk as we do. Were we living there we would walk as they do. The people of that neighborhood, accustomed to rough and muddy roads, contract a resolute and determined tread, as if they would be superior to all obstacles, and would not allow themselves to be stuck. However deep or tenacious the clay, it could not hold them prisoners. The feet, like the fingers, are, though unconsciously, educated for their work. The preacher knelt for prayer. He tried to concentrate thought, when feet with such shoes came on those planks that 'rang hollow from beneath,' but the inevitable effect on a mind in such frame was to say, 'You might as well get up,' and so he did. Sinners as well as saints went to our churches, and they did not always ponder the duty of 'walking softly before the Lord.'

"Besides, that sanctuary was the resort of other living things than human beings. The Psalmist says, 'The sparrow hath found an house, and the swallow a nest for herself, . . . even thine altars.' Well, wasps had made their homes in that meetinghouse, and there were more of them than of worshipers, and even weak things will become strong by numbers.

"The text was taken. The preacher was doing his best, under the circumstances. But his words lacked point; his watch chain was pendent; a wasp warmed out of his nest by the fire had settled upon the chain, and as the hand touched it that little creature spent all the power of his single weapon, and imparted to the preacher a celerity of movement that showed there was no want of pungency in a wasp's sting, if there was in a young preacher's words.

"Of course, this is only to show what a weak creature the preacher was in his first circuit; albeit, even now, with fifty years added, he would rather in preaching get far enough away from a wasp's nest, and he hopes never again to see a 'meetinghouse' that wasps would preempt, not even excepting the pulpit.

"The preacher had experience in study on his first circuit. The junior preacher at that time lived among the people. With them he had to make arrangements for his work with his books, and the young preacher sought the best opportunities that he could obtain. In some places it was convenient; in others it was not. In the present instance there was all that he could ask. It was in the delightful home of Mr. Cazier. His habit was, when practicable, to retire at nine and rise at four. The hour had come for rest, and he found it. The moon was full-orbed; waking from his slumber, he bounded from his bed, with the reproach of his conduct for sleeping so long, as from the light he supposed it was nearly sunrise. Dressing with speed, he was about falling on his knees to pray, when he took out his watch, and saw it was one o'clock. But fearing if he did not remain up he might oversleep himself, he prayed, made his fire, and burnt out his candle before daylight. Need enough there was for early rising. Need enough there was for hard studying. But this was of a sort that intelligence could not long justify. Some of his study was on horseback, some in the bed, and all places had their suggestions and influence, if the mind was in the right frame.

"The preacher's depression in his work, and timely encouragement, must be noticed. All men, of whatever age, have various experience in the ministry. There were times when this one was cheerful and strong. There were other times when he thought rather of what he wanted to do than what he did. He had been reading Bramwell's Life, till he had little life left in him. This man, so wonderful in his piety and achievements, had by comparison brought him lower than humility required. In this state of feeling he went with his colleague to attend an extra

meeting at North East. It was remarkable for its success.
Among the converts were two elegant young ladies, the
daughters of Dr. Bryan. John Chew Thomas, the eldest
son of Thomas S. Thomas, was then also brought to Christ,
and gave a grand life, though brief, to the Philadelphia
Conference. At least one of the daughters of Mr. Thomas
was brought in, and the town was alive to God. Never
did Edward Kennard, the preacher in charge, show more
of the power in prayer, exhortation, and preaching that
God gave him than at that meeting. Among those attending, not of the place, was Cyrus Oldham, one of the
most intelligent men on the circuit—a gentleman by instinct, education, and association. After one of the
services he desired the young preacher to walk with him.
He was an official man. He said to the young preacher,
'Tell me how you are feeling.' He told his heart. He replied, 'I thought you felt sad,' and added, 'I want to tell
you of the fine effect and the commendation of your service
at Ebenezer.' The spell was broken. 'As cold water to a
thirsty soul, so is good news!' Those 'kind words will
never die.'

"The young preacher was sure to meet a sufficient offset
to all this. House's and the Union were appointments
that filled the fourth Sabbath in the preacher's round.
The congregation at House's was not full; that of Union,
or Dickey's Factory, was overflowing. It had many strong
men in it, and among them the two brothers McComb,
then local preachers. The young preacher thought he had
made his best preparation. The hour came; the house was
crowded. The text was taken, 'Thou, Solomon my son,
know thou the God of thy father.' He had thought he saw

a great deal in that text. The sermon on the circuit usually occupied about an hour. At the end of twenty minutes the matter of his mind was exhausted. He thought, 'If I stop here everybody will know it is a failure; if I can talk on for a time some may not know it.' Twenty more minutes came heavily and went slowly, and the preacher closed. He went home with an exhorter. Tea was ready, and the blessing was asked, but the host observed the preacher did not eat, and asked if he was not well, and remarked, 'Any way, you gave us a good sermon.' It is said Dr. Sharp, of Boston, had preached to his people in a way that greatly depressed him, and he went to bed. The colored man who served him came into his room to ask him to dinner. He said he wanted none. The man said, 'It would have done you good to hear what beautiful things the people said, as they went by, about your sermon this morning.' The young Dr. Sharp found the bed was no place for him, and ate a good dinner. The young preacher did the same, and found his food both good and necessary. He thus moralized: 'Why be distressed when you have tried to do your best? Even if, from your own standpoint, you have failed, some may have derived good from your effort, and think well of it.'

"But this was not the end. Shortly after, he was calling on Rev. William McComb, and *he* was depressed from a failure in preaching in the same place, from the text, 'Charity never faileth;' he told his sorrows. The young preacher had heard him, as he had the young preacher, and said, 'You should not feel so; there was nothing to justify it.' He then turned on him, and said, 'Do you think you ever did as badly?' and he replied, 'If you never heard me do as badly I should be glad.' Then said McC., 'When? Was it when you took "Thou, Solomon my son"?' The young preacher thought, 'There it is; he knows it.' From that time the preacher had the feeling, 'I will let somebody else advise a Solomon.' In after years, when McComb was in the Conference, he would recall this fact, and say, 'John, do you remember preaching from "Thou, Solomon my son"?' and John would as promptly ask, 'William, have you forgotten that "Charity never faileth"?' Like many of our troubles that formerly made us weep, they now allow a laugh!

"The young preacher's first quarterage is a well-remembered fact. Among the leading men of the circuit was Charles Wilson, of Elk Ridge. He was the most influential man in the appointment. He was an excellent local preacher, and the treasurer of the board of stewards. His wife was a lady of equal excellence in sense and piety. It was at the time of the third quarterly meeting, and the presiding elder and young preacher stopped at his house. He called the preacher into his room to pay the quarter's salary. This was just after the preacher had received a rebuke from his elder for putting a book down on the settee, pages downward, rather than turn a leaf. The elder said, after asking who was reading that book and having been told it was I, 'If that were my book I would not want you to do it.' Matthew Sorin was a wonderful preacher; but if he ever relaxed it is unknown to the writer, and his words, not in themselves, but in their manner, could be like lancets. A glance of his eye burned you. His touch was not abrasion, but incision. Smarting under this rebuke, the young preacher entered the room of Mr.

Wilson, and when asked, 'Do you feel satisfied to take this money?' his heart aching, said, 'What next?' and added, 'No, sir, I am not satisfied; but I have no private means, and if I go on to preach I have to take it.' Then said the good steward, 'You don't understand me. We owe you twenty-five dollars, and have only twenty.' 'Satisfied!' exclaimed the young preacher with the mountains removed, 'I am satisfied with anything as to amount; but I feel as if I should rather pay you for letting me try to preach than be paid for doing it.' It may excite no wonder that both wept.

"The young preacher parted with the presiding elder at the end of the third Quarterly Conference with bruises and maceration, but no bones broken. It is just to say of Mr. Sorin it was his way. On earth the young preacher had no friend to whom, perhaps, he owed more, and no man had a greater admiration of him than the young preacher. Mr. Wilson saw how his words had pierced, and told how he had replied to him, though his host. Mr. Sorin did not intend to wound either of us.

"The first ordeal of the young preacher came. Another quarter came. It was the last of the year. There was assembled that large and remarkably strong body of official men. It was like a small Annual Conference. One trial took it into two o'clock Sabbath morning, and the presiding elder said, 'It cannot be helped. It is the necessary work of the Church.' It was not then considered proper to give the time of God's day to such work. They did not go home to dinner, but met after the Saturday morning sermon and hardly took time for tea. The preacher of fifty years has never seen another such trial in a Quar-

6

terly Conference. The charge was immorality, and it was against one of the keenest minds and best talkers of the circuit, or any other place. He was expelled.

"But it was the Quarterly Conference to recommend or reject the young preacher as an applicant to the Annual Conference. The examination began. It was winter. The stove was hot, and the young preacher's brain was burning. The presiding elder began. The young preacher answered, answered, answered. Then came a queer question about baptism, presented in a form utterly novel, and the brain on fire began to reel, and the man staggered. The elder saw he was about to faint, and exclaimed, 'This room is hot enough to fry lizards.' It was not far from true. But it was an ice house compared to his question. The young preacher asked the privilege of retiring for a few moments, and was taken in the loving arms of the late Rev. William McComb; and they went out back of the church among the graves, where the young preacher had his 'meditations among the tombs,' as really as James Hervey, whose works he had, a little time before, been reading. With his friend, after some fresh air, he came in, not much inflated, but in the spirit his father taught him—'Never give up the ship'—and said to the elder, 'I am ready, sir!' It is said on one occasion Patrick, true to his instincts for fun, said to one of his companions on shipboard in the absence of the commander, 'Let us shoot off the long Tom; but so as not to make much noise; you just touch it off lightly,' and it came near being Pat's death. Powder touched off will make a noise. The young preacher had virtually said to his presiding elder, 'Fire away,' when he knew that as a target he could be riddled by that master

in ecclesiastical gunnery. Nor was it the custom of this
elder to fire blank cartridges. But the young preacher
would not 'play baby.' He did, however, think that even
Matthew Sorin tried to 'touch it off lightly.' He was recommended.

"In retrospect the preacher thinks that in his first six
months he saw all types of character that he has ever
known—all types of the physical, social, intellectual, and
moral. There, though he 'made a covenant with his eyes,'
he saw a form and a face of beauty that he has never seen
transcended; one that might have been some apology for the
battles of Troy, if found in her who bore the same name as
the lady of the first circuit. There he met intellect as keen
and as penetrating, there he met refinement and rudeness
as confessed, as anywhere; there, moral virtues were as preeminent as in other places. There were the ardent and
frigid; and there he saw persecution—the husband of his
wife—more painful than he remembers elsewhere. There,
too, he saw revival! And it is a fact that trials in the pastorate there, presented themselves in a way to make the
duty seem the most repellent.

"As on the first day he had an experience in his fall from
his horse such as all other riding never furnished, so in his
first circuit he had experiences of the work that were best
calculated to repress desire for the itinerancy. But in the
midst of all, God and his people sustained and blessed him.

"His colleague, Edward Kennard, was in talent, in devotion to duty, in deep piety of heart and life, the equal of
any that after circuits gave; and he had a wife of taste and
devotion to God, and of influence in her sphere, that made
her an ornament wherever she went.

"As the result of the kindness and confidence of Port Deposit Circuit the young preacher left in good condition in March, 1835, and attended the Philadelphia Conference, held in 'the Union,' beginning April 8th, 1835. These were received on trial: Charles H. Whitecar, William K. Goentner, John D. Onins, George Lacey, Samuel Jaquette, John McClintock, Jr., Wesley C. Hudson, Henry Matthews, Isaac Adkins, William Hanley, George Barton, John A. Roche, Benjamin N. Reed, Joseph Carlisle, Henry Sutton, Isaac Cross, Ignatius T. Cooper, Pennel Coombe, John T. Hazzard, Stephen Townsend (20). Of all these men of God, of such tender and precious memory, with all their hopes and labors and successes, with all there was in their natural talent, with their acquired knowledge, with their broad and commanding influence, by the pulpit, by the press, by the magnetism of their contact, and by the inspiration of their presence—of all these only the following remain: Charles H. Whitecar, Samuel Jaquette, George Barton, Joseph Carlisle, Benjamin N. Reed, and John A. Roche. Of those who entered at that Conference, only John A. Roche is in the effective ranks.

"The preacher who writes of 'My First Circuit' has traveled other circuits. They have all had their points and persons of interest. Other circuits are remembered with pleasure and profit. Other circuits have their records before God as really and as full as 'My First Circuit.' But for the susceptibilities of the preacher, for the force of novel facts, for the impressions produced, for the influence of the period and the place upon the preacher, no other circuit compares with the first. It required no bushel to conceal this light in the pulpit. A breath might have extinguished it. A word of men and the oil of grace have kept it burning for more than fifty years."

The autobiography contains an interesting reference to the weather:

"As I went in September, 1834, and remained till the spring of 1835, I had the whole winter in the circuit. It was a remarkable winter for its severity. Hon. Alexander H. Stevens, in his *History of the United States,* page 352, says: 'The winter of 1834-1835 was noted for its great severity throughout the United States. On the 4th of January, 1835, mercury congealed at Lebanon, N. Y., and at several other places. The Chesapeake Bay was frozen from its head to Cape Charles and Cape Henry; on the 8th of February the thermometer fell to eight degrees below zero as far south as 31 degrees north latitude. The day before, the 7th, is remembered as "the cold Saturday" to this day. The Savannah River was coated with ice at Augusta. Orange trees were killed on the coast of Georgia. The ground in the interior of the State was covered with snow for several weeks. The falls of snow in Georgia on the 14th of February and 3d of March averaged from eleven to thirteen inches.'

"This was my first winter on my first circuit on horseback, and that 'cold Saturday' I proved its severity in a ride of several miles to fill my appointment on the Sabbath. But I retain a blessed memory of God's supporting hand. Though there were trials of the flesh, I could say of them all, 'None of these things move me.' My concern was to be equal to my work and 'serve my generation by the will of God,' before I fell asleep. Nor, indeed, was I inclined to compare these experiences with the case of other positions, but rather to compare them with what were called the hardships of the earliest Methodist preachers. But I needed God, and had him.

"My first Conference appointment was by Bishop Emory. It was the first and only time he ever presided at the Philadelphia Conference. He had been made bishop in 1832. I was sent to Snow Hill, Md."

In 1885, when the Wilmington Conference met in Snow Hill, Dr. Roche, at the request of the editor, contributed the following to the *Peninsula Methodist* on "Snow Hill in 1835:"

"It requires little arithmetic skill to determine the number of years between 1835 and 1885, that compass my connection with an Annual Conference. Fifty years in prospect suggest eternity; in retrospect it is as 'an handbreadth.' I was sent to Snow Hill Circuit in 1835. It was my first appointment by the bishop. The Methodists of the town had been trying to 'glorify the Lord in the fires.' A few months before a fearful conflagration had burned out the heart of the village, and our people were among the chief sufferers. In a few hours was consumed all that industry and economy presented as the product of nearly a lifetime. The writer, when the fire occurred, was on Port Deposit Circuit, under the presiding elder, the late Dr. Matthew Sorin, who had traveled Snow Hill Circuit some years before, and knew the condition of the people. Through his intelligence and suggestion we took up collections to help the sufferers of Snow Hill. . . .

"When in the following April I reached Snow Hill as my field of labor I had knowledge of these facts. The late calamity was oppressive. The evidences of desolation were all around me, but 'the Spirit did not fail' in our people; the center of the town was measurably rebuilt. The church was an old frame edifice with a bell. The preacher in charge was William Connelly. He was genial and popular; had excellent health, and a firm voice. He was a sweet singer, and was powerful in exhortation. He was not only zealous to save souls, but was great in building parsonages, and soon showed this skill in Snow Hill. As he, the married preacher, lived in the town, most of my time was spent about the country appointments. The junior preacher of the year before was Mr. James L. Houston, of whom I heard so many pleasant things as to tempt the thought that I could never satisfy the people. But God has his own way and Methodism its own plans; I was there by highest authority, and Brother Houston had the honor of a station at Elkton.

"Levi Scott was the presiding elder of the Delaware District, in which Snow Hill was comprehended. He was a model man in the office. In the estimate of preachers and people he was never greater. His preaching was distinguished for clearness, soundness, and unction, and there was a power that prostrated, roused, and quickened the soul. He was an example of all he preached.

"The leading members of our society were Mr. Dymock, Cord Hazzard, George Hudson, Steward Nelson, Mr. Matthews, Mr. Heath, Mr. Townsend, and James L. Compte. John Handy, of one of the most influential families, and clerk of the county, was not literally a member, but was a constant attendant, and his wife, and daughter Maria, were among the most devoted ladies in the membership of the church. The late Dr. Stephen Townsend had been a local preacher there, and his family still lived in the town, though he that year had entered the Conference as a probationer, in the class with the writer, and was the preacher on Princess Anne Circuit, filling forty-two appointments in four weeks.

"The Protestant Episcopal church had its rector in Mr. Wiley, and the Presbyterian church had, only a little while before, been served by T. B. Balch, who was distinguished for talent and eccentricity. Many stories were told of him illustrating the latter characteristic, but never at the expense of character or the marring of his influence. Once, preaching on the man going down to Jericho and falling among thieves, he became very graphic. He represented him as waylaid by men who concealed themselves in 'locks of the fence,' with firearms ready for the execution of their diabolical purpose, and when the man came within gunshot, off went the weapon of death—representing the sound as well as the act. The poor man ran for his life, and from another 'lock of the fence' off went another gun, and so on till, scared almost to death, he fell wounded in the way. Then 'they stripped and robbed him, and left him half dead.' Irving Spence, one of his most cultivated hearers, sat and wondered, and soon after called on him and said: 'Brother Balch, what did come over you Sunday night? How could you make such a description of that man, and of his attack by his pursuers? Do you not know that gunpowder was unknown, and firearms were not invented?' Whereupon poor Balch threw up his imploring arms, and said: 'Brother Spence, spare me; I know it all, and I am going to stay in my study all the week and fast. I will do penance.' As Solomon Sharp used to say sometimes

of himself and of other Methodist preachers, Mr. Balch
had got into the bushes, and he was very much tangled up.
But the fact lacks its full force till heard through the lips
of the naturally witty and sometimes waggish George Hudson. Before me is a volume of sermons which Mr. Balch
published while pastor in Snow Hill. They are entitled
Christianity and Literature in a Series of Discourses.
They show fine taste, broad culture, and in style may be
placed beside Hugh Blair.

"A Methodist Protestant church was in process of erec-
tion by the means and energy of Mr. Quinton, a devoted
member. Besides the church he was building, he had fitted
up a camp ground with remarkable adaptation to its purposes. A fence surrounded it, and there was an imposing
gateway. To this camp he invited the most eloquent ministers of the body. Hence came glowing accounts of the
sermons of T. H. Stockton and Webster, the president of
their Conference. For the expense of all Mr. Quinton was
responsible. He had no children, and seemed willing to
give his last dollar to the cause so dear to him. Indeed,
it was said that he declared he 'did not care if the last
johnnycake was on the board when he died.' Ministers
of this day do not know the friction, to use no stronger
word, that was felt when the Methodist Episcopal and the
Methodist Protestant Churches were touching each other
all along the line of their labor on the Peninsula. Over
the door of one of the Methodist Protestant churches I now
see, as of yesterday, the words painted, 'Be not ye called
Rabbi: for one is your Master. Matt. xxiii, 8.' That
motto opens a volume.

"The colored people had no church of their own; they

worshiped with the whites. The gallery was assigned them; they heard the same sermons, spoke in the same love feasts, communed at the same table of the Lord, and were led in class by the same circuit preachers. The conduct of Nat Turner, a colored preacher who led the insurrection of Southampton, Western Shore, Va., only a little while before, had induced rigor in the conduct of meetings by a white person. The late Governor II. A. Wise had acquired fame by voluntarily engaging to defend the Rev. William Lee, of Onancock, when accused by a distinguished citizen of having 'allowed the blacks too much freedom in their worship.'

"Snow Hill had an academy, of which Mr. Valandingham was principal. In this academy John Moxcey, one of the holiest members of our church, taught. Thence as a student came James Allen, who, after teaching for a short time at Horn Town, became a member of the Philadelphia Conference. The court had for judges Tingle and Spence; and the bench was proud of their purity and wisdom. Nor had the bar cause for shame. Irving Spence was lawyer, writer, and historian of the Presbyterian Church. The charge in Snow Hill furnished rich material as the first station of Presbyterianism in the county. Dr. Martin was an elder of that church, and few physicians have the lives of their patients committed to them with more confidence than had this man of God. The writer has cause to remember him. When ague had shaken him, as if it would be satisfied with nothing less than throwing down the house of clay; when fever had flamed, as if intent upon 'dissolving the earthly tabernacle;' when Nature had said, 'This conflict must cease, or the bones will soon be ashes;' when the failure of others to cure had asserted, 'You are physicians of no value,' then Dr. Martin took me in hand, and in one week the tortures disappeared, and the heart leaped in the joy of deliverance. Law, medicine, and divinity had their places in Snow Hill.

"Two memorable events marked the period of my labors there—the death of Bishop Emory, who presided at the Conference when I was received, and the burning of our 'book room,' in New York. In the painful death of Emory by casualty, I thought the Church had lost its greatest leader. At the burning of the 'book room' the winds seemed to waft in sadness the calamity suffered. It was said at the time a fragment of a burned leaf of the Bible was found as far off as Staten Island, and on it were the words of Isa. lxiv, 11: 'Our holy and our beautiful house, where our fathers praised Thee, is burned up with fire: and all our pleasant things are laid waste.' The death of Emory might only be deplored, but the ruins of the 'book room' could be repaired; and the people of Snow Hill, who had so recently needed great aid, now extended help to others, and the writer with the people of the circuit had the privilege of contributing to the same 'Book Concern,' though not to the same structure, that now fills so conspicuous a place in New York.

"Never having had an opportunity to see the Sabbath congregations in the other churches, I cannot tell their comparative sizes. But while I am sure the Presbyterians had more wealth, I doubt whether they had as large a congregation as the Methodist Episcopal church. If I may speak of the circuit as associated with Snow Hill, the following may represent our work. I give from memory, as the memoranda of that time are lost and the journal I kept is destroyed. Each preacher filled the pulpit in Snow Hill once in four weeks, on Sabbath morning and night, besides leading a class or classes, and preached that same afternoon at the Furnace, some five miles out in the country. One Sabbath was given to Horn Town in the morning and Swansgut in the afternoon; another Sabbath, to Newtown in the morning and Williams's meetinghouse in the afternoon; the last Sabbath of the four, to Newark in the morning and Wesleyville in the afternoon. Classes were met at all these places by the preacher of the day. Alternate weeks had labor and rest. One week we preached at Conner's, Spring Hill, and Sandy Hill; the other week gave us Acquongo, Queponco, St. Johns, and Coulbern's. The last named was the private house of a local preacher by that name. We met classes at every appointment. At Wesleyville lived the mother of Rev. John S. Porter, now of the Newark Conference. Was ever hospitality to a Methodist preacher more quiet and pure than that which Mrs. Porter and her daughter Jane dispensed?

"There are facts of which gratitude precludes oblivion. Did space allow, it would be a pleasure for me to name many who come to mind as I write. Three books I obtained on Snow Hill Circuit—a miniature Greek lexicon, from that godly man, John Moxcey; a folio copy of Burkitt's *Notes,* from Mrs. Captain Berry, of Horn Town; she was to me as a sister, and the book a treasure. From Maria Handy, that Christian Lydia, I had the present of Homer's *Iliad.* Language, poetry, and divinity were embodied in these books. For forty-nine years they have gone where I have gone. They have had an abiding place in my library. But in a warmer and more sacred place abide the friendships of 1835. The hands will take down the books, and the fingers turn the pages, but the heart holds on to the treasures that Christian character gives. How often has mine communed with those 'whose names are in the book of life'! May the Snow Hill of the present and the future crown with greater glory the Snow Hill of the past!"

The autobiographical thread is thus resumed:

"From Snow Hill Circuit I rode horseback in three days a distance of one hundred miles to Smyrna, Del., the residence of my sister, Sarah Ann Woodall, and went thence to see my mother in Kent County, Md. She lived on the large farm with Mr. Short, her third husband. Many good things she had ready for me, and with her own fingers knit me a pair of silk stockings. Thence I went to the Philadelphia Conference—by stage to New Castle, and thence by steamboat—and in due time met the committee for examination in the first year's course of study. While in Smyrna, on my way to Conference, I met Rev. George Lacy, who was of the same class, and we spent a night together at Judge Daniel's. Perhaps more of it was passed on our studies than in sleep. He had a fine verbal memory, and had studied the books, and he passed an excellent examination. I was greatly concerned about my preparation in its results before the committee. I knew I had done my part with prayer and care and constancy. On grammar, one of our first books, I feared no examiner, and I soon found I had no cause to fear in my other studies as compared with a class of twenty. On the Bible we were examined from Bishop Emory's *Hundred Questions.* Some of them were very difficult, and on one of the geographical questions—the settlement of the various tribes on the east and west of Jordan—I walked the floor and taxed my memory, at the Widow Porter's, for hours together; and yet, when the Rev. Henry White, who examined us on the Bible, came to this question, from which I hoped for high honor, he just skipped it, and my hard work counted for nothing. This series on the Bible my second wife, Mary Caroline Osler, before I knew her, studied with equal success.

"Wesley's *Notes on the New Testament* I had studied till there was hardly a variation in his version that I could not give. I soon found myself quite at home on the books; a good report was made, and I was by the vote of the Conference continued for the second year.

"At this Conference, held in 'the Union' Church, I was sent to Accomack Circuit, Va. This was the next circuit south of Snow Hill. John S. Taylor was preacher in charge. This circuit was famed for its hospitality and its kind treatment of the young preachers. In those days the junior preacher was not expected to remain more than one year, while the preacher in charge was supposed to continue two years—then the full period of service, according to the *Discipline.* This was also, like Snow Hill, a circuit of fourteen appointments. Princess Anne then had forty or forty-two, all of which were filled in four weeks by the two preachers. Two weeks after the senior preacher the junior filled the same appointments. Thus the people had the circuit preachers every two weeks. The appointments at other times were filled with local preachers, who were business men and received no salary. If local preachers did not fill the appointments they held prayer meetings and class meetings, and the fire was kept burning from week to week round the circuit. The traveling preachers each made the circuit in four weeks. They preached through the week every other week, and usually twice or thrice on the Sabbath, and sometimes twice in the same place. Mr. Taylor was a man of genial spirit, popular manners, and excellent influence among the people. He was devoted to his work, and was commended as a preacher. His residence was in Onancock, and had been given to the church by William D. Seymour, Esq. Drummondtown was the county seat of Accomack. At its bar was fine talent. Henry A. Wise, Thomas H. Bayly, and George Scarboro were members of the bar. On the edge of the town Hon. Henry A. Wise, then in Congress, resided. Of his ability and character judgment is formed from his career at the bar, his governorship of the State, and as general in the war of the Union. As a duelist he appeared on the 'field of honor,' when he wounded Mr. Coke, his competitor for Congress; and as the second in the Graves and Cilly duel, when Cilly fell, and filled the country with greatest horror at the practice. I was in Virginia at the time. Rev. Henry Slicer, of the Methodist Episcopal Church, then chaplain to Congress, preached a sermon of great power against duelling. Mr. Wise challenged Hon. Thomas H. Bayly to mortal combat. Mr. Bayly declined the challenge, on grounds that men of honor accept. Mr. Bayly, after Mr. Wise, represented the district in Congress. In the vile conduct of Mr. Wise, in his attempt to horsewhip Mr. Stanton, a member of Congress, the country was full of indignation at this time. Mr. Wise was a man of great compass of character. He had his good points, and they were good. He had his bad points, and they were bad. On entering Congress, at about the earliest age allowed by the Constitution, he showed readiness and boldness of speech, and as a man was pronounced fearless; as an orator, independent. Some thought he was ambitious to be a second John Randolph. He certainly attracted great attention. We used to see him, when at home, in the Methodist church, and at camp meeting, and once I came very near to asking him to get down off the fence that separated the white and black people. Mr. Wise had religious impulses and convictions. His first wife was the daughter of the Rev. Dr. I. Jennings, a distinguished Presbyterian minister. She died when I was on the circuit. My first wife knew her well. As Mrs. Wise was about to pass away Mr. Wise stood over her and exhorted her to put her trust in the God of her fathers, and of her youth, and of her own heart, assuring her He would not forsake her as she passed 'through the valley of the shadow of death.' Wise could be chivalrous.

"The Rev. William Lee, of Onancock, Va., had been present, according to the demand of the law, that some white person should be in the assemblies of the negroes. Though Mr. Lee had met the conditions of the law, a distinguished citizen of the county arraigned him for violation, or for some failure, as he claimed, of attention to the law. Mr. Wise offered his services to Mr. Lee, and it was said he gave the prosecuting fellow-citizen a most fearful castigation, though he was one of his near neighbors and one of the most prominent men of the county.

He spared him in nothing. Grandly he vindicated Mr. Lee.

"Another case may be given to show the man. The Rev. Thomas J. Burroughs, of Philadelphia Conference, had slain his brother-in-law. Mr. Bishop, the person killed, had threatened Mr. Burroughs, who, passing in his carriage near Mr. Bishop, was arrested by Mr. Bishop's seizing the bridle of the horse. Burroughs shot and killed him. The trial took place in Snow Hill. Mr. Wise undertook the defénse, and cleared Mr. Burroughs. It was said Mr. Wise, after examining the Methodist *Discipline*, pronounced it a little book of great concentration of thought, and as embracing the soundest principles for the government of its people. While he used this at will, he quoted from the Scriptures like one who was a daily student of their contents. Mr. Bishop was of a family that showed great influence as well as spirit in the case, and it was said if the jury failed to convict Burroughs the life of Mr. Wise would not be safe. He was warned and advised to have a guard on leaving Snow Hill. The verdict was rendered, Burroughs was cleared, Mr. Wise called for his horse, and, refusing any guard, mounted and rode away in disdain of all danger. This was the man who, when as governor of Virginia he could hang John Brown, would add he 'admired his pluck.' Pluck and honor quickly made their appeal to Henry A. Wise. His son, O. Jennings Wise, who fell at Pittsburg Landing, was a son of Mr. Wise by his first wife, and was named after his grandfather.

"On the Accomack Circuit I commenced the study of Greek, which I pursued four years and more. My other studies commanded all the time and attention necessary

7

for the examination, which, if satisfactory, and no other objection was found, would enable me to secure admission to membership in the Conference, and also deacon's orders. On both I was honored at the ensuing Conference. The examination was severe, and some of our members were denied orders, and continued on probation.

"Accomack was a strong circuit. Among many other interesting families I may be allowed to name James White, the brother of Rev. Henry White, a man of great influence in the Conference; Frederick Conner, one of whose daughters married Rev. James Hargis, father of the present J. H. Hargis, D.D., of the Philadelphia Conference; Rev. Garretson Burton, local preacher; William E. Wise; Colonel Poulson; James Poulson; Colonel Bagnell; Dr. Cropper; Dr. R. W. Williams, local preacher; John Law, local preacher; Wesley Elliott, local preacher; William D. Seymour, local preacher. I recall, too, the names of James Garretson, Mr. and Mrs. Arbuckle, Mr. and Mrs. Proll; and their daughter, who was studying Greek, as I was doing amid my multiplied duties.

"The family of Mr. Seymour was one of the most intelligent and devout that I have ever known. Mr. Seymour was a graduate of law, though he did not practice it. He had an only brother, Dr. Hugh G. Seymour, practicing in the county, who was one of the most ardent Episcopalians, and, I think, a lay reader. William Seymour was one of the most conscientious men that I have ever known. His wife, who was a Miss Bayly, was equally consecrated to God; and the family was under as exact government as if John Wesley ruled it. His house, built by his father, a local preacher, had every comfort, and was named Wesley. Mr. Seymour, who had slaves, though emancipated, was accustomed to retire at nine o'clock and rise at four. Then, with his pocket Bible in his hand, he might be seen regularly going to the quarters of the colored people to have family prayer before he had it in his own family. To them, day after day, in their devotions, he read the word of God. In the family also were three sisters, unmarried—Miss Eliza, Miss Leah, and Miss Margaret Seymour. Miss Margaret was an earnest Episcopalian, and was a lady of fine intellect, of fondness for literature, and of refined manners. She was afterward married to Mr. Ames, of Washington, the father of Mrs. Charles H. Hall, wife of the present and distinguished rector of Holy Trinity, Brooklyn, N. Y. Mr. Ames was also father of Rev. A. H. Ames, D.D. Leah Seymour married Carrington Cropper, son of General Cropper. Eliza, a holy lady, never married.

"With Mr. Seymour also lived the only sister of Mrs. Seymour, Elizabeth Upshur Bayly, in intellect, mental culture, refined manners, and entire devotion to God one of the first ladies I have known. She and her sister, Ann Upshur, and John H. Bayly and James Bayly constituted the family. The father, Edmund Bayly, was brother of Richard Drummond Bayly and Colonel Thomas Bayly, the father of the late Hon. Thomas H. Bayly. The father and the son at different times filled the same positions as distinguished members of Congress from the same district. All the brothers were lawyers in Drummondtown. The mother of the Misses Bayly was a Miss Upshur, cousin of the late Hon. Abel P. Upshur, who was Secretary of State under John Tyler. Mr. Upshur was killed by the explosion of 'The Peace Maker' on the *Princeton*. I married Elizabeth Upshur Bayly on the ninth day of February, in the year of our Lord eighteen hundred and thirty-seven, at Onancock, and for the few weeks before Conference boarded with Dr. Williams, from whom, with his wife, we received great kindness.

"In this circuit, at an early period in our history, Methodism had suffered by the unguarded conduct of some of the leading members in arresting and imprisoning Mr. Robert Curtis for some alleged misconduct on our camp grounds. The administration was sued, and heavy damages were obtained by Mr. Curtis. Mr. Seymour, the father of William D., as a man of means, had a heavy share in the money required for the mistake. Mr. Curtis was still living when I was on the circuit, and the influence of our incaution was felt to our injury as a church. For many years this fact was quoted. But God had many wise and good men that held up his banner of Methodism and saw it prosper.

"We held a camp meeting at Knox Branch, beginning August 5th, 1836, and saw much fruit of our labor.

"In April, 1837, I received my next appointment, with Rev. George Wiltshire, to Northampton Circuit. This was the next south to Accomack and extended to Cape Charles, the lowest part of Northampton County. This and Accomack were at an earlier period one circuit. The habits and characteristics of the people in the two circuits were much the same. There were hospitality and kindness to the ministers. Mr. Wiltshire was an Englishman and a man of striking peculiarities, but was one of the best men I ever knew. I greatly revere his memory. I knew him in his noble instincts, his pure spirit, and his power with God in prayer. Of course, though he was never married, his age placed him in charge. I boarded for a time with Joshua Turner, and for some months with Mrs. Floyd.

"Mr. Turner, with whom we boarded, was successful in business, and had purchased a large brick house built by General Pitt, one of the first citizens of the Shore, and we had excellent accommodations and a happy home. Mrs. Floyd was as kind to my wife in her sickness and suffering as if she had been her sister.

"Mr. Wiltshire, though in charge, wished me to attend to some of the duties that properly devolved on him, and among them that of 'seeing that the society be duly supplied with books.' This I did; and with Bibles, hymn books, commentaries on the Scriptures, Wesley's and Watson's works, and Christian biography, and our various Methodist publications, I sold about five hundred dollars' worth of books. As I was now married, besides my salary of one hundred dollars, and the same amount for my wife, I was allowed one hundred and fifty dollars table expenses. This would make three hundred and fifty dollars. This was not fully raised, but the books I sold yielded nearly thirty-three per cent, and my expenses were met.

"There were many interesting and influential members of the church on this circuit; among them J. Simpson, Colonel Nottingham, Mr. Brickhouse, Rev. Montclare Oldham, Peter Williams, and Mr. Dolby. And there were some ladies of great influence, both from their social positions and their Christian character. Among them were two sisters of the Hon. Abel P. Upshur. Mrs. Elliott, the older sister, was not literally a member, though in the congregation. The other sister, the widow Nottingham, was a member at Johnson's Chapel; and there was Mrs. Dr. Frankard, one of the most active and useful members in the great revival at Johnson's Chapel.

"In these days, excepting the places the Baptists filled, the Methodist Church had the people, and our houses of worship were full. The Protestant Episcopal Church at Hungar's Parish had a fine glebe, and many persons of wealth attended it, and they could offer such support as invited excellent talent. Among them, however, was a local preacher of the Methodists—a blacksmith, but a fine speaker—and they called him, after due preparation, to be the rector of their parish. As the Methodists in Accomack had something to humble them in the treatment of Mr. Curtis, so the people of Hungar's Parish had their trials in some rectors that they had. In this circuit resided, as a supernumerary of the Philadelphia Conference, Rev. William B. Snead. He was a friend to me in my early ministry. He married a daughter of Rev. Mr. Gardner, a rector at one time of Hunger's Parish.

"On this circuit were some fourteen appointments. Having been ordained deacon, I went before the court at Eastville, the county town of Northampton, to obtain, according to the laws of Virginia, liberty to solemnize matrimony, and was required to give my bond and security under oath that I would marry only such persons as the law allowed; but I did not, and I think my colleague did not, marry a couple the whole year. The fact was that local preachers had deacons' orders, and in their neighborhood married nearly all the people that we as Methodists married. The circuit preacher was at all points on the circuit, and was not called on for this service. Though I was required 'to swear allegiance to the Commonwealth of Virginia,' I received nothing to pay the cost. While on this circuit, we had a visit from Bishop Waugh. He had been made bishop in 1836, and had his residence in Baltimore. He cherished a wish to visit that Shore, as Bishop Emory had done only a few years before. He was in my care, and for some ten days I took him in my carriage that, being married, I had now purchased. I shall never, while memory lasts, forget that godly man, that courteous gentleman, that modest but able minister of the Gospel. He preached at Drummondtown from 'Thus it is written, and thus it behooved Christ to suffer, and to rise from the dead the third day: and that repentance and remission of sins should be preached in his name among all nations, beginning at Jerusalem.'

"The sermon was an hour and a half long. But its merit was much longer, for with me, at least, it has lasted fifty-five years. It was a great sermon. He preached in our various appointments and addressed the societies after preaching, guarding them against certain temptations and urging them to Christian holiness, enjoining temperance —though he said he did not go into 'the culinary department'—reading the Scriptures, secret and family prayer. Preachers and people felt how high were the qualifications that he showed for this exalted office. I took him to Cape Charles, where we touched the lowest point on the Peninsula that a Methodist bishop ever reached. There was nothing cold in his intercourse; though dignified in bearing, he was genial in spirit, and could and did relax in anecdote. He was mighty in prayer. I have heard him preach when he was not great, but I never heard him fail in prayer. The memory of his addresses, not to the audience, but to God, even now serves to warm my heart. One of the most interesting evenings I ever spent in social life was with the bishop at Wesley, the residence of William D. Seymour, Esq. At the fireside, the pastor Rev. John S. Taylor, was present; and as we sat around the room the bishop, with ease and dignity, began to speak of the work of God and Christian experience; and as all in the circle were Christians and Methodists excepting one—Miss Margaret Seymour, who was an Episcopalian—the bishop made some inquiry of Brother Taylor, then of Mr. Seymour, that no one might be taken unprepared. Then, as far as he felt his way clear, he called out different ones to speak. I heard no one hint that there was bad taste in the exercise. I think of this man of God with a heart full of gratitude. One trial I had with him; that was of preaching in his presence at Onancock, one of our leading appointments.

"A feeling of pathos may be allowed as I think of that family of Mr. Seymour's; every one of whom, and all that company of the evening named except myself, have left the world that they so honored. But the hope of meeting them all in a better world is the joy that no one can take from me.

"Northampton Circuit that year took in a part of the Accomack Circuit, the one I was on the year before. We held a camp meeting near Capeville, some five or six miles above Cape Charles. But such was the storm that even the courageous Henry White, presiding elder, thought we might better 'pull up stakes and leave.' We remained: but little was done. We held another camp meeting higher up on the circuit. At first some of the 'hot bloods' gave us trouble. My colleague spoke to them kindly, but to no effect. For a time we suffered it. Then I felt 'forbearance ceased to be a virtue' and went out among them and remonstrated. They were not disposed to hear; but this was the end of their bad conduct. Everything seemed against us. My colleague said I must preach at night. I took my text, 'The wicked shall be turned into hell.' When the text was announced my colleague, Mr. Wiltshire, exclaimed, 'My Lord!' I did not represent hell as a place of questionable anguish, or of doubtful duration. I had what our fathers called 'great liberty.' The people heard with awe, and drew near the pulpit. The Rev. William B. Snead, supernumerary of the Conference, unable to go into the pulpit, remained in the tent. But as I advanced he came out and stood, and when I was reaching a fearful climax and exclaimed, 'Shall I say more?' he cried out, 'More!' Then I broke forth in the language of Pollok, 'Methought I saw a lake of burning fire,' and quoted the passage at length. A young woman in the congregation shrieked, rushed toward the pulpit, and fell in prayer at the altar, and in a short time it was filled with souls crying for mercy. My colleague, who had, on hearing the text, exclaimed, 'My Lord!' now asserted, 'The devil has left the ground;' and from that time there was a wonderful sweep of God's power. This was one of the most manifest triumphs over the power of darkness that I have ever witnessed. God had the ground.

"At the end of this year I went to Conference under great embarrassment. Our firstborn was about six weeks old; my wife was suffering; I was on my third year, and my Conference studies must be met, or I must at least lose a year. Trusting in God, and the best attention that my wife and babe could have in Mrs. Floyd and the nurse, I left for Conference, held at Asbury, Wilmington, and passed my examination in the office of Dr. Samuel H. Higgins, then in the practice of medicine, but who afterward entered the ministry of the Conference.

"My appointment for 1838 was for Reading, Pa. My dear colleague with whom I had passed a happy year in Northampton was sent to Tamaqua.

"Reading and Pottsgrove Mission stood together on the minutes, and the announcement by the bishop was 'J. A. Roche and M. D. Kurtz.' This for me was removal from the appointment farthest south in the Conference to one not far from the farthest north. In those days we knew nothing of the appointments till they were read out. I was not dissatisfied; but much was involved in it. I could not for about three weeks attempt the journey on account of the condition of my wife and babe. And then how should we reach the appointment? By stage? That would be death. By a schooner to Baltimore? It might get on a bar, as I had once proved and lost a visit to Baltimore after the detention of a week. And what accommodation could we have on the boat? I could not attempt that. The only other way was by steamboat from Pungoteague. That went every other Sabbath at one o'clock P. M. I was unwilling to go thus, and yet I felt God would not hold us guilty. My reason told me this was the only way, and my conscience commended it. We thus reached Baltimore. As the Eastern Shore of Virginia receded from my view I lifted my hat and bowed, full of the memories that it furnished. Nearly fifty-six years have elapsed, and with all the good I then received I have not touched that Shore since.

"In 1838 the railroad was not laid from Baltimore to Philadelphia. My wife and nurse and myself took the steamboat to Frenchtown: thence by railroad to New Castle, and thence by steamboat to Philadelphia. The railroad from Frenchtown to New Castle was laid in 1832. This helped us. On reaching Philadelphia I met Rev. William H. Gilder, the father of Richard Watson Gilder. Mr. Gilder's health had failed, and he had gone into the drug business with the late Samuel W. Monroe, who had not then entered the ministry. Mr. Gilder hearing me ask for a boarding house, wished to know for what purpose, and on being told for myself and wife and babe and servant, replied, 'This must not be; you must go to my father's house.' I told him I could not think of such a tax on a friend. He insisted, and took us there. It is true they had a large residence in Colonnade Row, Spruce Street, but equally true it seemed too much to expect. There we were cared for as tenderly as if we had been his own family. In those days our people in the cities entertained Methodist ministers as if they thought they were God's angels, and some of their houses were always open for them. Mr. and Mrs. Gilder had two sons, Rev. John Leonard and Rev. William H., in our ministry. But now we were fifty-two miles from Reading, and the railroad was not yet laid. How should we reach Reading? There were two canal boats for coal, black enough; but could I, with safety to my wife, take one of them? Then there was a railroad from Ninth Street and Green, Philadelphia, to

Norristown. This we took; and then the stage, as the only way to Pottsgrove. As if Providence had us in view, that very day the railroad was opened between Pottsgrove (now Pottstown) and Reading, and we had this. On our way the babe took the whooping cough! A fine-looking gentleman in the stage we were compelled to take made a remark, to the effect that 'our troubles were often blessings.' I took it to heart, and hoped to find it so in the present case.

"We reached Reading, after a journey of three hundred and ten miles, about a month after the appointment had been read. The official brethren met. They were just on the eve of giving us up. Brother Kurtz had preached on the Sabbath, and had been among the people. We boarded for a week, and then began our experience in housekeeping in a little frame dwelling. The house, originally one story, and so remaining, was, by the filling up of the street, left three or four steps below the surface of the pavement, and from the street I might almost touch the roof. My predecessor, Rev. Allen Johnson, excellent preacher, had lost his wife, and it was not known that another house would be needed; and neither my wife nor I was in the spirit of finding fault. In a little time we had a better house, but the rent was eighty-five dollars, and this was too much for the society. Sabbath came, and I preached my first sermon. The church was originally a one-story brick dwelling; they had added to its depth, and Rev. Joseph Ashbark, a former pastor, called it the coffin. The form suggested the figure. The ceiling was possibly eleven feet high. Among our members sat Mrs. Judge Banks, an elegant lady, whose husband afterward ran for the governorship of the State. Mrs. Banks had been but a short time from Meadville, Pa., the seat of Allegheny College, where she sat under the preaching of Rev. Henry B. Bascom. I can hardly write of this period without tears. There was such a felt responsibility. Reading, now a city of possibly seventy thousand population, was then a borough of eight thousand people. Our society was fifty-eight whites and two colored. Excepting Mrs. Judge Banks, Mr. Daniel Rhein, Henry Goodheart, Andrew Gussler, and a Mrs. Smith, our society was very poor; and those not poor were far from being rich.

"The church was in debt, and failing to pay its interest. We held a little Sabbath school up in the attic of the church, under a sharp-peaked room that in summer gave us all the heat that ordinary natures could stand; and there, on colored as well as white children we tried to make as good an impression as we could. I was only in my fourth year; was not through my Conference studies, and could not, as a deacon, administer the Lord's Supper. Rev. James Smith was the presiding elder, and to him we had to look for that sacrament. It was soon concluded that Rev. M. D. Kurtz should take the 'Pottsgrove Mission,' and that I should remain in Reading, though both places were under my charge. Brother Kurtz was educated as well as born among the Germans, and could speak the language, and I could not. He was an excellent preacher. In this borough Summerfield had preached, and George G. Cookman had in an orchard delivered his holy message in his attractive style and manner. Thomas Sovereign, Joseph Ashbark, and Allen John had served as pastors. Repeated efforts had been made to build a church and had failed; and it was now associated with Pottsgrove, 'as a mission,' and one hundred and fifty dollars appropriated. My first year I received a salary of two hundred and twenty-seven dollars. Nearly all Reading was German; their preaching, in the German and Lutheran Reformed churches—that took in nearly all the people—was German; their schools were German, though English was taught in some; and there were German Methodists, and their preaching was in German. There was a St. Peter's Protestant Episcopal Church, whose devoted rector was the Rev. R. U. Morgan.

"Our society had suffered in the reputation of some who had been among us, but I soon found the talk of building was by such as could do nothing but talk, and I knew that would not build a temple for God. I determined I would not be governed by such men, and that no one in the future should reproachfully point at me and say, 'This man began to build and was not able to finish.' Then, my pulpit called for two sermons every Sabbath. On a circuit a man has no such necessity for this number of new sermons. In those days we had few stations except in the cities; and here I was, with the study the pulpit required. A few years before this the Book Concern under John Emory, D.D., afterward bishop, had published the *British Sketches*. These were very common among our preachers; I had a copy. In those days hardly any preacher wrote sermons. I had written two or three. These sketches suggested subjects, and though I memorized no sermons of any author, nor any sketch, they helped me in sermonizing. They who unqualifiedly condemn such means do not commend their conclusions to my judgment.

Mechanics have patterns as well as tools. Artists have models as well as material, and professional men study one another, and the unwise learn from the wise—not to be those men, but to be themselves improved by the wise.

"In finances a great commercial crisis occurred in 1837, occasioned, it was said, by reckless speculation. During the months of March and April the failures in New York city alone amounted to one hundred millions of dollars. So distressing was the condition of the country that petitions were sent to the President from several quarters, and deputations of merchants and bankers of New York waited upon him in person, and solicited him to defer the immediate collection of duties for which bonds had been given, and to rescind treasury orders requiring duties to government to be paid in specie. They also asked that an extra session of Congress be called to adopt measures of relief. He granted their request so far only as to suspend suits on bonds which had been given for the collection of duties. In a few days after his response to this deputation was known in New York all the banks of the city stopped specie payment, and their example was soon followed by nearly all the banks of the State. Mr. Van Buren was compelled to convene an extra session of Congress to provide for meeting demands on the treasury with legal currency. 'To meet the exigency of the treasury as well as to provide for the public relief as far as to them seemed proper, Congress passed an act authorizing the issue of treasury notes to the amount of two millions of dollars.' It was indeed a time of financial gloom. It became the period of an issue in Pennsylvania known as 'shinplasters.' It might be a small note of five or ten cents—a handful might make little more than a dollar or two. Prices fell to nearly half their former figures, though the former were not high. This was the condition of the country when I was sent to Reading.

"What, then, could encourage hope of building? The few that had a little money feared the undertaking, as they supposed it would appeal to them beyond their ability; and the complaints of those unable to give against those who had a little did not make the case more promising. I saw, young as I was, that we must have those with us in the movement that could render some financial aid. When I had been with them about six months I found that I could have the cooperation of those who would be of real help. I began by calling a meeting of the society, and at once remarked I would not begin, to go back and abandon; but wished them to consider whether it was God who was impelling us, and assured them if it was He there could be no failure if we did our part. I wished them to act together, and with the understanding we must have all the help that they could give. We took a vote, and the church stood committed; eight hundred dollars was subscribed. I then went out into the town to collect. General George M. Keim was one of the leading men not only of the borough, but of the State. He was then a member of Congress, and subscribed twenty-five dollars, and said, 'If you need me call again, and I will give you more help.' General De B. Keim, his uncle, subscribed twenty dollars. Mr. Whitiker, partner of General George M. Keim in the iron business, though claiming to be somewhat of a friend, said, 'I am opposed to building brick churches.' As I saw his mind was cheerful I thought mine could be a little free, and though I was young and he was old, I playfully replied, 'O! you would have them iron.' He took it well, and said he would give me a keg of nails that would be worth twenty-five dollars. I refused to call on no man for his dignity or his poverty, if I thought there was any chance.

"I hastened to Philadelphia with a purpose of getting money enough to clinch the resolution of the church, so that they could not go back on their purpose. This only saved us from that result. Rev. T. J. Thompson, D.D., then stationed in Harrisburg, was in the city before me, begging for a church in the capital of the State, and the Rev. James Neill, who went out from Philadelphia a popular preacher, then stationed at Lancaster, was also in Philadelphia, begging for a new church. I determined not to ask collections in churches, but to call on the pastors in various charges, and I soon found I could not ask the names of persons able to give, as their members would reproach them if they gave them. I plunged into the ocean, sink or swim, and with no past experience. Through John Gilder, Esq., I was introduced to the mayor of the city, who, by the way, was of my name, and he gave ten dollars, as Mr. Gilder did—and each with a blessing. I saw Richard Benson, Esq., father of the bankers of that name. I met him at the book room in Fourth Street, and told him I had wished to call on him, as he was one of our great men in clearing and improving our church property. But I added, 'I have heard of your gift to Harrisburg of one hundred dollars, and I have not the heart to ask anything.' But I carefully stated our case. The next week after returning from Reading, to which I had returned to preach

8

on Sabbath, meeting Rev. William H. Gilder at the book room, he said, 'I congratulate you.' I asked, 'For what?' He replied, 'Mr. Benson is going to give you fifty dollars.' He did so. It gladdened my heart.

"I asked no man's pulpit, but Dr. Charles Pitman, stationed at Eighth Street, then a new church, with perhaps the finest congregation that we had in the city, made me preach for him on Sabbath morning, and then urged his people to help me. I called on the late Bishop James, then stationed at Nazareth; and he afterward met me, and though he, with all the pastors, thought the times and circumstances forbade hope, he now said he heard I 'had almost miraculous success.' I called on Isaac Lloyd, then with a block of houses in process of building. I went from store to store, from house to house. I rushed on in the vigor of my purpose, and when I had a tooth aching as if it would leap from its socket I stopped in the market house, then in the middle of Market Street, and, like a common drayman or porter, asked for a glass of milk and a slice of pie, asked my blessing, drank and ate, and said my prayer as I walked the street. At the end of four weeks I raised there and at Germantown six hundred and thirty dollars. This was thought to be unexampled. Money was scarce, as we have seen. I, for example, called on C. W. Stratton, in dental business, and one of our most-liked men, who said he could give nothing; teeth would not build a church. Then I asked him to give me teeth, and I would see they were sold, and the money should go to the church. He gave me a handful. They were sold, and the money resulting was, I think, twenty-five dollars. My treasurer wanted one, and for that one I got a dollar. A young man gave me a breastpin. I sold it. Another man, when I was in Wilmington, said he had nothing to give except shoes, and they did not sell. Then I said, 'Give me shoes.' He gave me a pair of slippers. I asked him the price, and took them for myself, and paid the money to the church.

"While begging in Philadelphia I was absent from my pulpit on two Sabbaths. I would leave Reading on Monday morning; and in those days the ministers traveled on that railroad free of any charge. I would pass one Sabbath in Philadelphia, and then on the following Saturday return and preach twice in my own pulpit on Sabbath, and then next day go as before; and in that time I accomplished the result I have named. I went to Pottsville, one of our strongest charges; I went to Carlisle; I went to Easton, Md.; to Centerville. I attended camp meetings. I knew no limit, but that of possibility. O, how I thought and prayed! I took a violent cold. Dr. M. Sorin, then stationed in Ebenezer, Philadelphia, saw me and said, 'John, you must go home and attend to that cold, or your work will soon be done.' On going home I called on one of the best physicians and most accomplished gentleman that I have ever known, Dr. Isaac Heister, and he fairly commanded me to put flannel next to my skin and never go without it. This I did, and for all these years have not failed for a day to follow his direction. I lived through all. At Carlisle, the seat of Dickinson College, the daughter of Bishop Emory and afterward wife of Dr. Crooks, collected money for me; and Dr. Thomas C. Thornton, then pastor of the church, in the camp meeting that he was conducting, when I preached, spoke to his people from the pulpit and said he believed God had sent me to them, and they should give. More than fifty-five years have passed, and did I ever obtain in anything else that I have ever done as much character and commendation as I received in the church in Reading as a beggar? They declared my equal could not be found in three Conferences. In all this I honor God, for it was he that was working in me mightily.

"The ground for the church was bought in one of the best localities. The house was fifty by sixty-five feet. It was dedicated in December, 1839. Joseph Lybrand preached in the morning, Bishop Scott (as he was afterward) in the afternoon, and Dr. John Kennaday at night. Dr. K. remained with me two or three nights, and a good extra meeting followed. At the end of the year there was a debt on the church of two thousand five hundred dollars. They owed me on salary two hundred and sixty-six dollars. I owed them on subscriptions twenty-seven dollars. Mine I paid. They felt ashamed to take it, as they were unable to pay me. The second year they paid me about four hundred and fifty dollars. I attended to all parts of my work as pastor and preacher, and when Conference came was not found wanting in my studies, and received elder's orders.

"But the deepest gloom came over me in this charge, when at midnight I heard a cry from my wife, who had so cheered me in all my work, and, though raised in the most refined society in Virginia, never complained at anything as a hardship. At first I had the greatest need to hold hard to God. She lived more than two years after this. But the stroke of that night was on me. Rev. Mr. Morgan, of St. Peter's Church, called on me in my distress, and was to me such a blessed man of God; and Dr. Isaac Heister was all that a mortal and a man of science could be.

"I got through our church building well. There was a time when I had a good deal of money in hand. I did not know whether there was more than one man that had a bank account, and he was one that they had not been able to get into the work. I knew the time would come when I might need some one to advance money, and now I could give him a good deal that he could command, and I knew that with him all would be safe. I had him made treasurer, and he gave fifty per cent more than those wishing his aid had ever thought to ask him to give. So far was I from losing my hold on him, he so loved me that when he was nearly ninety years of age he came walking through the middle of the street, because of the sleet, to visit me, when, in 1853-54, I was stationed in Fifth Street, Philadelphia. I mention his name with honor; this was Daniel Rhein, one of our first members, who, because of our earnestness as Christians, left the German Reformed Church to join us. This was an epoch in the history of our church in Reading. In about six years a second Methodist Episcopal church (St. Peter's) was built, and now I understand they have a new church that is one of the grandest in the State. I trust it will be as honored in its zeal for God as was the church we built and called 'Ebenezer.' That was the name I gave it, as I wished to perpetuate the fact that 'hitherto had the Lord helped us.'

"I have tried in every field to do my duty. But when I consider all the facts I know of no charge I have ever filled where I did, under all the difficulties, a better work than I did in Reading, between the springs of 1838 and 1840. When I left it I was followed by Rev. Dr. Samuel Hall Higgins, who was very popular as a preacher, and he said to me the only discredit on my labors was in the fact that I had given twenty-seven dollars to the church that owed me two hundred and sixty-six. But the reproach gave me no pain for my conduct. Souls, too, were brought into the kingdom of God; for without these nothing could satisfy me.

"My next appointment, in 1840, was to Norristown, Pa. With this Evansburg and Lumberville were associated. This was as unexpected to the people as to the preacher, and it was not pleasant to either. Norristown had been a circuit. They had no knowledge of any purposed division, and they were not in a position for a station. They had no parsonage, and at the first Quarterly Conference, with a statement of the case by the presiding elder, James Smith, they hired a house for me and furnished it with articles temporarily supplied by members of the church. Norristown resolved to stand alone and retain me as their pastor. Evansburg and Lumberville formed a separate charge, and the late Rev. John Street, then in business in Market Street, Philadelphia, was called out to fill the charge, which he did with the pleasure of the people and with success in his labors.

"Under such circumstances the appointment was trying to me. Yet I had a happy year and many conversions. For the period we had a fine church. It was the county town of Montgomery, Pa., with a population of two thousand five hundred. The Baptists were strong. The other churches had positive influence. We were not numerous, and had no wealth. The hard times were still on us. Many of my people were in the factories and mills, and these were stopped, or running on half time. My members could get only a little money for work done, and were compelled to take pay in orders on the stores. When we came together in leaders' meeting my men were pained to say we had next to no money. 'What shall we do to pay the preacher? We have little but orders; by these we have to live.' I said, 'By that on which my people have to live, I will live. Pay what money you can, and then pay me as you are paid, in orders.' We had a large Sunday school, excellent prayer meetings, and great congregations. I received for salary about two hundred and eighty dollars. But I had a field and a devoted people.

"In 1841 I was sent to Cohocksink, then really a village, at the northern end of Philadelphia. The church was new, the society was small, the means of support utterly inadequate. We had excellent members, but the congregation was small, and there was no community to make it large.

"This, too, the year before, had been in a circuit—the Philadelphia Circuit—with one remarkable man and one talented youth on it. The man was Caleb A. Lippencot, distinguished for his zeal, his force, his popular talent. He had done an excellent work in building the church. The talented youth was James McCarter: he was bright, earnest, and eloquent. We had a successful extra meeting, and some of the fruit of that meeting has given me great joy. It is in one there converted, and called of God into a useful ministry.

"Several of us ministers resolved that we would unite

to help each other during the extra services. The band included the late Thomas Jefferson Thompson, stationed at St. Paul's, four or five miles away in the southern part of the city; C. A. Lippencot, at Asbury, West Philadelphia, about an equal distance; Elijah Miller, at Salem, Southwest Philadelphia, nearly as far away; and myself. We were all to be at all the meetings of every charge. In those days we had no surface cars, and except on Market Street we had no conveyance but what locomotion supplied. But God was with us, and the 'people had a mind to work.' The meeting was four weeks long.

"To the nation and to the Church this was a year of gloom. Early in the year William Henry Harrison, President of the United States, after being in office only a few weeks, died. He was followed in office by his Vice President, John Tyler, of Virginia. This year Rev. George G. Cookman was lost in the *President*, in a visit he was making to his relations in England, whence he had come a few years before. He was one of the most popular preachers of his country. He had just served as chaplain to Congress, and in that body of distinguished men commanded great influence for his piety, his prayers, and his magnetic power as an orator. The ship was never heard from after she left port.

"In 1842 I was sent to Germantown. This was a strong charge; the salary was five hundred dollars—excellent in those days. Besides Germantown, where we preached morning and night on Sabbath, we also, every two weeks, preached at a mission chapel at Chestnut Hill, where at that time we had no church, and our membership was seventeen. In October I began an extra meeting that was crowned with even wonderful success. For the time I gave myself almost wholly to this place through the week. Lutherans, German Reformed, Presbyterians, and Protestant Episcopalians showed as much interest as did our own people. In the early stages of the meeting I would invite the members, and any others that would, to come and kneel with me at a bench we placed before the stand—for we had neither pulpit nor altar—and those of the other churches would as readily as my own people come and kneel with me to seek God's richer blessing. The people came five and six miles, and about one hundred souls professed religion. I preached nearly every night for about eight weeks, and visited through the day. I went to Philadelphia for help, and, failing, would rise to preach, when too tired. Seizing upon a text which I had not time to find, I would say, 'You will find the text by obeying the command, "Search the Scriptures." ' I would then announce it from memory. O, what days of visiting, of prayer, of preaching, of urging the people to labor! They hardly needed urging to come out; some could scarcely wait from one night to another. It was a glorious day! We had a successful extra meeting in Germantown. But as 1843 drew near the Miller excitement about the coming of Christ was very great. There was one of my leading men, one whom from my relation to him I had great cause to respect, who had at various times talked with me on the subject and whom I had not opposed, thinking he had the right of private judgment. But he determined to have a leading advocate give a lecture in my church, and asked my consent. I refused. He persisted in his wish, and I persisted in my purpose not to have it. I had heard of the bad results in the churches. I suffered for the refusal. In those days ministers of families were to be taken care of, and I had none but a babe and a housekeeper, and it was argued they needed the charge for one with a family. I was made to feel a very great change. Rev. Samuel Harsey, president of the Germantown Bank, and one of our most honored laymen, was a local preacher in the charge, and also Rev. Samuel Y. Harmer, who afterward went West and entered the itinerancy.

"In 1843 I was sent with C. J. Crouch on Radnor Circuit, just on the edge of Philadelphia. Brother Crouch, as the older preacher, was in charge. It was, from its location and membership, an interesting circuit. Here I remained one year, making my residence at Kingsessing.

"On the 17th of August, 1843, I was married by the Rev. James Smith, Jr., my presiding elder, to Miss Mary Caroline Osler, of Gloucester County, N. J. She was born near Merchantville, not far from Camden, on a farm that had been in the family for more than two hundred years, a part of which is still in the possession of some of the family. Miss Osler I found a member of the church when I became pastor at Germantown; she was then in a very choice seminary, conducted by the Misses Latimer and Parker. It originated with the Rev. William Neill, D.D., former president of Dickinson College, the last Presbyterian president before it came into our hands. Miss Osler was studying languages, and various branches—music included—to fit herself for the best position as a teacher. She was at the same time teaching a school in Germantown; she had previously had a seminary in Pemberton, N. J. She was with me on the circuit from August 17th till

Conference. The circuit had about fourteen appointments, and some of them, especially Radnor, were of the early preaching places in the days of Bishop Asbury. Salary, of course, was small, and that year I was compelled to spend more than I received, and thus drew on private means. But souls were saved. As Conference approached it was suggested by brethren to make Kingsessing a station, though it was only a small village, and I was spoken to about serving the place.

"In 1844 I was appointed to Kingsessing as a station. I was living in the circuit and had no need to remove. I collected money for them outside the community, and though my salary was about two hundred and eighty dollars, my wife saved fifty dollars, and we lived as well as ever and had help in the family. We never took boarders, as some have felt constrained to do. We had an excellent revival. Thus I was in this place two years. Though I went to it as a station for the first time, there was no doubt among the people as to supporting me. A petition was prepared to ask for my return, if the law of the Church would allow it. This was the year of that General Conference that enters so largely, if not honorably, into our history, when as a Church we divided over the painful fact that Bishop Andrew had by marriage become a slaveholder, and the Church South would not allow him to resign his office, though it was known the Church in the North would not accept his services on account of his holding slaves. My account of this is found in the *Life of Dr. Durbin.*

"In 1845—Levi Scott, D.D., being presiding elder—I was stationed at Asbury, West Philadelphia. Here we had an excellent society, and the salary was five hundred dollars. Hestonville was an afternoon appointment, and there every other Sabbath afternoon and night we preached. Thomas Hunter, Esq., and his family attended Asbury in the morning, and took me in their carriage to their hospitable home, where I dined and preached and held class in the afternoon. I then took tea at Mr. Scott's; or Frederick Sauber's, who, after my filling the night appointment, sent me in his carriage to West Philadelphia. On one occasion the horse ran away, and I had enough care for my life, but a Providence of mercy kept me. Here began an acquaintance with the family of Thomas Hunter, and his sons and daughters, that I have enjoyed nearly fifty years.

"Messrs. Rose, father and son, were much to Asbury what Messrs. Hunter and Sauber were to Hestonville. We had a good work of revival in both appointments, and in that charge I spent two happy years. Our parsonage was on Oak Street.

"Having ended the period of my pastorate at Asbury, I was sent in 1847 to St. Paul's, Philadelphia. Here we had a fine large church: one of the best, if not the best, parsonage in the Conference, and a grand congregation. Here, on September 29th, 1847, our bright and beautiful boy Emory Fisk was taken from us. I was out in my charge visiting and praying with my people, and when I returned the doctor met me at the door and told of the fact, but conveyed the idea the chances were in the child's favor. There was no 'chance.' In a few hours that sweet life went out, and he was with the angels.

"This charge, from many facts, has ever been very dear to me. I had great trials there, but great triumphs also.

My salary was seven hundred dollars, with many marriages. Salaries in those days in our best churches were not as now, and our people, being numerous, were not expected to give as they are now required to do, to support the Church and her institutions."

In the issue of *St. Paul's Faith and Works* for January, 1898, Dr. Roche reviewed his labors at this church in the following letter:

"*To the Editor of St. Paul's Faith and Works:*

"DEAR SIR: Your remembrance of me awakens thoughts of the past in relation to St. Paul's that may interest others if you will permit them a place in your intelligent and interesting periodical. In the spring of 1835, after serving as a junior preacher on Port Deposit Circuit, I went to Philadelphia—which I then saw for the first time—to attend the Conference of April 8th, at the Union Church, between Market and Arch Streets, where, in those days, it was uniformly held. There and then, with nineteen others, I was received as a probationer in the Conference. There, by God's providence, I remained twenty-two years, till 1857, when transferred to New York East Conference. As an utter stranger it was my happiness to fall under the care of the St. Paul's people for entertainment, and during the Conference I had one of the most delightful homes at the residence of the late John Whiteman. In this I was associated with the Rev. William Weir.

"St. Paul's had been organized only a short time previously. The Rev. Lawrence McCoomb, one of the mighty men of God in his day, was as a supernumerary in charge of the church, and the Rev. William Wurie, one of the most attractive young preachers, was with him to do the work. They then worshiped in a church that had been built for the Methodist Protestants, or was used by them for some years. It was located on South Fifth Street, near Catharine. Ebenezer had long been the only Methodist Church in that part of the city, and had great strength in numbers and influence. But as at a former period 'Union' left St. George's, the mother church, on the question of having 'stewards' as well as trustees, influential members of 'Ebenezer' desired a like government. After frequent discussions it was determined by strong members that a new church should be formed, as the 'Union' had proved a great success. John Whiteman, who, from his early membership to his latest life, was one of the most intelligent and active members of the church, rose in the congregation of Ebenezer, and expressed his purpose to leave, and some of the best people of the charge responded to his statement and joined him, among whom was Nicholas Toy, Peter Hortz, and Mr. Jackson, men of age and moral strength. Then, also, or about that time, Charles Perrine and wife identified themselves with them; soon thereafter the families of Nesbit and Caramder.

"At once St. Paul's took an influential position among the churches of the city, and some of the best men of the Conference were placed in charge. For a short time they were under the care of the late Dr. William Cooper. William A. Wiggins, for so many years the honored secretary of Conference, was one of their first regular pastors. The esteem in which he was held, and the great admiration of his labors and success, were enough to make one who, like the writer, heard the expressions of his people feel that if privation and persecution came with the ministry

there was something compensative in the kindnesses of
those he served. In St. Paul's the pastor and the flock
were one, and a strong one it was. For several years the
writer, from Conference to Conference, was given homes
in Almond Street with the members of St. Paul's; then
with Messrs. Whiteman, John Scott, Bickerton, and
Walker. While still pursuing his Conference studies, he
could without embarrassment to the families work, till two
o'clock in the morning saw his mental exercise end in welcome sleep. This was in the days when all our churches
in the city had preaching during Conference every night,
and St. George's in the morning. At night the houses were
filled, the pulpits flamed, the altars glowed, and the songs
of victory over souls converted drew others not of the
church. The pulpit and the altar filled the churches with
the inquiring and the devout.

"The progress and promise this young charge presented
in a short time directed the attention of Paul Beck, Esq.,
one of the rich men of Philadelphia, to its future need.
Edmund J. Yard, one of the holiest men, was in Mr. Beck's
office, where from day to day he exerted his influence, till
Mr. Beck, who had lands in the locality of St. Paul's,
offered them lots for a new church, and with them ten
thousand dollars, provided they built such a church as
the community ought to have. The promise was given,
the church was built, and the donor added to his other
gifts a lot for the parsonage, that when finished was pronounced by the Rev. Levi Scott a 'Methodist preacher's
palace.' The church and property were such as induced
visitors to the city to call and see, admire and commend.

"The picture that St. Paul's pamphlet of *Faith and*

Works now presents eloquently reminds us of those days when our churches were built for capacity and conveniences. Material magnificence and architectural attraction exerted little power. Plain as St. Paul's edifice now appears, it was, when built, one of our finest churches in the city. It had a centerpiece in the ceiling a little more showy than usual, in the style of the day, and caused Father Hillsey to complain as if 'they had taken away his Lord.'

"The dedication of the church was a great occasion. One of the sermons was preached by Edmund S. Janes, afterward bishop, but then a member of the Philadelphia Conference. His text was 1 Cor. iii, 5: 'Who then is Paul?' He did not fail to tell who *Paul the apostle* was in language to rouse the soul, and was by no means lacking in information, that he freely used, as to who *Paul Beck was;* and the place of their worship became St. Paul's. So may it ever continue, if God's providence and grace direct! Time, talent, and task exert their power! All is right when God bounds the realm of our thoughts and keeps our ambition in his control. Our people desired that holy spot for future homes. Directly opposite to the church Mr. Whiteman built a residence that he retained till removal after several years took him to another part of the city. Others built in the location, and the church greatly prospered.

"William Barnes, one of the most eloquent men of the Conference, a pastor, followed the Rev. William A. Wiggins. After him was sent Levi Scott, afterward bishop, and as *his* successor Rev. Thomas Jefferson Thompson, who was worthy the episcopacy twenty years before God took him.

"The Conference of 1847 appointed the writer to the

charge, and never did he feel so honored when, as pastor, he faced one of the finest congregations of Philadelphia. The happy memory of the services he tried to render, the encouragements and supports he there received, must abide while memory has place. But as in St. John xix, 41, 'There was a garden, and in the garden a new sepulcher,' so, amid the charms of the premises of St. Paul's, my suddenly summoned and beautiful son Emory Fisk sleeps, and tears and joys had their turns. Of some honored pastors before my days, and of many since, there is no need for me to write, as they are fresh in the memories of those who still live.

"I cannot tell the pleasure it gives me to know that Mr. Charles Perrine and his equally devoted wife are still among the living, and also to find the name of T. C. Nesbitt among the trustees of St. Paul's.

"The writer has taken the liberty that your kindness offered to narrate facts in St. Paul's history that he thinks no other living minister could give. Sixty-three years brings an oblivion of much that it may do us good to cherish or to study. So far as the writer knows, Mr. Perrine is the only living man who can reproduce the early facts of which we have written. With earnest prayer that Dr. Foster, your present pastor, may witness success that will be to him a crowning glory in his ministry of so many years, and that St. Paul's may be equal to the work that now induces so natural a care, and rise superior to the difficulties that face us in all great service for the Master and Lord, and with profound respect.

"I am, dear brothers,

"Yours in Christ,

"JOHN A. ROCHE."

9

Dr. Roche continues his narative as follows:

"At the end of my pastorate at St. Paul's, Rev. T. T. Tasker and Rev. D. H. Kollock, two of the strongest local preachers in the city, and both members of Wharton Street —a very large church—waited on good Bishop Waugh, who construed West Philadelphia to be Philadelphia; by which fact—the law of the Church at that time allowing no preacher to remain more than four consecutive years in the same city—I was not allowed to serve that grand church.

"This rule began about the time of Bishop Waugh's entering the episcopacy, and ended about the time of his death. He thought preachers were allowed to remain too long in a city. He was great on the change that our system recognizes. What would he now do with one who, like me, has been in New York and Brooklyn for the space of thirty-six years?

"In 1849 I was sent to Smyrna, Del. Thence I had gone out as a preacher fourteen years before, and I thought I would rather preach to any other congregation in the Conference than to this one. There was that man of so much wisdom, Judge Davis. There was my old class leader, Dr. Perkins, and there was the Rev. Piner Mansfield, a local preacher that had gone to school to my father. Smyrna had one of the most excellent societies that I have ever known in any place. I had a good time there—excellent revival. Never was I more kindly treated by a people, and no kindness was greater than that received from those before whom I would be the slowest to preach. My salary was five hundred dollars. My mother and my sister Sarah Ann lived in Smyrna, and were in my congregation while

I was pastor. My sister married Mr. Raughley before I left.

"The Conference, through my influence, had been invited to Smyrna, and it cost me no little thought to make the best arrangements possible. There I spent two happy years. There where I had gone as a boy in my fourteenth year, there where in my sixteenth year I was converted to God, there where I had prayed so much, labored with energy, and studied with such solicitude—there I felt I could be glad to spend my life.

"This year, 1851, I was sent to Asbury, Wilmington. This was one of the great churches in early Methodism, and here had been stationed some of our bishops and many of our most talented ministers. It was a strong society. But scarcely was I in the charge before my son Alexander was taken sick with typhoid fever; on the 29th of May, 1851, God took him from us, at the age of seven years and four days. He was a promising child. He was in a private school of the Rev. Mr. Mansfield, an Episcopal minister, and in spelling was said to be the best in his class. A committee from the seminary, with Bishop Lee's son as one of the members, waited on us and presented resolutions of sympathy passed by the school. The death of that child was a heavy stroke. When ill he said to his mother, 'Mother, what is the meaning of that scripture, "But some man will say, How are the dead raised up, and with what body do they come?"' and as he had been forbidden to call anyone a 'fool' he stopped at that word. His mother continued the quotation, and tried to tell him the meaning, and he said, 'I understand.'

"While in Asbury. Dr. Hodgson was at St. Paul's, and

we had much care about our 'Young Ladies' Seminary.'
Rev. Solomon Prettyman, who was its originator, lacked
financial success, and had given up the school. Dr.
Hodgson and I had heard of Professor George Loomis,
who had been a success as chaplain in Canton, China, and
we went to Trenton, the seat of the New Jersey Conference, to consult Professor Loomis about the vacancy. He
came on to Wilmington to make observation and hear prop-
ositions. We met, and after long discussion I made a
proposition, when we were on the eve of failure. My
proposition was accepted, and Professor Loomis was secured; and most happy selection it was. He was genial,
careful, a disciplinarian, and knew enough of the world,
and had enough of taste and prudence, to make him the
man for the place. God had made him one of the noblest
specimens of a human being. He was about six feet two
inches in height, and his form was perfect symmetry. He
was a man of fine spirit and dignified intercourse, and the
institution rose and was strong under his government.
By an act of the Legislature it became 'The Wesleyan
Female College.' Before leaving this charge Mr. (afterward Chancellor) Bates, with others of the trustees, desired me to select a library for the college; and after I
had done so Mr. Bates paid me the compliment to say he
would like to have me collect a library for him. This expression from such a man as Mr. Bates was the best kind
of praise for my care and labor. This college for many
years did grand service in the education of ladies in our
Church, who were a power for intelligence and purity,
and some of them for the missionary field. We had great
revivals in this charge—a great congregation. When my

time was nearly out Mr. Bates waited on me, with desire that I should be appointed to their charge, St. Paul's. This to me was very pleasant.

"I had had delightful intercourse with the people of St. Paul's, and I was greatly interested as an officer and trustee of the college. I could have wished to stay in Asbury, or in the city of Wilmington, till called to heaven. At Asbury my salary was eight hundred dollars. While in Wilmington my mother died in the residence of my sister Sarah Ann Raughley: she was in her sixty-ninth year; she died December 19th, 1851, from pneumonia. She was a blessed mother to me.

"In 1853 I was sent to Fifth Street, Philadelphia. This at the time was probably the largest Methodist congregation in the city. Dr. D. W. Bartine had been transferred from the New York Conference to serve them, and, popular as he generally was as a preacher, perhaps he was never more successful than here. I was greatly concerned about the result of my appointment. I knew they had been anxious for Alfred Cookman, who I am sure they had just reason to seek. But he was not sent to them. Cookman was appointed to Harrisburg, that year the seat of the Conference. I hastened home, fearing the results. In those days protests were facts that told. A letter came to the house. My wife said, 'Mr. Roche, it is from Philadelphia.' Then thought I, 'This may be a protest.' But no! It said that 'at a meeting of the official members of the church I was, by a unanimous vote, desired to inform you we cordially receive you as our pastor.' Tears of joy stood in my eyes, if they did not flow down my cheeks.

"On Saturday I went to the city and was entertained by

a dear friend, Samuel Aldrich, Esq., then one of their richest and most active members. That night, in his parlors, the official board met. Around those parlors sat one of the finest-looking official bodies that I have ever seen. On Sabbath I preached. The presiding elder, Dr. Castle, was present, and on the following Thursday they gave me and my family the grandest reception at the parsonage that I had ever witnessed. In those days receptions, if given, were very modest. I had two blessed years here. I was told when I went there it was an 'ice house.' To me it was warm in the best of senses. Our extra meetings were excellent. Our membership was large; and when about to leave I looked through the charge and said, without calling on another church to help, I could accommodate the Conference in Fifth Street. The treasurer told me their finances were never so good.

"In my congregation were several captains of the sea, one of whom wished to know my full name; I gave it. I afterward found he had built a three-masted schooner of three hundred and eighty tons and called it *John Alexander Roche;* as he had named another *Edmund S. Janes,* from a former pastor who afterward became a bishop. About this time, having some money in the hands of Mr. Seymour, whose health forbade him to keep it, to save the trouble of collecting interest, and with a hope that it would yield well, I was induced to take an interest in three land associations, to be paid for from week to week; and I took an interest in the *Roche* to enable me to meet the demands of the associations. The *Roche* sank. I lost about fifteen hundred dollars, but told nobody and showed no sadness. The real estate did not yield as much as ordinary interest.

While here, through Dr. George Loomis, I invested about one thousand dollars in Iowa lands.

"In this Fifth Street charge I was waited on for a transfer to the New York East Conference, to become the pastor of Allen Street Church. I replied, if the bishop wished to transfer me I would go, but should desire to remain in my Conference, with cordial thanks for the honor done me in the wish expressed. My pastorate in Fifth Street was a very happy one. My salary was one thousand dollars. Then, I had on Saturday night a grand Bible class.

"In 1855 I was sent, by invitation from the charge, to St. George's. This was the 'cradle of Methodism in Philadelphia.' In an historic aspect it is to-day, from its early place in the Church, the most interesting charge in the denomination. But I did not wish to go. I had had at St. Paul's a great deal of trouble from church trials; and as it was evident that much of that was before the man that went there, I wished to avoid it. Dr. Hodgson, whose term was just expiring, was called down twice from Conference held out of the city, to attend church meetings. I was sent. The church divided. This was the origin of the 'Central Church.' I had agony. I did my best. Dr. Castle at the close of my pastorate, in 1857, said in Conference the 'old ship at St. George's' was under glorious way. She survived the storm. My salary was one thousand dollars. While here I studied and was graduated in medicine, and also studied Hebrew, under Professor William M. Willets and Dr. Murphy.

"As my term of service was soon to expire at St. George's, I was again waited on by a committee from Allen Street, New York, to serve that charge as pastor. The committee consisted of Benjamin F. Camp, William R. Foster, and Francis Godine. At that time the four years' rule in the city would require me to leave Philadelphia for four years. I was invited to St. Paul's, Wilmington, with sufficient ground to expect to return to Asbury in that city when my time was out at St. Paul's. This was the pew church, and nothing could be more flattering to me. I talked with my wife, and she said, 'Mr. Roche, if we can return to Philadelphia in four years or in eight years, I will consent.' I said, 'I can assume nothing as to that.' She consented if I did. I replied, 'Neither my wife nor I will do anything to oppose it, but you must not expect me to do anything to effect it.'

"I was sent to New York East Conference by transfer, and to Allen Street Church. Allen Street, at that time, was a great charge. My first sermon was in the afternoon of Sabbath. My text was Zech. iv. 6: 'Not by might, nor by power, but by my Spirit, saith the Lord of hosts.' Our first meal as a family was with Dr. Palmer, who, with his family, received us as God's servants. Our first week while the parsonage was being prepared was spent with James L. Stewart and family, and the memory of those hospitalities is very warm.

"In Allen Street I followed that noble man of God, Heman Bangs. I gave him the morning sermon of my first Sabbath, as he suggested to me he would take either. I always hung upon his words.

"In October, 1857, we began an extra meeting. It continued twenty weeks lacking three nights. Much of the time I preached every night. About two hundred and twenty-five souls professed religion. We had in the charge a wonderful working force. Rev. Wakeman H. Dikeman was constantly on hand. Professor George W. Collord, local preacher, was at the time superintendent of the Sabbath school. They were ready for any service. Dr. Palmer and his wife, Mrs. Phœbe, and Mrs. Lankford were members; and who ever knew of a greater helper in such service than Samuel Halsted? O! we had an outpouring.

"After the meeting had been going on with great success some six or eight weeks John B. Dickinson, a princely man, came into the parsonage as authorized by others, and said, 'We did not invite you here to kill you, and I wish to say you must have help.' I replied, 'You don't know how much I can stand without death.' He replied, 'It is not to be argued; the meeting must stop, or you must have help.' 'Well,' I answered, 'if I am to call in pastors to fill the nights, with obligation to return their services, I would rather preach three sermons in my own charge than one in any other.' 'No,' he replied, 'we told California Taylor'—the present Bishop of Africa—'that we would call on him in the extra meeting this year, and we will pay him.' 'O!' I said, 'rejoiced to have him.'

"He, in great faithfulness, was with me four weeks. A blessed man of God I found him. His preaching was direct, earnest, and effective. The Holy Spirit, and 'plenty of oxygen'—ventilation—were always in his mind and speech. I think of him with joy that I had his faithful labors for so long a period. He sold his book to repair a loss from the fire in San Francisco. I think he received altogether about two hundred and fifty dollars. I should have been glad had it been more. We raised our missionary collection from one thousand dollars—the highest that they had ever collected—to fifteen hundred dollars my first year, and to two thousand dollars the second year; Bible collection, one hundred and fifty dollars; for superannuated preachers, two hundred and fifty dollars. Other collections showed well. My salary was made fifteen hundred dollars, the most they had ever paid by three hundred dollars. My second year they had money in the treasury, from the mode of collecting that I suggested—by cards; and it was proposed to me by a leading member to raise my salary the second year, but I told him 'No.'

"In 1857 there was a wonderful turning of the minds of the people in all positions to the need of religion. It seemed like a moral instinct that asserted itself, and the wish to repress was absent. Noonday prayer meetings were held. Then began the 'Fulton Street Noonday Prayer.' Prayer meetings were held in offices, in stores, and in Burton's Theater; great throngs attended. Our churches were full. Religion seemed to be the sovereign demand of the soul. Then there were 'showers of blessing.' While in this charge began 'the National Association of Local Preachers,' through the efforts of the Rev. W. H. Dikeman. With Samuel Halsted, also; then began 'The Flying Artillery,' as the 'Praying Band' was called, and Brother Halsted was the leader of this power.

"From the spring of 1859 to the spring of 1861 I filled the charge of Seventeenth Street, New York. As my time was expiring at Seventeenth Street I was waited on by a committee to serve as pastor next year at Carlton Avenue, Brooklyn.

"I was sent to Carlton Avenue in 1861. This church

edifice was not such as the congregation should have had. But the times forbade attempt to build. We had a large congregation, and among the members perhaps as much talent among young men as in any congregation that I have served. It was a pregnant period. Fort Sumter had been fired on the preceding week, and on Saturday before my first day in the pulpit was the great 'uprising in Union Square.' That day my son Watson enlisted to go down with the Thirteenth Regiment of Brooklyn, in Company G, to the defense of Washington. It was a day of darkness. If ever I prayed in the pulpit, I did at that time, for the Union of my country. But there was enough to keep us disturbed. 'So I prayed to the God of heaven.' War was everything. Then Sunday papers found an entrance, and the liberty then taken is still followed, to the pain of the Christian. Women walked the streets in dresses of red, white, and blue. Flags were made and sent to the army with the kisses of some who made them, and with prayers by others that they might wave in triumph over an undivided country. We had a splendid Sunday school, and one of the most interesting Bible classes that I have ever known. We had a good work of God both years.

"In anticipation of the future I was waited on by a committee from Allen Street to return to them as their pastor, and in 1863 again was sent to that charge. It was greatly changed. I had a good time, despite difficulties that none would deny. We had good congregations. We had many and excellent converts, and it was my ambition to get the missionary collection back to what I first found it—one thousand dollars; we reached above twelve hundred dollars.

"From Allen Street I was invited to First Place, Brooklyn, and was appointed to that charge. It was a pew church, and largely made up of families. It had talent and material means, and in the centennial year of American Methodism, 1866, we raised six thousand dollars for the purposes of the collection. There I followed Dr. A. S. Hunt, one of the most devoted, as one of the most faithful and honored, pastors and preachers. We had in the charge, as local preachers, William B. Barber and Jacob Lewis and another minister who had traveled in the regular work. We had quite a number of conversions, and the history and memory of them give me great joy at this day. Here the twenty-fifth anniversary of my marriage to Miss Osler occurred, and though we made no occasion of it, the friends did, and presented a silver service that was calculated to keep them daily in our minds.

"From First Place I was invited to Forsyth Street, New York. To that charge I was appointed in 1869. This had been one of the grandest charges in American Methodism. But the days of its decline had come. Yet they had one of the finest official boards that I ever knew. We had a good Sabbath school; J. H. Ockershausen was the successful superintendent. Our extra meetings were good. We had as a teacher of the Bible class, Robert Sinclair, then city editor of the *New York Times*, and he had a remarkably large and promising class of young men and women.

"In this charge was the Rev. Joseph Sandford, son of the distinguished Dr. Peter P. Sandford. John H. Ockershausen, though but an exhorter, cultivated and displayed much of the talent and real functions of a preacher of the Word; and never was man a better treasurer than he.

"At the end of two years I was summoned, in 1871, to South Second Street, Brooklyn. While in Forsyth Street charge I received from the Asbury University, Indiana, the degree of Doctor of Divinity; but it has not made me any wiser. I shall be glad if it has made me any better. It certainly has not made me proud, though I do not despise the honor; for such attention the university has my thanks.

"South Second Street, Brooklyn, was at this time a strong appointment. Its membership was large and able. It was a fine field and a large congregation. They were earnest and active in Christian work. The Sabbath school was large. We had grand extra meetings. My dear friend Samuel Halsted was with me part of the time, in all his mental and spiritual vigor. Many were brought into the church. Both my extra meetings were successful. In my third year I had contracted heavy cold; I suffered from nervous prostration, and I concluded it would be better for me to ask a supernumerary relation.

"I left South Second Street, and for the first time in forty years sought rest. I determined not to preach for some time; I did not. But scarcely had I changed my relation before I had a most eloquent appeal from St. Paul's, Philadelphia, to become their pastor the next year. I thought it unwise to encourage hope of transfer.

"In 1878 I resumed work, and was sent to Parkville, through Edward Ridley, a local preacher, superintendent of the Sabbath school. I attended to my work in Parkville as carefully as if I had lived there. I went out on Sabbath morning, and after preaching dined with my dear friends, Captain Lowber and his wife and family, and never was hospitality more prompt or cordial. Through the influence and generosity of Mrs. Ridley a fair was held, and one thousand dollars raised. Though expected back the third year, the appointing power was urged by a committee from Flatbush, who had waited upon me, that I might be appointed as their pastor.

"This appointment, like that of Parkville, was within easy approach of my residence. There the society was small, also the congregation. I remained here but two years, though invited back the third. We held extra meetings, in which quite a number professed conversion.

"In 1882 I was appointed to St. Luke's, Brooklyn. This was a new charge. Though it had appeared on the minutes, it had received no preacher from the Conference. It was a mission, and some friends from St. John's had built up a Sunday school, that was doing well. Dr. North, a local preacher from St. John's, had charge of it as superintendent. We worshiped in the stone church at the junction of Harrison and Division Avenues. There we had good congregations. Here were some of the most faithful men that I have ever known. While in this charge, on March 8th, 1884, my son Richard Watson died, and now sleeps near his mother in the burying ground of Haynes Street Methodist Episcopal Church, Germantown, Philadelphia.

"In 1886 I was sent to Forsyth Street, where I had previously served. We had an excellent Sabbath school, and many were brought into the church. My predecessor, Rev. W. W. Gillies, had formed a society of the young people for mutual improvement. This I regularly attended and found very interesting, both for the young and myself. Various and valuable tokens of their kindness were received by the pastor. There I spent three happy years; was expected back; was asked for by a unanimous vote of the official body, but Bishop Foster thought, from the condition of things, I ought to go to Washington Street, Brooklyn; they had been in great trouble.

"In 1889 I was appointed to Washington Street. I knew what I had to meet. The society was greatly reduced in number. The Bridge was calling for the block on which the church stood. By an act of the Legislature it was condemned, and was finally sold for one hundred and thirty thousand dollars. After paying the debts the money was, by a vote of the society, given to the Brooklyn Church Society. In this charge I lived in the parsonage. Here, on the 8th of January, 1891, the wife of nearly forty-seven years, after a painful and protracted illness, went to God. On the 12th the funeral services were held in the Washington Street Church, Dr. A. S. Hunt making the address. Many of the prominent clergy of Brooklyn were present; among them, Dr. Charles H. Hall, of Holy Trinity, and Dr. T. DeWitt Talmage; there were also many Methodist ministers. The church was filled—the largest assemblage I had witnessed there. On the same day she was buried in Woodlawn Cemetery, in good hope of a blessed resurrection.

"While in Washington Street there was a dear personal friend, though not a member of any church—Mr. Purnell— who, with his wife, gave generously for my work. This friend, whose only child's funeral I attended years before, abounded in liberal offerings.

"I remained at Washington Street till Conference, 1893.

"My last appointment had been filled. I expected to take no more appointments from the Church of my youth and from the Conference of which I had been a member for thirty-six years. It was to me a pathetic hour. And at the Conference at Danbury, Conn., Bishop Ninde presiding, on Tuesday night, April 11th, just before the close of the session at the call of supernumerary members, I arose and asked my relation changed from effective to supernumerary, adding, 'No man could reach this hour with the experience I have had without deep emotion.

" 'The dream of my life is ended. The romance and reality of our itinerancy of fifty-eight years and six months with me closes to-night. I cannot in truth say I am a supernumerary in the sense of the *Discipline,* for neither in mind nor body am I disabled. I have physical vigor to climb the highest tenement and to descend the darkest and deepest cellars. My faculties of mind, memory, imagination, and inventive power, as far as I know, are unimpaired. But I am so situated as not to be able to take such work as I might receive. I have not spoken to bishop or presiding elder about any appointment since Conference began. Though not in a position to take an appointment, I do not feel that I should ask a location, and as I know how the relation of supernumerary is granted I can honestly ask it.

" 'I was received on probation in the Philadelphia Conference of April 8th, 1835. I labored in its bounds twenty-two years. I was transferred to this Conference in 1857, and though repeatedly invited to other Conferences, have remained here doing the work assigned me. My life is like a miracle of God's mercy and might. I am astonished that I live, and that I am so well; I have had but one ambition, and this has been as positive as was that of Hannibal when he would cross the Alps. I have had no ambition but to preach Christ; and no office in the Church, not even that our president the bishop fills, could have been a temptation to leave the ministry as associated with the pastorate. I leave the work that has been the glory of my life. Nineteen years ago, 1874, I asked and received a supernumerary relation. Then I was suffering from nervous prostration. This is not now my case. Of my Conference class of 1835, if I be not the solitary survivor of twenty that then entered, for several years I have been the only one in the effective ranks. With such statement I may ask the change of my relation now proposed.'

"As I took my seat Dr. Pullman moved my relation be superannuated; this would entitle me annually to five hundred and forty dollars. To this I promptly objected. Thus ended my utterances at the Conference.

"Soon, alas! came one of the great sorrows of my life. I, with my daughters, had spent one week at the World's Exposition at Chicago. On the day we were to leave for home, the 13th of September, 1893, as my daughters were preparing for breakfast, I heard my daughter Sallie Alethia say, 'Lie down, May.' I started, and Mary said, 'Call father! quick, quick, quick!' and spoke no more. She was seized with apoplexy, and in twenty-three hours died. Nothing could have been more sudden or more unexpected. My dear child had not the slightest intimation of approaching illness. She was like a picture of health. She was to me so much. There was no care she would not take; no labor she would not perform; no sacrifice for

10

which she was not ready. An unselfish spirit, and boundless energy, with skill in all she attempted! With her instincts, with a refinement that made her intercourse a charm, and with a readiness to every good work on earth! God, who gave her, took her. To me it was one of the most crushing blows that ever fell, and still I stagger under the infliction. I trust in all my sorrow I have not refused to be 'still and know that He is God.' On the 14th of September she who so honored him went to her heavenly Father; she joined the mother, whom she had so recently lost, where death never comes, and parting and tears are unknown. I pray God that we all may be made better through this bereavement. For all other deaths in my family I was prepared by indications; for this I was prepared by none; but the will of God is always better than that of erring man. To him we bow, and kiss the hands that smite, though with streaming eyes and an aching heart. I will thank God for the daughter left and sons to be my comfort.

"Next to the wonder of her death was that my dear daughter Sallie Alethia was such a heroine in the gloom and anguish that were on us both, a thousand miles from home. The two sisters so fully lived in each other's confidence and affection, they were so largely one, that I could hardly expect anything from my younger daughter but a powerless prostration and consequent inability to do anything. But she rose as with moral majesty and did everything with the mental control that would astonish the wisest. Only God enabled her.

"On September 18th the funeral services were held in St. Peter's Church, of which my son Olin is rector, and with whom my daughters and I were making our home. Large as the church is, it was nearly full. Dean Hoffman, of the General Theological Seminary; Dr. Backus, rector of the Church of the Holy Apostles; the Rev. Mr. Mottet, rector of the Holy Communion Church; and Rev. Alfred W. Griffin, at that time curate of St. Peter's, took part in the very impressive service. There was also a large choir. Quite a number of persons whom we had been with only about twelve days before at Saratoga were present in the church and showed their deep sympathy. When the cemetery was reached, late in the afternoon, the sky was threatening and black with clouds; just, however, as the body was being lowered into its last resting place, and while Rev. Mr. Griffin, a friend of the family, was saying the committal, the sun suddenly burst through the clouds, lighting up the whole place. In Woodlawn, beside her mother, sleeps the just pride of a father's heart, Mary Caroline Roche.

"After a ministry of nearly sixty years and a membership in the Church of nearly sixty-five years, I may be allowed a glance at the past. If the man of business feels a loss when he ceases from his secular position; if such a man feels the change, even when he has enough of this world for which he was laboring, how may a true minister of Christ be supposed to feel when he retires from the work that has been on his heart from youth, and in his heart all the time of his toil, and when not money, but the race for whom Christ died, is his care, and when their salvation has been his glory? Then my feelings may be judged. I am at the end of my calling as a traveling Methodist preacher. As such I have had appointments to try the feelings, and others, and many of them, to give me great comfort. It is my joy to know that all through my ministry I have been trying to improve. I still have opportunities to preach, but I have no people. For this I do not allow myself to mourn; when I have served the Church as best I could I have that consolation.

"It has not been my habit to keep account of converts, so as to be able to say how many I have taken into the Church. The case of David's numbering Israel has always been before me. But I have enjoyed great victories. From the account given in the centennial of Asbury, Wilmington, I think it was shown that in all its history there was not more than one pastorate in that church, remarkable for revivals, that was equal to mine.

"My membership in the Church covers more than half its history since 1766. My ministry is more than half of the period since our organization as a Church. I knew Mr. Duke, the second man, after Mr. Watters, that from this country entered our ministry. I was for about twelve years member of the Philadelphia Conference with Ezekiel Cooper, who was present at the Baltimore Conference of about sixty preachers in 1784, when the Methodist Episcopal Church was organized. Solomon Sharp, who was on the Smyrna Circuit when I was converted, joined the Conference in 1794; others of like date I knew. I know the ministry of this day. As we see the pulpit of to-day we certainly, in the matter of education, are not like the same people. Excepting Dr. Coke from England, I fail to find one of the sixty in the Conference of 1784 that was a graduate of a college. At the time of my conversion I have not been able to trace more than five ministers among us who were graduates of colleges. John Dickins, our first book agent, an Englishman, was probably our best scholar. He for a time was in college in England, and had some knowledge of the languages. Now our college graduates are filling our Conferences.

"But if the question of power in the pulpit over any or all classes of hearers be the question, I am pained to think that, with all the advantages I so fully appreciate in the college and theological seminary, we have cause to fear power has not increased with culture.

"The Church of to-day gives money as it did not and could not in that day. We have now men of great wealth who are such givers as other times did not know. If spirituality increased in proportion to the grandeur of our places of worship we should indeed be as 'terrible as an army with banners.'

"When I was converted Methodism was very earnest in prayer meeting, class meeting, love feast, and God was always in the public assembly to impress with his grace and power. Many changes have taken place. Lay delegation, over which so long and hard a fight was made, is not now resting in all that was then asked. Some would have women for our legislators, with a claim of right to be preachers and pastors and even bishops. My trust is in God. But I know men have their duty, and if they fail of their high responsibility to God in following the teaching of his word, then the Church that has had and desired such honor must suffer for the temerity or the false theories that appear in its conduct.

"It is my joy that in my advanced life, now above eighty years of age, and without an appointment, I am not to want. This I owe to God's good providence, and to in-

vestments I made without leaving my work or impairing
my ministry. But in this I can never fail to give honor
to the wife of so many years, who, with such faithfulness
to her husband and children, and with the culture of her
mind, practiced economy in her home. With nothing of par-
simony at her table or in her gifts to those in need, with
a house that in Philadelphia extended as broad and warm
a hospitality as any other preacher's house that I have
ever known, with nothing mean in dress, in furniture, or in
the help, with an expenditure for books in the library by her
husband that few ministers have equaled—by her wisdom
and economy and constant service we have what we have.

"And when I think of the condition of the various members of my class in Conference I cannot think of one in
all the number who, for his appointments, for his children,
for his length of service, for the health of body and mind,
and for his condition in this world, has been more favored
of God than I have been. Wherefore, 'I offer unto God
thanksgiving,' and pray that he may give me a heart of
greater gratitude. I have had dark days. I have buried
two wives—remarkable women. I have buried five children.
I have met these trials under circumstances to make me
feel them. I have sustained material losses that pressed
hard at the time. But we have never been wanting for
bread. I looked for nothing but souls and poverty in
entering the ministry. I have had many souls, and no
poverty, for which the Lord be praised!

"I am now passing a happy life with my younger son,
Olin Scott, rector of St. Peter's; and my only daughter is
with me.

"'What is your life?' Alas, that to me it has been so

little! I have now passed my eightieth year. I find a note made when I was in Fifth Street, Philadelphia, on August 30th, 1854. It says: 'This day I have attained my forty-first year of age. This is strange to narrate, almost impossible to believe! I have been viewing myself as a young man. Indeed, the feeling of boyhood has seemed to remain with me. And yet I have reached that age which, according to the thought of my youth, would exhibit mental prime. I shudder at the thought that I have come to my prime. What have I done? for myself? for the Church? for the world? When Alexander the Great, whose name I bear, was in the country that his valor had given to his ambition he was humbled to remember that right there a female had done more than he. And he was not then as old as forty. I have given twenty years to the ministry of the word. I have striven to be faithful. Time is short. My mother is dead since December 9th, 1851. I cannot awake her out of her sleep, or see again in the body her that bore me, the one through whom I first breathed. and the stopping of whose breath it once seemed to me would be the end of my breathing. But I live on. My oldest sister is dead. My youngest sister is dead. My first wife and one of her children are dead. Yet I still live.'

"If I thus wrote when forty-one years old, how should I now feel when, on the 30th day of last August, 1893, I attained my eightieth year?

"In the review of my ministry all that have known me would, I think, say I was an earnest man in the pulpit; and one of the most faithful ministers who followed me in one of my largest charges said, 'No man can ever keep up with Roche as a pastor.'

"My humiliation in the retrospect does not arise from the feeling that I have been an easy-going, pleasure-seeking preacher. This I am sure I have not been. But my grief is that I have not been able to do more for Him who has done so much for me. I have spent little time in writing except for improvement in my work. I wrote the *Life of Dr. Durbin,* with a hope that thus I might be of some use to young ministers, to whom I dedicated it—that thus Dr. Durbin, being dead, might still speak, and that possibly I might also speak in the book for the glory of God when I could no more speak from the pulpit."

THE CLOSING DAYS.

DOCTOR ROCHE's health may be said to have been unimpaired till after his eighty-fourth birthday. His mind seemed more energetic and productive than ever. During the summer of 1897, after his address in connection with the commencement exercises of Dickinson College, and particularly after a visit to his old home in Smyrna, he developed a sickness from which he never fully recovered. On reaching his home he applied himself with great assiduity to his literary labors, finishing the *Life of Mrs. Palmer* early in October. About the same time he attended the Methodist Preachers' Meeting, and read the resolutions he had prepared on the death of Dr. Abel Stevens; this was his last public utterance. A gradual loss of strength followed.

On November 29th he was sitting languidly before his table in the study. He said: "I eat enough, but I remain weak. I am radically weak. I can only explain it as a premonition of the approaching failure of the vital forces. I am sadly thrown out of order by any attempt at hurry."

On Sunday, December 5th, the two sons exchanged pulpits in the evening. Dr. Roche attended the service in St. Peter's, and afterward spoke with his old-time vigor, with fatherly affection and even elation of what he had heard. Returning to the rectory, the arrival of the other son from

Brooklyn was awaited.   At half-past ten, he having come, all went to the dining room, and at the table his conversation reverted to the dear ones who had passed away.

The next morning all were on hand for a reasonably early Monday breakfast.   Dr. Roche went first to his study, where he took a cup of tea, coming then to the table.   He had family prayer before the meal.   For the lesson he read a single verse, "Be ye therefore perfect, even as your Father which is in heaven is perfect."   He ate lightly, but talked well, and then went into his study and lay quite still, well covered with a thick robe.   When he had rested his children sat with him as he read the papers or talked. They were interrupted by the boy from the publisher, who took away the last of the corrected proof for the *Life of Mrs. Palmer.*

On Monday, February 7th, 1898, his eldest son had the last Monday talk with him.   Dr. Roche's pleasure was great in the presence of his children and daughter-in-law. A son mentioned that in the autobiography there was a remarkable omission, in a matter involving the reputation of some of his parishioners who had been dead for a generation.   None who heard it can ever forget his answer; it was suave, reserved, forbearing, merciful.   It was, too, in his most diplomatic manner.   He was reduced to the necessity of fencing with a questioner, and all his powers were enlisted in the endeavor to treat his son with civility and the old church with courtesy.   While adhering strictly to facts, he allowed no embarrassing revelation to trickle through his expiring intellect.   He gave no sign of making any special effort, his manner being simply the familiar one to those who knew him, where with veracity, urbanity, and the impenetrable evasions of a Bismarck or Metternich he was resolved to give no offense and no information.

His final intellectual exertion was the avoiding of information, disclosures of tarnished, smirched names, and the revival of old scandals. He passed to other themes: "There are two varieties of language—the language of earth and the language of heaven. I am pretty nearly through with that of earth; I shall soon learn that of the kingdom of heaven." As he moved uneasily one inquired if he were in pain. "I am not in pain; it is not a question of pain, it is rather privation; I feel as if smothering."

About half-past six he bade us all gather around; then motioning to us to sit on the bed, with his hands grasping all our hands, he prayed that if it were his Father's will he might depart at once. Releasing his hands, he waved them, saying faintly, "Hallelujah, Amen. Even so, come quickly, Lord Jesus." Then lifting his right hand as in command, and in a voice with less of awe and more of sweetness and grace, he said, "Do all you can for the glory of God and for the good of men."

After this he was quiet for a few moments. When he again spoke his mind showed knowledge of his condition. But as the fever in which he had been for some space left him, the retiring tide seemed to carry reason away on its bosom. Very quickly it could be seen that his mind wandered, and these aberrations increased to the end. Up to the last day, however, there were seasons of mental clearness.

He was confined to his bed about three weeks, and the pain which he endured was borne with Christian fortitude. The son and daughter with whom he lived scarcely left him day or night, and his other son, who resided in Brooklyn, spent much time at his bedside. One asked him, "Father, what can we do for you?" The answer came with the swiftness of an arrow, "Angels from heaven could do no more." Speaking of his physician, Dr. Kemp, he said, "He has been prompt, steady, intelligent."

Some of his remarks suggested drollery: "My son, guard me from needless conversation. I was nearly talked to death yesterday. I was almost a dead man." One said, "You have been sleeping well." He replied, "You know nothing about it."

The closing days were marked by longer and longer periods of sleep, silence, or insensibility. The bell in the great tower of St. Peter's rang out the hours through light and darkness, but he heeded it not. The children and grandchildren moved softly through the room, but he knew it not. Fewer and shorter were the words, lower and slower the breath, till on Tuesday, the 15th of February, just as the twilight of the winter afternoon changed to night, the busy life on earth ended, the long and honorable career was complete.

On Friday evening the burial service was read in St. Peter's Church, West Twentieth Street, New York, of which his son Olin was rector; the Very Rev. Dr. Eugene Augustus Hoffman, dean of the General Theological Seminary, Rev. Dr. William Jones Seabury, Rev. Dr. Thomas Gallaudet, Rev. Alfred W. Griffin, formerly curate of St. Peter's, now at Trinity Church, New York, and the full vested choir of the church taking part in the service.

Saturday morning, at St. Paul's Methodist Episcopal Church, on West End Avenue, funeral services were held; Bishop John P. Newman, Dr. William V. Kelley, Dr. Thomas L. Poulson, Dr. F. M. North, and Dr. Eckman, pastor of the church, participating, the music being under the charge of Mrs. Joseph F. Knapp.

At a later hour in the day the body was committed to earth, in Woodlawn Cemetery, the final prayers being offered by Dr. Poulson, a close friend during many years.

On Monday, March 7th, a memorial service was held by the New York Preachers' Meeting, at the Book Concern, when several of his former friends spoke.

THE TRIBUTES.

FROM the address of Bishop John P. Newman, D.D., LL.D., at the funeral services held at St. Paul's Methodist Episcopal Church, West End Avenue, New York, Saturday, February 19th:

"As I reflect on my intercourse with Dr. Roche I am reminded of the value and pleasure of conversation. One of the greatest pleasures of life is talking with a friend, when mind answers mind, and thought responds to thought. When two persons of active intellects and congenial tastes exchange ideas each is broadened and inspired to better effort. Such delightful and uplifting acquaintance was I permitted hours together and year after year in Saratoga, the place where both of us were accustomed to spend our summers. As he talked on any theme it was seen that his reading had been kept up to the latest publications, and that his powers acted with force and brilliancy.

"Great as was the charm of his private conversation, it was in the pulpit that his temperament, his abilities, and his culture shone with the greatest splendor. As a preacher, he has a memorial in Wilmington, Philadelphia, Brooklyn, and New York, where he was recognized as foremost, as an orator and as a preacher. His gift of language was always remarkable for its affluence and its precision, expressing the wealth of his thought.

"With the exception of Bishop Simpson, Dr. Roche excelled in our Church in the unction of an orator. His power over his auditory was entrancing. This was largely due to the vastness of his information, and the readiness with which he recalled facts of history and science and biography; he was emphatically a preacher of illustrations, and he drew from the universe his illustrations—from the flowers beneath us and the stars above us. Nature was to him as a library of books, with which he had grown familiar, and it was difficult to refer to any subject on which men had written, whether in prose or poetry, whether in science or theology, with which he was not familiar. Such was his reputation among the clergy of our Church that whenever Dr. Roche was announced to preach his brethren always looked forward with the anticipation of an intellectual treat.

"With such a man the earnest and lifelong study of eloquence, when vitalized by intimate friendship with some of the most distinguished preachers of the age, would naturally lead to quickening authorship. Fortunately for us, he was personally acquainted with that matchless orator and preacher, Dr. John P. Durbin. He admired him with enthusiasm. It has been my luck to hear great orators both in this country and in Europe, those of the pulpit and those of the forum, and I do not hesitate to say that Durbin reached the very highest standard of success, both in the use of the voice and in the rhetoric of oratory.

"In his *Life of Dr. Durbin* our friend has given to the world not only a noble life of the famous divine, with an appreciative estimate of his versatile labors, but what is even more precious, an analysis of Durbin's matchless eloquence, and an unrivaled disquisition on the sources, conditions, and laws of oratorical power. He has done for our age, in my opinion, what Cicero has done for all ages in his analysis of oratory; and it may be doubted if any writer since Cicero has presented a more philosophical statement of the subject. It is a standard work, and our Church has not only honored the names of Roche and Durbin by placing the volume in our course of Conference studies, but also has prepared the means of education for years to come in qualifying our ministers to be efficient preachers of the Gospel. Had I a young minister to educate that book would be the first that I should place in his hands. The work has already been of the greatest value to our preachers and students, and long after we have gone to our rest Roche's Durbin will be acknowledged a superb and permanent work of Methodist literature, and one of extraordinary power in lifting men toward the place where Durbin and Roche stand in marvelous possession of the secrets which help men to mold the minds and hearts of great audiences.

"Mrs. Lankford Palmer was a dear friend of mine, as well as of Dr. Roche, and our distinguished friend, in the mission of the pen, has added to the literature of our Church by giving us also the *Life of Mrs. Lankford Palmer,* who, with her sainted sister, as Mary with Martha, will be recalled in ages to come. Perhaps no two women of Methodism have exerted greater influence upon the religious life of our denomination, both in this country and in Europe."

At the memorial service held by the New York Preachers' Meeting, at the Book Concern, Fifth Avenue and

Twentieth Street, on the morning of March 7th, 1898, the following paper was read by the Rev. Thomas L. Poulson, D.D., the article afterward appearing in full in the *Minutes* of the New York East Conference for that year:

"John A. Roche was born at Still Pond, Kent County, Md., August 30th, 1813, and died at the residence of his son, the Rev. Olin S. Roche, rector of St. Peter's Episcopal Church, New York city, on the 15th day of February, 1898.

"His early education was acquired at schools in Chestertown and Baltimore, Md. Subsequently he prosecuted further studies at the College of Medicine of Philadelphia, and the Union Theological Seminary, New York. He received the degree of M.D. from the former institution, and that of D.D. from Asbury University of Indiana.

"He possessed an omnivorous taste for literature, and was a persistent and thoughtful reader of books, particularly those of historic and religious character. His library was soon richly and amply stored, and continually replenished with the latest publications, the assiduous perusal of which ever kept him abreast of the most advanced lines of ethical thought and progress. He was to the end of his terrene toil an ardent student, especially of moral science and of Church polity, with fresh and vigorous views on all cognate questions, and remarkably alert on the spur of the moment to express his opinions intelligently and impressively, making him a keen and ready debater in Conference or convention.

"At an early age Dr. Roche gave his heart to God in the town of Smyrna, Del. Immediately thereafter his reflections and convictions were turned toward the Christian ministry, for which he diligently employed every available

11

opportunity for preparation. He was received into the Philadelphia Conference in the spring of 1835, and was regularly assigned to the following charges, respectively, namely: Snow Hill, Md.; Accomack and Northampton, Va.; Smyrna and Wilmington, Del.; Reading and Norristown, Pa.; Asbury, St. Paul's, Fifth Street, and St. George's, Philadelphia. Thence he was transferred to the New York East Conference in 1857, and stationed at Allen Street, Seventeenth Street, Forsyth Street, again at Allen Street, Thirty-seventh Street, again at Forsyth Street, New York city; Simpson, First Place, South Second Street, St. Luke's, Parkville, Flatbush, and Washington Street, Brooklyn. From 1874 to 1877 he sustained a supernumerary relation. Again in 1893 he became a supernumerary, and in 1895 he passed to a superannuate, and thus remained to the time of his decease.

"In 1889 Dr. Roche published the *Life of the Rev. John Price Durbin, D.D.*, in which volume he clearly and strongly presents his ideas of sacred eloquence and ministerial faithfulness. This biography is a luminous and eloquent portraiture of a genuine Christian minister. Recently he also published the *Life of Mrs. Sarah A. Lankford Palmer*, wherein he exalts and magnifies the Christian character as exemplified by that elect lady, paying a just and beautiful tribute to the sweetness and usefulness of her life and work. He has been a frequent contributor to the columns of our denominational organs on themes connected with the doctrines, discipline, and usages of the Methodist Episcopal Church.

"He retained his physical and mental vigor to an extraordinary degree up to the extreme age at which he was translated, and was therefore in constant demand for sermons and addresses on special occasions. These services were rendered with the same sweep of comprehension, scope of thought, copiousness of diction, fluency of utterance, and attractiveness of manner which characterized his public efforts in the very prime of his manhood.

"Since the death of his wife seven years ago, while he was in charge of Washington Street Church, Brooklyn, he has resided with his son, the Rev. Olin S. Roche, in this city.

"Dr. Roche married Miss Elizabeth Upshur Bayly in Virginia in 1837. She lived only a few years after that event. A son of this marriage, Richard Watson, who died in 1884, was at one time secretary of the New York Central Railroad. In Germantown, Pa., he married Miss Mary Caroline Osler, in 1843. Three surviving children are the fruit of this union—the Rev. Spencer S. Roche, rector of St. Mark's Episcopal Church, Brooklyn; the Rev. Olin S. Roche, rector of St. Peter's Episcopal Church, New York; and Miss Sallie Alethia.

"No prince imperial ever possessed a truer title to nobility than the royal subject of this memoir.

"His intellectual equipment, commanding presence, courtly bearing, chivalrous spirit, gentlemanly deportment, respectful intercourse, conversational gifts, polemical expertness, oratorical inspiration, rhetorical accomplishment, superbness of poise, preaching afflatus, parental affection, devotedness as a husband, faithfulness of friendship, and Christian consistency were qualities and endowments that eminently fitted him for large influence and usefulness, which he everywhere and always wielded to a remarkable extent.

"We know of no style of genuine gentleman of fiction or history surpassing that invariably exhibited by Dr. Roche. Don Quixote held women in no higher esteem; John Storm was not truer to spiritual convictions; Dr. MacLure was not more self-sacrificing; Donal Grant had not a purer soul; John Halifax was not more considerate of or merciful to the poor and sinful; Jean Valjean was not more heroic in his upward struggle; nor was King Arthur more eager for service. These exalted ideals of regal manliness presented by their famous authors were more than actualized in our departed brother. Lord Chesterfield himself could not have exceeded Dr. Roche in polished grace of manners, or elegance of conversation, or in courteous consideration of the rights and feelings of others.

"His pastoral ministries and relations were of the most affectionate and helpful type, and his friendships were riveted as with bolts of steel. His ear and purse were ever open to the cry of need, and his emotions were always stirred by the sigh of pain. While his prime intellect never failed to charm those who were brought in contact with him, his large-heartedness at once captured their confidence and love. His refusal to receive the yearly stipend from the Conference fund for worn-out preachers, to which he was entitled, in order that there might be more for those who were in greater need, was but a characteristic display of his magnanimous nature. While his sermons corruscated with intellectual brightness and breadth, they were overwhelming in their emotional force, usually storming all citadels of doubt or hesitation. Dr. Roche incarnated Emerson's affirmation that 'character is higher than intellect.' Yet, judged by the most rigid standards of excellence, he doubtless ranked with any score of the most successful Gospel ministers of his day, from whatever grades selected. His ministerial course, from the Eastern Shore of Virginia to Long Island, a tract of about two hundred miles by an air-line, was gemmed by a continuous stream of revival interest and power as clear and definite as the trail of a sunbeam.

"Dr. Roche traversed the classic territory of that garden spot of Methodism on the peninsula lying between the Delaware and Chesapeake Bays when our denominational legions swept and shook the plains under the invincible leadership of those sons of Anak—Sorin, Lawrenson, Coombe, Thompson, White, Allen, and others. This is also the section that gave us two bishops—Scott and Hurst—and yielded an immense growth of bishop timber. Those were the days when the Red Lion, Tangier Island, Deil's Island, and other camp meetings of that region were world-wide in their fame as populous centers of pentecostal revivals. Among the memorable sermons, scarcely one of them less than two hours long, at those historic localities and occasions, from the silver-tongued Bartine, the eccentric Barnes, the logical Hodgson, the elder Cookman and his saintly son Alfred, the Boanerges Slicer, the graceful Sargeant, the polished Sewell, the peerless Stockton, none were more magnetic, overmastering, and far-reaching than those by the kingly Roche.

"During the twoscore consecutive years of his connection with the New York East Conference his picturesqueness and unique personality have been indelibly stamped not only upon the deliberations and discussions of the body, but also upon the minds and hearts of the individual members who have come and gone during that period. In every forensic contest in this arena during those years he took an active part, and his silver-crowned head, like the white plume of Henry of Navarre, was the guidon that marked the decisive point of each battle royal.

"He was ingenuous and generous to a fault; not only in his unostentatious and opulent dispensations of helpfulness to his brethren, but in his estimate of and conversations concerning them. We never heard him utter a word of detriment or detraction toward anyone, but frequently listened to his gracious laudation of the commendable traits of the absent whenever occasion offered. In the interviews it was our privilege to enjoy with him while on his deathbed his mind was clear and in complete repose, and his soul was 'calm as summer evenings be' in contemplation of the anticipated *dénouement* that would instantly transfer him from labor to reward. He was perfectly conscious and self-possessed until very near the closing moments of his life on earth. His last hours of spiritual triumph made the apartment where he passed away a delightful exhibition of Young's ecstatic vision:

> "'The chamber where the good man meets his fate
> Is privileged beyond the common walk
> Of virtuous life, quite in the verge of heaven.'

"The departure of Dr. Roche is the removal of another link of that chain which binds the other days of mighty Gospel preaching to the present time of much *dilettante* sermonizing and hypercriticism in our pulpit ministrations. May the precious memory of his winsome manners, kindly voice, genial companionship, and intellectual vigor long remain with us who survive, to cheer and strengthen our hearts for the contests that await us, and when the summons comes to us as to our lamented brother we pray that our thanatopsis may be as bright as his!"

The following address by Rev. George A. Phœbus, D.D., of the Wilmington Conference, was also given at the memorial service:

"The eulogy which has just been so sweetly pronounced is correct, according to my own knowledge of the dear one, in every particular—a character that we all may emulate, a hero in every strife, a joy in every circle where he moved, one in whose light multitudes have seen light, one through the opening of whose mind astonishment and glorious good has welled forth to make the hearers around him feel that there was power in God's appointed servants, and life and liberty to those that are doing his work.

".A ship was loosed from her moorings in the city of Bristol, making her way to our city of Philadelphia, up the waves of the Delaware River. As she moved onward with prosperous gales, with full spread sail, the ship made rapid headway, but ever and anon there were the changing winds, and then the zigzag course and the sails drawn to the angle made the progress difficult; but onward, onward she went.

"So was it with our dear beloved brother. When in public life he started forth and all was fair, with full-spread sail he moved on with rapidity. but when the opposing gales drove him, when the zigzag course must be produced, he moved still forward, onward, onward, ever conquering, ever succeeding, ever getting higher. 'The ship entered the Delaware,' said Thomas Rankin—for it is he whom I quote. 'I never experienced so delightful a sensation in all my life; I never saw anything like it. As we approached nearer the shore the land on both sides, the trees, the bushes, the waving fields, the green corn of June, the tender flowers beneath the feet, all inspired me with a delight that I never experienced before in all my lifetime.' I thought of Dr. Roche in social life. There was the violet, but it was never too low for him to see the flower; there were the shrubs, but they were always in such bloom as that he could enjoy the fragrance; there was the poly-chrome chestnut, but he was equal to the condition of so-cial life that was above the shrub, or the violet at the feet; there were the giant oaks, rising higher and higher still, but he was above them all. He could see them all, and in every phase of social life, from the lowest to the highest. he stood, the friend of the humble, the friend of the exalted.

"I do feel here to-day as though it was but appropriate for me to indulge in one phase of his life that is sweet and precious to us all. I refer to his religious life. I knew him in the social circle, I knew him in the halls of learn-ing, I knew him in all the walks of common life; but in his religious life he is yet to be properly appreciated—his eloquent prayers, his deep, yearning devotion to God; and I claim that he rendered such devotion to God as to make him a privileged human being walking in perfection be-low. His last volume tells us about that. 'O,' says some one, 'is that possible?—in the midst of the scenes through which we are passing is that possible? In all earth's sur-roundings and scenes is perfection possible? Can the na-ture be sanctified in order that there may arise a constant day of spirit life?'

"If God preaches to us in nature, and preaches to us in this blessed book the doctrine of perfection, let us stand with Dr. Roche, who would rise to his feet to-day and say, 'And the very God of peace sanctify you wholly; and I pray God your whole spirit and soul and body be preserved blameless unto the coming of our Lord Jesus Christ. Faithful is he that calleth you, who also will do it.' "

From *The Christian Advocate,* March 3d, 1898:

"Frequently for more than forty years there might have been seen in the bookstores, especially where old books are kept, a tall, dignified, graceful man, obviously a gentleman of the old school; and while he peered in the window or held close to his glasses some work which had attracted his attention, a stranger would be in doubt whether he was a clergyman, or professor of systematic theology or Church history, but would not suspect him of being other than a devout and learned person, accustomed to literary surroundings. If occasion led him to speak, the stranger would at once be impressed with his courtly bearing, quite unlike the freer manners of the present day, and in his speech would discern a mingled graciousness and condescension which, together with his self-possession, would lead him to wonder who he was. New York has many fine old gentlemen, of every conceivable type; some born in other lands, and others native to this country but much molded by foreign travel; but not one among them all could be found to remind an acquaintance of the patriarch whose more than eighty-four years of life, and nearly sixty-three years in the ministry, terminated on February 15th.

"In the pulpit, to the last, he was as erect as a strong man rejoicing to run a race. His voice was a baritone of wonderful depth and strength, and at the recent services in connection with the dedication of St. Paul's Church, at which he offered one of the prayers, it resounded through the building like the tones of an organ. Not one orator in a thousand at forty-five years of age has such a voice as he retained until after he had passed fourscore years. He was a student of rhetoric and elocution, a survivor of the golden age of American oratory. With the works of Robert South, Robert Hall, Archbishop Tillotson, Bishop Sherlock, Jeremy Seed, and Isaac Barrow he was as familiar as with the current literature of the day. His own vocabulary was inexhaustible. His rhetorical style was more French than English, more Ciceronian than French, and his delivery Demosthenic in fervor and force. His nature was exceedingly sensitive. Courtesy he considered one of the fundamental elements of true religion, and in etiquette he was an expert and an authority. His temperament was peculiarly oratorical. A modern congregation to which he was unknown would be surprised by his fervor and vigor; and, though loud, his delivery never reached vociferation.

"Unlike many orators in whom the linguistic element is so conspicuous, he possessed unusual power in debate. The mysteries of parliamentary law were simple to him. His readiness in repartee was the envy of those to whom it was sometimes a terror. A restriction in time somewhat embarrassed him, as the same rhetorical elaboration which characterized him in the pulpit seemed a necessity to him in debate; but he did not object when his time expired; indeed, as he foresaw that it would soon be exhausted, with

a mighty effort he condensed his ideas, and would sometimes be more effective by a few quaint terms as he was
taking his seat than he had been in his previous utterances.
At all times he was ornate, and his style would have been
ostentatious had it been affected, but being natural to the
man, its absence would have been deplored. To every
pathetic situation or thought he instantly responded. In
him also a mystical tendency existed. He delighted to
find hidden meanings in every scriptural reference to spiritual experience; these he interwove with his own testimo-
nies and appeals. In public prayer all his mental and
moral characteristics were displayed. Great was the sorrow of New York when the eloquent and the popular Dr.
Thomas M. Eddy, one of the missionary secretaries, died,
after an illness so short that few were aware that he was
in danger. The ministers of the Church assembled at
their customary meeting in the Mission Rooms, and when
the information was given, Dr. Roche was asked to lead in
prayer. We listened to the words as they fell from his lips,
and wondered at their fitness. They were stenographically
reported, and published in *The Methodist;* and a study of
them showed no place where a word could be added or a
word changed without putting a less fitting one in its place.
That, judged by the standards of the present day, he was
somewhat diffuse in his public lucubrations is true, and
he could not easily accommodate himself to the changes of
style which took place in his life; but it was not the dif-
fuseness of repetition or verbiage: it was the luxuriousness
of a rich vocabulary, each word bearing a new idea; the
only defect of the whole, like that of most oratory of forty
or fifty years ago, being that it did not leave sufficient to

the imagination. Dr. Roche confined himself almost entirely to the exposition of the word of God, and the building up of those to whom he ministered in the knowledge and love of God and of his Son Jesus Christ. There was great variety in his preaching, but his themes did not transcend the bounds of moral and religious teaching established in the period in which his career began.

"Of the higher Christian life, known among Methodists as 'entire sanctification' or 'Christian perfection,' Dr. Roche was an advocate, accepting without reserve the views of John Wesley and John Fletcher, testing and afterward attesting them by his own experience. In the three months' debate held in this city thirty-two years ago, in which Daniel Curry, Randolph S. Foster, Hiram Mattison, and many other able theologians and debaters participated, most of whom preceded him to the highest realm, he took an active part, and his oration on that occasion, for such it was, was afterward published in a volume which grew out of the debate. After entering the ministry he was impressed with the destitution of the poor of the city of Philadelphia, and devoted much time to their welfare; and that he might assist them with advice and, in emergencies, with medical attention, he pursued the study of that science and was graduated; but at no time did he employ his confessed skill, in competition with the regular profession, or use his knowledge in derogatory criticism. Some years since he prepared a work entitled *The Life and Times of John P. Durbin,* by doing which he met a felt want, and incidentally gave his own views of sacred eloquence. His reputation as a preacher and pastor for more than twenty years in Philadelphia and vicinity, led to his being called to this city and his appointment to the pastorate of one of the largest churches. Such was his moral and physical energy to the last that he will be greatly missed by his brethren in the New York East Conference and in the weekly assembly of the ministers of New York and vicinity; the eye will miss his expressive features and familiar gestures; the ear will no longer vibrate in unison with his thunderous, but not unpleasant, tones; and the heart will feel the absence of his kindly glance and warm salutation."

From the *Philadelphia Methodist,* February 26th, 1898:

"Dr. Roche was born in Kent County, Md., in 1813, and served his time with Mr. Benson, of Smyrna, who was a carriage maker. Dr. William Cooper was apprentice with this same party. Dr. Roche was from the beginning of his ministry a close student, and always made thorough preparation for the pulpit.

"His style was marked with the grace of oratory, at times reaching the sublime. His speech was impassioned, and the fervor and incision of his appeals would awaken the deepest interest, and most gratifying results attended his ministry.

"He was the peer of Kennedy and Hagany, and ranked with them, preceding or succeeding them in the order of his appointment. He was a voluminous writer, contributing to the Church and other papers. His relations with ministers of other denominations were most pleasant and cordial.

"His service in the Philadelphia Conference began in 1835, and covered over twenty years. From its beginning to its close it was one of decided prosperity, and grew in importance as the years went by. He was greatly beloved by both the laity and clergy, and after he was transferred to the New York East Conference he was repeatedly called back for service on great occasions, and this was true up to a very recent date.

"He had power with God and men, for his devout disposition ever sought communion with God, and the prayers he offered were characterized with an unction that caused all hearts to bow in adoring love before the throne he supplicated. Heaven seemed ever near to him. He walked with God, and took hold upon the horns of the altar, and prevailed mightily.

"Many will recall those remarkable prayers clothed with majesty and grace. He seemed to have entered the presence chamber of the King immortal and invisible, and held converse with God, like as one having the most intimate acquaintance. His whole being was electrified, and he lifted the audience into communion with God, until the place in which they met was the gate of heaven, and glory crowned the mercy seat.

"His gentlemanly bearing, courteous manner, and brotherly regard made him a welcome guest in every company. He expressed appreciation, and gave encouragement to those who least expected it, and his commendation was most gratefully received.

"His transfer from us we greatly regretted, but both in Brooklyn and New York he proved a tower of strength, and for more than twenty-five years filled some of the most important appointments, and repeatedly was returned to the same churches when the required term of absence expired. He was remarkably well preserved, and his vigorous mind lost none of its brilliancy, nor his voice its compass and power.

"Fourscore and five years rounded out the life of one we loved to call friend and brother. His best literary production, *The Life of J. P. Durbin, D.D.*, who was his intimate friend, gives evidence of a fine discrimination and cultivated taste and exact biography—a chaste writer and a classical scholar."

From the *Brooklyn Daily Eagle* of February 17th, 1898:

"The Rev. John Alexander Roche, M.D., D.D., one of the most widely known men in the Methodist denomination, died at the residence of his son, the Rev. Olin S. Roche, rector of St. Peter's Episcopal Church, Manhattan, late on Tuesday afternoon. Dr. Roche was in his eighty-fifth year, and up to a recent period was in constant demand for sermons or addresses on special occasions. He was always a conspicuous figure at the sessions of the New York East Conference. His last pastorate was that of the Washington Street Methodist Episcopal Church in Brooklyn, which was sold to make way for the bridge improvements. Dr. Roche was born at Still Pond, Kent County, Md., on August 30th, 1813. He entered the Philadelphia Conference of the Methodist Episcopal Church in 1835. During the sixty years of his ministry he served the churches at Snow Hill, Md.; Accomack and Northampton, Va.; Smyrna and Wilmington, Del.; Reading and Norristown, Pa.; Asbury, St. Paul's, Fifth Street, and St. George's, in Philadelphia. In 1857 he was transferred to the Allen Street Church, New York city. He was placed subsequently at the Seventeenth Street Church and at Forsyth

Street; again at Allen Street, and for a short term at Thirty-seventh Street. In Brooklyn he had been pastor of the present Simpson Church, First Place, South Second Street, St. Luke's. Parkville. Flatbush, and Washington Street.

"As a preacher, debater, and author Dr. Roche was widely and favorably known. Four years ago he rested from active work, becoming entitled to a pension from the Conference of over five hundred dollars a year. The entire sum, aggregating more than two thousand dollars, he voluntarily relinquished for the benefit of the general fund for aged preachers' support. Since the death of his wife, seven years ago, he lived with his son, the Rev. Olin S. Roche. Another son, the Rev. Spencer S. Roche, is rector of St. Mark's Church, Brooklyn. The only other member of the family surviving is a daughter, Sallie Alethia; another daughter, Mary Caroline, died in Chicago in 1893.

"Dr. Roche married in Virginia in 1837 Miss Elizabeth Upshur Bayly, who lived but a few years. A son by this marriage, Richard Watson, who died in 1884, was at one time secretary of the New York Central Railroad. In 1843, at Germantown, Pa., Dr. Roche married Miss Mary Caroline Osler. Three children, already named, now represent this union."

From the *Smyrna Call*, Smyrna, Del., February 22d, 1898:

"Dr. John A. Roche, one of the oldest Methodist preachers in the New York East Conference, died at the residence of his son, Rev. Olin S. Roche, Tuesday evening last, after a lingering illness, of general debility.

"The loss of such an able and eloquent preacher will be keenly felt by that Conference, as few men possessed such qualifications needed in a pastor as the deceased. He was a godly man and beloved by all who knew him. Dr. Roche had few equals in his chosen profession, and during his many years of active service in the Church accomplished much good. He was widely known as an eloquent orator and forcible writer. The doctor had been gradually failing since the sudden death of his daughter, Miss Mary, while visiting the World's Fair. He continued preaching, however, and only gave up work last year at the earnest appeals of his sons to do so. Last September he came to Smyrna to attend the funeral of the late Joseph Reynolds, his boyhood companion and lifelong friend. He was not at all well then, but insisted upon coming, as Mr. Reynold's death left but one member of the crowd of young men prominent in Smyrna in 1830—himself. He keenly felt the death of his old friend, and while here was taken sick and confined to his room. He insisted on returning to New York the following Saturday, as he had some business to attend to. He soon began to fail rapidly, and when he died a man who had spent sixty-five active years in the Methodist ministry had won his promised reward in heaven.

"John A. Roche was born in 1813, at Still Pond, Md. He was a son of John Roche, a prominent man of that section who came here from Ireland. When fifteen years of age his father died, and he came to Smyrna and started clerking for Duhamel and Lambdin, whose store was located on Commerce Street, where Frank Reiman now lives. He gave that up in a little while, and apprenticed himself to Benson and Catts to learn the carriage-trimming business.

12

He employed much of his leisure time in reading, and at the age of nineteen years entered the Methodist ministry, having made enough by extra work to pay for his time from his employers.

"He was converted in the great revival which was held in this town about seventy years ago, the late Joseph Reynolds also being one of the converts. That revival turned out seven ministers, Dr. Roche being one of them, and he survived them all.

"His first charge was on a circuit in the lower county and extending into Virginia, and from there he went to Reading, Pa. In 1850 he was pastor of the Methodist Episcopal church of this town. A few years later, having made an excellent record in this part of the country, he was transferred to the New York East Conference, and has been the pastor of some of the leading churches in that Conference.

"Dr. Roche was married twice. His first wife was Miss Elizabeth Bayly, of Virginia, his second wife being Miss Mary C. Osler, of New Jersey, who died about seven years ago. The deceased leaves three children, Rev. Spencer S. Roche, rector of St. Mark's Episcopal Church, Brooklyn; Rev. Olin S. Roche, rector of St. Peter's Episcopal Church, New York; and Miss Sallie. Dr. Roche came of educated ancestors, and his family has given a long line of ministers. His father was a Roman Catholic, and was educated for a priest, but ran away from his home in Ireland and came to this country. He had several near relatives who were Roman priests, and his two sons decided to enter the ministry, but connected themselves with the Episcopal Church. Seldom does a son of Roman Catholic parents become a Methodist minister, but such was the case with Dr. Roche.

"The deceased was a writer of great ability, and was a student until his last illness kept him from his study. He wrote the *Life of John Price Durbin, D.D., LL.D.,* with an analysis of his homiletic skill and sacred oratory. This work is now a text-book in all Methodist colleges. The *Life of Mrs. Palmer,* another work of his pen, is just from the press.

"Dr. Roche leaves a good estate. It was his habit from the first year of his ministry to save something each year, and he owned several valuable properties. Although eighty-five years of age, sixty-five of which had been spent in the ministry, he never asked the Conference for a cent in his old age, and was well able to take care of himself. A full history of this noble man's life would make an interesting book. He was well known in the Wilmington, Philadelphia, and New York Conferences, and his death, although daily expected, was a shock to his many friends, and he had a host of them, both old and young.

"Interment was made Saturday in Woodlawn Cemetery, about fourteen miles from New York, Mrs. Mary Hoffecker and Miss Emily Spruance, of Smyrna, relatives of the far-famed divine, attending the funeral services."

From the *Smyrna Times,* February 23d, 1898:

"Intelligence of the death of Rev. John Alexander Roche reached us just before going to press last week, and was so announced. He was born in Maryland in 1813, but came to this town when a boy, to go out of it in 1836 into the Methodist ministry. He always maintained an interest in Smyrna and its people, and possibly the name of no one not a resident was more revered in the community than his. He dates back to the 'heroic' days of Methodism, and was the last one of the great revival of 1829, that so strengthened the Church and sent seven men into the ministry. When he came to Smyrna last fall to participate at the funeral of Joseph Reynolds, the last survivor of his youthful associates, the feeling was general on the part of his friends that they would never see him again. Though possessing a wonderful endurance, it was seen that feebleness was taking possession of his frame, and his death was not a surprise.

"His coming was always a source of pleasure to his friends, who regarded him as strong as a preacher and wonderful in prayer, and his personal presence was always felt a benediction.

"He was no less able as an author than as a preacher, as was shown in his *Life of Rev. John P. Durbin,* and the *Life of Mrs. Sarah A. Lankford Palmer,* finished a few weeks since.

"An unmarried daughter and two sons survive him, both of the latter being clergymen in the Episcopal Church."

From the *Transcript,* Chestertown, Md., February 24th, 1898:

"Rev. John A. Roche died at the home of his son, the Rev. Olin S. Roche, on Tuesday, in the eighty-fifth year of his age. He was the son of John and Sarah Roche, and was born on the farm known as 'Camels Worth More,' near Still Pond. His father kept store in Still Pond, and taught school in Chesterville five years. In his early youth he went to school for a short time to Mr. G. B. Westcott, and was always proud to call himself a son of Kent.

"Upon the death of his father he went to Smyrna and clerked with Duhamel and Lambdin. He then apprenticed himself to Benson and Catts to learn carriage trimming. During the great revival of 1829 in the town he was converted, and at nineteen years of age bought out his time and commenced preaching. He was pastor in Smyrna in 1849-50; was then sent to Wilmington; from there to Philadelphia, and then transferred to New York East Conference. During his sixty years' ministry he filled many of the finest appointments in both Conferences.

"Several years ago he was appointed by the Conference to write the *Life of Dr. Durbin;* he also wrote the *Life of Mrs. Palmer.* This book is just from the press.

"Dr. Roche visited Chestertown during the Methodist Episcopal Conference last year, went to the place of his birth, and renewed acquaintance with those of his old friends who remained in the county."

Extract from a letter received from the Rev. Alfred William Griffin, sometime curate of St. Peter's, now of Trinity Church, New York:

"In recalling a few of the distinctive traits of your father, there is little that I can supply which is not already familiar to your mind.

"No representation of what he was can, I think, be either fair or complete unless strong emphasis is laid upon his advantages of person and bearing.

"In appearance he was truly striking. Tall and stately,

with a face full of command and an address both dignified and courteous, he compelled at once respect and reverence.

"In a congenial party he was at his best; his varied knowledge, refined taste, and power of expression made him a most interesting conversationalist. Familiar with the current events of daily life, problems confronting the Church, the affairs of the State and of society, his talk was wonderfully rich, witty, and helpful. One found in him a ready and attentive listener who seemed to want to get beneath your words, and ascertain your inmost thoughts.

"Added to these characteristics was a freedom and a naturalness which set anyone meeting him for the first time quite at ease, and often thrilled one with pleasure. It was his exquisitely natural courtesy, together with such dignity of presence and feeling, which, as much as anything else, quickly won the heart.

"I remember also on more than one occasion his keen sense of humor, and the apparent delight with which he told or heard amusing anecdotes and reminiscences. He enjoyed the narration of the little entanglements of daily life; I can see him now fairly bubbling over with delight at some diverting incident told, and can almost hear his quick and interested exclamation, 'Tell it again, tell it again; it does my heart good to hear it.'

"I love to dwell on your father's entertaining and charming manner, especially in the society of young people; he would enter into their joys and pleasures with the greatest enthusiasm, evincing a warm-hearted benevolence, a sunny disposition, and a buoyant spirit that drew them to him, and enabled him to do them untold good.

"His deep piety and strong religious temperament appeared to me especially during my curacy at St. Peter's, when Sunday after Sunday he worshiped in the old church, sitting in the rector's pew with his daughters. No one who saw him as I did at such times could fail to have noticed his devout attitude, his intense earnestness, his ready and hearty responses. It was the attitude and demeanor of one who firmly realized the nearness of God to himself, and witnessed to his inherent belief in the blessings to be vouchsafed.

"I might speak of other traits—his deep sympathy, the strength and simplicity of his character; but these have already been noted by others, whose knowledge of your father extended over a greater number of years than mine. It was indeed a privilege and a blessing to have known him, and of him it may be said, as of one of old, 'He being dead yet speaketh.'"

SERMONS.

SERMON I.

THE JOY OF THE LORD.

The joy of the Lord is your strength.—Nehemiah viii, 10.

WITH nations and churches, as with individuals, "there is a time to weep and a time to laugh." In ancient times (Deut. xvi, 15) the feast was to be kept with rejoicing. The context presents an occasion that justified intensest joy. We witness one of the sublimest spectacles in the world's history. God's chosen people, long in captivity, have returned to Jerusalem. They who by the rivers of Babylon sat down and wept, when they remembered Zion, are back in the city of solemnities. Male and female—all of understanding—assemble, as upon a plaza before the water gate, and ask Ezra the scribe to bring the book of the law of Moses. He stood upon a pulpit of wood, and read and caused them to understand. He blessed the Lord, the great God, and all the people, with uplifted hands and bowed heads, answered Amen. Memory awoke, gratitude glowed, hearts melted.

Can we imagine greater joy except with those who return and come to Zion with songs and everlasting joy upon their

---

*Preached at the centennial of the Asbury Church, Wilmington, Del.

heads? Nehemiah wished the people to appreciate their condition—to "eat the fat, and drink the sweet, and send portions unto them for whom nothing is prepared." He desired others to sympathize with the occasion and share in its delights. The day was holy unto the Lord, and it forbade sorrow, and urged joy *as their strength*. With a like spirit, this honored church of a hundred years asks its friends far and near to rejoice with it and profit by the holy services of its first centennial. They would not eat their morsel alone. They rather say, Eat, O friends, and drink. Yea, drink abundantly. Magnify the Lord with us, and let us exalt his name together.

Appropriating the language of the text to the child of God, we shall endeavor to show that the joy of the Lord is the Christian's strength.

Joy is a delight of the mind to which men of the world are not strangers. It may arise from riches gained, from learning acquired, from stations reached, and from influence at their command. This delight may be largely of the animal spirits, or it may be mere mental buoyancy. It may be the joy of success, or of deliverance from danger— as men enjoy in time of harvest, or as when some great evil has passed. But the text presents "the joy of the Lord." He is its source, its substance and its support. At one time it may be expressed as serenity and satisfaction. At other times it rises to transport. The inhabitants of the rock sing; they shout from the top of the mountain. Christian joy is rooted in faith, grounded in love, and increased by exercise. "The Lord Jehovah is their strength and their song."

We sometimes say of a man he is strong in logic, or in

eloquent speech.   This man's strength is in grasping great principles, and that man is strong in the administration of government.   The strength of the athlete is in his muscle. The strength of the philosopher is in his mind.   The strength of the millionaire is in his coffers.   But the joy of the Lord is the strength of the Christian.   He may be the scholar, the statesman, the man of wealth and of earthly power; but joy in God distinguishes him as an heir of heaven.   He has the best cause for joy, and its cultivation is both his duty and his interest.   There is a joy of the world that from its origin and excess is followed by lassitude and depression.   It reacts.   Not so the joy of the Lord.

Let us consider divine joy as an element of power in Christian character.

1. As the highest inspiration to noble deeds.   Of joy in general we may say it is an *inspiration*.   Gloom enervates. A depressed spirit has enough to do to attend to its own sorrows.   But the faculties of the mind, the passions of the heart, and all the forces of nature respond to joy.   It is the sunshine of the soul in which things appear in the best light, and all the fruits of the spirit ripen; even the dearest relations of life fail to exert their due influence when sadness is allowed.   The parent, the companion, the child, each of whom should be happy in the relation subsisting, experiences none of the delights that should distinguish the place and condition.

In business life the wheels of commerce stand still when depression paralyzes.   The mariner would make no voyage, and except in desperation the soldier would fight no battle.   An officer received orders from his superior to take a stronghold. He replied, "It is impossible." He was relieved. To another the commander said, "Take that fortification." The reply was, "I am unable." To a third was given the order. He saw the difficulty, but answered, "It shall be done." He marched; he charged; he fought; it fell. The one was buoyant, the others depressed.

The sculptor had his ideal. Before him lay a rude mass of marble. What was in that block more than in many others in the same quarry? He took his chisel; devoted his skill; labored in faith. The form, the features came out; the links, the chain, the manacles were revealed, and before an admiring world stood "The Greek Slave." The ideal was actualized, and the voice of freedom was heard from lips of stone. It immortalized the artist who worked with cheer.

In art, in science, in literature, in government, in all the departments of thought and action, joy is a power to be confessed. It kindles the imagination of the poet, it fires the heart of the patriot, and causes the tongue of the statesman to flame with consuming eloquence.

If such is the influence of earthly joy, what shall we say of the "joy of the Lord"? It is more exalted in its origin, more intense in its action, more certain in its results. The soul under its power is ready, if not eager for any work. The young man hears God say, "Go ye into all the world and preach the Gospel." One of observation sees he is exercised about his duty, and ventures to say, "Pause; you have talents that will distinguish you in law, in medicine, in commerce; your talents qualify you for the grandest spheres of human action." Talk to a rock! you may as soon move it. Assure him of the estate of an Astor or a Vanderbilt; of the preeminence of a Webster or a Gladstone; name to him all the difficulties of a divine vocation; you do not deter him for a day. He says, The Everlasting God is my portion, and they who turn many to righteousness shall shine as the stars forever and ever. Hear Melville B. Cox. Africa is on his heart. A friend says, "Such a mission is certain death." "Then," replied he, "when I fall come over and write my epitaph." "What shall I write?" inquired he. "Write, Let a thousand fall before Africa is given up." He went! He fell! He rose! He lives, the inspiration of the missionary of the cross.

What is it to-day that makes Bishop Taylor the grand man that he is on the Congo? A wonder of labor in advanced age! A hero in suffering and danger! "The joy of the Lord is his strength." There is a young lady who has been reared and educated in the refinements and luxuries of one of the most distinguished families in New York city. The cause of missions stirs her. She marries one of like mind, and they go as missionaries to a distant and dangerous field. Her husband dies. With an infant she is left among a people whose only claim to her love is that they have souls. Her father wishes her return to the comforts at home, but she remains amid the privations of her condition and place, that she may do the work that her missions afford. What animates her? What sustains her? It is the joy of doing good! This is a strength worthy the name. Behold the action of this element in the apostle Paul. He is just converted. He had great and protracted sorrow. Now he has indescribable gladness. Joy thrills him. Love to Christ consumes him. He cannot be restrained in the exhibition of his zeal. He would be like an angel flying with the everlasting Gospel to preach to men on earth. When Edward Taylor, the eloquent mariners' preacher of Boston, would describe a converted sailor in his haste to save sinners, he said, "It was as if you had put spurs to lightning; hardly had he kindled the holy fire in one port before he was off to another to set it on blaze." We know how it was with Andrew. He first found his brother, and brought him to Jesus. This joy prompts the adoption of all means available to the divine purpose. Time, talent, and treasures are at ready command. Paul shows this in the church (2 Cor. viii, 1) of Macedonia, "how that in a great trial of affliction, the abundance of their joy and their deep poverty abounded unto the riches of their liberality." "For to their power, yea, and beyond their power, they were willing of themselves;" "praying us with much entreaty" to receive the gift and minister to the saints. So now there are laymen who, though they cannot be missionaries and ministers, give much of their time and talent and secular gain to the advancement of the cause of Christ, and who, like Zaccheus, are ready to give half their goods to feed the poor.

Joy in God makes a ready and cheerful offering. Nothing is difficult to him who acts under its power. Who shall describe this joy in the first realization of the beauties and blessings of vital piety? It sparkles in the eye, speaks in the voice, shines in the countenance, and is itself a quiet demonstration of the influence of the good. Joy that is the highest inspiration of genius secures the sublimest manifestation of the saintly devotion, and affords the clearest evidence of its presence in strengthening and sustaining Christian character. Did not David show a just judgment when he said, "Restore unto me the joy of thy salvation; . . . then will I teach transgressors thy ways, and sinners shall be converted unto thee"?

2. The joy of the Lord is a support of the Christian in the labor and trials to which he is called. As there are efforts that would never be put forth if the joy of the Lord did not impel them, so there are difficulties that we could not overcome if joy did not sustain us. The minister enters his study with the "burden of the Lord." The missionary goes to his work with a knowledge that he lacks the success he seeks. The Bible reader, the Sabbath school teacher, retires from the lesson and the class with the feeling that nothing seems to come from all this effort. The exhorter, the class leader, the laborer in God's vineyard, in whatever department, is tempted to say, "What good?" The tear falls; the heart aches. He enters his closet; "he prays to the Father." The soul struggles; faith reaches up; the hand grasps the arm of Jehovah, and Omnipotence yields to importunity. A voice from the throne proclaims, "As a prince hast thou power with God and with men, and hast prevailed." Now comes the sustaining power of holy joy. Behold Elijah when sorrow takes him to the juniper tree, and then God so feeds him that he goes in the strength of that meat for forty days.

Holy Samuel Rutherford, amid the imprisonment to which his preaching Christ subjected him, writes in his joy, "From Christ's Palace at Aberdeen." This joy in God sustained Francis Asbury on this Peninsula in the season of his "dumb Sabbaths," when in the Revolution of 1776 he was pursued by those who did not comprehend his mission and character. This joy kept Freeborn Garrettson faithful to the ministry that he had received of the Lord, when in his native State he was beaten by his persecutors and left unconscious on the highway. And who can ever forget the joy of Paul and Silas, that gave them songs in the night, when an earthquake shook the prison and the jailer was made an heir of heaven?

In whom can we find a fuller illustration of the sustaining power of Christian joy than in the apostle to the Gentiles? He declares: "God has set forth us the apostles last, as it were appointed to death: for we are made a spectacle unto the world, and to angels, and to men. Even unto this present hour we both hunger, and thirst, and are naked, and have no certain dwelling place; and labor with our own hands: being reviled, we bless; being persecuted, we suffer it: being defamed, we entreat: we are made as the filth and offscouring of all things unto this day."

Think of a man of such origin, education, endowments. Think of him with such capabilities of worldly distinction. Think of him as such an apostle of Jesus Christ, and yet subjected to such contempt. Think of the extent of his labor, the character of his solicitude, and the fierceness of his persecutions. Take his own account: "In prisons more frequent, in deaths oft. Of the Jews five times received I forty stripes save one. Thrice was I beaten with rods, once was I stoned, thrice I suffered shipwreck, a night and a day I have been in the deep. . . . Besides those things that are without, that which cometh upon me daily, the care of all the churches." What unaided mortal could bear this with mental serenity?

But amid these diverse and trying experiences he maintained a courage, revealed a wisdom, and achieved results

to which God alone could make him equal. With a moral
heroism that showed the real grandeur of the man when so
sustained, as if disdaining the thought of cowardice, as if
utterly superior to all thought of regret at his course, he
eloquently declares, "None of these things move me, neither
count I my life dear unto myself, so that I might finish my
course with joy." What orator, poet, philosopher, or divine
can tell the strength to labor or endure of him whose "sufficiency is of God"? Only the infinite can gauge the soul
that grace fills. The Lord alone can measure the depths
and heights and breadths of that love that passeth knowledge.

We know that the Christian has tribulation as well as
joy. But we have not forgotten the words of Him who
said, "Ye now have sorrow, but I will see you again, and
your heart shall rejoice, and your joy no man taketh from
you." Thus in the past have the children of God been
enabled to perform the most difficult service and withstand
all the fiery darts of the devil.

There are those around us to-day who stand as the beaten
anvil to the stroke; and the hammer will break, and the
arm that wields it fall powerless before the soul shall yield
to the strokes, though the heaviest that were ever given.

3. The joy of the Lord is our strength as a means of
turning souls to Christ. Is there anything in the Christian that attracts attention and awakens desire in those
not saved like a cheerful and exultant spirit? The desire
of happiness is innate; one exclaims, "O happiness, our
being, end, and aim." The rich seek it; the poor long for
it; the good have it. Dr. Samuel Johnson says: "The
habit of looking on the bright side of things is worth a

thousand pounds a year." The Scriptures declare a "merry heart doeth good like a medicine."

May we not assume that the religion that does not invite by its benignity repels by its austerity? Religion is supposed to make us at once good and happy. And we so present it. If in this it fail, we fail. A man was recommending his medicine for a particular disease. The patient looked and said, "I perceive you have the same trouble; why does not your medicine cure you?" It killed the cure. Joy is diffusive, and there associates with it a sweetness and suavity that admit no counterfeit. I had almost said there is in the very manners of some Christians a divine urbanity as unlike merely artificial courtesies as the sun's rays are unlike the beams of the moon. "They saw the face of Stephen as it had been the face of an angel."

The book of Daniel tells of Nebuchadnezzar's wish to have some of the children of the captivity trained for superior wisdom and service. They should be fed with meat and wine from the king's table. They refused and asked only "pulse and water." After ten days they were examined and were fairer and fatter than those who ate at the king's table, and they were ten times wiser than all the magicians and astrologers. Zech. viii, 23, speaks of ten men of all languages that shall take hold of him that is called a Jew, saying, "We will go with you: for we have heard that God is with you." It is not the form but the spirit of religion that wins. Who will long prefer a bird of plumage to a bird of song?

Joy was a distinguishing characteristic of early Methodists. The witness of the Spirit to adoption into the

13

heavenly family, and the earnest it gave of the inheritance that is incorruptible, undefiled, and that fadeth not away, justified their highest expressions of delight. Lady Hastings, converted through Mr. Wesley's influence, declared to Lady Huntingdon, "Since I have known and believed in the Lord Jesus Christ for life and salvation I have been as happy as an angel!" Such an experience must win. It did in Asbury Church in its earliest history. It does to-day. In your graveyard and in your records may be found the names of some of the leading families of this State, and through Delaware and this Peninsula, Methodism in her first efforts was instrumental in the conversion of some of the most distinguished laymen that have honored her history. The spirit she revealed won not only the poor and uneducated, but the rich and learned.

When Whitefield asked an unbeliever in Christianity what it was in his sermon that convinced him of the truth of religion he replied, "Nothing;" but added, "As I was passing from the church an old woman was about to fall; I caught her; the look that she gave me and the 'God bless you' that she pronounced convinced me that she had something that I had not."

The truth is many Christians must either be strong in joy or in nothing. They are not strong in learning, in riches, in worldly fame or position. They can only say, "By the grace of God I am what I am." What I am not by grace, I am not.

Two Christians I observed in my youth to be impressed by them. I marked the contrast in them: one sighed, the other shouted; one told by his life that grace is not gloom and sanctification is not sadness. It drew me, won me.

On my first circuit there were two members of the charge who inspired me by their joyful spirit. They were a power! When they prayed the heavens bowed. When they spoke in love feast the assembly shook.

Who confesses not the power of sacred song? Who that heard it in the united voices of the congregation that our fathers addressed will doubt its benefits? It came from the holy joy that lifted the soul of the singer. This joy is the very thing that all want to make life happy, death welcome, and heaven a thing of certitude.

The late Samuel Halsted, of New York, a man of precious memory as one of the most successful laymen in bringing souls to Christ, was in nothing more distinguished than in his ardent zeal, his cheerful spirit, and his practical and earnest exhibition of what he called "good religion," that made him happy in every place and service. The sight of him to many persons was a benediction. He gave a narrative of two men who spoke in love feast. One was in a complaining mood. The preachers, the members, the times received his censure. To a warm meeting it was like a cold douche. The other man was in ecstasy, and regretted that he who had just spoken lived in "Grumble Street." He confessed that he was once there, but he disliked it and left it. It was narrow and not clean, and he had bad neighbors. Now he was living in "Thanksgiving Avenue" and was delighted there. It was wide and clean. The air was pure, he had good neighbors, and he was happy all the time.

Who that reads Christ's life does not see that, though the world's moral woes were on him, he carried joy wherever he went? He gave joy at the wedding feast; to the woman at the well; to Zaccheus, who received him joyfully; to the two disciples as they walked to Emmaus. And in his presence children by the wayside shouted "Hosanna!" Do not facts justify us in saying with Dr. Young, "Retire and read thy Bible to be gay"?

There is a moral gayety that grace induces. There is that exhilarates more than wine. Peter defended the disciples of Pentecost against the charge of drunkenness, by quoting from the prophet Joel, in relation to the pouring out of the Spirit in the latter days. These days we see. Will it, then, be deemed harsh to say, " 'Tis impious in a good man to be sad"?

Would that we could be properly impressed with the fact that the Christian and the Church that fail in the joyful prosecution of their work deny to the world one of the most influential means of bringing it to God!

4. The joy of the Lord is our strength in the conquest of our final foe. Death is before us; it meets us in every avenue of life. It comes under all circumstances and in many forms. To human nature it is an event of perpetual revulsion. The old as well as the young, the poor as well as the rich, would shun it. It is the King of Terrors and the terror of kings; but there is no discharge in this war. "We must needs die." But how shall we meet death? With nothing but manly courage? With nothing but human philosophy? Will it be enough to say, "The sword devours one as well as another"? Will the death of the many change the death of the individual? Alone I must meet God; alone I must be judged. If David Hume joked as death approached did it prove exemption from fear? His levity not less than another's gravity was a recogni-

tion of that which he would fain disguise.   The affectation
meant apprehension.

Men brave in battle cower in the sick room.   Behold the
sinner as he faces death.   His anxiety increases the solicitude of his friends.   What will they do?   Will they enu-
merate his social, domestic, and political virtues?   Will
they tell the orator of his eloquence in the Senate, or the
financier of the skill by which he saved the credit of a
tottering government;   or will they emphasize the unequaled wealth of him that is about to depart?   Would
not the dying man say, "Miserable comforters are ye! I
am entering a world where these things do not avail"?
This is true.   The wreaths of earthly immortality wither
before the tomb.   Fame has no voice in the silence of
the sepulcher, and flattery cannot soothe the dull, cold
ear of death.   Now is wanted what the dying man has
not.

If God has made it possible for a departing soul to
triumph over death, then that which he has provided is a
boon worthy of universal and profoundest gratitude. Grace
in the heart, through the death of Christ and by faith in
his blood, is the death of death—the funeral of our sorrows.
Here where unaided human reason fails, where philosophy
hangs down its head, and skepticism carps no more, religion wins her brightest trophies and reveals its sovereign
power.   In yielding the ghost the Christian is more than
conqueror.

Bunyan represents the pilgrims as entering the land of
Beulah.   The air is sweet and pleasant; the birds sing;
the flowers appear, and the voice of the turtle is heard in
the land.   The sun is shining night and day; they are out

of the reach of "Giant Despair," and cannot so much as see "Doubting Castle." They are in sight of the city, but there is a river, and there is no bridge over it. All save Enoch and Elijah have had to cross this river. Doubt makes Christian sink; joy makes Hopeful brave. One is troubled with apparitions, hobgoblins, and evil spirits, but Hopeful says, "I feel the bottom." Christian in his doubting has a fainting fit, but when he believes, "the enemy is as still as a stone;" they see the shining ones enter heaven and are safe.

So have I seen a saint go up to God. Glory filled the room, and she said, "The angels have come;" with them she went and left us. Is there not strength in such joy of the Lord? Hear Paul when martyrdom was before him: "I am now ready to be offered, and the time of my departure is at hand. I have fought a good fight, I have finished my course, I have kept the faith: henceforth there is laid up for me a crown of righteousness, which the Lord, the righteous judge, shall give me at that day: and not to me only, but unto all them also that love his appearing." Joy to the last, and culminating joy in the final conflict. Yes, yes, "the joy of the Lord is our strength," and the more we have the stronger we are to do, to suffer, or to die.

Who wonders, then, that such facts should inspire the genius of even Alexander Pope to write:

> "Vital spark of heavenly flame,
> Quit, O quit this mortal frame;
> Trembling, hoping, lingering, flying,
> O the pain, the bliss of dying!
> Cease, fond nature, cease thy strife,
> And let me languish into life.

> "Hark! they whisper: angels say,
> 'Sister spirit, come away!'
> What is this absorbs me quite—
> Steals my senses, shuts my sight,
> Drowns my spirit, draws my breath?—
> Tell me, my soul, can this be death?
>
> "The world recedes—it disappears;
> Heaven opens on my eyes; my ears
>   With sounds seraphic ring!
> Lend, lend your wings! I mount! I fly!
> 'O Grave, where is thy victory?
>   O Death, where is thy sting?'"

Is this dying? O, this is beginning to live with grander capabilities and for a higher realm. Call this transport! beatitude! call it the gate of heaven, with much of heaven in it!

People of Asbury! honored members of the charge of a hundred years! we cordially congratulate you in your history. You have no cause to blush at your origin or to be ashamed of your record. The temple where you worship perpetuates the memory of "The Apostolic Bishop" of earliest Methodism. No church in the denomination can boast of nobler names than those of your first pastors. Yours was the ministry of Ezekiel Cooper, distinguished for logic, illustration, and strength; of John Emory, afterward bishop, and one of the ablest men that this country has produced; of Lawrence McCoomb, the Boanerges of the Conference; of Solomon Sharp, the colloquial, the expository, and the patriarchal; of Lawrence Laurenson, who rose to the heights of impassioned eloquence; of the pathetic and searching Henry White; of the courteous and fascinating John Kennaday; of the majestic Matthew Sorin,

and of the seraphic Joseph Lybrand. These are a few of
the men of the first half century. All these I personally
knew. Those who have filled your pulpit in the second
half century, some of you know as well as the speaker.

Of the thousands of souls—I mean thousands—converted at your altars we need not tell you. Their names
are in "The Book of Life." In this, where is the church
that transcends you? Nor is it the least of the facts of
which you may exult that God has made you the mother
of so many churches. The light of their knowledge and
purity is shining all around you, and yet in the brightness
of their beams you are not eclipsed or obscured. He that
holds the seven stars in his right hand will cause you to
shine on. In all that constellation there is no "Star called
wormwood," whose fall makes the waters bitter. Organizations do not, like saints, have crowns in heaven; but
Asbury is crowned on earth. Shall we say with eleven
stars?

O, to-day as you are about entering upon your second
century, resolve that with additional opportunities you will
give it a character not less exalted for wisdom, for virtue,
and for usefulness. Let it be seen that the ardor of your
zeal in the past is equaled by the fires of your love in the
present. O, honor your origin. Emulate the graces of
the fathers, and still exhibit the energy that made you
what you are. Increase if you may—if you may not, multiply the successes of the past.

May the pulpit be as true to the truth! May the altar
glow with intenser fires! The living this day celebrate the
victories of a hundred years. But the dead, the ascended
saints—have they no share in this great interest and as-

sembly? It seems not fancy, but fact. It is vision. The veil lifts, and I behold a cloud of transported witnesses. They look with love; their shining faces tell the "joy of the Lord above," even greater than we are having below. I recognize many of them. Some seem incapable of perfect rest till they see us crowned. Rest! rest, departed ones, we will join you; in the race where you ran run we; on the field where you fought we are making our arms tell. We have the same great enemies that you encountered; some of them seem even stronger, but by the means of your conquest we shall be victors. Even now our hearts are saying, "Thanks be unto God, which always causeth us to triumph in Christ, and maketh manifest the savor of his knowledge by us in every place."

SERMON II.

Christ Is All.

**Where there is neither Greek nor Jew, circumcision nor un-
circumcision, Barbarian, Scythian, bond nor free: but Christ is
all, and in all.—Colossians iii, 11.**

Christianity, like every other system of religion, has
in it that which is essential to its existence. This, like the
first link in a chain, draws after it all parts with which it
is necessarily connected. In natural religion this principle
is the "being of God." In Islamism it is that Mohammed
is his prophet. In evangelic religion it is that "Christ is
all, and in all." He is the Alpha and Omega, the beginning and the end, the first and the last. This triplication
of the same thought gives emphasis to the fact. The Jews
are said to express the whole compass of things by the first
and last letters of the Hebrew alphabet. John, writing in
Greek, takes the first and the last letters of that alphabet
to convey the same idea: that we are in our possibilities
and hopes complete in Christ; by him we may not only
spell out the way of life, but "read our title clear to man-
sions in the skies." "There is neither Greek nor Jew, circumcision nor uncircumcision, Barbarian, Scythian, bond
nor free: but Christ is all, and in all."

This golden sentence from the pen of Paul now leads us
to consider

The preeminence of Christ in human salvation.

1. In the redemption wrought.

We do not teach that Christ is nowhere but in redemption. He is in creation and providence. "By him were

all things created, that are in heaven, and that are in earth, visible and invisible, whether they be thrones, or dominions, or principalities, or powers: all things were created by him, and for him: and he is before all things, and by him all things consist." He laid the foundations of the earth; and the heavens are the work of his hands. He spread the floor and reared the dome of this vast temple. His Spirit kindled and his arm suspended the ever-burning lamps of the sky. He started the sun out of his chamber, and made him rejoice as a strong man to run a race. "He penciled with beauty and perfumed with fragrance the flowers that bloom." Wind and wave assert his presence: the mountain and the molecule utter his praise.

It is not meant that Christ is alone in human salvation. For "God so loved the world, that he gave his only begotten Son." And the Spirit guides us into all truth. Yet in the atonement it was Christ who was made an offering for sin.

When the foundations of nature were out of course, when ruin rested on the fairest of creation, when the breath of the Almighty's indignation blasted earthly hope, when Adam and Eve were driven from Eden, and the "flaming sword turned every way, to keep the way of the tree of life," when the gloom of guilt covered the moral horizon, the first gleam of hope that gladdened the exiled pair was the promise given, "The seed of the woman shall bruise the serpent's head." Christ "was manifested to take away our sins." "Who is this that cometh from Edom, with dyed garments from Bozrah? this that is glorious in his apparel, traveling in the greatness of his strength?" Who? None of the tyrants of antiquity; none of the thunderbolts of war; none of the rods of God's anger; none of the hammers of the whole earth. Who is this? "I that speak in righteousness, mighty to save." "Then said I, Lo, I come: in the volume of the book it is written of me."

"Herein is love, not that we loved God, but that he loved us, and sent his Son to be the propitiation for our sins." Herein is love that is pure, disinterested, and un-exampled—love to the unlovely; love that would shut hell and open heaven; love that calms conscience and exalts man. He saw when there was none to help, and wondered that there was none to uphold; therefore his own "arm brought salvation." He defeated the hosts of darkness. His expiring cry proclaimed his victory, and the cross now stands, and will forever stand, the bloody trophy of his conquest. O Bethlehem, we look to thee! O Calvary, thou art our only hope! Christ's cross presents the corner stone, and his resurrection the keystone, of the arch that makes the temple strong enough and wide enough for all the race.

2. In the attainment and fullness of the grace offered.

It is one thing for atonement to be made, quite another thing for it to be applied. It is one thing to be placed in a redeemed state, quite another to be saved; one thing to make pardon and purity possible, quite another to make them our experience.

Christ does not render human effort superfluous. He does not repent and believe for us. But who moves first in our salvation—Christ or the sinner? "It is God which worketh in you both to will and to do of his good pleasure."

He is first in our salvation. With the outward eye men can read the Bible. With the ear they can hear the Gospel, with the mind they can ponder truth, and yet sinners are perishing despite the atonement. It is Christ who opens the eyes of our understanding, who touches our will, who bends our purpose. It is he who makes the heart soft and impresses his own image.

When the converted Sandwich Islander was asked how he was converted he answered, "By thinking on Jesus."

That flaming herald of the Church of Scotland, Robert Murray McCheyne, when writing to a young Christian lady who was much disposed to dwell upon her unworthiness, advised her, for every look she took at herself, to take ten looks at Christ.

As in pardon, so in purity, Christ, who is the author, is also the finisher of our faith. He "of God is made unto us wisdom, and righteousness, and sanctification, and redemption."

Thus the royal law is fulfilled. We love God with all the heart, and with all the soul, and with all the mind, and with all the strength. There is nothing withheld from Him who is the head of all principalities and powers. It is said that at a time when Christianity was making a deep impression on the Roman empire there was a motion made in the Senate of Rome that Jesus Christ should have a place among the other gods. To this there was prompt opposition, on the ground that if Jesus Christ had a place there he would never rest till all the other gods were cast down and he alone was on the throne. It is a fact that idols must fall before God's ark, and that the Saviour of mankind allows no rival. He will not have the heart he enters to be divided. To the Christian and to the sinner he says, "Thou shalt have no other gods before me."

Our first experience of grace may be compared to the entrance of some of the early settlers of this country. The Swedes, for example, who entered Delaware and Pennsylvania took up their abode along the rivers and water courses in the hope of deriving much of their support from fish and fowl. Gradually they went further into the country; but in their own localities, what knew they of the vast treasures not yet opened, of the soil in its richness, of the mines in their wealth, and of the land in its territory? So it is with young Christians: "There remaineth yet very much land to be possessed." God wishes us "to comprehend with all saints what is the breadth, and length, and depth, and height; and to know the love of Christ, which passeth knowledge," and so be filled "with all the fullness of God." We go on to perfection. Thus when Christ has his full place in the heart we say, as the sky overarches every spot of earth, so does the sense of our responsibility to God cover every faculty, function, and force of our renovated nature. We realize those wonderful words of Paul: "I live; yet not I, but Christ liveth in me."

3. In the means instituted for the highest good.

a) The Church.

It is "the pillar and ground of the truth," which Christ "hath purchased with his own blood." He was in the tabernacle and in the temple. The Church, with all its means of instruction and Christian support, is nothing without Christ. It may have learning in its ministry, and wealth in its membership, and splendor in its places of worship; and yet they who minister at her altars may be as "the scribes and the Pharisees" who sat in Moses' seat, whom Christ condemned. So far may the Church fail of her functions and abuse her advantages that Christ may again say, "Come out of her, my people, that ye be not partakers of her sins." With Mary Magdalene of old we may say, "They have taken away my Lord, and I know not where they have laid him." Lo! may it not be amid the lore of antiquity, the pride of circumstance, the pomp of power, and the devices of men?

Sirs, Christ must be a "wall of fire round about, and the glory in the midst of her."

b) What significance or efficacy have the sacraments without him? What is baptism without the Father and the Son and the Holy Ghost? It may be by sprinkling, pouring, or immersion; it may be with water from the Jordan, or even in the Jordan itself, where Christ was baptized; it may be by a bishop's or an archbishop's hands; but it is Christ alone that gives the grace and blessing for which the means were instituted. We take the Lord's Supper—the communion—in accordance with his own command, "This do in remembrance of me." Yet the church of Corinth showed that even this holy sacrament might be received without benefit. His remembrance should be vivid, tender, and grateful. It is in such a manner that we should show forth his death until his coming again. Yet in the very days of the apostles there were those who ate and drank to their condemnation.

c) What are the Scriptures without Christ?

His own words are, "Search the Scriptures; for in them ye think ye have eternal life: and they are they which testify of me." They certainly do; and their testimony is clear, full, and convincing. They testify by types, and figures, and facts of abiding utility. We see him in the ark that was launched upon the flood, in the altar when Isaac was ready for sacrifice, in the brazen serpent set up to heal the stricken Israelites, and in the ladder that reached from earth to heaven. And O! sirs, amid the burning, consuming thirst of the wilderness, and the exhausting hunger of his ancient people, we see him in the rock that was smitten, and in the waters that gushed: "they all drank of that spiritual Rock that followed them: and that Rock was Christ." Nor did the manna that they gathered every morning more certainly nourish their fainting frames than does the bread of Christ our own souls and our spiritual life.

In Moses we see him who is the deliverer; and in Joshua we have him with us to go over the Jordan, and to usher us into the promised land.

Now take the ritual types of the Mosaic dispensation, and compare them with the spiritual doctrines of the evangelic system; and as in the former the Saviour's blood virtually mingled with every sacrifice of the altar, while his intercession was typified in every incense cloud before the mercy seat, so in Christianity there is not a doctrine but contains Christ, no sacrament but enshrines him, and no Christian but partakes of him. Think of the promises of Scripture so helpful to us amid our losses, griefs, persecutions, and tribulations! "All the promises of God in him are yea, and in him Amen, unto the glory of God by us." An old Puritan has said: "If the promises are the field, Christ is the pearl hid in the field. If the promises are the golden pot, Christ is the manna contained in the pot. If the promises are the alabaster box, Christ is the precious spikenard that sends forth its grateful odor. If the promises are the golden candlestick, Christ is the olive tree that drops its fatness into it, and the light that shines from it." If the promises are the glass, Christ is the beautiful face; and "we all, with open face beholding as in a glass the glory of the Lord, are changed into the same image from glory to glory, even as by the Spirit of the Lord."

d) What is the Gospel without Christ?

Christ bade us go into all the world and preach it. Luther calls it God's grand ordnance. "It shakes one world with the thunders of another." St. Paul, who preached it to all sorts and conditions of men, whether at Corinth, or Rome, or Athens, preached "Christ crucified, unto the Jews a stumbling-block, and unto the Greeks foolishness; but unto them which are called, both Jews and Greeks, Christ the power of God, and the wisdom of God."

A devout Scotchman had a son whom he educated for the ministry. The young man delivered a trial sermon. The father heard it. The son was anxious to know his father's estimate of it, and therefore asked him. He met with candor. "John, my lad," was the response, "it would have answered if you had only had Christ in it." Slow to discern, the young man thought of the Christ of rhetoric, and said, "O, father, if he had come in my way I would have had him!" Then the good man exclaimed, "O, my lad, if you knew Christ as you should you would have had him in your sermon, though you had 'run through a troop or leaped over a wall to reach him!'"

14

e) What are any or all the means of grace without Christ?

We call them channels, and so they are. But if Christ be not in them they are channels without streams; they are wells without water; they are clouds without rain; they are trees without fruit; they are shadows without substance. As easily might we conceive of an artery in our physical organization without connection with the heart, or imagine a planet in the solar system with no relation to the central orb, as to suppose means, the Church's instruments, have any power without Christ, who is their very basis and foundation stone. We hesitate not to say that "without Christ the Bible is a dead letter, the sacraments are unmeaning ceremonies, and the Church is an ecclesiastical corpse." With Christ in them he is the end of the law for righteousness, the end of prophecy for fulfillment, the end of miracles for their justification, and the end of all that God has instituted for the broadest and grandest benefits to man, and for the sublimest display of his own glory.

4. "Christ is all, and in all," in the rewards of the saved.

"Come," said one, "and I will show you the glory of Greece. When thou hast seen Solon thou hast seen all." Our heaven on earth is in being in Christ. Our heaven above will be that Christ is its fullness. For "the God of our Lord Jesus Christ, the Father of glory, . . . raised him from the dead, and set him at his own right hand in the heavenly places, far above all principality, and power, and might, and dominion, and every name that is named, not only in this world, but also in that which is to come:

and hath put all things under his feet, and gave him to be
the head over all things to the Church, which is his body,
the fullness of him that filleth all in all." Why is it that
there, there is no need of the sun, nor of the moon, nor of
the stars? It is because Christ, who is the Lamb, is the light
thereof. To him the harps of heaven are struck. To him
the jubilant chant of the ten thousand times ten thousand
is raised. The elders round about the throne fall before
him, and any other note than that of praise to God would
fill heaven with discord. Angels honor him; the redeemed
extol him; and if possible to speak of profoundest hell, the
very devils howl his sovereignty while they believe and
tremble. He that placed the heavens above us and his own
divine Spirit within us, while around us is the vast theater
for the display of his benignity and power, shines forth in
all his unobscured glory upon the throne. Look at the
trees that bloom and bear their twelve manner of fruits!
Look at the jasper walls and pearly gates and crystal river,
and tell us what invests heaven with its glory and fills it
with the shout of an eternal jubilee? "We praise thee, O
God. . . . The glorious company of the apostles praise
thee: the goodly fellowship of the prophets praise thee:
the noble army of martyrs praise thee. . . . Thou art the
King of glory, O Christ. . . . When thou hadst overcome
the sharpness of death, thou didst open the kingdom of
heaven to all believers." To all who enter there thou art
"all and in all." Let us feel then as we should to-day,
and, shouting, say:

> "All hail the power of Jesus' name !
> Let angels prostrate fall :
> Bring forth the royal diadem,
> And crown him Lord of all."

SERMON III.

THE PLEASANTNESS OF RELIGION.

Her ways are ways of pleasantness, and all her paths are peace.—Proverbs iii, 17.

LET us never be judged by our adversaries. Truth is too precious a thing to be determined by her foes, or even by her misguided friends. They have shamefully repressed the cause of vital piety. That which in itself is full of brightness and beauty is made gloomy and repulsive. Satan himself, transformed into an angel of light, seeks to transform religion into an angel of darkness.

In the context religion is given its proper aspect. It is personified as Wisdom; "Length of days is in her right hand; and in her left hand riches and honor." Another figure of grandeur is used: "She is a tree of life to them that lay hold upon her: and happy is every one that retaineth her." This is the lesson impressed, and that we shall seek to exhibit:

THE PLEASANTNESS OF A LIFE OF RELIGION AS A COMMANDING ARGUMENT FOR ITS ATTAINMENT.

1. Religion is here presented as wisdom, and the way of understanding: "For the merchandise of it is better than the merchandise of silver, and the gain thereof than fine gold. She is more precious than rubies: and all the things thou canst desire are not to be compared unto her."

The pleasantness of a religious life—comprehended in "her ways"—is explained only by the moral transformation of human nature through the working of divine grace.

Vital religion is not in the flesh and blood, the loins and

sinews, the nerves and muscles of the human frame—
though it does not ignore or disparage these members as
an essential part of our nature for the purposes of our
being. The carnal mind is not religious, but none the
less it should be governed by religion. In itself "the flesh
lusteth against the Spirit." St. Paul says, "I know that
in me (that is, in my flesh,) dwelleth no good thing." We
do not disguise the fact that the attainment of piety is
only through painful exercise. For pardon of sin the
heart has bitterness, and the soul may know agony. The
unpardoned spirit has guilt and fear and the dominion
of unholy passions. Guilt awakens remorse that eats as
canker. Fear of final anguish often gives present torment. Unholy passion forges chains that reason and resolution fail to break, when we "condemn the wrong and yet
the wrong pursue." But saving grace in the regenerated
heart gives abiding joy and peace. "If any man be in
Christ, he is a new creature; old things are passed away;
behold, all things are become new." Of this transformation we say, in the language of another: "While under the
dominion of sin all the passions were in dreadful unison
and diabolic concord; all gave forth sounds grateful to
the ear of Satan, and every note was attuned to his mind
and well fitted to increase the chorus of the condemned.
But now, O glorious change! O new creation! The passions of the soul, newly adjusted, have changed the mode
of their music; all now is the harmony of holiness, and the
strings, swept by the breathing of the divine Spirit, swell
out in notes of solemn praise that are borne on the wings
of heaven and carried to the ears of the Almighty."

2. The transformation thus effected, through saving

faith in the merits of Christ, renders all things pertaining to a holy character both welcome and satisfying.

a) Piety undoubtedly has its trials and restraints. But the change from darkness to light, from the power of Satan unto that of God's own Son, imparts such desires and aspirations as affect the whole of life—influencing its entire course and current—so that at length it can even welcome what hitherto it had regarded as rocks and shoals and tempests. The Christian does not shrink even from crosses; if under the cross he sees a crown—if in the trial of faith he beholds a final victory—he can bear his hardships with equanimity. The child of God even glories in tribulation, "knowing that tribulation worketh patience; and patience, experience; and experience, hope: and hope maketh not ashamed."

Trials in life to the Christian? Certainly! To whom in life are trials unknown? To the merchant in his losses, to the patriot in his love of country, to the student in his high and just pursuit of knowledge, to the man of honor as he maintains a course of consistency and uprightness? In all such cases there are sufficient reasons for constant trial and incessant struggle. Without labor and conflict there could be no real strength; without these there could be no genuine nobility of character. Moses, "choosing rather to suffer affliction with the people of God, than to enjoy the pleasures of sin for a season," presents us with a sublime spectacle. It was a very wise man who said, "God forbid that I should glory, save in the cross of our Lord Jesus Christ, by whom the world is crucified unto me, and I unto the world." Certainly there is something compensative in losses sustained, in troubles encountered, and in things from which unsanctified nature shows its aversion. Even St. Paul's thorn in the flesh, which at first filled him with perplexity and consternation, was welcomed when God declared his grace would be sufficient.

b) Religion enjoins duties that for the best of reasons the Christian accepts and discharges. We are to pray. But it is to our "Father which is in secret," who rewards us openly. We are commanded to "search the Scriptures." But what mines of moral wealth do they open to those who seek for the "unsearchable riches"? We are called to worship the Lord in the beauty of holiness. Is it in public worship? But what saint does not esteem a day in God's courts as better than a thousand? The service held, the hymns sung, the word preached, the sacraments administered, all these fill us with hope and happiness. In the sanctuary we have sometimes found days of heaven upon earth. "I was glad when they said unto me, Let us go into the house of the Lord." There faith is increased; there love abounds; there we are filled with high aims and noble ambitions; there, if we are faithful disciples, we exercise that charity, beneficence, and kindliness which the Master enjoins, and we receive that reward which he has promised. Surely the paths of religion are strewn abundantly with pleasantness and peace.

3. The transformation that fits for heaven does not unfit for earth.

Christians are in this world as citizens with all the responsibilities that their relationships involve — whether they be social, domestic, secular, or political.

The pious youth is not indifferent to the necessary improvement of his mind by study. The young man in business loses none of his mental perception, energy, economy, skill, or perseverance from the fact that his conversation is in heaven. The woman who has consecrated her life to God feels her responsibility to society increased thereby; and the man who has given his heart to his Saviour feels that he should attend to his daily vocation with added heartiness.

In domestic life where is there a happier home than that where the family altar stands, and day after day sees the bended knee of a Christian father? Where do we find a community of more quietness, honesty, and truth than that one in which Christianity prevails? And is any land ever so blessed as that one where Christ's religion holds sway?

Is there aught which health requires or mind demands that religion forbids? If relaxation or amusement add to health, God in nature is not opposed to God in grace. Nay, in the use of proper means we realize that "a merry heart doeth good like a medicine."

The delights of mental application and culture are not diminished, nor the realm of proper thought limited, by the fact that God reigns in the heart. The universe is God's, and its study does not harm the soul. Never are the forces of the mind keener than when roused by piety to the sense of duty. Genius as really flashes its fires in the brain of the righteous as in the thought of the undevout.

The study of science, the charms of art, the pursuits of literature, the reasonings of philosophy, are facts that the religious are not forbidden. No good thing is denied them that love the Lord. The intellect has its freedom in all the fields that divine wisdom opens. Livingstone and Stanley in Africa are honored in the object of their ambition. Newton in philosophy, Gladstone in statesmanship, and Milton in poetry can be as great in piety as men of less contracted spheres of action. If the flames of war inspired a Homer's "Iliad," so did the fervor of religion give birth to a "Paradise Lost." And eloquence that has its highest themes in the facts of revelation may have and often has had its sublimest exhibitions in the sacred desk.

The greatest pleasures of the mind are said to be found in objects of beauty, novelty, and grandeur. And where are these qualities more abundant than in the statements, principles, and realities of religion.

Pure religion gives to learning its greatest value, to genius its sublimest exhibition, and to all moral virtues their highest claim. Will not all acknowledge that it is pleasant to be constantly advancing in that which should be our chief pursuit? The Christian daily grows in grace.

Believe us, religion, as the Bible teaches it, lays no embargo on the endowments of nature or the advantages of providence. It places no icy hand on the true joys of life. Supreme delight in God destroys no subordinate delight in the things he has given. It is as foreign from gloom as the sun is from darkness; as alien from roughness and severity as the gentle breezes of a summer eve are from the wild storm blasts of a wintry sky. Compared with this, mirth is like lightning breaking through a dark cloud and glittering for a moment, then leaving the mind in gloom the greater by contrast: but Christian cheerfulness is a perpetual light, and is filled with celestial anticipations. Pollok says:

> "About the joys and pleasures of the world
> This question was not seldom in debate,
> Whether the righteous man or sinner had
> The greater share of earthly good.
> Truth answers, nor needs to reason long,
> The righteous man; for what is there of earthly good
> Of which the righteous man may not partake?"

Would that we could show you religion as she really is: not as the monkish or melancholy make her; not in continuance of gloom and habits of austerity; but full of kindness, hope, and happiness. Here is not a tearless eye, a pulseless heart, a cold and motionless arm; here is a form of beauty, a spirit of innocence, and a soul of love. Religion calls for no fires from heaven, breathes no execrations, invokes the aid of no human policy, and disdains the violence of the sword; she advances by moral suasion, and triumphs in the grace of God. Behold this daughter of the skies, this mother of all the noblest virtues! Where she goes peace and prosperity smile, the heavens drop fatness, the earth teems with benefits; angry, mutinous, and tormenting passions expire; the renovated nature rises in holy contemplation, and all the movements of the soul are heavenward; the bosom is calm like that of Jesus, undisturbed by the agitations of time. In form, in bearing, in beauty, and in blessedness how worthy of a God! Her consolations are constant and unfailing; in labor a support, in suffering a solace, in society an ornament, in solitude a friend.

But her highest honor is not yet reached. The hour of her coronation advances, when God will lead her to the throne of heaven, and in the person of his Son. Hail, rightful empress of the world! Hail, consummate blessedness of eternity!

Will any, then, deny that Religion's ways of duty, of devotion, and of moral dignity are ways of pleasantness? Will any dare assert that her promises for futurity are not full of brightness and comfort and peace?

It is religion, beloved, that in the purpose of God is again to make paradise where sin now reigns. It is religion alone that is able, through the power of the Almighty, to convert and transform the world. Surely, then, every intelligent and responsive heart must feel the weighty inducement toward such a life. May God at length, through his grace and power, lead all mankind to adopt it!

SERMON IV.

PAUL AT ATHENS.

Then Paul stood in the midst of Mars' hill, and said, Ye men of Athens, I perceive that in all things ye are too superstitious. For as I passed by, and beheld your devotions, I found an altar with this inscription, TO THE UNKNOWN GOD. Whom therefore ye ignorantly worship, him declare I unto you.—Acts xvii. 22, 23.

LUTHER at Worms, Elijah at Carmel, and Paul at Athens stand among the most remarkable figures in ecclesiastical history; each was a man for an emergency, and each emergency was filled by the man. Paul in the context had a varied experience. In Thessalonica he had success and opposition. In Berea there was cause for joy.

He was now conducted to Athens, and while waiting for his fellow-laborers, Silas and Timotheus, he saw the city wholly given to idolatry; his spirit was stirred within him, and he at once began to dispute with those whom he met in the synagogue and in the market place. It was in this way that the interest and curiosity of the philosophers was at length aroused, and he was brought to Mars' hill, in order that they might have the opportunity of listening to what they chose to designate his "new doctrine." He seized the occasion for impressing the claims and merits of his Lord and Saviour Jesus Christ. Consider:

PAUL AT ATHENS ENCOUNTERING ITS PHILOSOPHY AND SUPERSTITION, AND SUCCESSFUL IN THE CONFLICT; OR, CHRISTIANITY ANTAGONIZING PAGANISM, AND TRIUMPHANT.

1. Paul at Athens.

a) Athens was the chief city of ancient Greece—the center of science and the emporium of art. It was distinguished for philosophers and poets, for warriors and statesmen. There Thucydides, the immortal historian, wrote. There was the Academy where Plato taught, and the Lyceum that Aristotle honored. Athens is said to have been to Greece what Oxford and Cambridge are to England. There the eloquence of Demosthenes burned and blazed. There towered the Acropolis covered with marble temples, the very remains of which awaken in modern travelers a feeling akin to adoration. There stood the Parthenon. Athens was the eye of Greece when Greece was the eye of the world. "If thine eye be evil, thy whole body shall be full of darkness." Full as Greece was of gods, it is said there were more in Athens than in all the rest of the land. The Roman satirist declared it was easier to find a god than a man. The citizens were regarded as the most religious people of all Greece. There was the high court. In sight were the plains of Marathon and the monuments of pagan pomp and superstition. Greece, the mother of science and mistress of art, owned no more favored child than Athens.

b) Paul at Athens was the man for the place. He was a citizen of no mean city—Tarsus, in Cilicia. Strabo, a contemporary, says the inhabitants were chiefly Greek, and cherished such fondness for philosophy and all branches of polite learning as to make them compare favorably with the people of Athens and Alexandria. His mental endowments, his intellectual culture, his Hebrew training, all fitted him for an eminent position among men of mind.

He was also a freeborn Roman citizen. He had education, eloquence, dignity, and genius.

To one of Paul's tastes and early habits Athens might naturally have been supposed to be a place of intense attraction and wide allurement. It might have been supposed that he would luxuriate in the splendor of the city, the abundance of its literature, the distinction of its people. But art, science, self were as nothing. It was the moral state of the masses that took hold of him, and all else sank into oblivion. He saw the city "wholly given to idolatry," and that "stirred" him. His mind could not rest; his heart could not be quiet; the solicitude of his soul made his whole being bend under the burden that the guilt of others imposed.

Paul had a soul to feel. There are irresponsive natures—natures that are so morally cold that no cause or calling warms them, so dead that no power vitalizes them; the circumstances and condition of things, be they never so critical, do not affect them. We may compare them to things inanimate. They are like prairies of the West, where there is so much of sameness, solitude, desertion, and gloom that, should you cry aloud because you were lost, there would be little likelihood of any response— where time itself seems to make almost no change. But as there are also landscapes where rises the mountain, stretches the valley, leaps the cascade, and rolls the river, so there are minds that appreciate facts, and souls that strive to correct wrongs—like God in at least the sense that they cannot look upon sin with composure. They are exalted by contact with the pure and noble; they are depressed by beholding the corrupt and injurious. Paul had a nature that was intense, and solicitude for the imperiled compelled his conduct. He had self-command, so that he could appear outwardly as calm as a summer's evening, and yet feel within him a moral power and a divine impulse, in violence like unto a tornado.

With what an eye could one who said, "God forbid that I should glory, save in the cross of our Lord Jesus Christ," behold a city "wholly given to idolatry"? He knew that the psalmist had said, "Confounded be all they that serve graven images, that boast themselves of idols." If Christians have eyes to see, and ears to hear, and hearts to feel, can they be indifferent to the moral danger of the perishing around them? Paul was troubled, and his heart would not allow his tongue to be silent.

2. Paul as he preached at Athens.

There was no work for God that he refused. Hard cares and difficult duties did not turn him aside. As a man he had intellectual faculties and mental culture that made him the peer of the greatest. But idolatry—a capital sin—was an evil that faced him, and roused his holy soul. In self-oblivion, as in utter forgetfulness of all beside, he stood, the Christian minister before pagan philosophers, beholding men "without God in the world." It was to him an eventful hour with regard to the treatment he should receive, and as to the doctrine he should elucidate. In the midst of Mars' hill stood the apostle of the Gentiles. It was a tremendous hour. The court before which he appeared took cognizance of high crimes, impurity, and immorality. And if ever a man had need to be wise as a serpent and harmless as a dove Paul had in that hour.

There was a recognized state religion. To introduce a

new one was death by law. For that alleged crime Socrates had lost his life; and Paul was now charged with being a setter forth of strange gods. It is a great fact when we can truthfully say, "God hath not given us the spirit of fear; but of power, and of love, and of a sound mind." Paul enjoyed this gift, and it was his preservation. Precipitate action might have wrecked all hope. He knew the difference between real philosophy and that falsely so called. He could distinguish between sophistry and sound reasoning. He had classical learning and could entertain by quoting from certain of their own poets, and by their utterances sustain the truths he declared. In the midst of idols, with superstition staring him in the face, solitary and alone he stood, to show verities, as, in the light of God, he saw them. With him superstition was a vile weed to cumber the soil and choke the growth of the seed of God. He knew that their philosophy was to the light of revelation only as a lamp of the sepulcher, shedding its sickly ray amid desolation and death; while the objects of their boasting were as the treeless, turfless desert, with nothing to invite a human soul. Now they who delighted in telling or hearing some new thing could from him receive only the Gospel, as old as Eden, but that would prepare men for a better paradise than Adam lost. It was not the time or place for rhetorical pyrotechnics, but for profound and robust reasoning, for arguments to rescue the deluded, for teachings to save the lost. Two thoughts filled the mind and heart of Paul. The first was to expose and overcome superstition. The second was so to present the true God as that they should seek and find and enjoy him. He had no desire simply to undermine their religion, to leave them in doubt and perplexity, so that they should say, like Micah of old, "Ye have taken away my gods which I made, . . . and what have I more?" Turning them from the false, he would show them the true.

To change a man's religious belief, even when differences are slight, is no easy matter. But when the distinctions are radical the labor is almost insuperable. The memories of childhood, the lessons of youth, the teaching of relatives, and the love of those departed make such effort of doubtful efficacy, if not utterly futile. Even when all arguments seem to have been answered, all prejudices swept away, habit and home lift their voice, tradition cries out for observance; the possible convert recoils from change, and persists in his error.

When John Baptist came preaching Christ there was more for him than self-denial, than simple food and coarse clothing. He saw valleys to be filled, mountains and hills to be brought low, crooked places to be made straight, rough ways to be made smooth. Still greater were the difficulties of Paul. Before him were towers of philosophic pride to be brought low, valleys of licentious conduct requiring a divine arm to close, and crooked things in purposes and practices to be made straight. Sirs, the hearts of the people of Athens were harder than the pedestals of her idols or the stones of her temples.

a) Paul's preaching was agonistic. It meant opposition to error. It meant authoritative declaration of truth. And he who disputed in the synagogue and in the market could not fail to show at Mars' hill intense earnestness and tremendous purpose. Enough there was to fill his mind,

15

to pain his heart, and to awaken all his energies. Paul did not know "comparative religions." With him there was but one—one God, one Saviour, one exalting, sanctifying, saving religion. It was this or nothing.

The issue was paganism as against Christianity. The Epicurean before whom he stood regarded pleasure as the chief good, and threw the reins on the neck of passion; virtue was but a name. The Stoics taught that happiness was to be found in insensibility to pain, and, like the Pharisees, boasted of their righteousness. The Epicureans were atheists; the Stoics were pantheists; and these were the oracles of this proud city. To them nothing could be more repugnant than Christ's atonement for sin. The first two of their teachers—Zeno and Cleanthes—were suicides. Such was the show of philosophy and superstition that Paul encountered. As the skillful commander arranges his battery so that he may capture the stronghold, so did Paul behold their superstition, and make the mighty discharge of truths to save the soul. Hear him as he says, "Ye men of Athens, I perceive that in all things ye are too superstitious"—in their way, too religious. "For as I passed by, and beheld your devotions, I found an altar with this inscription, TO THE UNKNOWN GOD." Now, thus spake Paul: That Unknown God is knowable, and him declare I unto you.

b) His preaching was evangelical. It comprehended morality, natural religion, and the redemption that is in Christ Jesus. He shows the immediate necessity of reformation; God "now commandeth all men everywhere to repent." John Wesley, in commenting on this passage, says, "The beams of God's eyes overshot" the days of ignorance, but rested on the present; he "now commandeth." He shows that the Godhead is not "like unto gold, or silver, or stone graven by art and man's device." He declares that God "hath made of one blood all nations of men;" and thus impresses the divine fatherhood. He declares also that God "will judge the world in righteousness;" and he preaches unto them "Jesus and the resurrection"— Jesus as Mediator, Redeemer, Advocate, Enlightener, Exemplar, and Saviour. What an avalanche of the mightiest truths did he bring down on the philosophers and the unbelievers!

It was Paul's hour; solitary and alone he stood facing these Athenians without trepidation—nay, with remarkable calmness, firmness, and courage. Thunder could not more certainly rouse apprehension, lightning could not more properly awaken terror, than could his clear and comprehensive arguments excite interest. It was said of Cicero that he lightened only when his mind was in flame and his words on fire. Paul was sublime in his declarations of the claims of Christ. O, sirs, think of the time, the theme, the place, the genius, the inspiration of Paul. Was there not a moral grandeur in his utterance and zeal, to which reverence and awe should pay homage? Believe us, the dogmatism of the pulpit is not of the preacher, but of God. It is the Almighty who imparts authority and inspiration. It is not the Gospel of men; it is the Glad Tidings of God.

c) This preaching was effective. It has always been true that "not many wise men after the flesh, not many mighty, not many noble are called." Paul met derision. "Some mocked: and others said, We will hear thee again of this matter." Indeed! Was there any argument in all this? If able to reply, they would have been only too happy to have done so without delay. Why did they not answer at once? I fancy I see the Stoic restless, despite his theory, and asking if the teaching of three hundred years is to be swept away by this stranger. The Epicurean says, "If what he declares is true I have misapprehended the purport of life."

But Paul had success. It was too soon for an abundant harvest. "Howbeit certain men clave unto him, and believed: among the which was Dionysius the Areopagite [possibly the judge, if not the president, of the high court of Athens], and a woman named Damaris, and others with them." Sirs, good is done even when our altars are not filled. In this congregation is some one man whose conversion might fill the place with exultation. Think of the conversion of one St. Augustine, one Athanasius, one Martin Luther, one John Wesley, or one Benjamin Abbot. Zaccheus was but one; the one woman at the well received Christ's care, and Paul was but one man; yet how much did these individuals accomplish!

Some have thought that Dionysius became the first Bishop of Athens; and hear it, O Church of God: in the ministry of Paul at this time and place we see the first great victory of Christianity over paganism. Nor was it long before Jehovah reigned, amid deserted temples and prostrate altars and fallen shrines; and Christianity, with the purple waving from her shoulders and the diadem sparkling on her brow, was proclaimed "empress of the world," in the throne of the Cæsars, where she had been arraigned as a criminal and condemned as an impostor. Hail, O hail, glorious Redeemer! thy trophies multiply;

and to-day in India, China, Japan, in Africa, and in the islands of the sea God is honored.

Remarks:

1. How mighty can God make a man whom he calls to a work! Think of St. Peter, St. Paul, Savonarola, John Huss, and John Knox!

2. Nothing so fits a man for the ministry as the "stirring" which the sight of sin gives him. Education is good; Paul had it. But it was the "stirring" that enabled him to accomplish what he did. We must *feel,* if we would make *others* feel.

3. In Paul at Athens learn how God moves men to duty, and blesses them when they obey.

4. The most difficult cases may be reached by patience and persistence.

> "Jesus shall reign where'er the sun
> Does his successive journeys run."

5. Let us give the people what God gives us—the Gospel. Amen.

SERMON V.

THE TRIUMPH OF THE GOSPEL.

He must increase, but I must decrease.—St. John iii, 30.

WILLINGNESS to be little may show a great nature; but the cheerful acceptance of obscurity after distinction is a rare exhibition. In the forerunner of our Lord this commands the highest admiration. He had filled distinguished places and done important service. He was a preacher of great power, and multitudes came to his baptism. Our Saviour received it at his hands, and said of him, "There has not risen a greater than John the Baptist." He was the connecting link between the old dispensation and that of Christ. Knowing the mission and might of Jesus, he declared he was not worthy to unloose his shoes. As the fingerboard points out the way for the traveler, so he pointed to the Son of God, and said, "Behold the Lamb of God, which taketh away the sin of the world." And in the text in sublime self-forgetfulness he declares, "He must increase, but I must decrease." There was no jealousy. There was prompt and unqualified subordination. It was the divine order. It was all right. Let us consider:

I. The increase declared.

There is that in Christ as the Son of God that cannot increase. He was manifested in the flesh to meet our condition, just as truly as God was God when he appeared in the burning bush and Moses took off his shoes. The Deity was before "the morning stars sang together and all the sons of God shouted for joy;" and Jesus Christ is "the same yesterday, and to-day, and forever." As the Divine Person we should see him in the greatness of his understanding, the extent of his natural dominion, the depth of his mercy, and the merit of his character. As God manifested in the flesh he engaged in the work of his heart. It was to make an end of sin and accomplish eternal redemption with the grand design of "bringing many sons to glory." His essential glory cannot be increased, but his declarative glory may be increased to the extent of his desires. This the text recognizes.

He is to increase in the diffusion of the knowledge of his moral merits, his holy achievements, and the conquest of the rebellion of sinful men. To him every knee shall bow, and every tongue confess.

They who have not heard shall hear; they who have not believed shall believe; they who have not obeyed shall obey, and as all souls are his by redemption, they shall be seen and sought and found, as the result of his purpose and plan.

He shall increase in the number of his followers, and in his influence on his disciples, who now, as in days of old, follow him afar off. His hold on nations and on individuals shall illustrate his increase in the estimate of his character, and in subordination to his claim. Clearly he saw, profoundly he felt, and eloquently John said, "He must increase." We argue:

II. The certainty of his increase from conscious need.

1. There is in us a moral necessity that argues his increase. We have a nature that is not merely of the flesh and of the mind. Heart and soul have place in us, and they are too big for any worldly, material, or social rela-

tions to supply. When we have all that gold can give, that office can bestow, that honor can indulge, there is still part of our nature that cries, "Give, give;" and only in the Messiah can we find the fulfillment of prophecy in the happiness promised the race. As we have a body with its members, and an intellect with its faculties, so we have a soul with its capacities and aspirations, a soul that can only be satisfied in the divine and the imperishable. Conscience has place, and it refuses to be displaced or ignored. It has a voice and pleads. It is not always alike powerful in its action to guard or prompt, and differs in different persons. But the suicides that we are constantly reading of tell us,

> "The world can never give
> The bliss for which we sigh."

We say, "All is vanity and vexation of spirit." Appetite, passion, distinction, and the best and happiest domestic relations do not meet demands that God has, and to which our moral nature responds.

We must go out of ourselves; we must go out of the mundane; we must go to God; we must see God in Christ reconciling the world unto himself, or we are as spiritual paupers. Bread for the soul is manna from heaven. Christ's blessing on what we have is essential to our hope and joy in God. Why did the common people hear Christ gladly? Why did Nicodemus seek an interview with Jesus and make the confession he did? And Agrippa with his throne for his earthly glory was almost persuaded to be a Christian. Christ is more than a scepter. Only Jesus Christ can say, "Thy sins are forgiven;" only he can be made unto us "wisdom, righteousness, sanctification, and redemption." Confucius had wisdom, Mohammed had policy, but Jesus Christ had infinite merit, and

> "In him all fullness dwelt,
> And all for wretched man."

And we may say,

> "Empty of him who all things fills,
> Till he his light impart,
> Till he his glorious self reveals,
> The veil is on my heart."

2. There is divine ability to secure increase.

God knows the springs of human action and how to reach them in order to produce the best results. God is as real in the power of grace as in the forces of nature. He can command facts with the individual, the family, the community, the nation, the world. These facts he can make tell according to his mind. Peter's vision on the housetop with all kinds of beasts shows Gentiles as well as Jews are to be saved. And when Jesus sent his apostles he said, "Go ye into all the world." Yes, there is power for all, mercy for all, fullness for all. God works "to will and to do of his good pleasure." Who shall set bounds to his influence and tell all the means and circumstances that he will subordinate to his purpose, and to our good? The Bible speaks his will. The Gospel tells his love. Prayer secures approach to him. The sheep is not too far in the wilderness for him to find, nor is the danger of its condition such as to detain the Son of God in seeking to save it. He may influence the prodigal to return to his Father's house, where the reception is ready and the provision is ample. It was the intense desire to secure our highest good that brought Christ from heaven and kept him on earth so long. To him what was the rancor of the Pharisees, the contempt of the scribes, the cruelty of Herod, the suppleness of Pontius Pilate, the treachery of Judas? In his coming to earth he brought life and immortality to light, and showed the eternal future as a fact to awe, to rouse, and to prompt to the proper action of dying man.

And the Father says: "Ask of me, and I shall give thee the heathen for thine inheritance, and the uttermost parts of the earth for thy possession." Daniel saw in "the night visions, and, behold, one like the Son of man came," "and there was given him dominion, and glory, and a kingdom, that all people, nations, and languages should serve him." And Jehovah says, "Surely the isles shall wait for me, and the ships of Tarshish first, to bring thy sons from far, their silver and their gold with them." "Thy gates shall be open continually." "The sons also of them that afflicted thee shall come bending unto thee; and all they that despised thee shall bow themselves down at the soles of thy feet."		.

And know ye not that God says, "Heaven and earth shall pass away, but my words shall not pass away."

To accomplish his purposes, fulfill his promise, and to show the subordination of all things to his power he has sometimes adopted means that we could not anticipate; and yet by his appointment they have been most efficient. He has planted the Church, opened the sacraments, and filled men for the very work to which he has called them. Sometimes, as in the case of Cyrus, who "meant it not so," he has been the Deliverer of his people. Do any ask, "Shall a nation be born in a day?" God only can answer that question. This we do say, "The Lord shall send the rod of thy strength out of Zion." Christ shall rule in the midst of his enemies. He "shall see of the travail of his soul, and shall be satisfied."

But the power that transcends all others is the Holy Spirit that enlightens, subdues, and sanctifies. This made Pentecost. This makes all true revivals. This preserves us blameless, and if we are "filled with the Spirit" one may "chase a thousand, and two put ten thousand to flight."

An illustration of the outpouring of the Spirit was seen in New York city in 1857. Twenty-seven banks closed in one day, and God so stirred the souls of the people that religion became the great interest of thousands who sought him, and of tens of thousands that were brought nearer to him. Noonday prayer meetings were held in the churches. Banking houses became the places of social prayer. Burton's Theater, then in Chambers Street, was made the resort of thousands who sought prayer, and many of whom found the Saviour. It was at that time that "the Fulton Street Prayer Meeting" originated. Who wonders if we thought of Revelation xx, 1, 2: "I saw an angel come down from heaven, having the key of the bottomless pit and a great chain in his hand. And he laid hold on the dragon, that old serpent, which is the devil, and Satan, and bound him a thousand years"? And who would not remember Joel ii, 28: "I will pour out my Spirit on all flesh; and your sons and your daughters shall prophesy"?

III. May not the facts of our day indicate the speedy and unexampled triumph of Christ?

It has been stated as a fact that "since the outgoing of the apostolic and subapostolic age there has been no such wave of God's light, no such magnificent sweep of worship, no such obedience to Christ's commission—on the two hemispheres—as in the last two generations. In the United States since the beginning of the Revolutionary War the increase of population has been elevenfold and the increase of churches thirty-sevenfold. The number of churches then was one to every seventeen hundred souls. Now it is one to six hundred souls. It seems that six churches are built every working day, and fifty millions of money are spent annually in objects connected with them. Besides, thirty-two millions of Bibles are printed and circulated every year" (Bishop Huntington's Bohlen Lectures, 89th page).

Let the earnest religion of such men as Brainard, William Bramwell, John Fletcher, appear; let the pulpit flame with the fire of "holiness to the Lord," as in the days of Benjamin Abbot; let laymen, like William E. Dodge, William and J. B. Cornell, offer money on God's altar, as well as their souls; let holy women, like Hester Ann Rogers and Adelaide Newton and Mrs. Palmer, work for the cause of the Redeemer with such examples as their lives furnished, and what may we not soon expect? Yes, yes, the world belongs to Christ. He redeemed it by his blood, and he calls all men to the enjoyment of his favor and to fitness for the kingdom of heaven.

O, sirs, if "the least in the kingdom of God is greater than John the Baptist" what may we not do? For what may we not hope in the near future? Like John Baptist, "sink self to exalt Christ!"

IV. The apostles of our Lord were confident of his "increase."

Look at Paul in energy, in faith, in self-sacrifice, in

self-oblivion; see him in his intensity of desire, in superiority to all obstacles, in the abounding, consuming love of his heart; hear him amid all difficulties and perils declare, "I can do all things through Christ which strengtheneth me." What can stand before such a man? And if we can judge Peter as he was at Pentecost, as he was at the house of Cornelius, can we not anticipate the final and complete glory of the cross? "These men" were the men to "turn the world upside down." Such men may still do the same. In classic Corinth, in Athens, in Philippi, in Rome, in idolatrous Ephesus, they gathered their trophies. In India, it is said, twenty thousand were converted to Christianity in one year; so Bishop Thoburn rejoices. In Africa Bishop Taylor has told the wonders of his work. In China and Japan we have seen and exulted in the grace of the Lord Jesus as displayed in the missionaries and their converts.

O, ought we not rejoice? "Robed in righteousness, radiant with beauty, and fired with energy divine," Christianity goes forth conquering and to conquer. The power seems cumulative. When we first entered Japan ten years were passed before three souls were converted. In the next ten years three thousand souls were brought to God. Yes, yes,

> "When he first the work begun,
>   Small and feeble was his day:
> Now the word doth swiftly run;
>   Now it wins its widening way."

O, what power is not at our command! If man is ever fully man, and woman is ever fully woman, if moral grandeur is ever to appear in human nature under the power of the grace of God, ought we not make a proper manifestation of it as workers for God and for the reward of millions of redeemed men now under the power of Satan? Alas that we do so little! John Hall said: "We raised five hundred thousand dollars for missions a year in one church, and we think it grand, yet it would hardly pay for the powder fired away every year in salutes to the distinguished of earth." What is a million dollars for Methodism? Think of eight hundred millions without the knowledge of God's Son.

I remark:

1. What are we individually doing to spread the Gospel among men?

2. What are we doing for increase in our own souls?

3. Think of the contrast of the world without God and the world with God in the abundance of his grace!

SERMON VI.

PAUL AND APOLLOS.

Who then is Paul, and who is Apollos, but ministers by whom ye believed, even as the Lord gave to every man? I have planted, Apollos watered; but God gave the increase. So then neither is he that planteth anything, neither he that watereth; but God that giveth the increase.—1 Corinthians iii, 5-7.

It was the wish of St. Augustine to have seen three things: "Rome in its glory, St. Paul in the pulpit, and Christ in the flesh." In neither of these could he be indulged. But in the text we see Paul in the best aspect of his character. If the carnal-minded disciples contended about the comparative claims of ministers, he saw that the latter were only as those who "plant and water," as those who dig and delve. They were nothing excepting as God used them. Any benefit through their instrumentality was to be regarded as properly coming from God. Pride springs from an earthly soil. Humility is a divine exotic. The true spirit of the man is before us. The "increase," which is the grand purpose of the laborer, is of Him who alone can save us.

Let us devoutly consider the facts here taught, that,

I. No distinction of talent, or assiduity of labor, can secure the success that the minister of the Gospel seeks.

II. No lack of ministerial power justifies doubt as to God's accomplishing his work.

We have here presented two of the most distinguished and diligent preachers of the word. Let us study them.

1. Paul.

Who was Paul? By birth, endowment, culture, citizenship, commission, and labor he was a remarkable man. He was by birth a Jew, a "Hebrew of the Hebrews," a student of law under one of the most renowned doctors of the day, and versed in the Jewish religion beyond most of his nation. He was a freeborn citizen of Rome. For a time he was a dire enemy of the Christians. His influence and rancor against them suggested him to the high priest as eminently fitted to be the leader in their persecution. The appointment was to his mind, for he "thought he ought to do many things contrary to the name of Jesus of Nazareth"—which things he also did.

While in the hot pursuit of his purpose, "breathing out threatening and slaughter," he was arrested by a Voice that he did not know; it was that of Jesus, whom he persecuted in his disciples. Prostrate before his Maker, with his spirit subdued and his rebellion conquered, his vengeful intent was succeeded by the deepest anguish. Three days of gloom attended his awakening, but pardon followed penitence. At once the Son of God gave him the highest commission—"to bear his name before the Gentiles, and kings, and the children of Israel." Christ sees in us more even than saints do. The disciples knew what Saul had been, but did not fully understand what he then was. The Saviour, however, assured them that he was a "chosen vessel," and should suffer many things for his sake. Paul lost no time in entering upon his work, in all the dignity and delight of his appointment.

As an ambassador of a nation is in his official relation more than in his personality, so Paul the apostle, as com-

missioned of Christ, was more exalted as the representative of God.

Let us think of Paul—

a) As to mind.

He had mental acuteness, compass, and vigor. He had
a memory well stored, tenacious, and ready. His judgment was a resource of strength. His will scaled mountains, crossed seas, dared dangers, if it did not invite martyrdom. He had an ambition for spiritual conquest equal
to that of Cæsar for military fame. He was remarkable
for his reasoning powers; and the chain of his thought was
formed by links that sophistry could not loosen nor violence
break. He kindled a fire in his logic that consumed the
"wood, hay, stubble" of false teachers. Besides, the inspiration of the Almighty kept before him things unseen
and eternal. Despite the disadvantages of his position,
he met superior minds with a moral majesty that swept
from under them all the foundations on which they stood.
The orator Tertullus felt the weakness of his own case;
Festus forgot himself; Felix, though a governor, trembled
as Paul reasoned; and King Agrippa was almost persuaded
"to be a Christian." The faculties of Paul were under discipline, and his resources were at his command. Thus he
was equal to any occasion, and superior to every adversary. Such was Paul as a man of mind.

b) His heart was equal to his head.

With God supreme in his affections, with all his passions
under control, he lived not unto himself, but unto Him
which died for him and rose again. The greatness of his
heart was next to that of his commission. Multitudes
with spiritual longings and aspirations turned to him for

16

hope; kings and nations found place in his soul; he declared himself a "debtor both to the Greeks, and to the Barbarians; both to the wise, and to the unwise." Despite the cruel treatment he received from many of the people, he declared he could wish himself "accursed from Christ for his brethren, his kinsmen according to the flesh." Who more than he resembled the Saviour of mankind, in self-sacrifice, suffering, and submission?

Paul had taste and tact and sympathy, and they fitted him for the best service in the work to which he was called. When the poet Cowper would describe the "faithful preacher" it was in the words, "such as Paul."

Who that admires sound doctrine and sterling character would not have been rejoiced in the ministration of such an one? Were he with us to-day would he not throng our churches, rouse our members, call home the prodigals, confound the skeptics, revolutionize the community, and fairly take perdition by storm? Would we not study his matter, admire his manner, commend his spirit? Would we not bring the frigid, that his zeal might warm them? Would we not seek the chronic complainers, that he might break up morbid associations? Would we not be tempted to do as some did in his day with his fellow-apostle Peter, bring "forth the sick into the streets, and lay them on beds and couches, that at the least" his "shadow might overshadow some of them"? Paul was great in preaching sermons, holding councils, writing epistles, and in doing all the work assigned him. By the seashore, or in the market place, to male and female, he had his message ready for the divine glory. He had a broad commission, and he filled every part. He could plant churches in any soil, and guard the seed from devouring fowls, of which then, as now, there were so many. He knew how to begin, and how to preserve his work. For breaking up the ground he had a subsoil plow, that made deep furrows in obdurate hearts.

But the one thing the agriculturist wants, and for which all else is intended, he could not give, namely, "increase."

Talk to the farmer about improved implements and the arts of husbandry as you may, he will value nothing so highly as the fruit of the soil. A full crop is his object; nothing else can take the place of that. Even "the king is served by the field;" and the faithful preacher is satisfied only by the highest moral results. Increase in the congregation, in collections, in influence, in the Church, and in the community, are things grateful to witness; but the supreme result he asks is "increase" in convictions, conversions, and the grace of God. This is his joy, and the lack of it is sometimes even his agony.

2. Apollos.

Apollos was a man of peace and power. He was a Jew, of Alexandria in Egypt, a place distinguished for great libraries and schools. Here were taught philosophy, poetry, logic, criticism, and eloquence; and of these advantages Apollos is supposed to have availed himself. Yet he was lacking in certain knowledge which the schools and libraries did not give. Good sense, however, marked his conduct, and he submitted himself to the instruction of Aquila and Priscilla, who taught him the way of God more perfectly. The Bible tells us he was "an eloquent man, and mighty in the Scriptures."

That which the Bible emphasizes justifies our study. Eloquence is here presented as a power in man to move others. Henry Clay said there was no power like the power of oratory. Cæsar conquered men by exciting their fears; Cicero by captivating their affections and swaying their passions. The influence of the one perished with the author; that of the other continues to this day. Speech is surely a tremendous power, when upon the breath of one hang with deepest interest the waiting thousands, who only stir as the orator moves them.

What secular eloquence has done the world's history has told us. If it has accomplished so much, with its theme, its spirit, and its utterance, what might we not expect as the result of divine eloquence—of that eloquence which God inspires?

If vastness of theme counts for anything; if weight of subject carries its influence, then should the sacred greatly surpass the secular. The one shows a world with eternal retributions for sin, and of endless rewards for holiness; the other tells of temporal ambitions, achievements, strivings, and failures. Apollos was an orator, who brought man face to face with the reality of the unseen and abiding; who told his hearers of death and of Him who could save from death.

Apollos was "mighty in the Scriptures;" that means not merely verbal might, but moral power. For the highest eloquence, what book compares with the Bible? The greatest orators of our day have drawn from its sacred pages ever the noblest illustrations for their secular themes, and from the fire it has kindled they have flamed in their influence. Think of the Bible as the fountain, for the purest streams that ever flow from human lips. Think of the words, the facts, and the spirit of the book. Think of

Isaiah in his glory, Jeremiah in his pathos, Ezekiel in his strength; of Moses as the sublimest of lawgivers; of Solomon in his wisdom; of David in his devotion. And can literature furnish more weighty sentences, or more mighty and subduing thoughts, than these: "The Word was made flesh," and "They crucified him"? What eloquence during nineteen centuries has ever transcended this, or what utterance, in its full import, has ever surpassed it?

For beauty, grandeur, and force one must go to the Bible, if he desires inspiration for himself or fascination for his hearers. Apollos was mighty in the Scriptures, because of the place they held in his esteem, in his devotion, and in his character. Can Ruskin, in his *Stones of Venice,* show finer word-painting than Job in his wonderful book? Such a question requires no answer. With the grandest themes, divinest vocabulary, and highest inspiration, surely the Christian orator has a wealth of material at his command, and has every advantage in the delivery of his message. We need not marvel, then, that Apollos triumphed over his captivated hearers. Doubtless he had much success and many adherents; otherwise we would not be told of his being "an eloquent man, and mighty in the Scriptures."

In Paul and Apollos we see two men of high mental attainment and of godly character, but also of strong individuality. They were not alike; their differences, however, added to their power; one was not a copy of the other.

Paul was mighty in logic, Apollos in eloquence. Paul convinced; Apollos captivated. Paul was a master builder; Apollos polished after the similitude of a palace. Yet the two, in themselves, lacked the "increase" power. They could not give the increase; and what was planting, or what was watering, without that? Paul excelled in planting, and Apollos doubtless in watering: but clearly they saw, deeply they felt, and candidly they confessed, the lack of what to them was most precious, and most sought after, namely, "increase." Yes, yes, Apollos could water as the faithful gardener, or as the gentle dew, or as the abundant shower; he could revive the fainting by words of hope and encouragement. Paul could argue and instruct; he could persuade and convince. But both lacked the supreme power, and saw that, excepting as Heaven helped them, "he that planteth is nothing, neither he that watereth, but God that giveth the increase."

The facts, as in the text inculcated by Paul, have been enough to impress men of greatest talent and earnestness with the thought that God is their sufficiency and only hope; that learning and human power must ever fall short of the grace which cometh down from on high.

But we come to the grand thought that,

II. No lack of ministerial power justifies doubt as to God's ability to accomplish his own work, and to give his own increase.

How many of God's faithful servants have been tempted to abandon their struggles—to give up their efforts—because of a seeming want of success! Even Moses, in a time of depression, exclaimed, "Lord, wherefore hast thou so evil entreated this people? Why is it that thou hast sent me?" Peter said, "I go a-fishing." He knew the nets, the waters, and the labor; but he was not prepared for failure in this new calling. Poor man! But listen. The other disciples said, "We also go with thee." Indeed!

Is the whole college, then, discouraged? O, who knows the temptation of the minister to leave the field—to give up the planting and the watering! Not for want of money. He can stand poverty and die, as one of the grandest bishops of Methodism did, without a dollar (Bishop Capers, after refusing a salary of thousands). All that he can stand, with persecution added; but want of fruit is the crushing, killing thing.

It is related of Narni, an Italian bishop, that he so preached that the people as they walked the streets exclaimed, "Lord, have mercy!" that in one week two hundred crowns were spent in self-invented penance; that when he preached before the pope, cardinals, and priests, he so represented the evils of nonresidence that forty priests went back to their cures; and that when in the pulpit of the University of Salamanca he induced eight hundred students to renounce the pleasures and honors of the world, and betake themselves to the different monasteries. But afterward, when the priests and people relapsed into indifference, Narni left the pulpit in despair. But O, sirs, God will help those who do their best. We go not a warfare at our own charges. Look at that same Peter, who was almost ready to give up in despair, who said, "I go a-fishing." Listen to him on the day of Pentecost. What might, what grace, what inspiration were there! So have we seen. Dr. Perkins once said, "Religion is at a low ebb in this place" (Smyrna, Del.); but almost immediately there fell two showers of revival and reformation that flooded the town, and six preachers came out of the scores converted. If God tarry, wait for him.

Let no one depreciate the earnestness of the trustful

minister, for God always does his part in saving men. He who commissioned Paul, and qualified Apollos, did it for appropriate service. What can take the place of the Gospel of God's dear Son? Art, science, learning, literature, have their office in the world; they refine and elevate society, but they do not bring pardon and peace and purity of heart. What makes the wilderness and the solitary places glad? Look and judge by those men once sunken in poverty through sin, who, under the conversion of the Gospel, have been raised to wealth and honor. Look and judge by those men once lost to earthly hope—those men that schools and colleges and society failed to reform, but who, through the preaching of the word, have been raised up and transformed.

God knows better than man what persons and what instrumentalities he shall employ. It is our joy that God works by us. Ask you, Who is Paul? The response is, One of the grandest men God ever gave to this globe. Let his epistles speak for him. Ask you, Who is Apollos? We answer, A priest of eloquence and a man to study. Ask you, Who is the faithful preacher? We reply, A man who, under the grace of God, might set the world on fire, remove its dross, and show it pure, noble, almost divine. What is he without God? A mere nothing. But what is a cipher without a unit? Put a unit in its proper place, and add ciphers, and it will finally show such millions as would make the Astors and the Vanderbilts ashamed. O, why should ministers and Christians yield to temptation and refuse to work?

Let us think of the reality, the certainty, the fullness, and the glory of the "increase." Amen.

SERMON VII.

Belshazzar.

In that night was Belshazzar the king of the Chaldeans slain.—Daniel v, 30.

Poor in the midst of affluence, humble amid the honors of a throne! Every king has his subjects, and Death has his subjects in all kings. There is a monarch higher than the highest of earth's sovereigns; there is a scepter that breaks all others to pieces. Place and power have their limitations, and the facts of the nearest future give no sign of their approach.

The feast in the context was royal, the assemblage mighty, the excitement intense, when forth from the wall came the fingers of a hand that wrote what a sovereign could not understand, but what immediately aroused his anxiety and his fears. Though he could not read it, it told of his wickedness, his judgment, and his doom. "In that night was Belshazzar the king of the Chaldeans slain."

Let us consider:

I. The facts the narrative furnishes; and,

II. The lessons they should impress.

1. Here is a royal feast in Babylon.

Babylon was the seat of the Chaldean empire, and was one of the most renowned cities of antiquity. Its foundation was early laid by Nimrod the mighty hunter. Under Nebuchadnezzar, Babylon became the seat of universal empire, and through him the city is supposed to have attained the magnitude and magnificence that made it one

of the wonders of the world. In his arrogance he said,
"Is not this great Babylon that I have built for the house
of the kingdom by the might of my power, and for the
honor of my majesty?" The least computation made
the city forty-five miles in circumference; Herodotus, an
eyewitness of its glories, says sixty miles. In this city
stood the Temple of Belus, or Jupiter, which some describe as a quarter and others half a mile square. It was
a species of pyramid composed of eight square platforms
placed one above another, diminishing in size as they approached the summit. The highest platform of all was
the observatory, by the help of which the Babylonians acquired such skill in astronomy.

It is stated that there Callisthenes, the philosopher, who
accompanied Alexander to Babylon, found observations
covering a period of nineteen hundred and three years—
extending back to within one hundred and fifteen years of
the flood.

At this period the city stood on both sides of the Eu-
phrates, and the eastern and western parts were connected
by a bridge. On either side of the river rose a palace.
That on the western bank was much the larger, and was
strongly fortified with three walls, one within another.
In these were the celebrated hanging gardens, consisting
of terraces, one sloping above the other till they were as
high as the walls of the city—the whole being eight miles
in compass. The entire city was surrounded by walls, as
some say, seventy-five feet high and thirty-two feet thick.
Herodotus says they were three hundred feet high and
seventy-five feet thick, which is deemed worthy of credit,
as the historian asserts six chariots could go abreast, or

that chariots of four horses could pass each other and turn.
These walls were encompassed by a broad and deep ditch
lined with bitumen. At the termination of the streets of
the city stood gates of brass, of ponderous size and strength.
Babylon was like a vast display of art, and also like a
great bulwark of nature. The French say, "There is no
France without Paris." There was no kingdom of the
Chaldeans without Babylon. Such was the city of this
feast.

Let us consider:

2. The sovereign and the occasion.

Belshazzar was a man who took great delight in occasions that were dissipating and demoralizing. The accounts we have of the king make him one of the proudest
and most voluptuous, one of the weakest and yet most
cruel, of monarchs. Xenophon says that he exercised his
barbarities upon some of the chief and most deserving of
his nobles; that he despised the Deity, and spent his time in
riot and debauchery. Isaiah xiv, 29, represents the Baby-
lonian dynasty as the scourge of Palestine; it styles Nebuchadnezzar a "serpent," Evil-merodach a "cockatrice," and
Belshazzar a "fiery flying serpent"—the last the worst of
all. It was once related of an old lady under the English
government that she prayed earnestly for the reigning
sovereign, though he was a very bad man. She was asked
how she could pray that the life of such a sinner should
be preserved. She replied that, being an old woman, she
had seen three kings; the first was a bad man, the second
was worse, and the third, the reigning monarch, was worst of
all; and she prayed that he might live, lest the devil himself should be his successor. Of such kind seems to have

been the succession in Babylon. Belshazzar was a moral
monster. His name was the synonym of arrogance, idolatry, and crime. Solomon says, "The name of the wicked
shall rot," but the stench of this king remains.

One of his daring deeds and idolatrous acts is set forth
in the context. The palace was a blaze of illumination.
A brilliant retinue surrounded the king. There were a
thousand lords, with their wives and concubines. According to Xenophon, the custom of having females at a
feast was peculiar to Babylon; it was unknown to other
nations.

Things at the feast of Babylon were to the monarch's
taste. He, of course, was the center of every eye, the honored of every voice. Interest was there to flatter, and
sycophancy was there to fawn. To add to the hilarity of
the occasion, the intoxicating cup was desired. Abundance of
wine was at hand, and for its consumption the king commanded to be brought the gold and silver vessels which his
father Nebuchadnezzar had taken from the temple at Jerusalem; and from them the king, his wives, and concubines
drank, in profanation of their use, and in disdain of the
God of Israel. While they drank they "praised the gods
of gold, and of silver, of brass, of iron, of wood, and of
stone"—every god but the true God.

"Reverence my sanctuary," says Jehovah. Of this the
altar is the most sacred place, the vessels the most holy
things of the altar. "Be ye clean that bear the vessels of
the Lord" is the divine command. Then what thunder
will be heavy enough for this temerity? Surely the light-
nings will not always play. The clouds will not forever
hold back the bolt that vengeance demands, and when the

bolt falls it will rend and tear, and grind to pieces. To the impious we may justly say, "Beware lest he take thee away with his stroke."

3. God's demonstration.

Amid this scene of gayety and guilt, when the heart of the king was lifted up in the midst of orgies that would exclude any thought of death, forth came the "fingers of a man's hand." The king saw the part of the hand that wrote—he saw not behind it. But God, who writes on the "plaster," writes also on the "fleshly tables of the heart." The king, who knew not the words, felt what they meant. Conscious guilt is something of an interpreter. The king's countenance was changed. His thoughts troubled him. His knees smote one against the other. In his fright he called for the Chaldean soothsayers and astrologers. They gave no help; for "the secret of the Lord is with them that fear him." Finally, Daniel was called. He is equal in knowledge and fidelity to the occasion. He reminds the king of the facts of a former reign; then calls up Belshazzar's sins, interprets the writing, and foretells the doom. He disdains the king's tempting offer, but shows him the mind of God. "In that night," so full of earthly splendor and of human guilt, "was Belshazzar king of the Chaldeans slain."

While the feast was in the fullness of its gayety, and at the height of its glory, two divisions of Cyrus's army marched into the city, one from each end. Having turned the course of the river, they took the channel, and, finding the gates of brass, intended to bar entrance from the river into the streets, left open through the carelessness and intoxication of the besieged, they met, and, marching into the heart of the city without opposition, surprised the palace before alarm could be given or resistance made. Having broken in, and slain Belshazzar, they proclaimed peace and safety to all who would lay down their arms. Thus the empire was ended with little bloodshed. So fell this mighty monarch. His eyes were closed, his tongue was silent, his arm was powerless.

Fancy the scene! But what imagination is equal to it?

> "With festive mirth resounds the regal dome,
> And luxury bedecks the banquet on the throne.
> Exalted, the proud Belshazzar sits; around
> A thousand nobles watch his envied smile,
> And on his ear more grateful than the sound
> Of heavenly music, tarnishing the soul,
> Breathe adulation bland; pride swells his heart,
> And in derision of Jehovah's name,
> The God of captive Israel, from the stores
> The consecrated vessels he commands,
> The spoil of Sion's temple. Yet forbear,
> Ere the full measure of thy sins o'erflow
> And rouse up slumbering vengeance! No, 'tis done!
> See the base herd of fawning sycophants,
> See the lewd train of wanton concubines,
> Taint with polluted lips the hallowed gold.
> And as they quaff the intemperate juice, extol
> Their idol god. What means that sudden start?
> Why drops the untasted goblet from his lips,
> And flies the color from his death-pale cheek,
> Trembles his frame, convulsed, and on yon wall
> His streaming eyes fixed motionless? Ah! there
> The hand of heaven in mystic characters
> Portrays his fall. From Elam, God hath called
> His servant, and the slaughtering sword no more shall
> Join the peaceful scabbard, until its charge
> Appointed, ends."

Behold, consider, and be made wise by the death of one of the haughtiest and most confident of men.

II. Some lessons from the narrative I would God that I had the mental and the moral power to impress.

1. When Massillon saw the death of his sovereign, Louis XIV, and beheld the demonstration in the grand temple where he was to speak to the mighty of the land — after standing in silence in the presence of an almost breathless assembly — he exclaimed, "Only God is great."

What is Belshazzar now? What is any dead sinner? The rods of God's anger are soon broken. "The hammer of the whole earth," the sovereigns of mankind, are as nothing before the Omnipotent. All the dead may say, "Art thou also become weak as we?" The living say, "Is this the man that made the earth to tremble?" Sirs, God will make us know that the Most High ruleth in the kingdom of men. Sirs, believe it, rivers and walls and fancied fortresses do not keep out God from a palace when he chooses to enter.

Death waits not our convenience, nor heeds our protest. He comes to us amid our brightest hopes, and in the scenes of our greatest delight—in the theater, where all is gay; in the church, where all is devout; at the marriage feast, to the sound of music; upon the bridal tour, or amid the summer's joy. Full of anticipation, the father leaves Washington with his son just at the opening of his vacation, and at Elkton on his journey meets death, where he had hoped for the face of friends. Great God, impress our hearts! Where has not death met men?

2. Are we ready for the final summons?

Alas, how many are no more prepared for death than was Belshazzar! Think of Jezebel, the queen, cast from the palace window! Think of King Herod, as the oration was warm on his lips, and the people cried, "It is the voice of a god!"

We have no throne. But are there no gods that we worship? none of gold? none of silver? none of flesh and blood? Yes, yes, there are still among us those who live in pleasure and are wanton. Join you never in scenes of dissipation, and in deeds of oppression? Sit you never in Mammon's temple? Bow you at no shrine but that of Jehovah? What if, in the night of thy loneliness and moral apprehension, thy spirit should move, and the hair of thy flesh stand up? What if, when thou art looking upon the desire of thine eyes and the pride of thy heart, thou shouldst feel the hand of death ready to strike thee powerless? What if, when quaffing the sparkling bowl, the poison should begin to circulate through thy system, and ere another day thy time should cease? What if, when thy passions burn and fury is in command, thou shouldst come to the end of all thy earthly hopes? What if, in the disaster by fire, by flood, by railroad or steamboat, God should call, and thy soul should be required?

May we not say that nothing could have been more unexpected or abhorrent than the death of Belshazzar in the place and prospect of the hour? May we not say,

> "He fondly dreamt his throne
> Through time's vast ages should endure,
> Fixed and unshaken as the solar orb.
> Vain boast! What is the city's towered strength
> Unless the Lord uphold it?"

O, what a speedy judgment upon Belshazzar in the night of his unholy revel! He goes from the sound of the viol and the mirth of the profane to the agony of the convicted and the shriek of the condemned—from robes of royalty to the winding sheet of fire—from fawning sycophants to accusing spirits—from the aspirations of a prince to the realization of a lost soul. Death strips the King of the Chaldeans as readily as if he was a poor man.

O, believe us,

> "There is a death, whose pang
> Outlasts the fleeting breath:
> O what eternal horrors hang
> Around the second death!"

3. Let no one say men have not sufficient warning of the consequences of sin.

God had said, "Babylon, the glory of kingdoms," the beauty of the Chaldeans' excellency, should be as when he "overthrew Sodom and Gomorrah;" that "the Arabian should not pitch his tent there, neither should the shepherds make their fold there, but wild beasts of the desert should lie there, and their houses should be full of doleful creatures." Nineveh, when threatened, repented; Babylon and Belshazzar did not. God says to every sinner, "O, wicked man, thou shalt surely die!"

4. Do any of us hold positions of honor or responsibility that make us forget our relation and duty to God? Is it politics, speculations, employments, riches, or poverty that induce forgetfulness of the coming of the Son of man? The manner of death is nothing; the readiness to meet it is all. The good man is prepared for any death. Water may drown him, fire may burn him, he may languish on the bed

17

of sickness, and wearisome nights may be appointed him, but in any case "to die is gain." The sinner, on the other hand, is never ready; and to him death is the eternal loss of all things.

Say, then, will you be a Daniel, in his purity to know and tell God's secrets; or a representative of the spirit of a Belshazzar, and with him suffer for your guilt? May the Almighty help you to make a wise choice! Amen.

SERMON VIII.*

THE VALLEY OF DRY BONES.

The hand of the Lord was upon me, and carried me out in the spirit of the Lord, and set me down in the midst of the valley which was full of bones,

And caused me to pass by them round about: and, behold, there were very many in the open valley; and, lo, they were very dry.

And he said unto me, Son of man, can these bones live? and I answered, O Lord God, thou knowest.

Again he said unto me, Prophesy upon these bones, and say unto them, O ye dry bones, hear the word of the Lord.

Thus saith the Lord God unto these bones; Behold, I will cause breath to enter into you, and ye shall live:

And I will lay sinews upon you, and will bring up flesh upon you, and cover you with skin, and put breath in you, and ye shall live; and ye shall know that I am the Lord.

So I prophesied as I was commanded: and as I prophesied, there was a noise, and behold a shaking, and the bones came together, bone to his bone.

And when I beheld, lo, the sinews and the flesh came up upon them, and the skin covered them above: but there was no breath in them.

Then said he unto me, Prophesy unto the wind, prophesy, son of man, and say to the wind, Thus saith the Lord God; Come from the four winds, O breath, and breathe upon these slain, that they may live.

So I prophesied as he commanded me, and the breath came into them, and they lived, and stood up upon their feet, an exceeding great army.—Ezekiel xxxvii, 1-10.

THE moral desolation of a great and honored people is one of the most painful thoughts that can be entertained. To this the text calls us, and we must seek the profit that

---

* After preaching on this text in Allen Street, New York, October, 1857, there was a revival, in which two hundred and twenty-five souls professed conversion.

it yields. The striking symbols and graphic expressions of this prophet are familiar to our minds. Ezekiel sees, and he makes us see. His figures so forcibly show facts and call us to duty that we may not decline. The bones of the house of Israel are dry and many. The oriental mind clothes itself in language appropriate to its thought, and allows little doubt as to its meaning. The inheritance of Israel was gone, their temple was defiled, their glory had departed, and their political condition was servile and abject. The text may have a broader application to the "gathering of the Jews now as a nation scattered and dead; to the souls of vast multitudes dead in sin; and to the final resurrection of all who sleep in the grave." Cyrus had place and power in the recovery of Israel, and God only can be our hope, by his Spirit, to do what the text commands.

Let us consider:

I. The spectacle presented.

II. The duty imposed.

III. The assurance given.

I. The spectacle presented—a valley full of dry bones. A revolting sight! Bones, the solids of the physical economy, are the last remains of the mortal part. The description represents the moral condition when all vitality is gone. In the text they are "dry;" thus it is with the human soul "dead in trespasses and sin." These bones are in the open valley. Rains wash them, suns burn them, winds waste them. Among the Jews an unburied corpse was a reproach. Here the bones are exposed in an open field, and the valley is full of them. Israel was in multitude like the stars of heaven; they are now scattered, as "when one cleaveth wood." Thus it is with Jew and Gentile when

grace does not animate.   Then what field is broad enough
to show them fully?   Where are they not found?   Ascend
the highest mountain, explore the widest continents, visit
the remotest islands, circumnavigate the globe, behold
heathendom in its hundreds of millions, nor fail to look
upon that part of the valley that stretches around us.
What millions have no proper realization of the God who
made them, of the Christ who redeemed them, and of the
Holy Spirit that cleanses the soul!   How much better are
they for the Bible they have, for the sanctuaries of worship,
for the Sabbath to give them special seasons for holy
service?   Not a pulse moves; not a heart pulsates.   The
morally dead in our streets are more in number than those
in the "cities of the dead."   Those that sin as Sodom, and
that promise no more than Gomorrah—they are not only
at Five Points, but in Fifth Avenue.

To this abhorrent spectacle God calls us in the text.
Ezekiel says, "He set me down in the valley."   Necessary
though painful position!   A visit to Central Park may be
more to our taste than one to Greenwood, but may not yield
as great a profit.   When Dr. Duff, the great Scottish missionary to India, was here, the ladies of Philadelphia desired him to speak at the largest hall in the city in behalf
of the Bedford Street Mission, answering to the Five Points
Mission in New York.   To have the proper feeling for the
occasion, he went to the scene of labor, and then, in his
great address in Concert Hall, he said, "I know whereof I
speak.   I have seen it with my own eyes."   God called the
prophet to go and see.   What ruins compare with those
of the "temple of the Holy Ghost"?   What an appeal do
they make where there is a heart to feel!   So, like "dry

bones," are some that it might be thought they were never vital. They throng our streets, crowd our homes, fill our parks, and in the surging, sweeping tides see you none in church fellowship? O, think, this rushing stream will soon pour into the ocean of eternity!

The searching inquiry, "Can these dry bones live?" Tremendous question! But God asks it, and we must answer, and the world must see. Consider what is comprehended in the inquiry! It is not whether a crooked limb can be straightened; science often does that. It is not whether a broken bone can be set so as to knit; surgery is equal to that. It is not whether a dislocation can be overcome, or a stiffened joint can be made supple. It is not whether resuscitation can be effected when animation has seemed to cease. Education, science, and skill have often satisfactorily answered these questions. It is not an inquiry whether depravity in a Christian can be removed, or a heart like an iceberg warm and melt. This, to the glory of God, we can see any day. But the question is whether such "bones" as are in that valley can ever live? God, who as no other knows the case, asks us, "Can these dry bones live?" Did we judge from the failure of men to show their real dignity, or from the efforts and results of the schools, we should say, No! no! The principle of life is gone, and it would be like making them over without a foundation to build on.

This would seem to preclude hope. Despite the best conditions of life they died. To the worst conditions they have been exposed. Amid multiplied miracles they have remained dead.

Look at Egypt, with all its learning, cleaving to idols, such as crocodiles, dogs, and cats. Lycurgus, as legislator, failed to purify the religion of the Spartans. The Chinese philosopher, Confucius, with all his morality and refinement, could impart no purity to his people; and Socrates, with the depth of his knowledge and the might of his character, could not save himself; and Cicero, with all his eloquence, could not change the manners or religion of the Romans; and Israel said, in sadness, "Our bones are dried up, our hope is lost; we are clean cut off." Civilization may shed a luster over our names, may give refinement to our intercourse and grandeur to our earthly achievements; we may have profound thinkers, able writers, brave soldiers, and renowned statesmen; but what vitalizes a dead soul but the grace that is in Christ Jesus? Has not civilization had the climax of its hopes in directing all our powers to the best results in our earthly condition and needs? Time enough has elapsed since Adam fell. Countries enough and governments of sufficient variety have exerted themselves to show any power they had to "wash the Ethiopian white." What country has done it? What legislation has shown the just moral elevation of man in the restoration of the likeness that Adam lost?

Nay, under the very droppings of the sanctuary unsanctified men have remained unsanctified, excepting only as they have looked farther and higher than earth.

> "O! dark, dark, they still may say
> Amid the blaze of Gospel day."

There are human beings with capacious minds and noble thoughts who for years have not felt a zephyr, or for a moment been warmed by the Spirit of God. Some of them to-day are beginning to think there is no such thing as the grace to purify and save. They weep under no sermon, feel under no prayer, and are roused by no exhortation; death in the family, their own sickness, hardly makes an impression. They are so unlike men that you might call them marble. The reasonings of the logician, the demonstrations of the deep thinker, the ardor of the minister in the sacred desk, all fail to restore the soul. That splendid scholar and worthy man, Henry Martyn, gave his life to mission work abroad and mourned over his want of success. O, sirs, "Can these dry bones live?" might shake us like an earthquake, and the fear that they cannot live is enough to make a moral universe shudder! "I answered, O Lord God, thou knowest." Only God knows!

II. The duty imposed. "He said unto me, Prophesy." Doubt, ignorance are not to influence us. But the command of God is to be followed in the face of any power, or as hindered by any influence. God's command always implies possibility. It means hope as well as obedience. If the wild olive can be grafted in, if of "stones God can raise up children unto Abraham," then dead members may be quickened, dead churches may feel a resurrection power, and communities and nations may present new and better aspects. They are all in the sweep of God's arm. O, believe us, God can gather the merest fragments of our moral nature and make a symmetrical moral whole. When little of conscience is left, when we fear the light of intelligence is well-nigh extinguished with regard to religion, when little trace of mortal and moral manhood is left, when we think of men as "trees twice dead and plucked up by the roots," yet even these wonders of mercy and might have been witnessed.

The late Samuel Halsted told of the conversion of an old man at Mamaroneck, whose very presence was next to disgusting, and of whom a minister, when asked for help to his moral condition, so sunk in sin, declared, "I can do nothing for him." He got into a great revival, and was brought into liberty from all his vices, and where death had reigned in all his members, life now appears in the full exercise of all his powers for the Lord of hosts.

The difficulties of the case are not with us. We are to "obey orders" and "prophesy." These, then, are the bones of a once cherished orthodoxy; but the firmness is gone. These are all the "dry bones" of a once robust manhood; but the relation to Jehovah has ceased. God says, Prophesy! Preach to them! Preach as if they had ears to hear. Impress truth. Inspire confidence. Say, "O earth, hear the word of the Lord"—though it is like talking to tombstones. Talk on. Tell them God lives, that the Spirit helps, that all things are possible to him that believeth. Tell them what they may, by hearing, escape of final woe; what, by proper hearing, they may at last secure in the presence of God and with holy angels. Remind them of the earliest offer of mercy to Jerusalem sinners, and tell them Christ wept over the city that he could not save. Tell them, All is not lost. Cry, Repent! Repent! Repent! Urge to prayer, to faith, to all holy obedience; make haste to do it, for time is short.

III. God's full assurance of the happy results of our fidelity. "Behold, I will cause breath to enter into you, and you shall live: and I will lay sinews upon you, and will bring up flesh upon you, and cover you with skin, and put breath in you, and ye shall live; and ye shall know that

I am the Lord." What more could be imagined? Is not this full recovery? Sinews, flesh, skin, and breath. That tells of life restored. Such results justify the prophesying, "God is able." So I prophesied, and the valley of dry bones became vital, a moving, mighty mass. We can think of the political changes, through Cyrus, to the Jews; and there was "noise" as they returned from Babylon. "Then was our mouth filled with laughter, and our tongue with singing: then said they among the heathen, The Lord hath done great things for them." Sirs, God's work makes a "shaking" among "dry bones" as really as in the mulberry trees. When victory is to crown conflict there must be noise. There was noise when Philip preached in Samaria. There was noise when, under the ministry of Paul, the "silver shrines" and the idolatry of Ephesus started men up for what they were about to lose. There was noise when Martin Luther became "the solitary monk that shook the world." Thus, too, it was when John Wesley saw the need of England.

Vitality has its degrees. There are lower forms of life in animal existence. It is so in piety as we see and learn it. As sinews are necessary to articulation, and the loins and muscles for locomotion, and flesh for circulation of the vital fluid, and skin to cover all, so the wind of the Spirit must be breathed for moral life into sinners as truly as breath was breathed into Adam's form. What is the body with all its members, however majestic and symmetrical, if the soul be not there? God shows his power in the elements presented. "The four winds" are to exert their power and secure the result. Pentecost had fire to warm, and melt and exalt in the tongues employed. There was, too, "a rushing, mighty wind." The wind is one of the greatest forces in nature, and Christ speaks of the work of the Spirit as resembling the wind that "bloweth where it listeth." What is the wind on the ocean? What is the wind on the forest? It is, in the moral world, like a tornado that carries everything in its course. With no thunder to alarm, no lightning to rend, it comes to invigorate and make dead souls live. O, think of the power that the wind of the Spirit gives, and of the contrast in the valley of dry bones; and think of God's means for effecting the change. The dead live, and bones show men real, vital, mighty, because God is in them of a truth—men clothed with flesh, endowed with reason, and fit for any service. Think of the contrast. Behold, admire, and confess the grandeur of the moral transition. Think of a vast battlefield where host sustained the charge of host, and crowns were staked and won; where lay the warrior with cloven helmet and broken spear; where bird and beast held carnival; but where now every eye opens, every heart warms, every hand is ready to grasp and every arm is strong to wield the sword for noblest conquest. The army moves with the majestic tread of the new creation, and all the force of souls filled with God.

O, think of a live church, alive in every member, alive in every part! It is the sacramental host of God's elect. This, this is the army that the Captain of our salvation commands, bloodless in victories but grand in purpose, plans, and achievements. You see no dancing plume, no gleaming spear, no slaughtering sword. "The weapons of our warfare are not carnal, but mighty through God to the pulling down of strongholds."

Live Christians, you see your work. You were once "dead in trespasses and sins;" now you are alive, and alive for what? For mental alertness, for vigorous action, for marching orders, for the moral conquest of the world. Look around and behold the world of living souls—souls alive to God's honor, alive to the deepest wants of our immortal nature. Depravity is not too great to be removed. Rebellion is not too violent to be conquered. The night is not so dark that God cannot cause light to blaze through it. O, listen to God. "I will cause breath to enter into you." The bloom as of Eden may cover the cheek. The energy as of paradise at first, may distinguish the action. The Almighty says, "O, my people, I will open your graves and bring you into the land of Israel, and ye shall know that I am the Lord."

Then, who will doubt the resurrection power at the last day, or who will say God may not gather the Jews? Whatever may be the case with others, let us be alive in every power God has given us.

SERMON IX.

EXCUSES.

And they all with one consent began to make excuse. The first said unto him, I have bought a piece of ground, and I must needs go and see it: I pray thee have me excused.— St. Luke xiv, 18.

MEN who decline duty are the ready apologists for their conduct. The context tells of a "certain man who made a great supper, and bade many: and sent his servant to say, Come; for all things are now ready." Moved by the same spirit, one after another said, in the words of the text, "I pray thee have me excused." Language this which expresses intensity of feeling and determination of mind, while there was a cherished wish that they might seem free from blame. So the Jews received Christ's messengers and treated his Gospel. We use this supper to represent the Gospel feast to which all among us are invited. The same disposition and conduct, however, mark some that this man that made a great supper encountered. We shall endeavor to notice their treatment of the Gospel invitation, and show that sinners, though ingenious to construct and importunate to plead excuses for delaying Christian duty, are, nevertheless, inexcusable.

We shall notice some excuses and their insufficiency:

1. There are difficulties pleaded in reference to matters of faith. One says: "I don't understand the Bible, the source of your faith, and therefore know not what to believe. Besides, my difficulty is enhanced by the fact that there is such diversity of belief among those calling themselves Christians." He is ready to say, "I believe that the

Bible is a book of many literary beauties, and that its moral precepts are incomparably excellent." Thomas Paine would confess the wisdom of the Sermon on the Mount. When the person wishing to be excused says he does not understand the Bible, what does he mean? that its depths are too profound? that its heights are too exalted? that its breadth is too vast for his intellect? Is it wonderful that an infinite mind should not be comprehended by one that is finite? Is there any great science in relation to which there is not something that you cannot comprehend? Can you fully grasp gravitation? Are not physical and metaphysical truths continually puzzling, perplexing, if not confounding us? Our frame—think of its delicate structure, its strange purposes, adaptations. Read Sir Charles Bell's Bridgewater Treatise on the arm and hand. Study the eye. Should you see the body as it is sometimes studied you would be almost afraid to move, lest the nerves, the vessels, the different parts of the system, by a jar or an irregular motion, would be thrown out of play. When you think of the accidents, the diseases, the multiplied and multiform avenues of nature, you would feel that it is "strange that a harp of a thousand strings should keep in tune so long." Did you know the human body as the physiologist presents it, in the elements of its formation, the sources of its being, and the origin of life itself, then you would say with David, "I am fearfully and wonderfully made: marvelous are thy works; and that my soul knoweth right well."

Dr. Samuel Judson, of Pennsylvania University, was one of the ablest physiologists of his day. On one occasion, when addressing a class of nearly five hundred, he came to a question as to the human organism; though it had been his study for forty years, he candidly said, "I don't know." Is it wonderful, then, that we should find some difficulties in the vast system of revelation?

But when he says he "does not know what to believe," what does the objection mean? Does he not know what the Bible teaches as to sin in this world—that it began in Eden, that in Eden it caused the ground to be cursed and man to be an offense to God, that Christ died for the sins of the world, and that in him we are made alive? Does he not understand that except we "repent we shall all likewise perish"? that "without holiness no man shall see the Lord"? that man's great duty is to "love God with all the heart"? We say to the sinner, "He hath showed thee, O man, what is good; and what doth the Lord require of thee, but to do justly, and to love mercy, and to walk humbly with thy God?" You speak of the differences among Christians as to belief. And is there no difference among scientists as to belief of theories? Is there never a difference among physicians as to disease? Is there never a difference among jurists in relation to points of law? Is there never a difference among statesmen and presidents with regard to administration, though they be of the same party? Is that a reason why science should be ignored? why medicine and law and government should be spurned and neglected?

Then, I ask, what is the difference among Christians? There are various denominations. Why? Often it is a simple question of Church government. Take any of the evangelical denominations, and see if they do not agree in the great essentials of religion—as when rebellion broke out the loyal States were one on the question of union. For example, do they not all say, "Ye must be born again"—"must love God with all the heart"? Do they not all agree that "without holiness no man shall see the Lord"? Ah! say you, right there, there is a great difference; some are fighting about holiness, and others say it is preposterous. I doubt not much of our difference upon this subject is in the use and understanding of Methodists. Methodists teach we may be saved from all sin in this life. Some others say we can't live without sin. What do you suppose they mean? That we can't live without the sin of adultery? No. Of drunkenness? No. Of stealing? No. They would turn a man out of the Church for it. Take the Protestant Episcopal Church. Does it not pray, "Cleanse the thoughts of our hearts by the inspiration of thy Holy Spirit, that we may perfectly love thee and worthily magnify thy holy name"? Methodism teaches no more. Do not other Churches teach that we are called on to repent of our acts of wickedness? that "the remembrance of them is grievous unto us"? Why? Does an engine ever shed a tear for running over a man and cutting off his limb? Does a locomotive weep for having killed somebody? Why not? It is mere matter, and can't do anything to be sorry for. Does a lion ever feel sorry for having torn a man to pieces, or does any beast repent for the indulgence of its passion or its appetite? But all Christianity teaches us to be sorry for sin. David shed many tears. All teach we must be holy, and we who teach you must be holy—must still use the Lord's Prayer, "Forgive us our trespasses, as we forgive those who trespass against us." The holiest man may trespass for want of knowledge. I may this moment be trespassing upon your patience and tempt your displeasure at the course and length of my argument. Yet I assure you it is not my design. Do not say, then, the differences of Christians keep you back from the feast. Do not say that you have not knowledge enough. Listen to the child's prayer, and see in it the elements of the system of faith that you surely understand well enough to be saved: "Now I lay me down to sleep; I pray the Lord my soul to keep." Then there is a Lord! Yes. He is our Keeper! Yes. "If I should die before I wake, I pray the Lord my soul to take." Then I have a soul. Then God takes it, or the enemy may, and I pray the Lord to take it. "All I ask for Jesus' sake." My prayer to God for my soul is through Jesus Christ! Sirs, there is enough sound theology in that prayer to make the most desolate island light in the Lord—enough to make the coldest hearts in heathendom glow with the fires of God's altar. My friend, you can't be excused on the ground of difficulty as to matters of truth, for in his "light you see light," and "wayfaring men though fools shall not err therein."

2. Some desire to be excused on account of the character of certain professors. They say, "Though I believe the Bible, the people who profess religion are no better than others, and whenever I think of the doctrine, the example of Christianity is a stumbling-block. There are many not in the Church just as good and even better than many in it." Let us look at your excuse. Do you make a fair comparison? If you say some in the world are as good as some in the Church, I agree with you. I will even say better. But what are you doing? Comparing the best you know in the world with the worst you know in the Church! Is that

18

fair? There is a man; he is moral, humane, kind in his family, a true patriot, and one of the most influential men in the community. Grant it. In all that goes to make up a citizen of this world he seems to be everything. But how about the world to come? Is there an experience of looking not at the things seen but the things unseen? Has man a nature for religion? Has he any of this spirit that is from above? I will find you many a man in the Church as kind to his family, as patriotic, and who, besides, will tell you, "I know I am of God. I know old things are passed away. I know that for me to live is Christ, and to die is gain." He will tell you of a love, of a peace, of a joy that the other knows not. Does he not live on a higher plane? Is he not possessed of a nobler nature?

Are you sure that you argue justly? You must remember, "The kingdom of heaven is like unto a net that was cast into the sea and gathered of every kind." Some taken in the Gospel net are poor fish when taken. They are persons, in some instances, of many vices and few advantages. Some were ignorant, rude, accustomed to demoralizing associations; and what if when brought into the Church you find them wanting in many things that religion does not impart? It doesn't always give refined manners, good education—or make one free from all mistakes. But you say, "There are even hypocrites! They join the Church to obtain notice that they would not otherwise receive, and to accomplish ends they could not in any other way reach!" No doubt of it. But is that a reason for you? Are hypocrites confined to the Church? Robert Hall was of the opinion that as some profess more religion than they have, so are there hypocrites in infidelity, that profess more unbelief than they feel. They may after a while get to "believe a lie." But they assume; they let on; and sometimes they show their insincerity. In sickness how do they repent? Are there no false men in politics, in medicine, in law? Is there, then, no statesmanship? no real science and government? Will you give all these up? I have known a man so deeply convicted that he could hardly keep from the altar, and at the same time he would declare he had no feeling, to induce the pastor to leave him. Come now, be honest. Do you not expect too much of some men? Is it not much like looking at a piece of statuary designed for a tower two hundred and fifty feet in height? From that elevation if it is to appear of the natural size it must be much larger than nature. So must some appear to others from the point where they view them. Yes, "Distance gives enchantment to the view," and nearness and familiarity sometimes take off respect. We must remember, "The best of men are but men at best." Hypocrisy, like a false issue of a bank, supposes there is the good.

I close this aspect by the question, Have you never known a single good man? a single holy woman? one that you believed had real religion? "O, yes!" say some, "my mother had." Say others, "My father had." Say others, "I have a son like the sainted John." And others, "My wife was almost an angel!" What made them so? Religion. Then there is a real religion? Yes. Get that. You have known some such; I have known some you have not known, and could I show them to you, you would believe in them as much as I. Whence their goodness? Not mere nature. "There is none righteous, no, not one." But human beings these. Then, O Christianity! these are the testing of thy reality, and the proofs of thy power, and the demonstration of Deity in man—God in us of a truth, turning out all that offends and making us meet for "the inheritance of the saints in light." Go to your natural religion for such arguments as these, forsooth! Sirs, we call on you not to be hypocrites, not to be formalists. We call on you to be "the sons of God without rebuke." That others are not so is our grief, is our humiliation. But this can never be used against the great feast. Say you, "I pray thee have me excused"? Look at the facts, and surely a man of your intellect, possessing your candor, with all the advantages of your mental and moral culture, ought never ask God's servant to have him excused. There is the feast. The food is good, the provision ample. Jesus Christ came down from heaven to provide it, and it is your own fault if you do not "take and eat and live forever."

3. Others ask to be excused because of the opposition they encounter in the way. True, you will have to take up a cross. You may be "hated for his name's sake." A parent may oppose; a companion may persecute. No man ever became good without effort. Christ knew what cost means when he left heaven to redeem us. He had his cradle in the manger. He suffered in the agony of the garden and the death of the cross; and he said, "If they have persecuted me they will also persecute you." And are you hoping for heaven without a tear, a pang, a persecution? Because you can't go to heaven on flowery beds of ease, then you will not go! Because you can't be a soldier without fighting you will not be a soldier! Because you can't reach a throne without a conflict you will give it up! "I pray thee have me excused." Now, say, will par-

don come without prayer, till purity is attained without effort? But because of opposition, or shame, how many young people—old people—are staying away from Christ?

4. Still others plead the magnitude of their cares as sufficient reason for excuse. Men in this world have business. They must provide for their own. This means work, vigilance, constancy. But what is the work that prevents piety? May not a good man "be diligent in business"? May not a good man be a lawyer, like Joseph of Arimathea? Has not a good man been a legislator, like Moses? May not a good man be a physician, like the "beloved Luke"? May not a good man cultivate fields and raise flocks, like Abraham? May not a devout man sit upon the throne, like David? Have me excused to be industrious, frugal, honest! If you have too much business for your time or health, reason, as truly as religion, says give up some of it. Can you wish to be excused that you may rob the fatherless, take advantage of the widow, oppress the homeless, and harm the abject? Have me excused that I may make a sharp bargain, or take from my neighbor his good name! Have you excused for that? But look at the context, and judge the validity of the excuse. One said, "I have bought a piece of ground, and I must needs go and see it." Indeed! and had he bought it without seeing it? Any Christian could have done business as well as that. Another said, "I have bought five yoke of oxen, and I go to prove them." And so had he bought them without trying them? A Christian of ten years could have done as well as that. Yet both of these said, "I pray thee have me excused." The third said, "I have married a wife, and therefore I cannot come." Curiosity was

pleaded by the others. This pleads impossibility. From the days of Adam a great many things have been said against "the women whom Thou gavest," but when with less reason than in the text? I think there is no proof that he could not have come and brought his wife with him. Certain it is that women can come to the Gospel feast. Women are welcomed by Jesus Christ, and we say, "Come thou and all thy house." Say, will an immortal being bring such arguments against an interest as high as heaven, as wide as our capacity, and as lasting as eternity? Sirs, there is no argument that religion or reason will accept for not coming to God. Such excuses come from depravity, and unwillingness to become the children of God. Suppose we feel there is something we might do, ought to do, but don't, there are so many subterfuges; but they avail not. How flimsy will all such excuses appear on a sick bed! How melancholy to perish for things which in themselves are lawful! You may see your ground, try your oxen, have your wife, and be a Christian.

With any apology the sinner is inexcusable. Will God, that so loved the world as to give his Son, excuse men? You have refused his blood. Will the Son, who has given his life and wept over Jerusalem? Will the Spirit excuse after "taking of the things of God," and knowing that you quenched his fires? Will the Church excuse you, when she had such right to hope that after all her prayers and solicitude in your behalf you would add to her influence and increase her honor? Will ministers excuse you, when they ventured, leaving all, that they might save your soul from death? Will angels excuse you after being so ready to rejoice in your repentance? Will you excuse yourself,

when from the lake of fire you shall "see Abraham and
Isaac and Jacob in the kingdom of heaven and you yourself cast out;" when you see a Lazarus whom you fed, a
parent, a companion, with the holy angels, and you shut
out; when you hear "the song of the hundred and forty
and four thousand," and witness all the glory of the New
Israel, will you excuse yourself, that for a piece of ground,
a yoke of oxen, for marriage, or for anything else, you
declined your duty? The difficulties of revelation, the in-
consistency of Christians, the persecution you fear, the
cares that absorb, will then appear as too little for an intelligent creature to name. Sirs, there is no excuse!
When those who were here invited pressed the excuse, the
master of the house was angry, and declared that not
one of them should taste of his supper. Your excuse will
avail no more. "I pray thee have me excused." O, sirs,
will you ask us as ministers to have you excused? "You
excused!" You of all men are the last. Were you of the
darkness of Africa, you might plead ignorance. Were you
of India, you might say, "False religions confused us."
But in this land of Bibles, Sabbaths, sanctuaries—no, no,
no, there is no excuse that a holy God will accept. Though
Noah, Daniel, and Job stood before him, you could not be
spared. You might pray for pardon and be converted in
a moment; you might pray for purity, and at once be
cleansed from all sin; but there is no plea that avails for
not loving God, for not having Christ, for not enjoying
the Spirit, for not "making your calling and election sure."
Peace with God, religion, is the great interest. You can't
be excused for not "seeking first the kingdom of God and
his righteousness." Then make no vain excuse; the sup-

per is ready, the invitation is out, the provision is ample, the guests will delight you, the Lord of the feast will honor you. The acceptance of this invitation will be the event of your history. You will never stop talking about it, of rejoicing over it, and of recounting the benefits resulting from it. Yes, a supper only inferior to that of the "marriage supper of the Lamb."

SERMON X.

Naaman.

So Naaman came with his horses and with his chariot, and stood at the door of the house of Elisha.

And Elisha sent a messenger unto him, saying, Go and wash in Jordan seven times, and thy flesh shall come again to thee, and thou shalt be clean.

But Naaman was wroth, and went away, and said, Behold, I thought, He will surely come out to me, and stand, and call on the name of the Lord his God, and strike his hand over the place, and recover the leper.

Are not Abana and Pharpar, rivers of Damascus, better than all the waters of Israel? may I not wash in them, and be clean? So he turned and went away in a rage.

And his servants came near, and spake unto him, and said, My father, if the prophet had bid thee do some great thing, wouldest thou not have done it? how much rather then, when he saith to thee, Wash, and be clean?

Then went he down, and dipped himself seven times in Jordan, according to the saying of the man of God: and his flesh came again like unto the flesh of a little child, and he was clean.

And he returned to the man of God, he and all his company, and came, and stood before him: and he said, Behold, now I know that there is no God in all the earth, but in Israel: now therefore, I pray thee, take a blessing of thy servant.—2 Kings v, 9-15.

MILITARY skill and achievement have always secured renown. Mighty generals live in history. The warrior who has secured the freedom, increased the territory, maintained the unity, or accomplished what in any way increased the glory of a country has not only received the plaudits of the period, but the honor of later time. To such are often given the highest civil distinctions. Our own nation has illustrated that fact, and "the first in war has been the first in peace, as first in the hearts of his countrymen." But there is limit to human power, and the conqueror of a great army in war has found his painful inability to conquer his own passions or overcome his own physical condition, and has been cut off by disease against which human skill and his own fame could accomplish nothing. Such has been the case in our own last and great conqueror, General Grant.

The text presents the hero of his age, Naaman, the "captain of the host of the king of Syria." "By him the Lord had given deliverance unto Syria." He was "a mighty man in valor," and prime minister. But he was a leper, and the king and the country could not cure him. The text shows him in his pain, his pride, and finally his cure. The passage suggests analogy that we shall trace.

Let us see this great man in his condition, in his pride, in his submission to the saving means prescribed, and in the gratitude manifested.

I. His condition was one of the most pitiable of our earthly kind.

Naaman was a great man with king and country, and accustomed to the most distinguished attentions from rich and poor. Yet he was a leper; he was suffering from the most loathsome disease to which flesh is heir. Bishop Hall said, "The basest slave in all Syria would not have changed skins with him, his office to boot." Bayard Taylor, in one of his letters on northern Europe, gives a most graphic description of four lepers on their way to the hospital with a piece of oilcloth thrown over them—the condi-

tion too revolting for further notice. From the melancholy
spectacle we turn with horror. Place was not allowed
them in society, and they anticipated only certain death.

In its origin, progress, and end nothing is more typical
of sin—small in its beginning, steady in its increase,
till it works throughout the system. At first only a little
spot, scab, scale, it required care and knowledge to tell
just what it was. So it is often with respect to sin. We
doubt the character, question if it is wrong. "The beginning of iniquity is as when one letteth out water," little
by little, as by percolation—the first drink, the first card,
first game, first oath—till, frightened at the depth to which
he has sunk, he exclaims, "Lord of my being, is this I?
Has this spot spread through my whole system? Is it
from the crown of my head to the sole of my feet?" Yes,
it is iniquity in heart and life and character and influence,
dangerous to meet as really as the leper to touch.

> "Vice is a monster of so frightful mien,
> As, to be hated, needs but to be seen."
>
> "Thy law demands a perfect heart,
> But I'm defiled in every part."

Leprosy and sin are incurable by human agency, and
bring certain death. It was only a question of time with
the leper. Money, that is said to answer all things, answers nothing here. Money cannot give power to his physician, and the king of Israel thinks that to send one to
him to be cured of his leprosy means a quarrel against
him. When the leper rose in the morning death was before him. When he retired at night it was the same. No
other care or wish or passion or appetite could shut out the
unwelcome thought, "I am a leper; my days are numbered!

No earthly power can reach my condition." When we say to the sinner, "O, wicked man, thou shalt surely die," do we say what he does not know? This, this is the gall in every cup of sweetness. It was the extinguisher of earthly light to the leper. It lay as an incubus on his soul. Sin and leprosy discrown royalty, and each has its own end.

Sin as a fact is followed by results more fearful than the pain and death from leprosy. "Sin kills beyond the tomb." Sin inflicts evil on others where there is necessary contact —the husband on the wife, the father on his child. Who sees it not in the gambling, dissipated, dissolute?

II. The pride that disdains the simple means for cure.

That his sovereign, who owed so much to Naaman's victories, should desire his recovery is perfectly natural, and, hearing through a Hebrew maid in Naaman's house that in Israel there was hope, he sends to the king, with letters and messages. He sends ten talents of silver and six thousand pieces of gold and ten changes of raiment—in the currency of our country seventy-five thousand dollars. But it availed nothing; the king said, "Am I God, to kill and to make alive?" Absurd wish!

The prophet of God heard of this, and said, "Let him come now to me, and he shall know that there is a prophet in Israel." A king may fill the throne; the prophet shows God. Naaman hears, starts, hopes; so he "came with his chariots and horses, and stood at the door of the house of Elisha." It was not a palace. It was very unlike the dwelling to which he was accustomed. But there are times when medicine is more than money, and food is more than sparkling gems. Who will deny that there are times when the righteous is seen to be more excellent than his neighbor?

Are there not times when prayer is more than a house, or than even a crown of jewels? There are times when "kings shall bow down before him, and gold and offerings bring"! God's prophets are not man's parasites, and Elisha is not anxious to see the face of his distinguished visitor. He knew poverty and was satisfied. The equipage made no appeal. He did only what the case demanded, did nothing for himself! He sent a messenger, saying, "Go wash seven times in Jordan, and thy flesh shall come again to thee, and thou shalt be clean." That was clear and full, and the promise should have satisfied in his extremity so far, at least, as to make the trial; but, alas for poor dying human nature! pride takes the place that humility should fill, and the direction was spurned and indignant utterance given. "Naaman was wroth, and went away, and said, Behold, I thought, He will surely come out to me, and stand, and call on the name of the Lord his God, and strike his hand over the place, and recover the leper."

Dignity is insulted. Accustomed to such honor from others, is this the attention he receives from one distinguished only as a prophet? He was wroth at such treatment. Mighty with the prince, why should he not be so with the prophet? Other men danced attendance. Is this all Elisha will render? Poor human nature! Now in its extremity, in the direst want, how will it assert its weakness and obstruct its own passage to the truest good! Yes, yes, great men have great ways. But philosophy as well as pride influences his conduct. He reasons, "Are not Abana and Pharpar, rivers of Damascus, better than all the waters of Israel? may I not wash in them, and be clean? So he turned and went away in a rage." Here was early rationalism and painful contempt of God. Thus he reasoned: If water is to cure, why go to the Jordan! Dr. Thompson says, "No one who has looked on the rivers of Damascus can wonder that Naaman despised the turbid Jordan in comparison with their sparkling clearness."

Thus men turn away from Christ as Redeemer, from prayer as a power that opens heaven, from faith rather than works as justifying us, and speak of the Church and sacraments as unworthy their confidence and devotion. With them doctrines are absurd, duties impracticable, and the institutions of Christianity unworthy the notice they receive.

The leper in his pride and anger did not see God in his prophet, nor the blessing of God in the waters named. God's greatness is not in circumstances, but in himself, in his order, in his means as representing only him. It is "not by might, but by my Spirit, saith the Lord of hosts."

It is a happy fact that a wise great man can be taught by an inferior, and it is to the honor of Naaman that he allowed his servant to say, "My father, if the prophet had bid thee do some great thing, wouldest thou not have done it?" Happily for this great man, his passion cooled, and he heard and thought and tried.

III. The cure that submission brought.

"Pride goeth before destruction," and "before honor is humility." Revulsion is not reason, and reason is not revelation. We must humble ourselves under the mighty hand of God if we would have him exalt us.

The cross, the altar, the confession may not be to our taste, but life and health and soul are to be remembered. The angry and disdainful Naaman bows his head and takes

the yoke. "Then went he down, and dipped himself"—
another couldn't do it—he "dipped himself." O, how much
was trembling in the scale! Down, down he goes, again and
again. No change! Give it up! No, "seven times" is
the command. The seventh dip! O, what a dip was that!
God was honored; the leprosy was gone. The "flesh came
again like unto the flesh of a little child, and he was clean."
Was not that a perfect cure? Think of the change: the
flesh not like the corrugated, tanned, seared flesh of the
battle warrior, but pure, sweet flesh as of the newborn.
It was a perfect work.

O, sirs, God's means may offend us, but his work tells of
his glory in our homes, our happiness, and our hope. How
like this is the change of the hardened sinner when "old
things"—the worst, the most humiliating and grievous
things—"pass away," and "all things become new"! How
many as they have come up out of the "fountain opened
for sin and uncleanness," as they have looked up to heaven,
have been ready to ask, "Is this I? Is this the old polluted
and offensive sinner? Am I the same person I was?"
O, no! it is a new creature. It is the "flesh" of one just
"born again." Naaman in vain might say,

> "Surely I thought my pomp, and train
> Of woes, and tears would notice gain."

But,
> "Christ as soon would abdicate his throne
> As stoop from heaven to sell the proud a crown."

The pride and unbelief of Naaman would have said, "Back,
back to Damascus! An end to such indignity." A better
thought influenced him, and in the result he could say, "I
am whole!" No! no! The Ethiopian cannot change his

skin, but Jordan—with God—can do that work. O Jordan, queen of earthly streams, when did the polluted soul find thee insufficient for the purpose of the hour? God's method may demand seven dips—it is enough if it cures.

In Wilmington, Del., I urged a lady to go to the altar; she said she had "gone sixty times;" but she went again, and that night she was made new.

If men will disparage the ways of God, and deny the supernatural, and refuse the miracles of our Lord, we cannot help it, but they must take the consequences of their own folly. How near to failure was the man in the text!

What gratitude was awakened?

1. "He returned to the man of God" with his company and stood before him and said, "Now I know that there is" a God in Israel. Do teachers of "comparative religions" know this now? Shall Christianity be tried by man's doubts, or their doubts be conquered by God's hands? God followed will convince any proud doubter of his love, his power, his benefits.

2. His gratitude prompted an offering. He got more than he could give; but the comfort of the prophet was in the work done, and he refused his gifts. O, the change! How long will men dispute with God! How many souls will rationalism keep from cure?

I remark, all this was the result of having one in the house that knew God! A Hebrew maid in pity told the means. "Would God my lord were with the prophet;" he would heal him. Again submission to God is an essential condition of obtaining what he has authorized us to seek.

> "I'm a poor sinner and nothing at all,
> But Jesus my Saviour is all in all."

SERMON XI.

THE SYROPHENICIAN WOMAN.

And, behold, a woman of Canaan came out of the same coasts, and cried unto him, saying, Have mercy on me, O Lord, thou son of David; my daughter is grievously vexed with a devil.

But he answered her not a word. And his disciples came and besought him, saying, Send her away; for she crieth after us.

But he answered and said, I am not sent but unto the lost sheep of the house of Israel.

Then came she and worshiped him, saying, Lord, help me.

But he answered and said, It is not meet to take the children's bread, and to cast it to dogs.

And she said, Truth, Lord: yet the dogs eat of the crumbs which fall from their masters' table.

Then Jesus answered and said unto her, O woman, great is thy faith: be it unto thee even as thou wilt. And her daughter was made whole from that very hour.—St. Matthew xv, 22-28.

THE Saviour said, "Many shall come from the east and west, and shall sit down with Abraham, and Isaac, and Jacob in the kingdom of heaven. But the children of the kingdom shall be cast out." And here comes a woman of Canaan, a stranger to the commonwealth of Israel and to the covenant of promise. The Phœnicians planted colonies in many places. They were gross idolaters and worshiped the images of dead men. This Syrophenician woman having a daughter possessed of a devil, hearing Christ's fame, entertained the belief that he could cure her, and with great earnestness asked him to do so. She addressed him as the "son of David," in recognition of his

19

Messiahship, "and worshiped him." Though for a time her efforts seemed unavailing, her persistence prevailed. She received Christ's commendation and blessing. "O woman, great is thy faith: be it unto thee even as thou wilt." While critics and doubters of God's word, men of the greatest advantages, fail of divine benefits, we will study the case of a heathen woman whose conduct reproves that of many a Christian even.

We would show the greatness of faith as illustrated in the narrative.

I. Her concern for her daughter.

Consider the magnitude of the mercy sought. It was a miracle of the greatest moral benefit. To heal the sick, to open the eyes of the blind, to unstop the ears of the deaf, to raise the dead, would not compare in blessing to casting out a devil. To curb a passion, to restrain a propensity, to inspire a noble purpose, to sustain a resolution wisely made, has often proven too much for a parent's power. How many fathers have mourned their inability to hold back their sons from sin! What mothers have deplored the fact that with all their care and labor their daughters have not been "corner stones polished after the similitude of a palace"! But here is a heathen woman asking Christ to cast the devil out of her daughter, a devil that vexed the mind, that tormented the spirit. She knew that no power but that of Messiah could cure her child. No incantation that heathenism taught, no skill that the physician possessed, no aid that friendship furnished could reach the case. It was asking the greatest thing that even a God could do. It was to save a soul from the dominion of the devil. It showed great faith.

II. The difficulties that her faith withstood show its greatness.

1. Christ's silence. "He answered her not a word." What did this mean? We speak of the silence of consent, and also the silence of contempt. She might construe Christ's silence to indifference or disdain. Has silence no voice to repress? Job said, "The moving of my lips should assuage your grief." He felt the need of some expression of sympathy. David had seen much of grief as the shepherd king. He conquered the bear, killed the lion, and slew the champion of the Philistines. Yet he said, "Be not silent to me, lest if thou be silent to me I become like those that go down into the pit." He could not trust himself without God's answer to his prayers; past experience would not do. But here is a woman just turning to God from idolatry; with little knowledge, but with deep sorrow applying to the Saviour, and receiving no reply. It seems unlike Jesus of Nazareth, who went about doing good. Two blind men sought sight. They were by the roadside as Jesus passed; they cried unto him, and though the multitude rebuked them and the Son of God was in his last journey to Jerusalem and his death so near, yet nothing kept him from compassion. He stood still and granted their wish. But to this lone woman "he answered not a word." There was Saul of Tarsus, a strong man and a persecutor. He asked nothing of Jesus, but did many things contrary to him. Yet to him in his madness Christ said, "Saul, Saul, why persecutest thou me?" Saul prayed, and Jesus converted him. But to this poor supplicant "he answered not a word."

2. Christ's reply to his disciples was calculated to shake

a strong faith. The disciples knew Christ well, and they might be supposed to have influence with him. They speak for the woman, saying, "Send her away; for she crieth after us." Some understand this as saying, "Bid her begone." But it looks as if they thought by blessing her as he had done the centurion she would be the means of inducing some of her people to seek the Saviour. His reply to them looks as though they wanted him to grant her desire, for he says, "I am not sent but unto the lost sheep of the house of Israel;" as if that was a reason for not doing as she wished. The time for opening the door to the Gentiles had not yet come.

If his silence to the woman was trying, his answer to his disciples was worse. Does it crush her? No. Does it exasperate her? No. Did it deter her? No. The commander of the army of the king of Syria was a leper. He was told of a prophet in Israel who could cure him. He started with horses and chariot; he stood before the prophet's humble dwelling. Then he sent his servant— went not himself: "Go wash in Jordan," and assured him his flesh should be as that of a little child. But Naaman was in a rage? Why? O! he had not received such attention as his position might suggest. Great men must have great notice. "I thought," said he, "he will surely come out, and strike his hand over the place, and recover the leper" (2 Kings v, 11). It required expostulation to induce compliance, though when he tried he found perfect success.

But here is a woman not at the head of an army, with a worse case, and "he answers her not a word," and then replies to his disciples in a way to repel her. Christians, have you never found it difficult to sustain the confidence of a seeker after God? Though reared in a religious family or community, and familiar with God's promise, "Ask and receive," and with the knowledge that many have knocked and found that the door was opened to them, who has not been ready to cease effort because the prayer was not at once answered? But here is a heathen woman with no such advantages, holding on to Christ as if she would not take "No" for an answer.

After Christ's reply to his disciples, "I am not sent but to the lost sheep of the house of Israel. Then"—right then; O, let the heavens hear! let the earth feel! let the Church wonder!—"then came she and worshiped him," as the Messiah—for that is the meaning of "thou son of David"—saying, "Lord, help me." These words, monosyllables all, were three arrows that, shot from a bow well bent, flew to heaven and hit the heart of God. "Lord, help me." O, sirs, mercy to a child is mercy to a mother. "Then came she and worshiped him." She came closer, as if to kiss the hand ready to smite, as if to grasp the arm about to inflict a blow, as if to throw herself on the bosom that showed no sympathy, as if to feel the pulsations of a heart that seemed adamant. "She worshiped him." I have read of a pursued sparrow that turned on rapid wing and flew into the sportsman's bosom, who then had no heart to harm it. I have heard of a babe who, when a murderer had raised his dagger, looked up and laughed, and the dagger dropped. But here is a woman who, when the Saviour seems to spurn her, draws near and worships him—a woman who, without a single ray of promise to dispel the gloom of heathendom, is an example of the tenacious hold that faith exhibits.

3. We come to Christ's direct answer to the woman: "It is not meet to take the children's bread, and to cast it to dogs"—an oriental term applied to those not of the faith of Israel. Well, well! this settles the matter! Go thy way, sad mother; thy misery does not move him. What though he has healed the sick, and even raised the dead? Thy case makes no appeal. Why linger, woman? Thy daughter needs thy care. Go thy way, sad mother, and soothe the spirit of thy child. "It is not meet to take the children's bread." O Saviour, may we reverently address thee? Thou calledst Herod a fox, and so he was; his cunning showed it. Thou calledst the scribes and Pharisees a generation of vipers, and so they were—stinging the best interests of men to death. Judas thou didst call a devil, and his treachery proved it. Now thou callest this woman a dog! Yet when did she fawn like a spaniel or bite or snarl like a cur? Does it look as if the Lamb of God had turned into a lion to destroy? Can the fountain of mercy stream blood? Yet she holds on, and, if a dog, will not be shaken off. O, who can tell the power of the human will when the extremity of a case says, "This or nothing; my all centers in what I ask, and here is my only hope"? The soul in its tension shows the soul in its might. Agony of soul is the soul of agony. Look at this woman. How alert and ingenuous! Her thoughts flash like lightning. Her words fly like projectiles. As the skillful logician turns the argument of his antagonist against him and conquers him on his own ground and by his own showing, so she seizes the very bolt of logic forged and flung as if to lay her prostrate, and hurls it back to annihilate the objection of Jesus. Hear her: "It is not meet to take

the children's bread and cast it to dogs." "Truth, Lord."
I don't dispute it. But no master has dogs to starve.
They may not be fattened on viands or fed on loaves. But
after the children have eaten they get the crumbs. These
keep them from starving. Lord, help us! It seems impossible to tell what this woman's notion of Christ's loaves
was. If casting a devil out of her daughter was only a
crumb compared to what she conceived of his power, had
she not "great faith" in Christ's resources?

Her conduct says, Thy crumbs to me are more than the
abundance of other households. Yes, there was one who
said, "Is not the gleaning of the grapes of Ephraim better
than the vintage of Abiezer?"

Sirs, in such an exigency, with such a pressure in an
appeal to the Son of God, something in heaven or earth
must give way. This struggle of desire will break of its
own weight, or the Almighty arm must reach it.

This brings us to

III. The commendation of Christ and the conquest of
the woman.

"O woman, great is thy faith." Christ passed no unmeaning compliments. He never calls a thing great if it
is not so in reality. If he speak of the "great command-
ment," or of a "great reward in heaven," his accuracy of
expression is not to be questioned. He who knows faith
in its nature, origin, support, and results, he who knew the
faith of Abel and Enoch, of Noah and Abraham, says, "O
woman, great is thy faith." Exclamations are not common in the life of Christ. Yet the Son of God seems fairly
nonplused by this woman's faith. He does not say, "O
woman, great is thy humility in not resenting being recog-

nized as a 'dog;'" he does not say, "Great is thy persistence in the face of discouraging facts;" he does not say, "Great is thy vigor of intellect when such a question is given for thy solution;" but, "Great is thy faith." He strikes at the root, whence spring the virtues seen. Christians, the plucking up of the sycamore tree and the casting of the mountain into the sea are attributed to the exercise of faith:

> "Faith, mighty faith, the promise sees,
> And looks to that alone;
> Laughs at impossibilities,
> And cries, 'It shall be done!'"

The greatness of her faith was seen in the conquest it made.

Sirs, when the cry of "crumbs" goes into the ears of Jesus Christ, no matter how he seems, it is a tremendous fact. "Crumbs" for my husband; "crumbs" for my wife; for my child; crumbs, crumbs, crumbs, crumbs! Either the storehouse of heaven is empty or there will soon be "bread enough and to spare." The pregnant hour has come. The mighty question is now to be resolved. Will Christ do for or deny the woman? Shall her daughter still be "grievously vexed with a devil," or shall he who came "to destroy the works of the devil" cast it out? Hear him now in his true character and as his heart speaks: "Be it unto thee even as thou wilt." There shall be no stint; woman, you have your wish. All that, no less. The grant is equal to the request. "And her daughter was made whole from that hour." O, what an hour was that? The mother was relieved; the daughter was delivered from a vexing devil. Did the sun ever shine on such a day to those before us? O, earth, wast thou to them ever so rapturous? Sirs, such is the triumph of faith in Christ. Nothing impossible to him that believeth.

A few brief remarks:

1. Admire the faith that Christ commends. As when we see genius break through the thickest clouds and shine with a splendor that transcends our utmost thought, so let Christians honor a heathen woman in her grasp of God.

2. Learn that Christ is not unwilling to answer when we ask, but that he will have us to be intensely earnest, and unyielding in our wish. Christ was in the woman's effort while he seemed not to pity her. "If he tarry, wait for him." "The kingdom of heaven suffereth violence."

3. We should learn from this heathen mother to go to Christ for our children. "Have mercy on me." Grace to a child is good to the parent.

4. The fullness of God's mercy in meeting our wants: "Be it unto thee even as thou wilt." "What wilt thou that I should do unto thee?" "Lord, that I may receive my sight." "Be it unto thee even as thou wilt." There, take the key and rifle my treasury. "The Lord will give grace and glory: no good thing will he withhold from them that walk uprightly."

5. Great occasions and necessities are calculated to reveal great character.

They make great generals and great Christians. Thus Washington, Wellington, and Grant were made. Thus Elijah, Daniel, and Paul were made. Christians, let our great wants and opportunities tell the world of how we rose supreme. Let the Syrophenician woman show us how to ask and act.

SERMON XII.

The Transfiguration.

And after six days Jesus taketh Peter, James, and John his brother, and bringeth them up into an high mountain apart,

And was transfigured before them: and his face did shine as the sun, and his raiment was white as the light.

And, behold, there appeared unto them Moses and Elias talking with him.

Then answered Peter, and said unto Jesus, Lord, it is good for us to be here: if thou wilt, let us make here three tabernacles; one for thee, and one for Moses, and one for Elias.

While he yet spake, behold, a bright cloud overshadowed them: and behold a voice out of the cloud, which said, This is my beloved Son, in whom I am well pleased; hear ye him.

And when the disciples heard it, they fell on their face, and were sore afraid.

And Jesus came and touched them, and said, Arise, and be not afraid.

And when they had lifted up their eyes, they saw no man, save Jesus only.—Matthew xvii, 1-8.

Trials and triumphs enter into the experience of the great and the good. The birth of Christ was in humiliation; so was the current of his life. The Son of man had not where to lay his head. His agony showed the burden of his soul. But his baptism was a source of glory, and his transfiguration transcends all other displays of his moral grandeur. As the sun that has been shrouded in the darkest cloud may shoot forth his burning beams, so he that asked, Was ever "sorrow like unto my sorrow"? may demonstrate an inherent and external splendor that confounds a Peter, who, amid the blaze of Christ's glory, "wist not what to say."

The transfiguration of Christ in its aspect and import is one of the most striking and stupendous facts in the history of our Lord. To this event we now ask attention, and may God influence my speech with reverence and wisdom!

The fact to be considered: The transfiguration.

1. When and where it took place.

The Son of God had been impressing some of those truths that are the most unwelcome to human nature—that to be his disciples men "must deny themselves," must put away their own carnality and unholy habits, and that each must "take up his cross daily." He had also asserted what Peter and others of his followers were not prepared to receive, that some were standing near him that should not taste of death till they saw his kingdom. This meant his death before their eyes. A few days after the statement was made "he took Peter, John, and James, and went into a mountain to pray." He would with these, in the mountain, have seclusion and companionship. Whether this mountain were Tabor, as St. Jerome says was a general tradition in his day, or Hermon, as later writers think, is of little importance. The questions of Christ's soul constrained his prayer, and he sought the mountain. A place is sometimes suggestive of great thoughts. The mountain in its towering heights, or in its massiveness, may waken powers not ordinarily brought into existence. The majesty of the place may add to the depth of our feelings. For some reason God that formed the earth has made mountains conspicuous in his work with men. On Mount Sinai he talked with Moses. Thence issued the moral law that extends over all time and is adapted to the good of all people. God's ark for preserving the race rested on Mount Ararat. He took Moses to heaven from Mount Nebo, and Aaron from Mount Hor. Christ's incomparable sermon was delivered on the mountain, and on Calvary Christ made an end of sin. "Mountains are a kind of natural mediators between the earth and the skies." There the clouds recover the exhalations from the ground and pay their tribute in the dew and rain that refresh, enrich, and beautify the earth. They are between earth and sky, and receive and give. But no cloud has ever rested upon a mountain and disclosed such benefits as that which rested upon the one where Christ prayed. There his soul was full of the future. There his soul was pressed by the present. There he was the immaculate Son of God as the Lamb ready for the slaughter, and full of his abounding work. He poured his petitions into the ear of the Almighty Father, and found then, as always, that there is profit in praying to him.

"In the mouth of two or three witnesses every word may be established." When Christ was in his agony there were Peter, James, and John. The same were present with him in the scene before us. Peter had just made the grandest confession of him: "Thou art the Christ, the Son of the living God." It was Peter to whom he spoke of the keys that open and shut; Peter was to be the preacher of Pentecost. James would be the first apostle to become a martyr for his Lord, and John was that disciple "whom Jesus loved," and that remained longest on earth to testify, and that more than any other saw and showed his glory. Of the apostles they were Christ's triumvirate. As all the disciples were not apostles, so all the apostles were not witnesses of this fact. "The condition of the Church requires difference." The crucifixion of Christ was before the world; the resurrection was witnessed at one time by five hundred; the transfiguration by three. How merciful was Christ in having those who were to be so weighed down in beholding his agony, to behold the sight of all sights in his history—his transfiguration!

2. The event.

Perhaps there is more to amaze us in the birth of Christ —in his mother, and in the manger—than in his transfiguration. The advent of him so born was announced by angels with the song of "Glory to God in the highest." A great contrast with his birth! This was the "Son of the highest." This was the Son of God. Was it really a thing to be wondered at, that he who from eternity had been in the glory of the Father, whose brightness had been concealed by the "veil, that is to say, his flesh," should at some time and for some good reason shine forth in something of the real glory that he always had with the Father? Should we be amazed at this? At his baptism God spoke out of heaven, and a dove representing the Holy Ghost descended upon him.

Now Christ is transfigured. His figure is changed, not, it may be, in form, but in glory. He was unlike what he had uniformly appeared to be, and yet more like his essential self. "The fashion of his countenance was altered." "His face did shine as the sun." "His raiment was white and glistering." "His raiment became shining, exceeding white as snow; so as no fuller on earth can white them." How better could God reveal the splendors of his Son? John in the apocalypse saw him with his head and hair "white like wool, as white as snow." Christ's body had long hid his brightness; now his brightness makes his body as a transparency. Nay, he is like luminosity, shining in his own light and in his own strength and in his own inherent glory, full of divine effulgence. No, no, this was no myth any more than was his birth. This was no optical illusion any more than was the "light that blazed on persecuting Saul." This was no mere atmospheric change. It was celestial radiance. As the word of man it could not be true. As the word of God it can't be false. Like his advent and his work, it was a miracle.

Let us name three great changes that took place in the appearance of our Lord: One, when he assumed our nature and was "God manifested in the flesh;" another, when he glorified that nature in his ascension to heaven; the third, when he was transfigured. In the first Divinity was humbled. In the second humanity was exalted. In the third we have the outstreaming glory Christ had with the Father. Some think he alluded to this when he said, "There be some standing here, which shall not taste of death, till they see the Son of man coming in his kingdom." As divine he had appeared. As human he now appears divine—as if the King put on his royal robes. "He that dwelleth between the cherubim shone forth."

It was a glorious demonstration in the mountain of prayer. Realize the grandeur and the solitude of the place, removed from the turbulence of the outward world. He breathes out his soul and receives into his Spirit celestial powers. He who by his example taught his ministers and disciples to begin their work of glorifying him with humble and consecrated prayer now prays till heaven is opened and the divine is manifest in the human.

Christianity puts the greatest honor on man. When Stephen was arraigned they "saw his face as it had been the face of an angel;" and after talking with God in the mount the face of Moses so shone that others could not look upon it but through a veil. Christ shows a fullness of God that never appeared in another.

3. Witnesses and participants from the other world.

Moses and Elias "talked with him." They "appeared in glory, and spake of his decease which he should accomplish at Jerusalem." Grand as is the transfiguration, is it more wonderful than the appearance and conversation of these two men? God had himself buried Moses. A dead man comes back, not like Lazarus after four days, not like the son of the widow of Nain, who revived as they were carrying him to the grave; but after fifteen centuries dead Moses is alive on the mount. And there is the veritable Elijah whom God took to himself in a chariot of fire. There is Elijah after being in heaven nine hundred years. Think of these men. Of all the world could two men be thought of that had greater place in God's economy? Moses the lawgiver of the Jews; Moses the leader of the Jews; Moses with whom God talked as never with any other man; Moses who said, "A prophet shall the Lord your God raise up unto you of your brethren, like unto me." The Jews said, "We know that God spake unto Moses." Moses was the most striking type of Christ. Moses, the oracle and deliverer of the Hebrew people, is with Christ in the transfiguration.

Elias was there—the man who by his prayer on Carmel

confounded four hundred and fifty prophets of Baal and vindicated the claims of Jehovah; the man that could shake the throne, and make a nation tremble, and start a Jezebel into diabolical frenzy; the man whom God made a living flame and sent a chariot of fire to bear to heaven—he is here in the "holy mount." These two men of such miracles were miracles of men—men who may represent those who die and such as are "caught up to meet the Lord in the air." They are with Christ in the mount. The giver of the law, Moses, and the restorer of the law, Elijah, are present in the transfiguration. The law and the prophets meet and pay their tribute to Him "who is the end of the law for righteousness and the end of prophecy for fulfillment." "What doest thou here, Elijah?" Art thou still jealous for thy God? Moses, though no man could find thy grave, art thou here to show that He who buried thee has retained thee in his custody, and art thou anxious to witness the glory of Him whom thou didst so vividly represent in thy concern and thy labor for the people? Back again, O, great legislator, to honor Him who ends thy dispensation, and so sublimely inaugurates his own? The appearance of these two men is a revelation of immortality and a refutation of the sleep of the soul that should awaken gratitude, establish essential faith, and do honor to Him whom his disciples had been slow to believe.

Their conversation is a tremendous fact. Note it well and note it all. They utter not a word of the bliss they had just left, of the companionship they had long enjoyed. They say nothing of the changes of the world since they left it. One thought absorbed them as essential to God's purpose, and the efficacy of which sent the tide of its bene-

fits back to Moses, and made Elijah the man of God that
he was. They "spake of his decease which he should accomplish at Jerusalem."

It was all about that event that is to save the race that
accepts it, from Adam to his latest son. It was not about
his example, his miracles; amid his glory they spake of the
"hour and the power of darkness." The Jews had come to
think of the Messiah not as one who was to be cut off for
his people, but as a King to reign on a throne. They had
rejected the idea of Christ's death. "Peter . . . . began to
rebuke him, saying, Be it far from thee, Lord: this shall not
be unto thee." Yet in truth "the dying Messiah is the
great article of true Jewish theology." Moses and Elias
emphasized the great doctrine of his death, and on the
mount of transfiguration the types and the antitypes meet.
We "take off our shoes" as heaven and earth meet in
Christ, whose death is to "the Jews a stumbling-block, and
unto the Greeks foolishness." In the estimate of celestial
citizens long saved by faith in his blood it is the trans-
cendent glory of the Messiah. If there were anything
greater, surely they were the men to know it and speak
about it. This is their theme, as it is ours.

4. God's authentication of the mission of his Son.

In that mount the disciples, "Peter and they that were
with him, were heavy with sleep." Whether this was the
effect of such a weight of glory, or arose from the fact that
it took place in the night, and after their watching with
Jesus, we say not. Peter, a representative and impulsive
man, and often the mouthpiece of the disciples—Peter
said, "Master, it is good for us to be here." None of us can
doubt that! But, added he, not knowing the import or
20

what was involved in what he said, "Let us make three
tabernacles—one for thee, one for Moses, and one for
Elias." In this, to the honor of Peter, it may be said,
there was no egotism, no magnifying of himself. These
tabernacles were for Christ and those with him. "While
he thus spake there came a cloud and overshadowed them"
—not a cloud from vapor, as those that descend in showers to water the earth, "but the shekinah cloud, the pavil-
ion of the manifested presence of God with his people on
earth, what Peter in his epistle calls the excellent or magnificent glory;" reminding us of the glory Moses saw—now
shining in the burning bush, now resting upon the tabernacle, now flaming on the mount where God gave the law,
now guiding Israel in the pillar of fire. "And there came
a voice out of the cloud, saying, This is my beloved Son;
hear him." Tremendous communication! God through
it speaks out of heaven to man on earth, to those whom
Christ had chosen to be with him, and God says what?
Three things of greatest might given from the divine mind:
First, "This is my Son:" not a mere man; no impostor.
Second, "My beloved Son:" as he elsewhere says, "in whom
I am well pleased." Third, the injunction, "Hear him!"
He speaks the truth; he is the authoritative divine teacher:
"Hear him." Hear him, to know; hear him, to believe;
hear him, to obey. It has been emphasized as a fact that
on no other occasion than in the transfiguration does the
Father address man. At Christ's baptism he addressed
the Redeemer, "Thou art my beloved Son." In the text
he addressed the three disciples, and through them, in the
revelation of the Scriptures, all men.

Sirs, that cloud has passed, and the voice that came

through it does not as then fall upon the outer ear. Moses and Elias have gone back to heaven, and Peter, James, and John are no more in person on earth. But adown the disparted skies, across the dispensations, rolling in the most distant lands, is yet heard the same authority, saying, with all the majesty that God can impart to the summons of his heralds, "Hear ye him." You and I are called to hear, as taught in these Scriptures, the brightness of the Father's "glory, and the express image of his person." "Hear him," that in the mount of transfiguration, by the incontestable proofs of his divine mission and authority, so speaks as to forbid a doubt that he is all that he claims to be. "Hear him." To subdue rebellion, to remove the burden of guilt, to calm the tumult of the soul, to impress the divine nature where the carnal has had control, and to make us meet for the inheritance of the saints in light, "Hear him." In the depth of your agony, in the wretchedness of an almost undone spirit, "Hear him." His voice is full of assurance; his heart is full of compassion; his hands are full of blessings; and he says so clearly that none can misunderstand him, "Come unto me, all ye that labor and are heavy laden, and I will give you rest." "Hear him," the source of all spiritual good, the basis of all holy hope, the "Alpha and Omega" of our salvation. Apostles are no more with us in the high functions of the ministry, but Christ says, "Lo, I am with you alway, even unto the end of the world"—with you, to apply my merits; with you, to save your souls.

"Hear him," and not false teachers; and in hearing know that some things are to be done. It may cost you tears, the agony that follows confession; but let there be no crying, Peace, peace, when God has not spoken peace. Let the proud Pharisee come down in the dust. Let the publican smiting his breast hear him say, "Look unto me, and be ye saved." Let those who "hunger and thirst after righteousness" at once be filled. Let the self-confident hear him say, "Except a man be born again, he cannot see the kingdom of God." Hear him when he speaks of the worm that dieth not, and the fire that is not quenched. Do not make "mincemeat out of the body of Christ's truth;" take it in its import, in its connection, in its design, and in its benefits. Hear him in all he inculcates, in the power he proclaims, in the blessing he now offers, in the reward he promises. "Never man spake like this man." Elijah spake, and idolatry fled. Moses spake, and the earth and sea attested his mission. The captain of the Lord's hosts spake, and Joshua fell and worshiped. "See that ye refuse not him that speaketh." Did not the heavens hear when the dove descended? Did not the rocks hear when "he said, It is finished"? Where is Jew or Gentile that will refuse the testimony to Christ's character and work? "Meridian evidence puts doubt to flight." Sirs, if the transfiguration has any voice it constrains conviction of Christ's claim and our duty. May it help us to hear him and live!

It is said Napoleon was once engaged in a sanguinary struggle with the Turks. The French under General Kleber marched with three thousand soldiers to encounter the Turkish army with fifteen thousand infantry and twelve thousand splendid cavalry. While the battle raged Bonaparte was standing on Mount Tabor. When ready to despair the thought of Christ's transfiguration on the top of that mount came over him and gave courage. The Turks were put to flight and were driven back toward the Jordan, where Murat was waiting to receive them.

What, then, is the power the transfiguration should impart to us in the battle of life?

1. Christians, we shall live forever. Death does not end all. Moses, dead fifteen hundred years, and Elijah, in heaven nine hundred years, are back.

2. The divinest attestations to Christ that could be given are furnished in this text.

SERMON XIII.

Not by Might.

Then he answered and spake unto me, saying, This is the word of the Lord unto Zerubbabel, saying, Not by might, nor by power, but by my Spirit, saith the Lord of hosts.

Who art thou, O great mountain? before Zerubbabel thou shalt become a plain: and he shall bring forth the headstone thereof with shoutings, crying, Grace, grace unto it.—Zechariah iv. 6, 7.

MANY have trembled for the ark of God, and some have felt a keener anguish when it has been taken or dishonored than they have suffered for their loved and lost. But God is the custodian of his own cause, and its interests are always before him. Nor is he ever lacking in means to compass his end. In the context he presents Zerubbabel, the governor of Judah, as a power by whom the walls and the temple of Jerusalem should yet be a glory to his humbled people. In our theme he is to serve as a type of God, in the building of his Church and the establishment of his cause.

The subject presents:

I. The greatness of the work to be done.

II. The insufficiency of human means to its accomplishment.

III. The sufficiency of the Spirit vouchsafed.

I. The greatness of the work.

The condition of Israel was sad. The walls of Jerusalem had fallen. The temple was in ruins. The captivity justified tears. By the rivers of Babylon they sat down, yea, they wept, when they remembered Zion—its changed condition, the loss of its privileges, the departure of their own dignities. But God saw their humiliation and sorrow, and in the context woke the prophet from his sleep to see a candlestick "with a bowl upon the top of it," and seven lamps with seven pipes, "and two olive trees by it," one upon the right side of the bowl, and the other upon the left side thereof, and these were continually dripping their oil into the bowl, and through the pipes supplying the light, so teaching his own divine and sufficient presence for all the work in the sanctuary.

Nehemiah was an instrument for God, and his blessing was upon him. The sword as well as the trowel was necessary in the work he had to do. In derision his antagonists said, "If a fox go up, he shall even break down their stone wall." But such words were idle. The narrative shows the force of the opposition, but it also tells of the success of the undertaking. Nehemiah pursued his work with constancy, and always in the spirit of prayer, and at length the walls were finished. In that the divine purpose was executed.

The Church of the living God, the pillar and ground of the truth, is God's plan; and his purpose is that it shall fill the whole earth with its benefits; that all shall come to its happiness and honor. Jesus Christ himself is "the chief corner stone; in whom all the building fitly framed together groweth unto an holy temple in the Lord."

It is to be as beautiful "as Tirzah, comely as Jerusalem, terrible as an army with banners." In the sublime sweep of Jehovah's plan men are to know him, from the least to the greatest. The Digger Indian, whom you can hardly distinguish from the brute, as well as the individual of the highest cultivation; the sovereign and the subject; the savage and the sage—all are to attain that saving knowledge. Jesus Christ, who came from heaven to redeem us and morally to reconstruct society, would declare the sublime results desired and foretold. This dark world should be enlightened; this corrupt world should be purified; and this rebel orb, out of its place in the moral galaxy, should shine with celestial splendor. Surely here was a work for Omnipotence!

Tourists look with awe upon the pyramids of Egypt; they think of the desert where they stand, of the massive stones in their structure, the men employed, the time consumed, the means expended, and the purpose for which they were reared. But to rear temples for God, to have them filled with the Holy Ghost, and then for all to be "joined to the Lord in one spirit," and form together the Church that fills the earth—this is something to awaken the greatest wonder, as the achievement of an Almighty Arm and an Infinite Mind. Think of the contrasts in construction. Think of the quarries whence these living stones are taken, and the condition in which they are found. Huge shafts, uncouth slabs, ponderous blocks, yet all to be joined together by Him who shall build the temple and bear the glory. By his own goodness and power, his is the polishing of them, after the similitude of a palace.

David on the throne and Lazarus at the rich man's gate form a part; the gross idolater and the educated skeptic. Alas, that so many are without God in the world, and that it is so difficult to impress the belief that there is a true Father in heaven, a real religion on the earth, and that in God's presence there is fullness of joy, and at his right hand pleasures for evermore! O, the breaches that sin has made between man and God—between man and his fellow-man! What difficulties face us! What chasms are to be closed! What mountains to be scaled! What radical saving changes to be accomplished! This is no artificial or superficial work. The world without is to be changed by changing the world within; the action, by changing the spring of action. We can only believe as we hear him say, "I the Lord will do it."

II. The insufficiency of human means.

1. It is not by the "might and power" of human organ-ization. We were made for society. The faculties with which we are endowed, the sympathies we naturally cherish, and the affiliations we seek, show we were not made for the cold and cheerless regions of solitude. In aggregation is strength, in segregation weakness. The Church is a body.

There are human organizations that are benign in their purpose and salutary in their action. By them the dis-tressed may be soothed, the sorrowful comforted, and the vicious reformed; the blessings of those who are ready to perish may come upon them, and they may cause the widow's heart to sing for joy. But however noble in their conception, or wise in their aid, they can never bring men from darkness into light and from the power of Satan unto God.

2. It is not by the might and power of legislative enact-ment. Government is of God, and is a necessity of our condition. Law is essential to its maintenance. It re-strains vice. It guards virtue. The statesman should know that the government which is wanting in the moral element that conserves is not without the immoral that

destroys—that "righteousness exalteth a nation," and that "sin is a reproach to any people"—that men rise to honor or sink to shame as they regard or disregard temper and probity and human obligation. But we cannot legislate men into the divine likeness. God gave a law amid circumstances of the greatest impressiveness; the thunder rolled; the lightning flashed; the mountains shook, and even Moses feared and quaked; and the law was a schoolmaster to bring us to Christ. But with all its lashes, did it ever scourge the old Adam out of a young sinner? How far do prisons reform? Alas, that so many are hardly out of one before they are in another! No, no. It is not by such means that of stones we raise up children unto Abraham.

3. It is not by the might and power of military prowess. It is not "by bow, nor by sword, nor by battle, by horses, nor by horsemen." It is not by the strength of a multitude, nor by the host of an army, that this desired end is to be accomplished.

We do not say that the sword of a country may not open to the Church, as it does to commerce, a door that it should gladly enter. But more is required for the salvation of the lost. The Crusaders, who journeyed so far to recover the place of Christ's sepulcher, could not restore his life or impart his spirit. Abraham Lincoln, as President of the United States, by a proclamation made four millions of slaves free; but this did not make one of them a saint. Who would imagine that the followers of Him who said, "All they that take the sword shall perish with the sword," could think that by an Inquisition they could secure heirs of heaven? In vain did the Arabian prophet stalk through the earth to conquer by butchery. No thundering anathema, no wrathful fulmination, no vengeful power can ever level the ramparts of sin, rear the walls of Zion, or conquer a single rebellious heart.

4. It is not by the might and power of ecclesiastical means or earthly auxiliaries. God has planted a Church. Christ has purchased it with his blood, and the very sanctuary is to be reverenced. But it has saving might, only as God is in it. He may say, "Come out of her, O my people." The scribes and the Pharisees sat in Moses' seat. Succession is not necessarily sanctity. Auxiliaries in God's plan in rebuilding the walls and rearing again the fallen temple of Jerusalem were found in Cyrus, in Darius, and in Zerubbabel the governor. But human power of itself is not enough. The Emperor Constantine hoped by his authority to do wonders for the Church. But the sunshine of his favor was followed by a denser gloom.

5. It is not by the might and power of natural resources. Yes, we have intellect, will, and a sense of right. But who has not deplored his want of power to conquer his tendencies to evil and to follow his convictions of good? Who has successfully said, I will make my heart clean? Who? Of the prophets, who? Of the apostles, who? What saith Jeremiah? "Though thou wash thee with nitre, and take thee much soap, yet thine iniquity is marked before me, saith the Lord God." "Can the Ethiopian change his skin?" Can he? When and where did he do it? Show us the case. Much less cannot we, accustomed to do evil, do well. Some other power must open our blind eyes, warm our cold hearts, inspire our best purposes, and enable us to draw nigh unto the divine image and likeness. Re-

generation is not from the ability within us, but from the power above us; when born again we are born from on high.

III. God's Spirit is our only sufficient hope.

The divine nature alone transforms the human, conforming men to the image of their Maker, and preparing them for the "house not made with hands, eternal in the heavens."

The world, the flesh, and the devil are triple forces, that education does not remove, and that human philosophy does not overcome. There is no chain in our earthly forge that can bind them. Depravity fuses and links habits which only the hammer of God can break. By his power adamant is shivered. God's Spirit means the third Person in the adorable Trinity. By this Spirit he will subdue the world to himself.

It is the Spirit that gives force to truth, pungency to conviction, reality to moral change. This is the tongue of fire that consumes the desires of the flesh; that destroys passion and transforms man's nature; it is the light, the life, the joy, the hope, the eternal felicity of the soul.

Look through history at the work of this Spirit in making man the glory of God. It was the breath of God's Spirit that in Eden made Adam the lord of the earth. It was its loss that drove him from Eden.

Think of the valley of dry bones and the Spirit that entered into them and made an army to march to the divine order; think of Pentecost and what it did for those who had been so closely associated with Christ! They had seen his example, heard his sermons, witnessed his miracles, and yet in spite of all these facts there was a time when they only followed him afar off—nay, a time when all the disciples forsook him and fled.

Christ, knowing the purpose and power of the Spirit, said: "It is expedient for you that I go away: for if I go not away, the Comforter will not come unto you." "When he is come, he will reprove the world of sin, and of righteousness, and of judgment."

Only think what that Spirit made of St. Peter! What bolts of hope did he forge and fling from those fires that consumed the "old man"! With what skill did he pour forth his arguments, and show the guilt of those who crucified "the Just"! "The same day there were added unto them about three thousand souls." Here was the hope of history. Here was the strength of our fathers. Here was the original of Methodism. Can we doubt this power? Can we refuse this aid?

The Church—the temple—does not yet rise in its magnificent proportions; but he who laid the corner stone will bring forth the headstone, with shoutings, crying, "Grace, grace unto it." The little stone is not taken out of the mountain with human hands, but it is to strike the image and fill the earth. "Shall a nation be born at once?" Ask God. Ask prophecy. "What art thou, O great mountain?" Who? The aggregation of all opposing forces; superstition, skepticism, governments, dominions, principalities, powers, spiritual wickedness in high places. Who art thou? All difficulties in one. Looking defiance from base to brow, from foundation to summit. What power can pierce thee? What arm can raise thee? What hand can annihilate thee? "Before Zerubbabel thou shalt become a plain." Nothing shall be left of thee. What mountain can stand before him whom God raiseth up?

Sirs, we know Him who has said, "Ask of me, and I shall give thee the heathen for thine inheritance, and the uttermost parts of the earth for thy possession." Ask, ask, ask. Hitherto, saith Christ, ye have asked nothing. Ask great things. Ask all God has promised, and hear him say, "I the Lord will do it." He has promised to make his servants his instruments; therefore let us be in earnest and do our whole duty. Then we need have no fear of the results; and of the good that is done in the earth we will say, "The Lord doeth it." Christians, believe it! The Spirit that to-day shines in the Scriptures, glows on the altar, and flames in the pulpit is able to cleanse the universe.

The prophet speaks of the "breaker" that is to come up and overcome the hardships of the Holy Spirit's work. May we not be as confident as others were of the means to their purpose? David triumphantly exclaimed, "From the blood of the slain, from the fat of the mighty, the bow of Jonathan turned not back, and the sword of Saul returned not empty." Jeremiah cried, "Thou art my battle-ax and weapons of war: for with thee will I break in pieces the nations, and with thee will I destroy kingdoms."

What power and success are here taught in the use of means, men understand. Know, then, that these are only figures of power, and that the true glory of the Church is not in the massiveness of her walls, or the height of her towers, or the magnificence of her palaces; it is not in the antiquity of her origin, or the number of her sacraments, or the learning of her priesthood; it is not in her social dignity or political place; it is not in the seminaries she builds or the universities she endows; but it is in this, that the Lord in her midst is mighty; it is in the truth that her walls are called salvation, and her gates praise; it is in the fact that the light of heaven streams in her assemblies, that the Spirit that raised up Christ from the dead dwells in her humblest members; it is that "of Zion it shall be said, This and that man was born in her: and the highest himself shall establish her."

Let the Church, then, remember that the Spirit in its plenitude is for every soul that hungers and thirsts after it, and for every Church that responds to the calls and claims of God.

> "What though the gates of hell withstand
> Yet shall this building rise."

Amen.

SERMON XIV.[*]

DEATH.

Forasmuch then as the children are partakers of flesh and blood, he also himself likewise took part of the same; that through death he might destroy him that had the power of death, that is, the devil;

And deliver them who through fear of death were all their lifetime subject to bondage.—Hebrews ii, 14, 15.

THESE are facts of universal concern and of the gravest importance. For such reasons the statement of the text must make the profoundest impression. The sublimest events of history are the Son of God's assuming our nature that he might die for our sins, and then his dying as proposed, and securing all the benefits for which he took part of flesh and blood.

From this Scripture we propose to consider:

The conquest of Christ as here presented; that he might "deliver them, who through fear of death were all their lifetime subject to bondage."

1. The fear of death is a natural passion. Life is sweet, and death has a sting to an intelligent creature. None is to be reproached for aversion to dissolution. It seems like a contradiction to the life God has given us for enjoyment and usefulness. Death involves enough to provoke horror and loathing.

We leave our early home where childhood was nourished, where relations were formed, where sights and sounds exert their memories, where education was eagerly sought and highly prized; and to it we cannot return to correct our

---

[*] This sermon was written January 18th, 1898, less than a month before Dr. Roche's death.

errors or improve our condition, though we may have cherished that desire through all the weary years of a long life. Even the exile in humiliation thinks of the playgrounds of his youth, and nothing utterly obliterates the thoughts of joy and innocence that gather round that place and period. The tourist who spends so much of his time and money in the delights of foreign lands would have no final resting place but near the region he calls home. No ashes are like those of his father, with which he would have his own mingle. Life is felt to comprehend everything that is in us and for us.

> "For who, to dumb forgetfulness a prey,
>   This pleasing, anxious being e'er resigned,
> Left the warm precincts of the cheerful day,
>   Nor cast one longing, lingering look behind?"

This to the dying! But what to the surviving? Mary and Martha remain, and at the grave of their brother "Jesus wept."

When David Garrick showed Dr. Johnson the mansion he had built, the garden and grounds he had prepared for his closing days, Johnson said, "Ah, David, these are the things that make it hard to die."

And whose life that has any value closes without unaccomplished plans, which, had they been carried out, might have brought great good to those left behind. It is stated that Dr. Johnson, in advanced life, declared he would gladly suffer the amputation of a limb could death be delayed a single year.

Bonaparte, who made all Europe to tremble, when stripped of renown, exchanged the pinnacle of fame for

21

the obscurity and degradation of banishment rather than suffer death.

Hadad the Edomite, in the slaughter of his countrymen by Joab, having escaped into Egypt, was well received by the king, and was honored in the royal family. Though but a child when separated from home, he no sooner learned that David and Joab were dead than he prepared to return. Pharaoh expostulated with him, and asked, "What hast thou lacked with me, that, behold, thou seekest to go to thine own country?" And he answered, "Nothing: howbeit," he added, "let me go in any wise." So much for country! So much for life!

We read of Hezekiah, king of Judah, who had lived long enough to see the world, but who with real greatness of soul and conscious integrity, at the approach of death, "wept sore."

2. But what shall we say of the "Unknown," that gives to death the lifelong fear? It makes no report of what it does. Death has reigned from Adam to the present hour, and its place in the world has always been associated with the thought of sin that caused it. The explorers or visitors of the most distant lands and seas—from even the "Dark Continent"—return to tell us of what they saw and learned; and the missionary has his story; but, excepting in the appearance of Moses and Elias at Christ's transfiguration, none has returned from death to tell us of the great "Beyond." Lazarus did not; the son of the widow of Nain did not; though Jesus raised them both. And what father has ever come back to his children to tell them of the great Unknown?

The patriot has been ready to die for his country. In

John Quincy Adams this land had such a man. For fifty years he filled such stations of honor and trust as to make him deeply interested in whatever concerned his people. He came to death in the American Congress with the words, "This is the last of earth;" but in the fifty years that have followed not a word has come from the patriot's lips to tell of the land he has entered.

Death takes whom and when it will, and makes no report from another state.

3. But beside the "Unknown" there is the "Apprehended." God, who is the author of our being, and under whose economy death has place and power, has given us in the Bible such a revelation of another state, and of different conditions and durations, as compel the deepest thought, and the fear that is lifelong. In the administration of God we see a law that we have violated, guilt that we have incurred, and penalty that we cannot escape. And even if the proudest of all earth's monarchs can look death unflinchingly in the face, without thinking of the possible anguish beyond it, shall we call him brave? One in Holy Scripture says, "My flesh trembleth for fear of thee; and I am afraid of thy judgments."

Boswell said to Johnson, "I have been to Tyburn to witness the execution of several criminals, and none of them seemed concerned." Johnson replied, "Most of them, sir, never thought of death." Boswell answered, "Is not the fear of death natural to man?" "So much so," responded Johnson, "that the whole of life is but a keeping away of the thought of it."

No one has ever witnessed a flood, a fire, a railroad disaster, or a sinking ship without learning something of the fear of death that is lifelong. Kant, the German philosopher, was asked before his death what he promised himself with regard to a future life; after reflecting a moment he replied, "Nothing certain." All are not disturbed with an equal fear; but still all are subject to fear at times.

The conquest.

The Son of God, knowing the enormity and the punishment of sin as no other could, and seeing that his purpose to secure to us the possibility of acceptance with God could be effected only through his atonement for man's transgression, assumed an immaculate human nature—flesh and blood. This he did without deifying the human or humanizing the divine; then by his own death he defeated the dire design of the devil who had introduced sin into the world to bring upon man all the evils of a future state, and so rob God of the glory that eternity should bring to his name.

Satan had the power of death, as introducing it into the world ·by sin, and still retains that power by the vices through which wicked men destroy their lives. Christ destroys him that has the power of death—not in person, nor in his efforts for men's ruin—for he still goes about as a roaring lion seeking whom he may devour—but he destroys him in that he enables his followers, by his grace, to overcome Satan's wiles.

Christ as manifested had power to lay down his life, and he had power to take it again. This he voluntarily did, and died "the just for the unjust," to bring us to God. That was the only way of taking us out of Satan.

Christ died. He rose. He ever liveth to make intercession for us; and heaven may be the eternal home of those whom the devil would shut up in hell. "I will ransom them from the power of the grave; I will redeem them from death: O death, I will be thy plagues; O grave, I will be thy destruction: repentance shall be hid from mine eyes."

Thus we have the death of death, in the death of Christ; and death that would have had eternal dominion over us has lost its power, in the victory of the Son of God. Men still die, and may at any age. But here is moral conquest. A better, higher, diviner life awaits the soul that participates in the Saviour's death.

What was the tent in the wilderness in comparison with the tabernacle? What was the tabernacle in comparison with the temple? What was the first temple in comparison with that which Christ glorified by his presence? And what is the human body that now is, in comparison with that which shall be, when made like unto that of the blessed Lord? The devil still has power to tempt; still has power to destroy the body; but after that there is no more that he can do, if we seek life from the dead. From the first paradise Satan could compass our eternal banishment; but Christ opens "the kingdom of heaven to all believers."

"Flesh and blood" in Christ take hold of us. A minister was called to see a man about to die. He found him in anguish for his sin, and with no hope. In vain he reasoned, till with a vigorous hand he seized the man's arm and asked, "Is not that flesh and blood?" "Yes," answered the man. Then added the preacher, " 'Forasmuch as the children are partakers of flesh and blood, He also himself likewise took part of the same; that through death he might destroy him that had the power of death.' " The sinking soul laid hold on Christ, and died in peace. Ever since the utterance of God—that the seed of the woman should bruise the serpent's head—faith has had its triumphs, and Christ his victory over the devil. Abel was the first righteous man to enter the spiritual paradise, and ever since his time the saints have been going up, through much tribulation. The promise gave the power. Now every Christian justly claims the victory, not of his own good works, but through the merits of Jesus. May we not ask,

> "Why should we start, and fear to die?
> Death is the gate to endless joy:
> Why should we dread to enter there?"

What is it for the Christian to leave his present and pleasant home? It is to go to his Father's house! His Father's house? In his life here has he been a stranger to his Father? Has he not daily entered his courts with praise? Has not the family altar, morning after morning, flamed with the fires that his breath has kindled? Since his conversion has not his conversation been in heaven? Is not dying going to the same place of which St. Paul spake when he said he had "a desire to depart and be with Christ"? Then, to die is gain. It is going to our eternal home. Reasons may exist why saints might, for a time, wish to remain here—the love of family, and the desire of helping others. Such ties might bind them to earth. But no mortal can tell the fullness and glory of Christ's conquest over Satan. He met the prince of darkness on the ground that had been crimsoned with blood-guiltiness in the successive centuries since the death of Abel, and his victory was complete.

It was the death of death, in the death of Christ. "Death shot its sting in the side of Christ, and there it lost it." Now, futurity has no fear for the soul that lives in Christ and dies with the benefits he secures. What is there, then, in death to dread, when its sting is lost? The Christian loses nothing in death but what this short life has given him. He gains the infinite riches that eternity pours in upon a redeemed and restored soul. Death is the end of mortality. It is the beginning of all that is comprehended in "mortality swallowed up of life."

Think of an immortal nature, a deathless soul, a spirit full of God, "ready to depart and be with Christ"—looking through the chinks of the clay tenement and asking only, amid pain that writhes the body, at what point of the path the loving Father will say, "Come up higher"! Think only of the exit, and how the door to heaven through death is to be opened! Behold the departing Christian as Christ's victory exalts him! Allow a few illustrations:

When Dr. Leechman—once principal of the College of Glasgow, and one of the ablest preachers of Scotland—in the crisis of a fatal disease, addressed himself to some young men meditating the ministry, he said: "You see the situation I am in; I have not many days to live. I am glad you have the opportunity of witnessing the tranquillity of my last moments—and not my tranquillity alone; it is my joy and triumph; it is complete exultation." His features kindled and his voice rose as he spoke. It was the voice of the victor. Rest in Christ's finished work can be seen in the absence of the "lifelong fear of death."

It is said that when the sentence of death had been passed upon the Duke of Argyle he seemed in no way distressed or disconcerted; that on the very night before his execution the doomed nobleman slept on in the quietness of conscience and in the calmness of faith; that on the opening of his cell his visitors looked with utter astonishment upon the perfect repose which was his, in the full knowledge of the block and the ax that awaited him. For "so He giveth his beloved sleep."

Of Christ's conquest of death for the Christian we may recall three cases. Life was full of interest and hope to them all. Their departure has suggested what vision of the upper glory, ere the spirit takes its flight, Christ sometimes grants the soul. All three of these dying saints declared that the angels were with them, and that they heard the songs of heaven.

Such manifestations of God, vouchsafed to some just leaving for their Father's house, caused perplexity to that world-wide physiologist, Professor Carpenter. Famed as he justly was for his knowledge of all that enters into the human frame, his endeavor to find out what it was in his great science that could account for the rapture he sometimes witnessed in departing souls was utterly unavailing. Good reason there was for his failure. The solution of that problem lay outside of his knowledge and profession. It was to be found in Christ, by his conquest of death. It was the opening glory of immortality.

We do not teach that all Christians die in equal knowledge of their departure, or with like expressions of transport; or that all sinners expire in equal moral anguish. But each has sometime the vision of futurity never to be forgotten.

May we be allowed to use in substance the language—

almost too terrible for utterance—of one who had led an evil life? He declared in his dying hour that facts that had been allowed to sleep awoke; and the expiring sinner saw God, saw himself in his past conduct, and saw eternity. All the neglected, slighted kindnesses of the Almighty came trooping through his memory to torment him; one and another raised its accusing voice and said, as said the ghosts to Richard III in Shakespeare's wonderful drama, "Let me sit heavy on thy soul to-morrow." Wasted Sabbaths, fleeting pleasures, foolish sins, that had taken the place of the Church of the living God, each as it passed glared on the dying sinner, and said, "Let me sit heavy on thy soul to-morrow." Worse than the ghosts of murdered men came the sense and anguish of eternal loss!

But how different is the experience of the dying Christian! He asks, "Is this death? Give me thy hand—my life has been in constant readiness for thy coming."

"Come, welcome death, thou end of fears! Give me thy hand! It is cold to nature, but the breath of God warms it. O, triumph of all triumphs! Heaven's arches are not too high, the songs of the redeemed are not too loud, and the joys of the celestial city are not too great, for the entrance of the ransomed ones!" O, death of death! It will require the full light of the future world to see all that Christ's death has secured for "them who through fear of death were all their lifetime subject to bondage." The saints shall enter and progress! Amen.

PRAYER

THE public prayers of Dr. Roche were remarkable for their appropriateness, fervor, and reverence. Many of them offered upon notable occasions were reported stenographically. The following has been taken from the files of *The Christian Advocate* for October 22d, 1874, by the courtesy of the Rev. S. G. Ayres, Librarian of Drew Theological Seminary.

The Church had been appalled by the sudden death of Dr. Thomas M. Eddy, the beloved and successful missionary secretary. At the memorial services held by the New York Preachers' Meeting, Dr. Roche, without warning, was called on to lead in supplication. He said:

"O God, our heavenly Father, we rejoice to know that thou art our Comforter and Guide. Our minds are too narrow, our knowledge is too limited, our experience is too confined, to interpret thy dispensations. Thou art thine own interpreter, and thou wilt make thy ways plain. We are but as worms of the earth; thou art the Sovereign in thine own universe; we are thy subjects—subjects of thy moral government, subjects of thy grace and mercy. We bow before thee—though the voice falter, and the mind is stung, and the heart ache, we bow before thee, and say in contemplation of thy ways, 'Verily thou art a God that hidest thyself.' Yet thou art our Saviour. The events that are so gloomy in their results may be sudden. but we

still know that thou art God. Thou takest away as thou
gavest, and none can hinder thee; and who shall say, 'What
doest thou?' We have our natural tastes, we have our social inclinations, and we have what may be called the convictions of our intellects; and under the influence of facts
that are positive we say, 'O my God, take me not away in
the midst of my days.' Yet thou dost cut off in the
meridian of life; the sun goes down while it is yet day—
while it would seem to be but noon—and we stand in solitude as we stagger under thy blow; we stand in solitude
that seems as wide as the world itself. But, O Lord, thou
art our Comforter; thou art our Guide and Recompense;
we look to thee; we trust in thee; we would remember that
thou art wise and good, though incomprehensible to us.
Thy blow has fallen not upon a particular Church organization, but it has fallen upon the general Church, and the
secretaryship of our great missionary interest, in one of its
active and efficient members, is vacant; the place that he
filled is unoccupied; and the Church mourns because thou
hast taken away one who was strong in his position, strong
in his influence, strong in his activities, and strong in the
moral results of his service. Thou hast taken him away
from the wife, from the son, from the daughter, from the
Church, which Christ has purchased with his blood; not
only from our own denomination, but from Christianity at
large. Thou hast taken him away whose heart glowed with
the fire of Christian zeal, whose tongue was eloquent in
the cause which he espoused, whose energies were directed
according to the wisdom of Christ—and at a time when we
were hoping for grander moral results. But it is God.
We remember that thou art the custodian of thy Church.

Thou wilt fill the sphere; thou wilt perform the service; thou wilt achieve the results; thou wilt glorify thy name.

"O Lord, we bow before thee. Have we sinned? have we done wrong in thy sight? We would lay our hands upon our breast, and we would be pure. If we have been sluggish in thy service, we would not be sluggish any more. If thy servant has fallen by overwork, we would not lapse by underwork. We would fill our office; we would make full proof of our ministry; we would save souls from death; we would hide multitudes of sins. But, O Lord, there is little that we can do for the family bereaved, little that we can do in the mere contemplation of the place made vacant —that can be done by others; that can be done by thee— but, O Lord, we can bow down heavily; we can lift our hands; we can raise our voices; we can open our hearts; we can ask thee that we be made more pure; that our devices be multiplied, our views be broadened, and our energies increased; that we may live nearer to God; that we may achieve more for the honor of the Prince of Peace.

"O Lord, thou hast called us to other services when our eyes were tearful and our hearts were heavy; but we are making a special service of this occasion. And for what reason but that we may get nearer to the Friend of sinners? but that we may be more perfectly conformed to the image of him who created us? If at any time we have been supine, let us be so no more; if we have failed in our work, let us fail no more; if our hearts have not glowed with Christian zeal, let them glow hereafter. Come near to us now while we beseech, while we plead, while we ask to be more like thee, while we ask to love Zion better, while we ask to be more completely conformed to the image of our blessed

Saviour. Draw near and stamp thine image upon each member of this meeting, upon the ministers who go hence, upon our bishop who is here, upon the president of the association, and upon all its officers. As he that came first weeping shall come again rejoicing, bringing his sheaves with him, so we would remember that the sad heart is not all sadness, that the darkest wave may have white foam near it, and the blackest cloud its silver lining. We would remember, Lord, that though thou hast taken away him whom we mourn, thou hast spared another of eminent position in the Church—thou hast raised him up; our senior bishop is with us this morning. The Lord be praised! Thou lovest and leadest Zion, and though thou workest in a way that is inexplicable to man, yet thou dost seem to bless us beyond what we have reason to expect or hope. Thou dost comfort us in the midst of our griefs. Spare our senior bishop still; spare the officers of the General Conference; and spare us all, that we may accomplish the end of our being, and glorify God in our bodies and spirits, which are his. And when thou shalt call us, may we be fully prepared to say, 'The resting time has come, the labor is all over,' and may we enter into that rest that remains for the people of God. For Jesus' sake. Amen."